Scandalous Weddings

Scandalous Weddings

BRENDA JOYCE
REXANNE BECNEL
JILL JONES
BARBARA DAWSON SMITH

St. Martin's Paperbacks

SCANDALOUS WEDDINGS

"In the Light of Day" copyright © 1998 by Brenda Joyce.
"The Love Match" copyright © 1998 by Rexanne Becnel.
"A Weddin' or a Hangin'" copyright © 1998 by Jill Jones.
"Beauty and the Brute" copyright © 1998 by Barbara Dawson Smith.

ISBN: 0-312-96657-1

Printed in the United States of America

St. Martin's Paperbacks edition / December 1998

10 9 8 7 6 5 4 3 2 1

Contents

Scandalous Weddings

IN THE
LIGHT OF DAY

Brenda Joyce

Chapter One

"A lovely day fer a weddin'."

The gleaming brand-new Packard purred as it idled in the circular, cobblestoned drive. Pierce St. Clare did not reply immediately, his gaze not on the small man beside him, who was driving the motorcar, but on the mansion facing them. Vast lawns and elm trees surrounded the four-story limestone house on this particularly glorious Sunday afternoon, and high wrought-iron gates barred the public from any access to it or the Fifth Avenue property it was on. Those iron gates were now wide open, as a few of the very last wedding guests continued to arrive in their handsome coaches and carriages, and were no cause for concern. But the trees disturbed him. They were very tall and level with the second story—they might interfere with his signal. "Keep your eyes open," he finally said.

He stepped from the motorcar, a tall, lean, inherently elegant man, clad now like the two hundred other gentlemen present, in a black dinner jacket and matching trousers, a dress shirt and white bow tie, a white carnation pinned to one lapel. Dark hair swept across his brow, carelessly combed into place. His eyes were a brilliant blue. "I should be no more than twenty minutes. Look for my signal, Louie." There was a warning in his tone.

The thin, middle-aged Louie, clad in tweeds, smiled at him from beneath his felt hat, revealing a silver front tooth. "Guvnor, a true piece o' cake," he said with a cocky wink.

Pierce eyed him then turned his attention upon the Boothe mansion. He strode briskly across the drive as Louie drove the Packard out of the way of the last few oncoming carriages. The invitation had suggested that one be prompt; the ceremony would start at precisely four P.M. Several couples were just entering the house as he fell into step behind them. The women were walking behind their escorts and had their heads together as they spoke in hushed tones, but he overheard their conversation anyway.

There was a queue, and it had stalled. Pierce stood very still, in spite of the fact that he was filled with restlessness and impatience.

"So fortunate," the lady in low-cut pale blue silk was saying. "I cannot believe that poor, poor Annabel's good fortune. I do mean, what an amazing turn of events! Who would have *ever* thought!"

The blond lady in silver chiffon agreed. "One would have *never* thought she'd land a husband. Good Lord, I mean, after all, she is twenty-three, is she not? Twenty-three with her two younger sisters already married for several years now—with little Elizabeth expecting! This is so fortunate for the so very unfortunate Annabel Boothe. I mean, Jane, I must admit, I truly thought she would remain a spinster for the rest of her days in spite of the Boothe fortune."

"I thought so, too," the brunette said. "After all, when one's father cannot buy one a husband, why, there is truly no hope."

"He must be smitten. Can you imagine? Why else

would Harold Talbot marry her? He has his own fortune, you know."

Pierce sighed, his gaze straying past the two women, hardly interested in the bride and her good—or bad—fortune. However, the Boothe fortune did interest him. George Boothe owned one of the most popular dry-goods emporiums in the northeast—if not in the entire country. G. T. Boothe's was the most fashionable destination for those women venturing out upon the Ladies' Mile. Recently, his net worth had surpassed that of John Wanamaker, his closest rival.

Pierce had already been a guest at the Boothes' Thirty-third Street mansion, but he scanned the interior yet again. The foyer was huge and circular, the floor and pillars marble. Directly ahead, he could see most of the four hundred wedding guests finding their seats in the vast, domed ballroom where the ceremony was to take place. Overhead, a dozen huge crystal chandeliers hung. An altar had been set up at the very opposite end of the ballroom, framed with arches of pink and white roses and brilliantly lit up with hundreds of high, wide ivory tapers. Rows and rows of benches had been assembled to accommodate the guests, on either side of the long aisle upon which the bride would walk down. Perhaps fifty tall, wide ivory tapers on high pedestals graced either side of the aisle, interspersed with more floral arrangements. It was visually breathtaking, but Pierce remained oblivious. The ballroom interested him as much as the bride. But just outside of the ballroom, to his right, were the stairs.

It was a sweeping staircase of brass and cast iron.

The brunette, who was very attractive, was looking at him over her shoulder with a smile. Pierce realized she had caught him studying the house and he smiled back at her. She demurely lowered her eyes, but now the other woman turned to stare. Her cheeks became pink and she instantly faced forward, ducking her head toward her friend.

"Who *is* that?" she whispered, but he heard her anyway.

"Ssh. Not now. I do not know." The brunette glanced quickly at him again.

This time, he bowed.

She flushed. Her wedding ring, the diamond at least eight full carats, glinted on her left hand. Purchased at Tiffany's, it had cost an astonishing seventy-five thousand dollars.

And then the line moved forward, and George Boothe was greeting the two couples. Pierce remained relaxed.

Boothe saw him and smiled widely. "My dear Braxton," he said, clasping his hand. "I am so pleased you could attend my daughter's wedding after all." He was in his late fifties, heavyset and jovial, with huge mutton-chop whiskers.

Pierce smiled, a flash of dazzling white teeth, by now quite accustomed to the name that was not his. "George, how could I miss the happy event?" His British accent was pronounced and unmistakable.

Boothe stepped closer and lowered his voice. "I am extremely excited about the merger we discussed. I have scheduled a trip to Philly to look at your emporium next week and my bank has assured me, pending my inspection of the premises and your books, that there will be no problems at all. It looks as if we shall be moving forward far sooner than anticipated, my boy." He beamed.

"I am very pleased, also," Pierce said emphatically, the irony of the situation not lost upon him—poor Boothe expected to make another million or two when all was said and done, and he, Pierce St. Clare, knew not a whit about retail merchandising and hardly owned the emporium Boothe would soon be visiting. However, Pierce had no intention of being anywhere in the northeast by the time Boothe put two and two together and realized he had been taken, and royally. Pierce did smile at the irony of that.

He moved on, handing his hat and gloves to a waiting servant and pausing just inside the ballroom without taking a seat—so he could slip out as soon as possible.

He lingered until everyone was in the ballroom then stepped just past the threshold. When the foyer was empty, not a servant or guest in sight, he took the stairs two at a time to the second floor. No one saw him. He made sure of it.

He was sweating. One quick glance out of the window showed him that Louie might not see his signal, but there was a backup plan. He checked several doors until he came to the master bedroom, which was unlocked—not a good sign—and he quickly let himself in. The suite was an onslaught upon the senses—reds and golds competed with silks and damask and marble and wood. He knew where the safe was—and even if he hadn't he would have been able to find it immediately, as the location was hardly original. The vault was behind the huge Tiepolo that was hanging on the crimson-flocked wall facing the draped, canopied bed.

He extracted a hearing trumpet from an interior pocket, slipped a ball of wax in his other ear, and got to work. Within sixty seconds he had opened the safe, feeling a surge of satisfaction as he did so. And then he stared.

It was empty.

Which explained why the bedroom had not been locked.

Pierce thought of Lucinda Boothe's good friend Dariella, an extremely loquacious woman in bed, and he cursed. She claimed that Lucinda kept all of her jewels in the safe in her bedroom, and by damn, she had been wrong. For one moment, he felt like throttling the beautiful redhead for her misinformation—as guileless as it was.

But he had no time to lose. He checked his pocket watch. Eleven minutes had elapsed since he had left Louie outside. He slammed the safe closed, replaced the painting, and tucked his hearing trumpet in one of the many secret pockets that lined the interior of his dinner jacket. He stepped to the door, cracked it, and was reassured that no one was about. He hurried downstairs.

There was another possibility. In the foyer, he paused briefly to compose himself, glancing at the guests in the ballroom, all of whom were now attentively and restlessly awaiting the start of the wedding ceremony. A male servant suddenly entered the rotunda. But the man paid no attention to Pierce, disappearing down another hall with very brisk strides. Pierce turned and strode in the opposite direction. As he did so, he heard the organ in the ballroom begin to play. He was relieved, and he smiled.

Four hundred guests and the Boothe family would be very preoccupied for the next half an hour or so.

The very solid teakwood door to the library was closed. Only four nights ago he had been drinking a very fine and very old port wine within its confines, with George Boothe himself. The notes of the bridal march washing over him, Pierce tried the knob and found it locked. Instead of being dismayed, a thrill washed over him. He extracted a ring of skeleton keys from one of his pockets, trying several. The third let him in.

Pierce quickly closed the door behind him, his gaze slamming on the verdant John Constable landscape hanging over the fireplace. He smiled. And when he removed it from the wall, the dark metal vault stared back at him. Again, Boothe's placement of his safes was hardly original.

In less than sixty seconds he had the vault open. His pulse surged when he saw the velvet boxes and pouches inside the dark interior. Quickly, he began dumping all of the contents out. There were rings and necklaces and earrings, a lifetime's worth of jewelry. He sorted through quickly, looking for one piece in particular. And at last he found it. The pearl necklace. Pierce quickly inserted it into the specially sewn pocket that lined his dinner jacket.

He closed the safe, lifted the painting, which he did not pause to admire, and set it back upon its hooks. As he turned, he heard a noise, and realized that he had company.

He froze.

And stared at the rotating brass knob on the library door. Someone was about to enter the room. Less than a second passed and Pierce moved, diving to the floor and scrambling over to the claw-footed green sofa, just as the door creaked open.

"Damn it," a woman muttered very unhappily.

He relaxed very slightly—a woman would be easier to deal with than a man. His mind raced. His hiding place was a sham. He could not get under the sofa, the bottom was far too low, and while right now it served its purpose, because the couch was between him and the woman, it would become useless if the intruder did not stay on the other side of the room.

"Damn, damn, damn," the woman moaned.

He stiffened again, because he could hear her soft footsteps as she entered the room, along with the rustling of her skirts. Worse, he had not heard her close the door and the dim light in the library had become brighter. The wedding march sounded far too loudly for comfort now. Why was this woman not with the guests? He glanced awkwardly toward the hearth. And he cursed silently. The Constable hung at an obviously unstable angle, a dead giveaway of the burglary that had just taken place.

Pierce gritted his teeth. He would have to straighten it before he made his hasty exit.

"Oh, God," she moaned again, as if suffering very greatly. Pierce shifted so he could gaze beneath the sofa in her direction and he froze. Her skirts were stunningly white, beaded, and covered with lace. If he did not miss his guess, the woman was the bride.

He almost cursed aloud.

"Oh, God, what am I going to do?" she cried.

He stared at her skirts, not many paces from the sofa. The bride was in the library, but she was supposed to be walking down the aisle. From her tone, it did not take a genius to assume that she had little intention of doing what was expected of her—at least not in the near future. Worse, she was walking toward the couch. A dozen excuses for lying on the floor raced through his mind. He dismissed them all instantly as absurd.

And then her white slippered feet veered away. Pierce froze again, shifting, turning his neck at an impossibly awkward angle—she was walking around the couch. He held his breath, prepared to be discovered at any moment.

But she did not walk around it to sit down. Instead, she ambled past the sofa and the table and chairs surrounding it, her long pristine white skirts and equally long sheer veil trailing behind her. His gaze was unwavering. But now he was surprised. For an open bottle of champagne was clasped by its neck in her right hand.

She halted at the window, her back to him, gazing out at the sunny afternoon, or so he assumed. "How has this happened?" she whispered, and she raised the bottle and swilled directly from it.

The bottle was, he saw, two-thirds empty. Goddamn it. The bride was unhappy, she was drunk, and she was never going to leave the library so he could make his escape.

He quickly considered the possibility of slipping out of the room without being detected while she drank at the window. It was too risky. He considered standing up, before she turned, and introducing himself. Again, too risky—he'd be accused of the heist later. These two options he analyzed with lightning speed, within the span of several seconds. As a third option came to him, she turned, once again drinking from the bottle like a common saloon girl.

He froze.

She swigged. And for another moment, as she clutched the bottle, he saw that she was drinking la grande dame of champagnes, a vintage year of Veuve Cliquot, and he gave her half a dozen points for her good taste and her ability to hold her liquor. She did not see him yet, but that would change in a moment. But where were her warts and birthmarks? Poor, unfortunate, just-barely-a-spinster Annabel Boothe was not what he might have expected—had he been expecting anything. She was blond, blue-eyed, angelically beautiful. Then he saw that she was staring at the painting that was hanging so lop-sidedly over the fireplace. "Oh, dear," she said to herself.

He grimaced, about to rise from his very awkward position on the floor.

And then her gaze moved directly to, and upon, him—where it riveted.

He smiled up at her, feeling rather foolish.

She gaped.

"Hello," he said, aware of using his most devastating grin upon her.

"Oh, dear! Are you hurt?" she cried, rushing forward.

"Actually," he said, seizing upon the excuse, "it is my knee. A bad injury, you see." He began to rise.

To his surprise, she put the champagne down and in the blink of an eye was actually assisting him to his feet, supporting his weight with her shoulder. "Did you fall down?" she asked when he was finally standing upright, her arms still around him.

He stared into her brilliantly blue eyes, a blue that even two thirds of a bottle of superior champagne could not dim. In other circumstances, he would enjoy her concern and take advantage of it. "Yes, thank you, I did."

"Here, let me help you to sit, then," she said, pushing him toward the sofa.

"No, I am fine." He resisted, and she was strong, surprisingly so for a woman of her size and attractiveness.

"But you are hurt."

"It is an old injury, actually," he said, smiling. "The war."

"The war?" She continued to press her body against his, trying to urge him to the sofa. "What war?"

"The—ah—er—a brief skirmish in South Africa, you see."

"South Africa? Of course, you are British. Your accent is quite pronounced. And—" Suddenly she stopped in mid-sentence. Her blue gaze was on his. He knew the moment she realized that she was embracing him and that he was a man—and an exceedingly rakish one at that. Or so many women had told him.

Her cheeks turned a very becoming shade of pink. She dropped her arms. "Perhaps you should sit," she said, low and huskily, now avoiding his eyes.

He could not help himself, he staggered, as if imbalanced by his bad knee without her support.

"Oh," she cried, with concern. Her arms went around him again.

He smiled at her as their gazes met. Poor, unfortunate Annabel Boothe? Inwardly, he did laugh. "Miss Boothe," he said, as gently as possible, not breaking contact. "Are you not wanted elsewhere?"

She remained flushed, her gaze holding his again. And as she grasped his meaning, her expression changed dramatically. It crumpled, and she stepped away from him. He wondered if he was about to have a weeping woman on his hands. Perhaps she would swoon. That would be convenient. "Miss Boothe?"

But she snatched the bottle and looked at him defiantly. "I am hardly wanted, sir," she snapped. But her tone was tremulous, ruining the effect of her glare.

"I am sure you are wanted very much, Miss Boothe," he said gently, wanting her to go her merry way. But now she was angry—a response he had not anticipated. "I have heard that the groom is smitten."

She gazed at him as if he had lost his mind.

He smiled again. "Smitten and with his own fortune, as well. A lady could hardly do better," he encouraged. And almost added, at your age.

"He is a worm."

He blinked. "I beg your pardon?" he asked.

Tears filled her eyes. "He is a spineless toad," she said, her full pink mouth trembling. "I cannot marry him!"

He was taken aback. "Perhaps, my dear Miss Boothe, you and your fiancé should have a heart-to-heart *after* the nuptials?"

She continued to regard him as if he were a traitor. And then Pierce realized what was wrong. The organ had ceased playing. There was no wedding march. "Damn it," he said.

"There cannot be nuptials or I shall be unhappy for the rest of my life," she cried, drinking more champagne.

He could not believe his dilemma. "My dear Miss Boothe. This is your grand opportunity in life. Every young lady wishes to marry, especially a fine young man like your fiancé."

"*I* do not wish to marry," she said. She pushed the bottle toward him. "Would you care for a drink?"

On any other occasion he would have said yes. "Miss Boothe. If you reject your fiancé now, you may not have a second chance," he said as calmly as possible.

"Do you refer to the fact that I am twenty-three and a half years old, sir?" She swigged again.

He smiled, and it was forced. "I would hardly be so bold."

"I am being sold off like a milk cow," she said.

"You are hardly a milk cow, Miss Boothe. You are attractive, well-spoken, gracious, why, you are what every man dreams of." There, he thought, that should do it.

"Are you well?" she asked. "I think you are delusional."

Most women did not have such a word in their vocabulary, much less even know its meaning, and he could only stare.

Pierce was actually contemplating commanding her to go to the ballroom when he heard a woman calling Annabel's name from outside the library. "Annabel?"

He jerked around, alarmed.

"It's my mother," Annabel muttered. "Oh, God, why does the entire world think I should marry him?"

He whirled again. "Because you should, you can," he said, his hands on her shoulders, "and you will." His intention was to push her out of the room, by damn, before they were discovered—before he was discovered. But he felt something odd on his hip. Something hard. Something that should not be there. At first he thought it was the champagne bottle that she continued to grip by her skirts.

"Annabel? Dear, please, where are you?" Lucinda Boothe cried from somewhere just outside of the library in the corridor.

It was not the champagne bottle. Pierce felt the object slide down his thigh. He glanced down just in time to watch the magnificent triple-tiered pearl and diamond necklace slipping along his black pants leg to the floor.

"What is that!" Annabel cried, her gaze on the glittering necklace as well.

"Annabel?" Lucinda Boothe sounded as if she were in the doorway—or very close to it.

Pierce met Annabel's accusing blue gaze, smiled, and grabbed her. With one strong arm he clamped her to his torso. "Do not scream," he said calmly. "Or I will break your neck."

She froze. For a brief instant, her disbelieving gaze held his. "You wouldn't!" she gasped.

"Do not test me," he returned, bending to retrieve the necklace. And as he did so, she shifted, bent, and tried to jam her elbow right in his groin.

Pierce realized what she was doing before she could succeed and he managed to elude her and prevent a very serious injury, indeed. He jerked her up hard against him again. And this time, he used his free hand to point a revolver at the base of her skull. "Miss Boothe. That was hardly ladylike. I suggest you cooperate. You are a very beautiful woman. I like beautiful women. I do not want to hurt you, but I have no desire to find myself in jail."

"Then you should not be a thief," she spat, very flushed and struggling wildly now. "You won't shoot me. You are no cold-blooded killer, sir!"

"Do not bet your life upon it," he said coolly.

"Annabel!" Lucinda Boothe screamed.

Pierce turned, hugging Annabel to his body, and he smiled at Lucinda Boothe, who stood just inside the library doorway. The plump blond lady was in the midst of losing all her coloring. "Madam, I suggest that you stand still. I will not hurt your daughter."

"I am fine, Mama," Annabel said stoically. "He has stolen your jewels," she added, twisting to fling a grave look at him over her shoulder.

Lucinda Boothe stared at them soundlessly, then slumped to the floor in a dead faint.

"Mama!" Annabel cried. "She needs her salts. She is always fainting."

"Thank God for small things," Pierce said, hustling

his hostage past the unconscious woman, out of the library and down the hall. He did not falter, in spite of the fact that two servants were in the foyer and they halted in their tracks, their eyes widening, their mouths forming O's.

"Help!" Annabel shrieked abruptly.

"Do not move," Pierce countermanded the staff, jerking on her. The servants remained frozen like statues. Annabel refused to move her feet so he dragged her across the foyer. His glance could not help but take in the ballroom. Heads were turning. Gasps were heard. Four hundred guests were becoming cognizant of the abduction of the bride.

Pierce himself could hardly believe what was happening. He propelled the now-silent Annabel and himself to the threshold of the foyer.

"Braxton!" Boothe cried from behind him in shock and disbelief.

Pierce halted, facing Annabel's father. "I will not hurt her. Do not move."

Boothe was incredulous, but anger quickly overcame him. "You son of a bitch! Release my daughter!" he shouted from the entrance to the ballroom.

A young man had come up beside him, as blond and blue-eyed as Annabel, clad in a tailcoat with a red carnation pinned to his lapel. "Oh, God!" he cried. "He is stealing my bride! Someone do something!" A dozen guests crowded behind him and Boothe now.

"As long as nobody moves, she will be returned to you no worse for wear," he said, briefly pointing the revolver at the crowd. Collectively they gasped.

Pierce replaced the muzzle of the pistol to Annabel's skull and dragged her out of the house.

"You will regret this," she cried, but now she was running with him of her own volition.

"I am sure that I will," he said. But he was not thinking about the bride. He had never signaled Louie from the second floor as had been the plan, but the backup plan had called for Louie to have the Packard waiting for a getaway in thirty minutes should Pierce fail to signal. He was certain that thirty-five minutes or so had elapsed, but the Packard was nowhere to be seen. Had Pierce had the luxury, he would have been in a state of severe disbelief. Louie had never let him down before.

"Damn it, Louie!" he said, hurrying with Annabel toward the drive.

"Who is Louie?" she gasped, tripping now over her skirts as he increased their pace.

Pierce had no intention of answering her, because the father of the bride, the groom, and at least a hundred guests were crowding the front door of the mansion, watching him as he fled with Annabel. And then, just past several parked coaches and waiting grooms, he saw the Packard. "Louie!" he roared.

And Louie saw him. The Packard had been idling, now it came to life, rolling forward. Pierce ran to it, Annabel clamped to his side. When he reached the motorcar, he released her, pushing her away. She fell onto her hands and knees in the drive as he vaulted into the passenger seat. "Go!" he said, as Louie shifted gears. And he turned to look at her. Sweat was trickling into his eyes.

She was rising. Grass, dirt, and gravel now stained her wedding dress, and her blue eyes were wide. She faced him, and their gazes locked. The tiara she wore, which held her veil in place, was slipping.

Pierce was sorry that he had ruined her wedding. But since she was so reluctant to wed, maybe he had done her a favor. He couldn't help feeling an odd regret. There was nothing unfortunate about Annabel Boothe and she deserved a real man, not that milksop he had seen in the foyer.

And the Packard jerked, backfired, and stalled.

"Damn it." Pierce turned to Louie, incredulous.

Louie was leaping out, to crank up the engine again.

Pierce jumped into the driver's seat and shifted. Half a dozen gentlemen were running from the house toward him, including Boothe and the groom. Murder was justifiably upon their minds. And Annabel just stood there, a few feet from the motorcar, as if she had turned into a statue herself, watching them running toward her in her spoiled and stained wedding dress.

The engine roared to life.

"Get in!" Pierce shouted at Louie.

Louie was already racing for the passenger door, but Annabel had turned and seemed to be doing the exact same thing. Pierce could not believe his eyes as the two of them collided. "Christ. Get in, Louie!" he roared.

They separated, Louie tripping on Annabel's voluminous skirts. Pierce watched the pack of men coming closer—they were twenty yards away. And then a flurry of white landed in the seat beside him, followed by his driver, who leapt upon Annabel. As she shoved Louie to the floor, Pierce slammed down the gas pedal, gritting his teeth, filled with anger, the veil flying in his face. He brushed the transparent material out of his eyes as the Packard leapt forward, spitting out stones from beneath its tires.

This was unbelievable.

The Packard sped wildly around the circular drive. A horse reared, backing up in terror, pushing its coach into another carriage.

Gripping the steering wheel with two hands, his gaze glued on the straightaway and Fifth Avenue, beyond that, Pierce saw, from the corner of his eye, Louie righting himself in the same seat as the bride. And then they were shooting through the wide-open front gates. Tires screeched as he turned the Packard so hard to the left that two wheels briefly lost contact with the ground.

Annabel was huffing and puffing and pushing her veil

out of her face and eyes. She did not look at him. Her cheeks were very red.

But Louie did, absolute amazement on his face, along with an obvious question.

He was driving very fast, passing carriages, wagons, a hansom, and a cyclist. The Holland House, one of the city's most fashionable hotels, was on their right. A liveried doorman was standing in the street to wave down a cab, and a pair of gentlemen were attempting to cross on the same corner of Thirtieth Street. A dray was also trying to cross Fifth Avenue. Driving was taking almost all of his concentration. Casting one brief glance of steel at the very flushed bride, he said, "Throw her out."

"Aye, aye, guvnor," Louie replied.

Chapter Two

Annabel gripped the smooth dark leather seat of the motorcar as the thief drove like a madman down Fifth Avenue, weaving in between coaches and carriages, wagons and drays. She was coming out of her champagne-induced daze. She could barely believe what was happening—that she had left her groom at the altar, with her family and friends and several hundred of New York's most prominent members of society. Oh, God.

But a small smile formed on her lips.

And then he commanded Louie to throw her out of the motorcar.

His harsh words made her whip her head around to stare at him in a combination of amazement and dismay. Had she misheard?

"Throw her out," he said again, as firmly.

The expression on her father's face—and her fiancé's—as they stared at her in the foyer while the thief dragged her out of the house seared itself upon her mind. She recalled the sight of the several hundred shocked and gaping guests. Her pulse raced with alarming speed. Her fingers dug more deeply into the leather seat. She was not going anywhere.

She had made her choice. She could not marry Harold

Talbot. Not now, not tomorrow, not ever. This was, must be, fate.

Louie's hands closed upon her shoulders.

Annabel realized what was happening and cried out as the motorcar veered wildly to the curb and came to an abrupt halt, throwing them all toward the dashboard. "Now!" the Brit shouted at his small, wizened partner.

Annabel was jerked onto Louie's lap. Her chin hit the door. His intention, presumably, was to open the door and thrust her out onto the street.

"No!" Annabel cried, jerking free of his grip immediately, pulling back and rearing up on her knees, one fist raised. She slammed it into his face, not thinking, just fighting for her freedom—for her life.

Louie's head slapped backward, his eyes rolling shut, his body going limp.

"Jesus!" the thief cried.

Even Annabel was surprised, although she knew that she was stronger than most women, for she was constantly walking, riding, bicycling, swimming, and playing tennis. But her shock only lasted a moment, because the thief grabbed her, now undoubtedly harboring the exact same intention as Louie.

Their gazes met. He gripped her by her shoulders, hesitating. His eyes were sky blue and determined. "No!" Annabel shouted, struggling against him, trying to push him away. But she knew that it was futile—for she had experienced his superior strength firsthand just moments ago, when he had taken her hostage at the house. "You need a hostage, don't you? How much luckier could you be?—For I am willing!"

His eyes widened. "You are insane," he muttered. And then a whistle sounded behind them, loud and shrill and piercing.

He cursed, releasing her, shifting into gear and gunning the motorcar forward. Annabel was slammed back against the seat and the unconscious Louie. She strug-

gled to right herself as another shrill whistle sounded
and she twisted around to gaze behind them. Still driving
like someone insane—or like a crook determined to
avoid capture—the thief turned the automobile hard
onto Twenty-seventh Street heading west toward Broadway. Annabel watched two mounted policemen galloping after them, in hot pursuit.

She stole a glance at her captor. His expression was
set, at once grim, determined, and fierce. His eyes remained glued upon the road—he was about to shoot
across the congested avenue of Broadway. He did not
seem frightened by their pursuit in the least. She had to
admire him, and not just because of his cool demeanor.
He was, without a doubt, one of the most striking men
she had ever laid eyes upon. Annabel twisted to watch
the galloping policemen again. "They will catch us," she
cried. "There's too much traffic on Broadway. You
should have stayed on Fifth!" She could see herself
standing at the altar with Harold.

He shot her a look of disbelief.

"The traffic was lighter on Fifth," she said defensively.

"Hold on," he ordered, his eyes on the intersection
ahead, his knuckles white as he gripped the steering
wheel.

She turned her gaze forward and all her admiration
for the man driving the Packard vanished. Her heart
slammed to a stop. Two cable cars were coming down
Broadway, one after the other, on their electric tracks.
If he did not halt and let the cars pass, it was obvious
they would all crash into one another. Their motorcar
could not possibly cross the path of the cable cars in
time to avoid a collision. "Stop!" Annabel cried, seized
with panic. "Stop or you will kill us all!"

It was as if he had not heard her. With one hand he
banged hard on the horn, so it sounded as one long,
incessant blare. And the motorcar shot into the intersection.

Annabel was clinging to the dashboard of the automobile. She could see the faces of the men and women in the approaching first trolley. It was but a few yards away. Expressions of incredulity gave way to panic and then terror. A blond woman screamed. A straphanger's eyes, behind horn-rimmed spectacles, met her own. Her own face, she thought, mesmerized, must be as white as his. She tasted fear. Saw twisted metal, blood, and death.

The Packard screamed over the electric rails as the first cable car continued forward, metal and brass missing brass and wood by mere inches. And then they were roaring up Twenty-seventh Street, leaving Broadway behind.

And Annabel, turned completely around in her seat now, her veil twisted around her neck, watched the second trolley continuing down the track, quite literally on the back fender of the first. It was effectively blocking the two mounted policemen from following them. She slumped against the seat back, her heart beating like a jungle drum, smiling. "You did it," she whispered. Then she was thrown against the driver as he turned the motorcar hard to the right, onto Sixth Avenue. Overhead, a train on the El thundered by.

Annabel disengaged herself as the thief drove beneath the elevated tracks, chasing young boys in knickers playing stick ball into the shadows of the surrounding five- and six-story tenement buildings. Briefly, his gaze met hers. "Are you enjoying yourself?" he asked.

Annabel settled down in her seat. "Actually, you are quite a good driver." She smiled at him. She was enjoying herself—now that they had eluded the police and a fatal cable-car crash.

He glanced at her again while turning so sharply up another cross street that a man pulling a two-wheeled fruit cart was almost run over. As they sprayed a muddy puddle in their wake, Annabel glanced back and saw the vendor, perhaps a Jewish immigrant, shaking his fist at them, his coarse wool jacket soaking wet. Pedestrians on the sidewalks, working women in ready-mades and young male clerks, were all turning to gape at them as they sped by.

"Thank you," he said, and he flashed his spectacular smile at her. "I have had a lot of practice."

Annabel found herself smiling back. This thief had nerve—lots of it. "I imagine you have. Who are you?"

He turned onto Seventh Avenue, still driving at a madcap pace. "You may call me Braxton." Two mounted gentlemen jerked their mounts out of their way, riding up onto the sidewalk.

She eyed him, aware of them racing past another motorcar. "Is that your real name?"

His smile reappeared, but briefly. "You are a clever girl." Suddenly he veered around an omnibus and pulled up at the curb in front of a store advertising suits for sale. A furrier's sign was hanging outside the second-floor window. "Now get out."

Annabel did not move.

He appeared relaxed as he sat there in the front seat, both hands lightly on the wheel. "I am not Louie," he warned. "And I do not need a hostage."

She wet her lips. "Yes you do. They will let you get away if you threaten to hurt me. I am certain of it."

He leaned toward her. "Aren't you frightened, Miss Boothe? Hasn't it crossed your mind that I might hurt you—or at the least get you killed accidentally?"

His gaze was mesmerizing. She could not look away. "I can't. I can't go back there. I cannot."

He was staring. His eyes were opaque, impossible to read. "So it is the groom who terrifies you—far more than myself."

He did not frighten her at all. Not really—even though he did make her heart race. And Annabel had never been at all seductive before. But she was desperate. And even though men always lost interest in her soon after the first introductions were made, because she could outride, outshoot, outtalk, and outthink them all, she was fairly certain that she was beautiful—she had been told so a thousand times. She was, in fact, considered the most beautiful of the Boothe sisters, and Melissa and Lizzie were both gorgeous. Of course, she was also considered the odd one, the mannish one, the bluestocking—the one who couldn't catch a husband even if her father gave away most of his fortune on her behalf. Annabel had never cared about her beauty before, it had never seemed important or even useful.

But now she cared. She needed this man's help. Very self-conscious, she leaned toward him, her gaze on his, at once earnest and intent, praying that this once she could manage a man the way her sister Melissa could. "Please."

For one more moment they stared at one another. The clanging of trolleys, the roaring of the elevated trains, the clopping of horses' hooves, even pigeons cooing on the nearby roof, all faded and disappeared. Annabel crossed her fingers. Instinct told her not to move, not to speak—not even to breathe.

"Do not bat your lashes at me, it makes you look like a simpering fool."

Annabel winced, afraid she had lost, not just that round, but everything she valued in her life.

He grimaced. And then he shifted hard into gear and drove back into the heavy traffic of milk wagons and freight lorries, horse cars and trolleys. He turned his hard blue gaze to the road, as if concentrating on driving. His strong, clean jaw was set. Annabel was faint with relief. But she thought she could feel his thoughts—and they were directed, not quite charitably, toward herself. She had won, but it was only the first round, and she did not fool herself. He intended to get rid of her, and eventually he would.

But she could manage with eventually. As long as it

wasn't just then. For she had not lied when she had said she could not go back.

If she went back now, they would try to marry her off to Harold Talbot. A fate far worse than death—or a tarnished reputation.

Annabel smiled to herself, shaking a little, the newly hatched plan having taken a firm hold on her. And then a thought occurred to her. She quickly pulled the veil from her head and stuffed it beneath the dashboard at her and Louie's feet. She winced, feeling guilty as she regarded him. "Why is he still unconscious?"

"That was some right hook," Braxton remarked. They were now on Ninth Avenue, driving directly beneath the El.

She smiled. "Thank you."

He eyed her briefly. "You should be ashamed of such prowess."

"Yes, I should—but I am not like my sisters or other women." She reached behind her and began to undo the many small pearl buttons on the back of her dress. It was excessively difficult without a maid. "I did not mean to hurt him, though. I guess I do not know my own strength. When I was twelve I got into a fight with Tommy Bratweiller. I gave him two black eyes." She noticed they were heading uptown at a good clip now, and were already at Seventy-fifth Street. She had never been this far uptown on the West Side. It was hardly like being in New York City—at least not the New York City she knew. Huge lots of land stood vacant amidst smaller buildings and warehouses. Through the gaps in the buildings, she could see the Hudson River to the west, and the cliffs of New Jersey soaring above it on the river's other side. She even glimpsed two goats in someone's backyard.

He looked at her. "Two black eyes, not one? Tsk, tsk." And then he obviously realized what she was doing.

She flushed but ignored him, pulling the bodice of her wedding dress off her shoulders and down to her hips. She was wearing a corset, chemise, petticoats, and drawers, everything lacy and trimmed with satin ribbons for the occasion of the marriage, so she was far from naked. Still, he continued to glance at her. She shimmied out of the dress. Her cheeks were hot. She ordered herself not to think about the fact that she was undressing in front of this man. Hadn't she swum naked in the lake up in the hills around Bar Harbor? In spite of her sisters' hysteria?

"What are you doing?" he asked in that oh-so-calm British way of his.

"I am too conspicuous in the dress," she said, feeling herself continue to blush. "I am sure the telegraph lines must be humming by now. As a bride, I am a red flag to the police."

"You are as conspicuous in your underwear," he returned evenly. Suddenly he turned off the avenue, into an alley between two barns. And he halted the motorcar, jumping out.

Annabel shivered, also climbing out over the still form of Louie. She eyed the small man. "Do you think he is all right?" She was worried.

He was opening the barn door. "I am sure he will revive in a moment or so," he said, returning to the driver's seat. "He used to box. Lightweight, of course. He never quite recovered. I think you may have gotten an old injury."

"Oh, dear." Annabel realized that he planned to hide the car in the barn. She said admiringly, "This is brilliant."

He slowly drove the automobile forward as if he did not hear her. Annabel walked into the barn behind him. She smiled at the sight that greeted her—a horse and carriage, the horse already in the traces. "Truly brilliant," she said, more to herself than him.

He stepped out of the car, slamming the door. This time, briefly, his glance met hers.

She watched him pull Louie from the vehicle, leaving him on the ground. He then took a medium-sized satchel from the carriage and slipped off his tailcoat. Annabel watched him removing the jewelry he had stolen from one small compartment sewn into the jacket's lining, transferring it to the satchel. "You have thought of everything," she said.

"I hope so. You might want to turn around," he remarked, removing his bow tie.

Annabel blinked as he reached for the buttons on his snowy white shirt. He smiled at her. She realized that he was undressing, and watched as his shirt parted, revealing a broad slab of chest dusted with midnight-black hair.

Immediately she turned her back on him. Of course he would change clothes. She berated herself for not realizing earlier that he would do so. But what had possessed her to stare? And she was certain that he had known that she had been staring.

She could feel herself flushing, and as she heard his clothes rustling—he was stepping out of his trousers, she presumed—she walked around the Packard to give herself something to do. He was tall and lean and handsome. He was bold and exceedingly cool. His accent was the coup de grâce. If Harold had been at all like this man, she wondered if she would have objected so strenuously to the match.

Not that her family would ever allow her to marry a thief. It was a ludicrous thought.

Besides, she did not want to marry. All women turned into fools when they married, endlessly redoing decor, shopping until dropping, planning teas and babies. That was not for Annabel.

"Done," he said cheerfully a moment later.

She turned and found him clad in a sack jacket and

paler trousers. His evening clothes had been stuffed in the front seat of the Packard. A huge oilskin tarp was folded up on the floor, nestled among bales of moldy hay. "If you truly want to help, take up that end," he said with a nod at the tarp.

Annabel hurried to obey. "Does anything scare you?" she asked as they lifted the tarp in tandem and settled it over the Packard.

"Very little," he said, with a smile.

"You like this," she said after a moment. "You liked eluding the police."

"Didn't you?" he returned.

She refused to answer. "You have thought of everything," she mused. "Do you do this often?"

"Often enough," he said with a grin. He had a dimple in his left cheek, a cleft in his chin.

She watched him kneeling over Louie, gently slapping his face. "So you are a professional thief."

"Hmm. I do not think I need to answer that."

Suddenly Louie moaned, his lashes fluttering. "Thank God," she breathed.

"Didn't want to be branded a murderess?" he said somewhat mockingly. "An accomplice, perhaps, but murder would be too much?"

She met his gaze. There was a gleam there, perhaps of amusement. "I had no intention of hurting him. Murder is never justified."

He folded his arms and stared. After a long pause, he said, "It is time for you to go home, Miss Boothe. And I am afraid you will have to make your own way."

She stiffened. "You would not abandon me now!"

"Not only would I, I am doing so."

Her eyes widened, her heart lurched.

"Gawd, wot happened?" Louie said, sitting up groggily, one hand going to the huge bruise on his temple.

"The lady dealt you a severe blow," Braxton said with

real amusement. "Change your clothes, my friend. We must be on our way."

Louie had now recovered enough to moan and glare at his partner in crime at the exact same time. Then he looked darkly at Annabel.

"I'm sorry," Annabel said, meaning it. She hurried to the thief. "You cannot leave me here—on the West Side—in my drawers and petticoats."

He smiled. "You are a fetching sight, my dear. I am sure that in no time at all you will be aided and abetted by some concerned and civic-minded gentleman and on your way back to the altar."

"I want to come with you! I can help—"

"No." He turned his back on her and reached down for Louie. "Let's see if you can stand," he said.

Louie stood with Braxton's aid and went around to the other side of the carriage to change his clothes. Annabel rushed over to the thief. "What must I do to convince you to let me stay with you—just for a few days?"

He folded his arms across his chest as he studied her. "You are very tempting. Just what are you offering, Miss Boothe?"

She swallowed. Did he mean what she thought he did? "I cannot return home. If I return, they will all try to force me back to the altar."

"That is hardly my problem." He was impatient now. "Louie! Hurry up."

"Aye, guvnor."

She gripped his arm. "Braxton. I will go back. But when I do, I must be ruined."

He was finally surprised. His eyes had widened. "Well, well. So you wish my services in this endeavor?"

She hadn't meant it literally. She had meant that she could not return until her reputation was smeared, enough so that no one would want her, and then she would be free to continue her life without interference from her father or all the silly, useless men he kept introducing her to. For then no man would want her. Annabel bit her lip.

His gaze was fixed on her face.

If she told him now that she meant she wanted to be ruined in name only, not in fact, he would abandon her, she was certain of it. She would tell him that later. "I cannot go back now. Not now. It is too soon."

Silence reigned as Louie reappeared from behind the carriage, clad now in a plaid shirt and corduroy trousers. He glanced from one to the other. "We got to go, me lord." He carried the clothing he had changed out of in his arms.

Braxton gave him a piercing look, which Annabel did not understand.

"Please," she said, stepping closer to him. Her heart beat wildly. She was not a fool. What if he ruined her, not in name, but in actuality?

There were worse things, she decided, than this man's kisses.

A lifetime spent with Harold Talbot, for one—or with some idiot just like him.

Braxton's jaw set. He strode to Louie, took his bundle of clothes from him, and shoved them at Annabel— against her chest. "You can dress in the carriage while we leave the city. Get in," he said.

Chapter Three

George Boothe paced his library with savage strides. He had removed his tailcoat and was in a waistcoat and his shirtsleeves. The John Constable landscape, which was usually hanging over the marble hearth, stood on the floor, propped up against a tufted ottoman. The metal vault above the hearth was open, forming a dark and gaping hole.

Another gentleman, clad in an ill-fitting suit and a bowler hat, sporting a handlebar mustache, sat on one of a pair of pale green velvet armchairs, a notebook in his hand. A brass-knobbed walking stick was at his side. Lucinda Boothe sat on the gold and green sofa in her gold evening gown, a cashmere throw over her shoulders, her daughters on either side of her. The two girls' husbands stood behind the sofa, also in their shirtsleeves. Lucinda was sniffing into a hankie. Her eyes were red from hours of intermittent weeping.

"Well, Boothe, I can only say that you have been had, and that this Braxton fellow has done a damn good job of it. Oh, excuse me, ladies." The mustachioed gent stood, snapping closed his notebook and pocketing both that and his lead pencil.

"I could have told you that, Thompson. What are you doing to get my daughter back?" Boothe demanded.

"As we speak," the city's police chief said, "patrols are being sent out. He will not be able to get off Manhattan Island, I promise you that."

"What about the ferries, the bridges?" Boothe demanded, pausing in his pacing only to glare at Thompson, arms akimbo, his red face flushed. "By now he could be in Jersey, by damn!"

"Sir, we have done this before. As I said, he will not be able to get off the island." Thompson smiled in satisfaction.

"Oh, my poor Annabel," Lucinda whispered, choking on a sob.

Melissa, sitting on Lucinda's left, made a sound—something very much like a snort. She was tall like Annabel, but her build was more delicate, her blond hair darker. It was, in fact—and to her horror—more brown than blond. "*Poor* Annabel jumped into the motorcar with the thief, Mama."

Lucinda cried out, bursting into tears again.

Boothe turned to stare at his middle daughter. "That is enough, Missy."

"Melissa," Lizzie said in utter consternation. She was petite and had dark hair and eyes, just like her father. It made a startling contrast to her porcelain skin.

Melissa made a face. "Well, she did. We all saw it. He pushed her away, but oh no. Annabel decided to go and run off with him."

"I do not think she was running off with him," Lizzie cried, standing and wringing her hands.

"Excuse me." Thompson stepped forward, facing Melissa. "Why on earth would your sister jump into the perpetrator's vehicle with him—of her own free will?"

Boothe came between them before Melissa could answer. "Annabel did not jump into that motorcar of her own free will." He gave his daughter an I-will-disinherit-you glare.

Melissa folded her hands demurely on her lap and smiled angelically at Thompson.

Thompson faced Boothe. "Sir, if there is any chance that your daughter has run off with this Braxton fellow, then I need to know it—if you want her back."

"She hasn't run off with anyone!" Boothe roared.

"Oh, dear." Lizzie popped to her feet and gently tugged on Thompson's sleeve. "She was terrified. You do understand, a bride's jitters. That is all it was. Even Annabel would not run away with a complete stranger!"

Melissa snorted again.

Her husband, John, laid a restraining hand on her shoulder from behind. Their gazes met. "Ssh," he said, low.

Thompson saw it all. "All right. What is going on here? What are you all concealing from me? I am now exceedingly suspicious. Perhaps your daughter and this man were in cahoots. Stealing the jewelry together. Why, what a clever plan!"

"My daughter is no thief!" Boothe shouted.

"Oh, no," Lizzie said, paling. "Never! And Mr. Thompson, I would swear to this upon the Bible, Annabel did not know this Braxton gent. She did not."

"Perhaps she did. And kept it from you. Why else would she go with him willingly?"

Boothe sighed. "Thompson, Annabel is impulsive. Unruly. Good God, that's why it's been so hard to get her married. She has a heart of gold, is as honest as a human being can be, but she is, well, unconventional. My own daughter did not steal from me. She did not know this thief, Braxton. But I will admit it. She was dragging her heels over her marriage. Just last night she told me she wanted to break it off, but I would not let her." Boothe's face fell. He walked over to his wife and sat down beside her, taking her hand in his.

Lucinda wept now. "This is my fault. If I had listened

to her, even tried to understand, none of this would have happened."

"Braxton still would have made off with Mother's jewels," Adam said. He was Lizzie's tall, dark, handsome husband.

"Annabel had to get married," Melissa stated. "We all have married, and she is the oldest. It is not our fault that she could not find true love!" She turned to smile at her husband. John smiled back and they clasped hands over the back of the sofa.

"Well, an unconventional woman is a reckless woman, and perhaps Miss Annabel met this gent, fell in love, and rushed off with him purposefully." Thompson nodded to himself.

"She did no such thing!" Boothe cried. But then he faced Lizzie. *"Did she?"*

Lizzie was white. "Papa, I am certain that she never laid eyes upon that fellow before this afternoon." But Lizzie's hands toyed with the folds of her evening gown. Her face showed dismay.

"You don't sound certain," Thompson said flatly.

"No one can ever be certain about Annabel," John muttered.

"She is truly impossible to fathom," Melissa stated.

"Miss Boothe?" Thompson prompted Lizzie gently but firmly.

Lizzie bit her lip. Tears had filled her eyes. "Annabel would never . . ." she began, then trailed off. The tip of her nose was turning red.

"Do you know something you are not telling us?" Boothe was roaring again, but his eyes were wide and he was aghast.

"I do not know anything. I only know that I love my sister and she is the most brave and daring woman!" Lizzie flung her hands up into the air, tears trickling down her cheeks. Adam rushed to her side, slipping his arm around her. "She never said a word to me about meeting someone, or falling in love. There was a time when she was trying very hard to convince herself that Harold was right for her, but a few days ago she gave that up. She was terrified of marrying him—of marrying anyone, truthfully. She did not want to wed!"

"Annabel did not want to marry," Melissa agreed. "Not ever."

"Well. This is quite interesting. A very unusual woman, hmm?" Thompson had pulled out his notebook and made a short, decisive note. He slipped it back into an interior breast pocket. "Miss Boothe. Was your sister capable of falling in love with a complete stranger and running away with him?"

Lizzie stared. Her hand slipped into Adam's.

"Miss Boothe? I am not asking you if she did such a thing. I am asking you if she was capable of such recklessness."

Lizzie remained mute. She glanced fearfully at Adam. "You need not answer," he said, but his own expression was strained.

"Oh, pshaw," Melissa said, waving one slim hand and standing. Her pale, cream-colored chiffon gown fell in rippling folds about her. "Not only does everyone in this room know that Annabel was indeed capable of just that, so do all our friends. Her character, such as it is, is hardly a secret!"

Thompson looked around him, taking in everyone's expression, and he nodded. He folded his thick arms across his chest. "Well."

Boothe rubbed his temples, standing. "If Annabel was seduced by Braxton, it is not her fault. I was seduced by him, by God. The man is charming and clever. I truly believed him to be who and what he said he was." He flushed again. "I want him behind bars!"

"He is a professional, that is obvious, and I am certain that in no time we will have a dozen or two possible makes on him. We have already sent a telegram to Scotland Yard. Have no fear, Mr. Boothe. Even if your daughter was an accomplice to this crime, a crime has been committed, and it is my duty to solve it and apprehend the perpetrators. And I shall do just that." Boothe nodded with satisfaction. "I shall notify you the moment they are found. And in the interim, do not be surprised if I return to ask further questions."

"Wait." Boothe stopped him just before he could walk out of the library door. "I wish to offer a reward for the return of my daughter. Post it immediately. Fifty thousand dollars."

Thompson's eyes widened. "Very well. I will post it—but for her return *alive*, Mr. Boothe. I am sure you would not want it any other way."

A small cry sounded. Both men turned to watch Lucinda slumping into a faint, her two daughters and sons-in-law rushing to her.

"There's a patrol up ahead."

Annabel sat on the front seat of the carriage beside Braxton, and she had just seen the mounted policeman herself. She froze, her hands gripping the leather seat, her heart sinking like a stone. But Braxton did not stop the carriage. He continued to drive forward at the same steady pace. It was a pace that precisely matched his previous, matter-of-fact tone.

They had been traveling north for about twenty minutes, through the wooded, suburban countryside surrounding Manhattan. Every now and then they had passed a farm or an orchard. Otherwise, homes were interspersed in the wooded countryside. She wasn't quite sure where they were, exactly, but she knew they were all about to be captured. "What are you doing?" she whispered, gripping his arm.

"Relax, Charles," Braxton said with a smile.

She stared at him. When they had left the barn, he had made her put some dirt on her face and Louie's cap

on her head, her long blond hair twisted up beneath it,
but she did not think she was going to pass muster as a
young man. And what about Braxton? A change of
clothes was hardly a disguise! His description, which
was hardly average, had to be everywhere and his very
upper-crust British accent was a dead giveaway.

He halted the carriage as two policemen came forward
on big bay horses. He was smiling at them. Annabel
thought her own cheeks were red. She was afraid to
breathe.

"I'm going to have to ask you to step out of the carriage, sir," one mounted officer with a big mustache
said.

"Afternoon. What's this about, officers?" Braxton
asked—in a clipped and nasal Yankee twang.

Annabel realized she was gaping and she shut her
mouth.

"Please step down."

"Glad to obey, got all the time in the world," Braxton
said, sounding as if he were a native Brahmin of Boston.
He stepped lithely out of the carriage.

"Boston, eh?" the officer said, dismounting. His tone
had changed, becoming less firm, softer.

"Born and raised, just like my father and his father
before him." Braxton was cheerful.

The officer nodded, then glanced at Annabel and
Louie. "Who are they?"

"Charlie is a distant cousin. He's an orphan—his
grandmother just died. I'm concluding a bit of business
in town, stocks, you know, and am bringing him home
with me."

"An orphan, eh?" the officer said. He was chewing
tobacco now and eyeing Annabel closely.

Annabel was afraid he could see through her absurd
disguise, or that he was going to ask her a question directly, and she felt herself turning redder still, but then
he looked at Louie. She almost swooned with relief.

Louie, meanwhile, appeared to have fallen asleep in the back seat. Annabel closed her eyes.

"My groom," Braxton said.

Annabel jerked, thinking of Harold, certain the thief, damn him, was doing this to her on purpose.

The officer nodded and turned away, mounting. "Sorry to bother you folks. But we're looking for a very clever Englishman and a young woman he has abducted." He tipped his hat. "Seems he also made off with a small fortune in jewels."

Braxton stepped up into the carriage. "Criminals these days," he said with a shake of his head. Annabel felt like killing him. "The nerve! Thank God we have men like you serving citizens like us. Astute and perceptive officers of the law, capable of protecting the innocent and apprehending the guilty."

Annabel looked at him with murder in her eyes.

The policeman smiled. "Have a good day, sir," he said.

Braxton smiled back, lifted the reins, and drove the bay gelding past the barricade. Annabel sat staring stiffly ahead. Her heart continued to beat with frantic insistence. Clop clop clop. The gelding trotted along, taking them farther and farther away from the policemen and the road block. She wanted to look back over her shoulder to see if the two officers had realized their mistake and were now charging after them.

"Do not look back," he said in his usual, aristocratic British accent.

She looked at him. He was smiling. Unruffled, unperturbed—as if this kind of hair-raising narrow escape was an everyday occurrence. "You are not even sweating!" she accused.

" 'E don't sweat," Louie said from the back seat.

He glanced at her briefly. "Aren't you supposed to say 'perspiring'?"

"You are laughing!"

"You, my dear, are the one perspiring."

Annabel took a deep breath and collapsed against the seat. "I admit to being afraid."

"Why? You had nothing to lose—unlike Louie and myself."

Their gazes had locked. "I told you, I cannot go back. Not yet."

"Yes," he said softly, still holding her regard with his. "You most certainly did."

Annabel felt herself stiffening. She thought about being in his arms, about receiving his kiss. Then she shook herself free of the thought. What was wrong with her? Tonight she would explain everything, and there was not going to be either an embrace or a kiss or, dear God, anything else. But her reputation would be ruined and she could return home, a free woman at last.

She thought about her family and felt a twinge of guilt, for putting them through the ordeal of her disappearance. However, far more than guilt claimed her now. Soon she could return home with her ruined reputation, and she felt nothing but dismay at the thought.

She did not want to go home. Being on the run with Braxton was exciting. Her life had never been this exciting before. And she did her best to make it unusual and entertaining; Annabel knew she lived a far more imprudent existence than any woman of her acquaintance. She was always doing something thrilling. For a while she had actually exercised racehorses at dawn. She had spent a year enrolled in a very Bohemian art class on the Lower East Side. She had even modeled for some of the artists—without her clothing. She had taken employment as a shop girl for two weeks in Wanamaker's department store—which was but a block away from her father's emporium. All of these endeavors, of course, had been found out. Missy was a snoop.

And then there was her tennis game, her books, and travel. She adored all three pastimes, but especially traveling abroad. She had been visiting Europe one or two times a year since she was twenty-one. Her father had actually encouraged such adventure, but Annabel knew he had done so only because he hoped she would meet an appropriate man and fall in love and come home affianced.

But nothing to date had been as exciting as being with this man.

"You are staring at me," he said softly.

She swallowed. Not only was she staring, she had been envisioning herself once again in his embrace. Except this time he had been unclothed. He had been long and lean and all hard muscle. Such a thought should be shameful. Annabel found it intriguing.

He was intriguing.

Annabel looked away. They were entering the village of Mott Haven. It was nothing more than a collection of wood-shingled homes, four- and five-story brick stores, and farms. She did not really see the town. She was in trouble, fairly deeply; Annabel knew herself too well. If she continued to think this way, she was going to become even more deeply in trouble than she already was—perhaps irreparably so.

She wanted to ignore the little warning bells going off inside her head. Usually, she did. And then she would be off and running with a new pursuit. The end result was always the same. Being found out, set down, grounded for a time. And being talked about. Poor, poor, unfortunate Annabel Boothe! Whatever makes her so wild, so reckless, so headstrong? Annabel smiled. She considered her peers to be the unfortunate ones.

But to start thinking about her life being boring in comparison with his, why, that was very dangerous, indeed. That could lead her farther astray than she had ever intended to go. Maybe, as Melissa kept saying, there was something wrong with her. Drastically so.

"Is something wrong, Miss Boothe?" He interrupted her thoughts.

Annabel started. "No! No. Nothing is amiss." She smiled at him, but it was strained.

His blue gaze was brilliant and searching. "Having regrets?"

She straightened. "I never have regrets," she said.

His only response was a long, inscrutable, and very wide stare.

Annabel smiled sweetly at him. And realized that night was falling.

Chapter Four

The cheerful and freshly painted white clapboard house was one of the last on Main Street. A white picket fence surrounded it and there was a red barn in the backyard. Braxton drove the carriage directly around the house and into the barn. Both wide, whitewashed doors had been left open.

"More remarkable planning, I see," Annabel said with a glance around. Of course another carriage was in the barn, as was another horse. He had left no stone unturned.

"You are as clever as always," he replied. Braxton's spirits seemed high. He stepped out of the carriage, as did Louie, the smaller man immediately going to their tired gelding and unhitching him from the traces. Braxton looked up at her and held out his hand.

Surprised, yet ridiculously pleased, Annabel was about to accept it when she saw the twinkle in his eye. She was dressed like a stable boy, with dirt on her face. She was not a beautiful woman now. She withdrew her hand and leapt down from the carriage exactly as he had done. He laughed and walked away.

Miffed, she watched him removing a satchel from the second carriage, this one large enough to contain quite a few clothes. "Is the house occupied?" she asked.

"Yes, it is," an unfamiliar female voice said from the barn doorway.

Annabel turned to glimpse a tall honey-blond woman in a navy skirt and shirtwaist standing on the threshold, smiling slightly—not at them, but at Braxton. An instant later he had crossed the barn and taken her hands in his. "Hello, Mary Anne," he said, and he kissed her cheek.

Annabel stared, her pulse drumming, thinking the worst and jealous about it, too. But the woman, who was perhaps forty and quite attractive, merely smiled at Braxton briefly then turned to look at Annabel. Anxiety filled her gray eyes. "Pierce, I did not know you were coming with a third person." Her tone was husky.

Braxton gave her a look. "I do hope you have some coffee brewing?" His meaning was clear—he did not wish to discuss this now.

Mary Anne looked from him to Annabel again. Annabel decided to take matters into her own hands. She strode forward, holding out her hand, aware of acting very outrageous and mannish. She was angry. Any fool would know that there was something—or had been something—between these two. "Hello. I am Annabel. And actually, Pierce did not quite know himself until the very last minute that I would be coming along." She managed a smile. At least she now knew his first name.

Mary Anne stared for a moment longer, then smiled quickly. "Hello. I'm Mrs. Winston. Well, do come in. I know you must all be very tired." Her eyes remained anxious.

They followed their hostess from the barn, both men closing the doors behind them, and headed across the lawn and into the house. Inside it was as cheery as it had been outside. Doilies covered the tables in the parlor, slipcovers the couch. The walls were flocked with red roses and pale stripes. Annabel was left in the parlor with Louie. Braxton followed Mary Anne into the kitchen, just down the hall.

Annabel folded her arms, frowning, wanting very much to know what was going on in the kitchen. Were they in a warm and affectionate embrace? Or a passionate one? She faced Louie, who had flopped down on the worn sofa and was browsing through a catalog from Sears. "Is she an old flame?"

Louie looked up and grinned. "Yer jealous, girlie, an' it shows."

"I am hardly jealous," Annabel said hotly. "Well, it's obvious that they care for one another."

" 'E's got lots of flames." Louie continued to grin.

Annabel turned and stared down the hall, toward the kitchen. She could not hear a sound. "I'm sure he does. Who is he?"

"I think you 'ad better ask the guvnor 'imself." Louie returned to the catalog.

Annabel did not hesitate. She left the parlor, but tried to move as soundlessly as possible, shamelessly hoping to catch the two of them in a torrid embrace. She pressed against the wall when she heard their voices in quiet conversation.

"Pierce, how could you bring her here!" Mary Anne cried, setting a kettle down with a loud clang.

"We will leave at dawn, you have nothing to worry about." His tone was very gentle.

"Nothing to worry about?" Mary Anne was incredulous.

Annabel peeked around the open doorway and saw Mary Anne putting muffins on a plate, her hands moving swiftly and angrily, her back to Braxton. He stood in the center of the kitchen, as relaxed and composed as she was not. He placed both hands on her shoulders from behind. "You are not in danger. I appreciate what you are doing for me, Mary Anne."

Annabel crept forward, staring at them.

Mary Anne turned to face him. "You know I had no choice but to help you, but dear Lord, I wish you would give up these mad escapades of yours—before you wind up in prison or dead!" Tears filled her eyes.

He tilted up her chin. "No one is going to die. What happened to Harry was an accident. A terrible mistake."

"That will not bring him back, now will it?" She used the corner of her apron to dab her eyes. "Annabel Boothe. Oh, God. Why didn't you throw her out somewhere in Manhattan? The countryside must be swarming with federal agents by now!"

He shrugged. "Poor judgment on my part, in that I agree." He turned and looked directly at Annabel. "Enjoying yourself yet again?"

Annabel flushed. "I was not eavesdropping. I was thirsty."

He made an expression of disbelief.

"Please, do come in," Mary Anne said, pulling out a kitchen chair. She looked worried. "You must be exhausted and frightened, too. I am so sorry you had to get caught up in this, my dear."

Annabel did not want to like her, but her sympathy and concern were clearly genuine. "Actually," Annabel said, walking into the brightly lit room, "I am neither tired nor frightened. But I am dirty. Could I bathe and change clothes? These are Louie's things and I am afraid they do have an odor."

Braxton stared.

Annabel avoided his gaze. She smiled at their hostess. "If it would not be an inconvenience."

There was only one guest room and it had been given to Annabel. It was on the second floor, across the hall from the master bedroom. Louie and Braxton were sleeping in the parlor, or so they claimed. Annabel wondered if Braxton was downstairs where she had left him and his henchman after supper, or across the hall with the too kind Mrs. Winston.

She sat on the edge of the narrow bed, clad in a nightgown that belonged to Mary Anne. Her temples throbbed. She should be relieved that she remained alone in the bedroom, more so if Braxton were comforting the pretty widow. This was what she wanted. To be ruined in name only—not in fact.

But she knew she would not sleep all night long thinking about it—about them.

Annabel finally stood and walked over to her closed bedroom door in her bare feet. Her heart pounded. She pressed her ear against the wood and strained to hear. But there was not a sound in the house—as if everyone were truly asleep.

Very carefully, she began to open the door. It creaked loudly.

She froze, then tried again. The door groaned now as she opened it.

She was breathless, her pulse continuing to drum and deafen her. But her door was wide open. The hall was pitch-black; not a single light had been left on. The door across from her was closed. It was a shadowy shape. Annabel glanced toward the stairs, but could not make them out in the darkness.

Annabel took one step into the hall and winced as the wood beneath her feet squeaked. Grimacing, she hurried across the short distance separating her door from Mary Anne's, and finally she pressed her ear against it. Once again, silence greeted her. Of course, the way her heart was beating, it was terribly hard to hear anything else.

Wood groaned.

Annabel stiffened, wondering if she had imagined the sound, which came from the end of the hall. She stared into the shadows, but saw nothing. After a few seconds, she decided it had been her imagination, or old wood settling. She leaned against Mary Anne's door again, pressing her ear to the stained wood. Her efforts were rewarded by absolute silence.

And then an arm clamped around her waist from behind, a hand clapped over her mouth. Annabel would have screamed in fright, but the hand covering her mouth was so firm and uncompromising that she was prevented from making a sound. She was pulled from behind against a man's solid body. His grip upon her was as immovable as steel.

"Jesus, it's you," Braxton said in her ear. His hand left her mouth, sliding across her jaw to her neck and shoulder, and he did not release her for another moment.

And in that endless moment Annabel was overwhelmed by the warmth and strength of him, by his sheer masculinity.

He dropped his hands from her person.

Annabel turned. Her back pressed against Mary Anne's door as she faced him, and because he did not move, there was not an inch between their bodies. His thighs pressed hers. His chest flattened hers. She was a tall woman, and her eyes were level with his mouth.

It was an exceedingly attractive mouth.

And his teeth flashed white in the darkness. "Might I ask what you were doing?" he asked, but in a whisper.

"I could ask you the same thing," Annabel said, whispering as well. It was very hard to think—her body was acutely aware of him, and she did not know what to do with her hands, which remained balled up at her sides. "I thought you were the police, or a federal agent," she breathed.

His gaze appeared silver in the darkness of the night. It searched hers. "I thought the same of you." Suddenly he stepped away from her, putting a safer distance between them. "Did anyone ever tell you, Miss Boothe, that curiosity killed the cat?"

She inhaled. She was trembling, her legs were weak. Air now caressed her where his warmth had a scant instant ago. She did not want him to leave and go back downstairs. There was no time to think. "I am not a cat. Curiosity has not killed me yet—I doubt it ever will."

He laughed softly. "You know," he said, and their gazes locked, "I like you. It is a shame that you are who you are. For you and I could have gotten on quite famously, I do think."

She stared. His voice had been low and sensual and intimate. "I like you, too, Braxton."

His smile disappeared.

Annabel wet her lips, images she knew she should not, must not, entertain dancing in her head. Of him leading her across the hall into her bedroom, of him removing her clothing, his large, capable, elegant hands smoothing over her skin.

"Go back to bed," he said harshly. "I will see you in the morning."

"Wait," she whispered, a desperate cry.

But he had not moved.

"Wait," she said again, as intensely. But she could not think of a single excuse to detain him, or a single way to seduce him.

He now wet his lips. "Do not offer," he said with anger, "what will turn out to be a vast mistake. For you certainly, and maybe for us both."

"I am not like other women," Annabel said hoarsely.

He stared.

She clenched her fists. "I don't ever want to marry. I only want to be free."

He remained motionless.

"Free like the wind," she said, tears suddenly coming to her eyes. "Not shackled to an idiot like Harold, not shackled to anyone."

His jaw flexed. His brilliant eyes never left her face.

"But you would not understand. Because you are free, you are a man." She was bitter. She felt defeated. He would go. And in the morning, their paths would diverge, never to twine again.

"I understand," he finally said. "Better than you think."

She tensed and met his brilliant eyes again. And watched his hands lifting—coming toward her. And in that moment she felt a surge of absolute comprehension—she had known that this would happen from the very first moment she had laid her eyes upon him in her father's library. He gripped her shoulders and pulled her slowly up against him. As his chest once again crushed her breasts, as his palms slid down her back, settling on her hips, she breathed, trembling with anticipation. His mouth cut off the sound.

Annabel clung to him tightly, stunned by the endless kiss. She had never been kissed this way before, but then, she had never known such a man before, either. She did not want the kiss to end; she could not seem to get enough of the taste of him, the feel of him. But he tore his mouth from hers abruptly, and their gazes locked.

She was breathing harshly, but so was he.

"Last chance," he whispered roughly.

It took Annabel a moment to comprehend him, and then she realized what he meant. "No. My mind has not changed," she said.

He took her hand and pulled her into her bedroom, releasing her to lock the door behind them. Annabel's heart was trying to beat its way out of her chest. She stood uncertainly beside the narrow bed. He turned. She had left the light on in her room and now she saw his expression—it was fiercely intent.

"What should I do now?" she whispered, dazed.

His smile flashed and he walked to her, hooking his thumbs under the plain straps of her simple nightgown. "You do nothing but feel, Annabel. And you leave the rest to me."

She could not breathe, could not move. The way he spoke, the look in his eyes, the touch of his fingernails on her skin, was bathing her body in flames. And she knew exactly what it was that she wanted—this man, deep within her, in a carnal way.

Braxton bent and kissed each shoulder where the straps lay, then he slid them over her shoulders and pushed her gown down over her breasts, her hips, her thighs. It pooled in a puddle of cotton at her feet. His gaze was admiring.

He stroked the pads of two fingers down her neck and chest, over her nipples. Annabel bit back a cry of need and pleasure. He looked into her eyes, his expert hands skimming down her sides and abdomen.

"You are very, very beautiful, and far too much of a woman for most men."

She could not speak. He was touching her thighs. "But not . . . for you?"

His gaze jerked up to hers. "You are probably too much of a woman for myself as well," he said, as if he had just thought of it and as if he meant it. And then he pulled her close for another devastating, tongue-to-tongue kiss.

And when, a long time later, their lips parted, she gasped, "This is not fair."

He was pushing her down on the bed. "Life is not fair."

She laughed as she found herself on her back, but shakily. "I have no clothes on. You are fully dressed."

His eyes widened and brightened at the same time. He stood, smiling. "That," he said, "shall be remedied momentarily."

Annabel sat up to watch him disrobe. He was exactly as she had thought, broad-shouldered, narrow of hip, all rippling sinew and lean muscle. She had never seen a man completely naked before. She stared.

"You are eating me up with those incredible eyes of yours," he said, not moving.

She lifted her gaze to his, feeling herself blush. "I have never seen a man before. I mean, not a living, breathing one—I have never cared to. I have never felt passion before, Braxton."

"I am glad." He sat down beside her, taking her into his arms. "My name is St. Clare," he said softly.

Annabel heard, but could not respond, because his mouth was on hers again, and she was on her back, his huge, flagrant manhood pushing up between her thighs against her vulva. His mouth moved down her neck. She heard herself moaning, found herself arching for him, as wide open as she could make herself. Her body wanted him so badly that it hurt and she had never felt so impatient for anything before. He tugged one nipple into his mouth. Annabel caressed him wildly, urgently. "Hurry," she gasped.

"No," he whispered, nuzzling her other breast. "There are some things we do not rush, my dear, and making love is one of them." He was stroking her inner thighs with his long, lean fingers. Annabel thought she would die if he did not touch her most private parts.

"Annabel," he whispered, making her closing eyes fly open. "I want to savor you."

"You have a way with words," she panted. And then he slipped his hand over her, palming her intimately. Annabel cried out.

"God," he cried, no longer sounding either suave or composed.

"Please," Annabel wept, raking her nails down his back.

"Ow." It was a growl. He caught her face in his hands and kissed her hard. There was a brutal demand in his kiss and somehow Annabel understood it—and him—completely. She wrapped her thighs around his waist, grasping his hips. And then he was pressing into her. For one instant it was awkward and he paused, in the next instant he was there, hard and swift and sure, thrusting deeply into her, time and again, making Annabel cry out with desperation and weep with joy.

And then she knew it was happening. She tensed, clawing his shoulders. "Pierce!"

His gaze met hers as he came into her again, his face strained with lust. "Now?" he asked, a demand.

Annabel's nod was brief, her explosion star-filled.

Annabel woke up thinking that Braxton remained in her arms, and she felt herself smiling. A bright morning light was pouring through the parted curtains. Its sunny brightness matched the joyous feeling bubbling up inside her. Annabel sighed, recalling his lovemaking, and then she realized that she was hugging a pillow, not Pierce. She sighed again, rolling over onto her back, looking at his side of the narrow bed. It was empty.

She stretched, smiling again. No wonder men and women chased one another like fools, she mused. Making love was indeed a wonderful experience, especially with a man like Braxton.

And they had made love. He had been tender, even in the roughest moments, and Annabel hugged herself recalling the way he had looked at her, kissed her, held her afterward. She was, for the very first time in her life, smitten with a man.

And it was deliriously wonderful. Annabel beamed at the ceiling. Braxton was wonderful, the rogue.

No, not Braxton, she corrected herself. His real name was St. Clare. Or at least that was what he claimed.

She sat up, not bothering to hold the covers over her naked breasts. The bed was so small that they had slept in one another's arms last night—when he had not been making love to her, that is. She grinned again, understanding now that particular feline expression cats wore after lapping up a bowlful of fresh cream. Did all men make love like that? He had touched her everywhere, and not just with his hands. Annabel did not think so, and she did not need to be experienced to arrive at such a conclusion. Braxton was a superior lover—just like he was a superior thief.

She sighed. Then, realizing how moonstruck she was

acting, she jumped from the bed. Shamelessly naked, she went to the window and parted the curtains more fully. Her happiness dulled, her smile faded. What time was it? It had to be mid-morning. Annabel grew uneasy. Her bedroom looked out upon the backyard. She stared at the barn. The barn doors were wide open. No one was in sight.

He must be downstairs, getting ready to leave. Why hadn't he woken her up?

Surely he did not intend to depart without her—not after last night!

Annabel rushed about the room, pulling on her drawers and chemise, forgoing both her corset and petticoats. As she dressed in one of Mary Anne's dark skirts and white shirtwaists, there was no avoiding her apprehension. She did not know what Braxton planned as far as the future went, but she knew she would go with him. She could not return home now.

Annabel picked up her shoes and stockings and dashed into the hall.

The house was silent. As if it were deserted, everyone already gone. That, of course, was impossible. Trying not to worry now, trying not to imagine the worst, Annabel pounded down the stairs and into the kitchen. The scent of fresh coffee permeated the room, and Annabel saw a plate of sugar buns on the table. A few small dishes were stacked up on the counter by the sink. They were dirty. Where was everyone?

Annabel walked to the back door and peered outside, but she could only see the side of the barn. Her pulse was pounding now.

"Hello."

Annabel started as Mary Anne entered the room, looking very worn and very tired. "Good morning," she said brightly.

Mary Anne was holding that morning's *World* in her

hand. Looking unhappy, she handed the newspaper to Annabel.

Annabel saw the headline and gasped. "BOOTHE HEIRESS ABDUCTED—MANHUNT ENSUES."

"Oh, my God," she cried. And then, as she scanned the article, she felt her heart sinking like a stone. "Listen to this," she said, with anger. " 'Annabel Boothe is widely known to be an imprudent and impulsive character, given over to inclinations not suited to a gentlewoman.' And then this writer goes on to list some of my inclinations!"

"I read the article, my dear," Mary Anne said softly, not moving from the doorway where she stood.

"Well, at least they got some of it right." Annabel was dismayed. "But I never performed on the stage! Who told them this? Acting has never appealed to me!" Annabel looked at Mary Anne, aware of being exceedingly upset. Yet people had been talking about her for most of her life. Why did this nasty article dismay her so?

Mary Anne was silent.

Annabel also fell silent. She looked again at the dirty dishes by the sink, her heart lurching with dread. Then, with shaking hands, she scanned the newspaper column again. She froze. The writer went on to claim that dozens of witnesses had seen her willingly jump into the thief's motorcar. "Well." She forced a smile. "Once again it will be poor Annabel Boothe. Except this time I will not be around to hear the whispers and see the stares." Her gaze met Mary Anne's. "Will I?"

Mary Anne's gaze was pitying.

"Why are you looking at me that way? And where is Pierce? I mean Braxton?"

"St. Clare left."

Annabel knew she had not heard Mary Anne correctly. "What did you say?"

"Pierce left. He left at dawn with Louie."

Annabel stared at Mary Anne. The other woman's image became blurry. There was a roaring in her ears, a tingling in her limbs. The light in the room dimmed, becoming gloomy. "No," Annabel whispered, stricken.

Pierce could not have left her behind.

It was an impossibility.

Mary Anne was lying.

"My dear!" Mary Anne cried in alarm, rushing forward and gripping her arm. "You are turning a ghastly shade of green! Are you about to be sick?"

"He did not leave." Annabel looked at the other woman, about to be violently ill. She fought to contain her roiling stomach.

"I am so sorry. He has become a cad, Annabel, a horrid cad, and I will never forgive him for what he has done to you!" Mary Anne tried to put her arm around her, but Annabel pushed her away, swallowing bile.

"He made love to me," she said, bewildered. And images of the night before filled her mind.

"I'm so sorry," Mary Anne whispered, tears forming in her eyes. "Pierce is not this way. I do not understand any of this."

The memories continued to flood her mind, memories of his touch, his kiss, his smile, the look of love in his eyes. *All lies.*

"Oh, God," she cried, and then she was running to the back door, throwing it open, and flinging herself onto her knees on the stoop, where she retched convulsively again and again.

And when the heaves ended, she found herself gripping the stoop, panting, tears beginning, splinters becoming embedded in her fingers. But that pain was nothing at all compared to the pain of his betrayal.

He had used her. He had left her. Last night had been nothing but a lie.

Annabel thought she might die.

Chapter Five

There was a mist in the air, and Annabel was quite certain it would rain.

She carried her shoes and stockings in her hand as she picked her way across the short stretch of beach which was behind the Acadia, the very fashionable resort where she had just arrived yesterday evening. The small inlet was very popular with the hotel's guests, Annabel had been told, but the rules were very strict. Male bathers were allowed until two in the afternoon, female bathers after that. It was not quite one P.M.

But there was no one about today because of the weather. Annabel paused at the head of the narrow path that would take her back to the hotel, glancing around and sniffing the fresh, slightly tangy air appreciatively. The small section of beach was a part of one of the island's many inlets, and everywhere Annabel gazed she saw soaring cliffs and pine forests. Not far inland, she could make out one of the island's tallest mountains. A pair of eagles were soaring overhead.

And for one moment she forgot the past and she smiled, watching the spectacular birds. Then her smile faded and she started up the sandy path that led to the sweeping lawns behind the hotel, her muslin skirts whipping around her. She was questioning her judgment in accepting Lizzie's invitation to join her sisters and their husbands for the month of August. Supper last night had been a disastrous affair.

She should have gone to Europe, alone.

Where no one knew her, by damn.

A drop of water landed on her forehead, another on her nose. Annabel increased her pace. The large, whitewashed hotel with its long verandah and green shutters was ahead. Annabel saw a few couples leaving the verandah as the temperature dropped and the wind picked up. Then she saw a woman in a bright yellow dress waving madly at her.

Annabel smiled because she recognized Lizzie, who was as big as a cow. Her second child was due in two more months. "Hi," she said, arriving on the back porch beside her sister.

"Isn't the beach beautiful?" Lizzie said, but she looked worried, despite her smile.

"Yes, it is," Annabel said, sitting down on a wicker chair to don her stockings and shoes. She had tar and dirt on her feet.

"Well, there you are, we are waiting for you," said a disapproving voice behind them.

Annabel looked up to find Melissa standing in the doorway, her hands on her slim hips. "You didn't have to wait for me," Annabel replied.

"Annabel, you are not allowed down at the beach until after two o'clock!"

Annabel stood up. "For God's sake, Missy, calm yourself. It's about to pour! No one was there."

"You will never find a husband if you continue to break all of the rules," Melissa retorted. "Sometimes I wonder just what goes on inside your head."

"I don't want a husband," Annabel said as sharply, pushing past her to walk inside. A huge green and gold carpet covered the library floor. The room was empty, for it was dinnertime.

"Please don't fight," Lizzie cried, following them as they left the library and entered the dining room. "But Annabel, maybe you should obey the hotel's rules. They are very explicit."

"Everyone thinks you are fast, Annabel," Melissa said.

Annabel paused and turned sharply, so that she was nose to nose with her lovely sister. She smiled sweetly. "I know. And I don't care. Besides, it's the truth, isn't it?" She stared, knowing she was being belligerent, but unable to stop.

Lizzie grabbed Annabel's arm. "Ssh! Everyone is staring. Please, do not argue now." And she gave Melissa a stern look. "And please do not use that horrid word again in conjunction with our sister."

"You are always on her side," Melissa huffed, and she went to their table, sitting down beside John, who had jumped to his feet.

Annabel and Lizzie exchanged glances. "Do forgive her terrible mood," Lizzie finally said. "You know how upset she is right now."

"I am trying to be compassionate, but she makes it so very difficult," Annabel said. "The fact that she cannot conceive is not my fault—yet she is taking it out on me."

Lizzie nodded unhappily and took her hand. "Just ignore her," she whispered as they approached their table.

Adam was standing, waiting for them, and he smiled at both Lizzie and Annabel, holding out their chairs for them. "Isn't this place spectacular?" he asked Annabel. "Have you ever seen such views?"

Before she could respond and agree with him, at least about the countryside, Annabel realized that two couples at the very next table were openly staring at her. They had been as rude last night at supper. The women were about her own age, but they sported huge diamond rings on their left hands and had several young children with their nursemaids at an adjoining table. They were talking in hushed tones, but Annabel knew what they were saying. She could hear them. She was quite certain the ladies wished for it to be that way.

"It is absolutely true. Marion knows someone who was a guest at her wedding. She ran away with a burglar two years ago. That *is* her. Can you imagine? Leaving the poor groom at the altar like that? Talbot, has, of course, long since married. He would have none of her when she returned. How can she show herself in polite society?"

"What nerve," her friend agreed.

Annabel twisted in her seat and leveled a cold stare at the women. "It is actually quite easy to partake of polite society," she said. "It hardly requires nerve. One makes a few reservations, gets on a train, and voilà, one arrives. But I would question whether this is polite society, actually." And she gave the flushing women her back. Annabel stared at her place setting. Her pulse continued to race.

As soup was served all around, Lizzie placed a hand on hers. "Don't let one rat get your spirits down. This is a wonderful hotel. Most of the guests are so very nice."

To you, perhaps, Annabel thought. "There is always a rat or two, everywhere I go, and I am thoroughly tired of it," she said. She was more than tired of hearing about how fast and willful she was, or that other popular refrain: poor, unfortunate, oh-so-wild Annabel Boothe. Other than the fact that she had been served up a very large dose of a broken heart by her own reckless nature, why, there was nothing unfortunate about her.

She did, after all, have her freedom. Which was all that she had ever wanted anyway. It was women like the two behind her who deserved pity, not herself.

Melissa leaned forward. "If you led an exemplary life,

perhaps everyone would forget the past, Annabel. You choose to defy every norm there is—and then you expect people to like and accept you? How can anyone forget, for goodness' sake, when you refuse to let anyone forget!"

Annabel stared at her sister. Was Melissa right? If one entertained Missy's perspective, then she certainly was correct, but Annabel knew that she could not live the way her sisters did, or the way that most of society did. *Was* something wrong with her? Why was her nature so inquisitive, so reckless? "I do not want to discuss this," she said, lifting her soup spoon. The split pea soup was far too hot and she set it down abruptly.

Curiosity killed the cat.

Annabel inhaled, stabbed by words spoken by someone she did not wish to identify, not even in her mind. She had no wish to remember either his words or him.

"Our soups are getting cold," Adam said firmly, also taking up his spoon.

For a moment they sipped in silence. Annabel stared at her pea soup, having lost her appetite. In Europe no one seemed to find her behavior so odd that it was worthy of censure. But in Europe, she did not frequent society. Annabel had spent the holidays in Paris, where she had run into an acquaintance from the art class she had taken several years ago. Melissa would die if she knew that Annabel had kept such late hours that she had not arisen until the late afternoon, that she had passed the evenings at the theater and afterward in bistros and cabarets, drinking red wine and brandy and smoking cigarettes and cigars.

He had not disapproved of her. In spite of what she had done.

Braxton was haunting her again.

Annabel stared at her soup. It had been two years since the fateful day of her almost-wedding. He still, from time to time, appeared in her mind, haunting her oddly with bits and pieces of the brief time they had shared. Her heart was no longer broken, so she could not understand why this ghost of a memory would not go away and leave her in peace. What was even stranger was the fact that his expression in her mind's eye was always the same. It was filled with regret.

Which was romantic nonsense. The man was a thief and a charlatan, and while Annabel now felt that she was as much to blame as he was for what had happened—she had, after all, seduced him—she would never forgive him for leaving without a word the next day, or worse, for pretending to love her that night.

But he had not disapproved of her then, and he would not disapprove of her now. Annabel had not a doubt.

She reminded herself that as he was a professional thief, he was hardly a suitable judge of anyone's character.

An unladylike elbow jammed in her side. "Annabel! It is that gent from last night, the one who invited you to play tennis today!" Lizzie was full of excitement. Her pretty cheeks were flushed pink.

Annabel looked up, saw a young, handsome fellow approaching their table, and felt her own cheeks go hot while her eyes widened in surprise. She watched James Appleton Beard as he wound his way through the dining room. Last night he had singled her out after supper, and after a brief chat, they had agreed to a tennis match the following afternoon. It had been ages since a real gentleman had shown any interest in her—it had been exactly two years, in fact.

James paused at their table, bowing. His cheeks were flushed. Hellos were passed round. Annabel regarded him but remained silent. And gazing at him, seeing his discomfort, she knew.

Her heart sank. She should have expected this, fool that she was.

"Miss Boothe." His smile was brief, strained. "I am

afraid the weather will prevent us from our match to-day." He avoided her eyes.

Annabel thought dully, he knows about Braxton. "Yes, the grass will be far too wet to play."

A silence fell.

"There is always tomorrow," Adam said. Annabel knew that he meant to be helpful. But the effect was the opposite.

"Actually," James said, growing more flushed still, "I have twisted my ankle this morning. Perhaps at the end of the week." He bowed and quickly turned, leaving their table.

Annabel knew her cheeks remained red. She picked up her spoon, resisting the sudden surge of anger that made her want to flip soup all over the table. She was fast. Unacceptable, an outcast. But this was what she had wanted, in order to be free. She had no right to feel sorry for herself, and by damn, she was not ashamed. Yet she had never known that such ostracism would be so painful.

An intense silence had fallen.

"He has probably heard that you are an outstanding tennis player. The poor fellow undoubtedly knew he would not stand a chance," Adam said kindly.

Annabel felt hot tears filling her eyes. She knew that she must not let anyone see that the stupid clod had hurt her feelings. Or had he? She was thinking about the damn thief again.

"Everyone knows that you are unbeatable at tennis," Lizzie said emphatically, agreeing.

"Well," Melissa began. "If Annabel ever wants to catch a husband she should lose at tennis a few times or so."

Annabel had composed herself and she looked up. "I will do no such thing." She locked gazes with Melissa.

"You are a fool, Annabel. No man wants to be with a woman who is stronger, smarter, and a better tennis player than he!" She turned to John. "Am I right, dear?"

"You are very right," John said, nodding.

Annabel had had enough. She was not hungry and she set her soup spoon down. "We all know that tennis is not, and has never been, the issue."

"Yes, let's do change this boring subject," Lizzie said quickly, her tone high. "Have you all heard that the Countess Rossini is arriving today? She is one of the wealthiest women in Europe!"

"I should hope so," Melissa replied, reaching for the bread. "She was seventeen when she married the count— and he was sixty-five. Everyone knows she married him for his money. Her family was quite impoverished. But no one expected him to live another fifteen years!"

"She is a widow, newly so," Lizzie said to Adam and Annabel.

Annabel had no interest in the countess or her money. She stood. "I am sorry. But I have a terrible migraine and I have lost my appetite. Please excuse me. I will see you all for supper." She pushed back her chair and swiftly left the table, aware of dozens of pairs of eyes in the hotel dining room following her as she crossed the room, which had suddenly become far too spacious. A gentleman was entering it as she was departing. They collided head-on.

"I am sorry!" They both cried at the same time, extricating themselves from one another.

"Miss Boothe!" The fellow was tall and a bit stocky, gray-haired with a darker mustache, about her father's age. He now smiled at her. "Have I hurt you?"

They had been briefly introduced the previous evening after supper. Annabel scrambled to recall his name. "Mr. Frank, no, you have not."

"You have finished dinner already?" he cried in disappointment, his smile fading.

"I am afraid so," Annabel said, preparing to walk around him. "If you will excuse me?"

"Miss Boothe." He detained her by his tone of voice. Then he swallowed. He was beginning to flush. "I would like to say that I so enjoyed making your acquaintance last evening, and I had hoped, the weather permitting, of course, that you might join me for a stroll along the beach later, or perhaps in town, if that is your preference." He smiled at her.

Annabel stared in dismay. Thomas Frank was interested in her? She recalled now that he was a widower. "I am not feeling well," she said quickly. "But thank you." And she lifted her pale, striped skirts and hurried from the room.

Relief filled her once she was in the large lobby. There the floors were dark oak and strewn with Persian rugs, the walls were paneled and covered with works of art, and three large crystal chandeliers were hanging from the high ceiling. Soft sofas and chairs in brocades and damask with occasional tables made the room very inviting, and it was usually filled with hotel guests, engaged in quiet conversation or sitting alone and reading. Through the tall windows, Annabel saw that it had indeed begun to pour, and in the drive outside, she saw a large, gilded carriage arriving. There were two liveried footmen standing in back, and watching the conveyance, drawn by four blacks, halt in the downpour, she felt sorry for the servants.

Annabel sighed. She had no headache, and hardly felt like locking herself up in her room. She plopped down on one red damask sofa, picking up yesterday's copy of *The Sun*, a New York daily which had been left lying about and which the hotel provided for its guests. She had barely scanned the headlines on the first page when she heard voices on the threshold of the lobby, behind her. A woman was talking, her Italian accent very pronounced. "How good of you to accommodate me and my staff with such short notice," she was saying. "I can hardly believe we have made it in this weather. I feel like a drowned cat." She laughed, the sound husky and pleasant.

"Contessa, I am so sorry that you had to endure such weather today, but please, let me assure you, anything you desire, it shall be yours."

Annabel openly regarded the woman as she entered the lobby with the hotel manager, whom Annabel recognized. She was a small woman fabulously dressed in gold velvet, but when she turned, Annabel saw that she was a gorgeous redhead with a perfect porcelain complexion. So this, she thought, was the infamous countess Lizzie had referred to earlier.

"You are too kind to me, darling," the countess purred. The manager bowed over her hand and kissed it before the countess could even remove her gloves.

And then he barked out orders. Annabel watched with some amusement and some fascination as trunk after huge trunk was carried by both the countess's staff and the hotel's through the lobby and into the elevators.

"My dear Contessa, you need not linger in the lobby. I have sent champagne and caviar to your suite, should you wish a bit of refreshment, and of course, we will keep the dining room open for you."

"You are too kind," she cried and, gold skirts swirling about her, she disappeared into one of the lobby elevators, followed by several ladies who were undoubtedly her maids.

Annabel watched the brass elevator door closing. Briefly, her gaze met the countess's just before the door closed.

She looked up at the dial above the elevator. The hotel had eight floors. The big arrow went from one to eight. But of course the countess would have a suite on the top floor.

Annabel was laughing softly to herself, unable not to be amused by the entire display, when she heard footsteps from behind her in the entryway, followed by the doorman's "G'day, sir." The lobby had settled down now that Guilia Rossini had gone to her rooms and was once again filled with quiet. Annabel reached for *The Sun*.

"I believe you have a room for me," a male voice said, the accent perfect, patrician, and British.

Annabel's head whipped up and she felt as if someone had punched her so hard that the air had been knocked from her lungs. *No!* This could not be—she was making a mistake.

Annabel could not move. She stared.

"The name is Wainscot," he said in that unforgettable voice of his.

Annabel slowly came to her feet. His back was to her. He was tall, slim, dark-haired. And she was not deluded. She did not have to see his face in order to recognize him. Even from behind, this way, she would recognize him anywhere.

Oh, dear God.

He bent over a register now, signing it. Annabel became aware of the alarming rate at which her heart raced, and the deafening roar in her ears. She felt faint.

He straightened, pushing the register at the clerk, turning slightly, so that Annabel could see both his profile and his hands. He was smiling. And she would never forget his hands.

Those incredible, capable hands.

"Mr. Wainscot." The hotel manager had appeared and was introducing himself and wishing Braxton an enjoyable stay. Annabel really did not hear. It was him. Braxton. The man who had taken her heart—and then thrown it back at her.

Annabel stared, not hearing his reply. Aware now of a huge and terrible anger—and also aware of the hurt. Incredibly, it had never fully gone away.

Suddenly his shoulders stiffened. Annabel knew, in

that instant, that he had become aware of being watched.

Braxton turned. He saw her instantly, and their gazes locked.

Chapter Six

He seemed to recognize her instantly. Braxton appeared
to be even more severely shocked than she. His blue eyes
were wide and his visage was white. Annabel remained
frozen, in disbelief.

His mouth opened and closed. As if he wanted to say
something, but abruptly changed his mind.

Annabel realized that she was shaking. Like a veritable leaf. He was here. How could this be? And why was
she reacting like this, as if he were still important to her?
What had happened had been so long ago—and she had
long since recovered. She should not care that they were
face-to-face!

"Your keys, Mr. Wainscot. Your rooms are on the
third floor. But let me remind you that dinner is now
being served, and the dining room is closed from four
o'clock until seven in the evening, when it reopens for
suppertime."

Braxton came to life, smiling and facing the manager.
"Thank you, my good man." He handed him a coin.
"My valet will need some help with his luggage."

"Certainly." The gent bowed and strode briskly back
to his office, around the corner of the front desk.

Which left Annabel and Braxton quite alone in the
lobby, except for the clerks.

He turned toward her, his regard level and steady, his gaze impossible to read.

Annabel clenched her fists. The urge to strike him was overwhelming. Instead, she remained immobilized. All her instincts screamed at her not to make a scene—that to do so would be a dire mistake.

He moved first—toward her—his strides long and sharp. And he dared to bow. "I do believe we are acquainted, Miss, uh, Miss Boothe, is it not?" His blue eyes held hers.

Acquainted. Annabel was as sick as she was furious. "Are we acquainted?" Even to her own ears, her tone dripped sugary sarcasm. "Oh, yes," she said in a rush. "We met, oh, when was it? It is so hard for me to recall!"

His smile flashed, but it was twisted. Very quietly, he said, "I believe we met at a reception in New York City in honor of the mayor."

She was so very ill. "Oh? Then your memory apparently serves you far better than mine does me!" Tears were interfering with her vision. Damn it. *Damn him.*

"Miss Boothe." His tone was gentle. "In case you have forgotten, the name is Wainscot. Bruce Wainscot."

Forgotten—in case she had forgotten! "I have forgotten nothing," she cried harshly. "But I thought the name was Braxton!"

He stared, unmoving, mouth grim.

And Annabel, afraid she was about to burst into tears, turned and ran—crashing directly into her sister.

"Annabel! Are you ill? What is wrong?" Lizzie cried, steadying her with a firm grip on her shoulders.

Annabel looked blankly at her youngest sister, hardly assimilating her words. Braxton was here, in the hotel, by God. How could this be?

"I am so worried about you," Lizzie was saying, her brow furrowed in that familiar way she had.

Annabel could not help herself. She turned, but Braxton was gone. He had vanished as effectively as any ghost. Of course, he was no spirit from another world, oh no. "I do have a horrible migraine," Annabel managed, and it was the truth.

And suddenly an image Annabel would never forget raced through her mind: numerous wedding guests, her father, Harold Talbot, and her sisters and their husbands all crowding outside the front door of their New York City home as she looked up from the lawn, on her hands and knees, making the most fateful decision of her life.

Had Lizzie seen Braxton? Had Lizzie recognized him?

"You never get headaches," Lizzie said, taking her arm. But her gaze lifted to the sweeping staircase. Following her regard, Annabel saw Braxton from behind as he disappeared on the next landing.

Annabel threw her arm around Lizzie and whirled her away from the stairs, her heart lurching. "I am going up to my room to lie down," she said. To lie down, and to think.

"Your room is the other way," Lizzie pointed out. "Annabel, you are acting so very strangely!"

Lizzie had not recognized Braxton or she would have immediately commented upon it. She had only glimpsed him for a moment, and that from behind. Annabel realized the source of her panic, and could hardly believe herself. She was insane to care if Braxton was recognized and carted off to jail like the very thief that he was.

Annabel studied Lizzie. Even if Lizzie did encounter him directly, she might not recognize him. But there was no way of knowing, not until such an encounter actually took place. And Annabel shuddered at the thought.

And there was also Melissa and her husband and Adam to consider. Missy was very sharp, unlike her dim-witted husband, and Adam was also clever. Annabel was dismayed. Someone would recognize him, the odds told her that.

And she should be glad. She should even identify him

herself. She could be the one to send him to prison. It would be her vengeance and his due. But instead, she was worried over his being discovered. It was preposterous.

"Annabel? You are miles away. Whatever is wrong?" Lizzie tugged on her hand, her dark eyes filled with worry.

"I am going upstairs to my room," Annabel said, forcing a smile. "I will be fine. I will see you all before supper." But she did not think she would be fine for a very long time—and certainly not for as long as Braxton remained on the same premises as she.

Lizzie nodded uncertainly. Then, before Annabel could leave, she plucked her sleeve. "Dear, I am so sorry about that boorish James Appleton Beard. He is hardly good enough for you anyway."

"I had forgotten all about him, to tell you the truth," Annabel said honestly, for her thoughts were consumed with Braxton now.

"I do think Mr. Frank is very set on you." Lizzie's tone was hopeful. "He seems so kind, Annabel."

Annabel blinked, finally focusing completely on her sister. "Liz, he is old, and kind or not, he is a bore."

Lizzie's face crumpled and she bit her lip. "You just won't give anyone a chance," she cried. "Sometimes I think you are pining for that thief—and waiting for him to reappear in our lives!"

Annabel could not believe her ears—or the utter irony of what Lizzie had just said. "I must go," she cried, kissing her sister's cheek. She paused. "And you are wrong, Lizzie, so very wrong. That is ancient history. Truly."

Lizzie regarded her sadly.

Annabel gripped her striped skirts and rushed up the stairs, her gait hardly ladylike or genteel. Lizzie was wrong. She did not continue to harbor misplaced affections for a man who had abandoned her two long years ago. On the other hand, she wasn't quite sure she wished to condemn him to a life of imprisonment, either—and something was surely wrong with her for not wanting to see him in jail. Annabel glanced down the hall on the second landing. If she were honest with herself, she would admit that she expected to see Braxton lurking about, lying in wait for her, eager to speak with her.

But the long, plushly carpeted hall was vacant, except for one uniformed housemaid with a cart of cleaning tools.

Annabel's room was on the fourth floor—the hotel had eight stories in all. She quickly let herself in and found herself locking the door. Then she unlaced and kicked off her kid shoes and flopped on her back on the bed.

Tears shamelessly filled her eyes.

Oh, God. Annabel flung one arm over her brow. It was impossible to believe that she still felt such anguish over that man and what he had done to her. She had been the one to seduce him. But never in her wildest dreams had she imagined that lovemaking could be the way it had been, or that afterward, he would abandon her, without even a good-bye.

Annabel wiped the tears from her eyes. Maybe Lizzie was right. There was a stubborn part of her heart that just refused to give up her love for Pierce St. Clare, aka Pierce Braxton. But how could that be? And how could she have fallen in love with an absolute stranger in less than twenty-four hours?

Poor, poor Annabel Boothe. With her wild, reckless ways.

Annabel wanted to clap her hands over her ears to drive away that too familiar refrain, but it was just like her suddenly to go off half-cocked, whether her passions were stimulated by a voyage to India or a con artist and a thief.

There was a knocking at her door.

Annabel sat up, her heart lurching with dread. Of

course it was not Braxton. Undoubtedly it was Lizzie, bringing her a dinner tray, or Missy, come to scold her. Or it might even be a hotel maid. Annabel stood up slowly, wetting her lips. Her pulse pounded. She turned to glance at her reflection in the mirror over the Chippendale dresser.

Her pale hair was spilling out of its chignon, her high-necked gown was wrinkled, and her face was very pale. In contrast, her eyes were so blue that they almost seemed black. Annabel walked to the door in her bare feet, unlocked it, and swung it open.

Braxton stared at her.

She had known it would be him. For one moment Annabel looked into his eyes, and then she hit him with all her might. The slap sounded loudly in the room and the hall outside her door.

Immediately Braxton stepped into her room, closing the door behind him. In the blink of an eye, he had locked it and pocketed the brass key. "Now that we have gotten that out of the way, hello, Annabel," he said.

She was trembling, with rage, she supposed. "Get out. Before I am ruined twice."

He continued to regard her very intently, but his eyes gave no clue as to his thoughts or feelings, and it was not at all like her dreams—she saw no sign of regret upon his features. "You have not changed," he said after a long moment.

"Have you?" she asked caustically.

"You are angry." He did not move. He stood against the door, inches away from her. "You wanted to be ruined, Annabel, or have you conveniently forgotten that?"

"I have not forgotten anything," Annabel flashed, clenching her fists. She had the wild, nearly uncontrollable urge to hit him again. While a crystal-clear memory of their lovemaking swept through her mind.

"Then why are you so angry? Because I left without a good-bye?" He studied her.

How to answer? Two long, painful years had gone by, and maybe Lizzie was right, maybe she had been pining for him, and God only knew how many more years might pass after this single encounter. Annabel said, "When a man makes love to a woman, at least a good-bye is in order."

"I am sorry," he said. "But a good-bye was not wise. For many reasons."

She folded her arms tightly across her breasts. "But then, you did not make love to me, did you, Braxton? Naïve idiot that I am, virgin that I was, I mistook your passion for some amount of feeling, of caring. So a good-bye was not in order, now was it?" Her eyes felt hot. She would kill herself if she cried now, in front of him.

He tossed the key onto her bed and walked past her to the window. Appropriately, her view was of the back lawns and the Acadia's three tennis courts. Beyond that, one could see the other side of the inlet, a peninsula of black rock and green pines sticking out into the Atlantic Ocean. "I am sorry." He did not face her. "I never meant to hurt you. I did what I thought was best."

"I do not believe you. I do not think you are a repentant man. Not in any circumstance," Annabel flared. "And you did what was best for you."

He turned slowly and their gazes locked. Annabel almost fell over because she saw regret now, and it was vast—and identical to the expression he had worn in all of her fantasies. "It was not easy for me," he said quietly. "You see, you were not as naïve as you think you were. I was very fond of you, Annabel. And I am a good judge of human nature. I had already summed you up—and knew you would impulsively seek to join me in my adventures. I did what was best for us both, Annabel."

"Don't you dare claim that you know me," she retorted, but she was shaken anew. He was right—she would have insisted upon accompanying him instead of returning home. But more importantly, had he meant what he had just said? Had he been fond of her then? She had no intention of ever trusting him again. If he had cared at all for her, how could he have abandoned her the way he had? And what about now—what about the present?

Annabel wet her lips. "How arrogant, how presumptuous, to make my choice for me."

"You are not the first to accuse me of arrogance," he said with a wry smile.

Annabel trembled. It did not seem like two years since she had last been with him, damn it. It seemed more like two days or two weeks. She did not want him standing there in her room, just a few feet away from her, with that smile and those eyes and his damn charisma. "I make my own decisions," she said.

"Few women, especially unwed ones, make their own decisions," he returned evenly. His gaze had slipped to her left hand, which was bare of rings. "Is your father here?" he asked abruptly.

Her cheeks felt hot. Foolishly, Annabel hid her hand in her skirts. "So that is why you have come," she said, unable to disguise her bitterness. "No."

His jaw flexed as he stepped forward. "I do not wish to go to jail," he said. "And that is only one reason I have come."

She was aware of him coming even closer. Annabel hoped he would not see how she was trembling. She tilted up her chin. "You want to know if your secret is safe with me."

He smiled. Annabel could hardly stand it. She backed away from him until her shoulders hit the door. "Actually, I already know that my secret is safe with you," he murmured.

"Even I know no such thing," she huffed.

"If you were going to finger me, my dear, you would have done so forty-five minutes ago." He continued to smile. But his gaze had dropped to her mouth.

"I hate you," she heard herself hiss. But she was thinking about his kisses. She had stopped remembering them long ago. She did not want to remember them now—or to despair because she would never be in his arms again.

"I don't blame you. I should have refused what you offered. I did try. But I admit, I did not try very much, Annabel. I do not think you have any idea of how unusual a woman you are. Few men could be strong enough to resist you if you set your cap for them."

He was thoroughly wrong, no man wanted her, but his words affected her so much that she pounced on the bed, grabbed the key, rushed to the door and began to unlock it. "I want you to leave. Now." He had been sincere and she was certain of it.

His hand caught hers, covering it, stopping her from opening the door. And their gazes connected wildly once again. "You haven't changed, and I am glad," he said, smiling slightly. "You are still bold and courageous, and more beautiful than ever." His smile was gone. "I would hate to see you subdued by society and men like your father."

His words thrilled her, but she did not want to be thrilled, and they also frightened her. She said, "No one, not even you, could ever subdue me, Braxton."

He was silent. A tension fell that was thick and heavy, and with it an absolute silence, in which only their breathing could be heard. "Is that a challenge, my dear?" he finally asked.

Annabel stopped breathing. Her heart drummed against her chest. "No."

He laughed. The sound was as rich as his voice, as tempting, as infuriating. "I think that was a struggle, Annabel."

"I hate you," she cried, slamming her fist into his

chest. "Now get out—and don't you dare come near me again!"

His laughter died. He caught her right wrist immediately, the action reflexive. And suddenly Annabel fell fully against him—and she was practically in his arms.

She became acutely aware of her hand in his, his fingers on her wrist, and his long, hard body pressing up against hers. She looked up. He had also became motionless. Their gazes locked.

Annabel knew he was going to kiss her. She forgot the past. Expectation—anticipation—engulfed her.

"I knew," he said suddenly, his tone low, his words slow, "that if I said good-bye, you would convince me to take you with me. That I would not be strong enough to resist you."

Annabel felt her gaze widen.

He still held her hand. But now he was clasping it. "I did not want to be responsible for ruining your life. You deserve far more than a life on the lam. You had your entire life in front of you, with so many possibilities. I did not want to take any of those opportunities away."

Annabel was stunned.

His reached up and touched her cheek with two fingers, a brief caress that sent shivers coursing over every inch of Annabel's body, followed by an intense longing—a yearning that had never completely died. "I honestly did not think I would ever see you again," he said, and his expression was twisted and odd. "I think I had better go."

Annabel was stunned by the entire encounter, but one coherent thought was clear in her mind—she did not want him to go, not so soon, not yet. It had been so long since they had been together, even just to converse with one another.

But she had pride, and never had she been more confused in her entire life. She watched him crack open the door. "The hall is clear," he said, pausing—as if he did not want to leave quite yet, either. His regard was so direct it was unsettling.

She found her sanity and her voice. "Then go." She swallowed. "Pierce. My sisters and brothers-in-law are here, as well."

He stared. And smiled, with his eyes. "Thank you for the warning," he said.

Annabel could not find an appropriate response.

His gaze held hers for another moment before he slipped from the room.

She stood in the doorway, staring after him, long after he had disappeared. Tears were falling from her eyes.

Chapter Seven

Pierce regarded the rain.

The downpour continued, unabated. It was accompanied by a heavy fog, making it almost impossible to see more than a dozen feet in any direction. Pierce did not see, not the rain, not the blanket of mist, nor the few evergreens poking through pockets of it. He only saw Annabel, barefoot and disheveled, and in spite of her courage, obviously so damn vulnerable.

How perverse life was.

He had not lied when he had told her that he had not thought to ever see her again. He was dismayed. He had not wished for their paths to ever cross again. Yet he was also elated, peculiarly so, and there was no denying it.

His pulse continued to pound.

He sighed, turning away from the window, clad only in his shirt and trousers, his sleeves rolled casually up. His single leather trunk, large enough to contain an average-sized man, lay on the floor. His single valise lay on the bed. His jaw set, he went to the black trunk and began removing his clothing from it. He had a job to do.

Which was why he could not leave. And it had nothing to do with Annabel Boothe, but everything to do with the Countess Rossini.

Annabel entered the salon where the guests mingled before supper. It was a large room with gleaming oak floors and Persian rugs, and two brass gaslight chandeliers hanging from the ceiling, which was painted moss green. The walls were papered in a tree-of-life print, and most of the furnishings were yellow or green. Her heart was racing far too wildly to be ignored. Annabel paused on the threshold, glancing around. Numerous guests were present, including her sisters and their husbands, the women in lavish evening gowns, the men in black dinner jackets. But Braxton had not come. She had known he would not, anyway, for it was far too dangerous. But her heart sank like a stone, filled with undeniable dismay.

Annabel realized she had been trembling, and she grimaced. Worse, she had dressed with great care for supper, in a splendid gown of creamy beige lace that was very bare, showing off most of her bosom and all of her shoulders. She wore a velvet choker around her neck, and hanging from it was one large and perfect South Sea pearl. Never one to care particularly about her appearance, tonight she had wanted to be beautiful, and in this gown and necklace, neither of which she ever wore, with her cheeks flushed with excitement, her blue eyes brilliant, her hair upswept, she had known that was the case. How foolishly disappointed she now was that he was not present to notice and admire her.

She saw several men staring, including James Appleton Beard and the elderly Mr. Frank. Annabel sighed, moving toward her family without looking at anyone else. As she passed a group of guests, she heard someone say, "Can you believe that is her?" in shock and incredulity, as if such elegance and beauty were an impossibility for herself.

"Annabel!" Lizzie cried, beaming. "I have never seen that gown before! How wonderful you look!" Lizzie was holding the hand of her two-year-old son, Evan.

"That is because I have never worn it." Annabel bent to tousle Evan's dark hair and kiss his plump cheek. "Hi, sweetie. How was your supper?"

He stuck his thumb in his mouth and smiled at her. "Goo'," he said.

His nanny stepped forward. "We were waiting for you, Miss Boothe. It is time for Master Evan to say good-night."

Annabel bent and hugged him, holding him against her chest for a moment. "Sweet, sweet dreams, Evan. I will play with you in the morning, I promise." She smiled at him.

"Play ten?" he asked, taking his nursemaid's hand.

"Yes, we shall play tennis, weather permitting." Annabel grinned.

Evan was led away. For one moment Annabel watched him, not hearing Melissa making a comment on how odd it was to teach a two-year old to play tennis before he could even spell his ABC's. And then she froze. Standing not far from the doorway, watching her intently, was none other than Pierce St. Clare.

Annabel could feel all the coloring draining from her face. Her heart, which felt as if it had halted, now resumed beating, but violently. She had never dreamed he would dare to show himself. Even if he was in disguise—somewhat.

He smiled slightly at her and inclined his head. Annabel turned abruptly away. Was he insane? He had added thick streaks of white to his hair, changing it from a lustrous blue-black to an iron gray. He had done something to his mouth, she was not sure what, but the bottom lip was fuller and protruding. His nose too had changed, it was larger and crooked. But as far as Annabel was concerned, he was quite remarkable, and anyone who knew him would recognize him instantly.

"So where *did* you get that dress, Annabel?" Melissa said petulantly.

Annabel blinked, only hearing her sister when she had repeated herself. "It was a part of my trousseau. You can have it if you wish."

"Really?" Missy brightened. "I would certainly wear it, again and again."

"Do not give that dress away!" Lizzie said, glaring at Melissa. Then, "Annabel, what is wrong?"

Annabel realized she was twisting her neck to get another glimpse of Braxton, damn his hide. But when she saw that her entire family was also turning to gaze in his direction, she abruptly looked away, filled with fright. She stared at Lizzie, her mind going blank, unable to respond. Had they seen him?

Had anyone recognized him?

"You look as if you have seen a ghost," Adam said, his tone kind. "Are you all right, Annabel?"

"I am fine. I, er, did think I saw someone I knew, but I was quite mistaken." She flashed a smile, certain the world could see how contrived it was.

Lizzie was regarding her, her scrutiny unnerving. There were few secrets Annabel could keep from her youngest sister. Then she glanced one more time in Braxton's direction. Annabel dared not turn. Finally Lizzie smiled and stepped closer to her. "Thomas Frank is staring at you, Annabel. He is going to come over here at any moment. And so is James Appleton Beard!" There was glee in her tone.

Annabel darted a glance over her shoulder, and saw Braxton in a group of men, chatting in a congenial manner. But the moment she turned, his glance found hers, and briefly they made eye contact.

Annabel put her back to him, extremely flustered. And Lizzie was right. Mr. Frank was approaching, smiling at her.

She stiffened, dismayed. She had no wish for Braxton to see her courted by an old man—as if she were an old maid herself. And then her gaze fell upon James. The moment their eyes connected, he smiled at her, blushing, and he bowed.

Annabel was not the least bit interested in him anymore, but she gave him her most encouraging smile and a graceful curtsy. An instant later he had entered their group, cutting off the advent of Thomas Frank. "Good evening," James said to one and all.

"Evening, Beard," Adam said, not smiling.

Lizzie nodded coolly. Neither one had forgiven him for the way he had treated Annabel earlier that day at lunch.

But Annabel smiled at him. "Good evening, James. How is your ankle faring?"

His cheeks remained red but he faced her with wide eyes. "Thank you, Miss Boothe, for your concern. Actually, I seem to be making a miraculous recovery."

"How wonderful," Annabel lied.

"Perhaps I will even be able to play a little tennis when the weather clears," he said, the hint clear.

"Well, I do hope that is the case," Annabel said, and she grinned at him, hoping her manner was alluring and filled with guile. She could not help herself, and had to glance over her shoulder at Braxton. Although he remained among the group of gentlemen, he was staring openly at her, watching her dalliance with the attractive and very eligible James Beard.

And how wonderful it felt! Annabel beamed at James and laid her hand on his forearm. "If you recover, I shall be more than glad to test your mettle."

James smiled widely in return. "I have heard you are a premier player, Miss Boothe. But I should be honored to have you test my mettle, so to speak."

Annabel attempted a coy smile. "Let's do speak on the morrow, for undoubtedly it shall be a pleasant day.

They are expecting good weather, I have heard."

James bowed. "On the morrow, then," he said, and he took his leave of their group.

Annabel felt quite smug, could feel Braxton's gaze on her back. Then she realized that Lizzie and Adam were regarding her very oddly. Melissa and John were also watching her. Melissa said, "Well! He has certainly changed his tune! It must be the gown."

Lizzie glared. "He has merely come to his senses," she said. She took Annabel's hand. "You are acting more strangely than ever. You were flirting with him! And I know you, Annabel Boothe. You would never give someone who has cut you a second chance. Whatever is going on?"

Annabel was as demure as she could possibly be. She lifted her eyebrows innocently. "I do not know what you are talking about."

Lizzie stared.

Annabel smiled at her and turned to see if Braxton continued to watch her. He did not. He was staring intently in the opposite direction, at the doorway of the salon.

Annabel followed his gaze. Her heart slammed to a stop.

The Countess Rossini had paused on the threshold of the room. She was so lovely, so striking, that everyone else in the room seemed to disappear. In fact, all of the guests had immediately noticed her appearance, and they were all staring—conversation had dimmed and ceased. Annabel also stared. The countess wore a stunning, narrow, extremely bare black lace gown, with the most spectacular diamond and ruby necklace dripping from her long, elegant neck. Annabel felt as if, in that one moment, she had been turned by a witch into ugly black stone. The countess, in contrast, was probably one of the world's most beautiful women.

The contessa smiled at the room at large and entered

it, followed by two couples and her escort, a very attractive blond, mustachioed gentleman. She nodded and smiled at those she passed.

Annabel tore her gaze from the countess's overwhelming presence to Braxton. He seemed as mesmerized as everyone else. Slowly, he looked from the Italian redhead to Annabel.

Annabel felt like sticking her tongue out at him. How childish she would then seem—when in reality, he must think her a child in comparison to the stunning and worldly older woman. Annabel could not believe how upset and unnerved she was. It struck her then that she was a complete fool. That she still harbored feelings for Braxton, strong ones, or she would never be so concerned about the other woman.

"Miss Boothe? Good evening."

Annabel was about to turn and respond when she saw Guilia Rossini stop and stare at Braxton. She made no effort to disguise her interest. He, in turn, smiled at her and bowed.

Annabel inhaled, stabbed with hurt.

"Miss Boothe? Might I mention that you are quite breathtaking tonight?"

Annabel watched Braxton purposefully approach the countess. Although she could not hear him, clearly he was introducing himself. The countess was smiling. He was smiling. She extended her hand and he took it to his lips.

Miserably Annabel turned away, to face her admirer, the ancient Thomas Frank.

As the hotel staff had forecast, that next day was clear. It was far too early in the morning to tell if it would be warm and sunny, for it was not even nine o'clock, but the rain had ceased and the clouds were lifting. Annabel paused beside a sprightly tree, not far from the beach. Behind her the path she had followed led to the Acadia's back lawns and tennis courts; ahead, it led to the swimming inlet on the beach.

She leaned against the tree, digging into her simple straw bag, trying to forget last night. She had made a fool of herself, she had no doubt, allowing Thomas Frank to escort her into supper and walk with her afterward in the galleria. Annabel grimaced, extracting a small box and from that a cigarette, hearing in her mind the gossips giggling over the old maid and the old man. She stuck it between her lips, digging deeper for a matchbox, wishing she had not behaved like an idiot. But then, how could she have not done so, when Braxton had danced attendance on the Countess Rossini all night long, until the countess's escort had exchanged such sharp words with him that the two men had nearly come to blows? Oh, how the countess had seemed to enjoy that!

As her fingers finally slid around a small matchbox, there was a sharp hissing sound behind her. Annabel whirled.

"May I?" Pierce St. Clare said with a smile.

She was so surprised by him that the cigarette fell out of her mouth. She caught it against her chest as the man she had no wish to see, not now, not ever, continued to hold out the flaming match. Trembling, angry, Annabel jammed the cigarette back in her mouth. She inhaled deeply as he lit it for her.

He watched her closely, shaking and dropping the match. "Since when did you become a smoker?" he asked.

"Oh, sometime after the abduction," she said tartly, between puffs.

"There was hardly an abduction," he returned, his tone as pleasant as hers was not.

"That is not what society says." She waved the cigarette airily.

"And since when have you ever cared what others

think? It is a part of your vast and unique charm, Annabel."

For an instant she believed that he was sincere, then she caught herself and blew smoke as directly as she could at his face.

He waved it away with his hand. "It's quite early in the morning for a stroll. Much less a smoke."

"I rise at six," she retorted. "And I have come down to the beach for a swim." That wasn't true, but Annabel was beyond analyzing herself. She wanted to do battle, and badly.

He grinned. "The ladies are not allowed to swim before two," he said mildly. "But then, I imagine you already know that."

"I do." She puffed harder than before.

"Does the kindly Thomas Frank know about this habit of yours?" There was laughter in his tone. "I don't imagine he would allow his wife to smoke."

Her eyes widened. "I beg your pardon. Nothing has changed in two years. I am hardly interested in marriage."

He stared, remaining silent.

Annabel felt herself blushing. He was clever, and he probably knew that no one would have her even if she did wish to wed. "I would certainly never marry that old man, kind or not."

"I know," he said.

Her heart turned over, numerous times. "You know nothing. And you followed me," she said sharply, unnerved.

"Yes, I did."

"What's wrong?" She was snide. "Did the countess throw you out of her bed before breakfast could be served?"

His gaze was searching. "Your jealousy is showing."

"I am not jealous," she flashed, throwing down the cigarette.

He eyed her, then ground out her smoking butt with his heel. "You could have fooled me, Annabel."

"It is Miss Boothe to you."

"Actually, I am flattered, that after all this time, you still care enough to be jealous of another woman."

"I do not care at all!" she cried, turning her back on him and starting rapidly down the path.

He fell into step beside her. "Well, in truth, I have not been in the countess's bed, although I doubt you would believe me."

"I don't."

"You also have nothing to be jealous of."

Annabel snorted.

When he did not reply, merely kept pace with her, she had to look at him. If only he were ugly. "She is probably one of Europe's reigning beauties."

"Probably," he agreed.

Annabel wished he had denied it, so her stride quickened. She could see the two of them entwined. It more than upset her—it infuriated her and it hurt her. What *was* wrong with her? How could she still care?

"Ten years ago," Pierce said, his tone conversational, "I would have enjoyed the attentions of a woman like Guilia Rossini, but call me jaded if you will, she offers little for a man like myself now."

Annabel harrumphed. "Why are you trying to placate me?"

"Perhaps because *I* care," he said.

Annabel stumbled. He caught her arm. She pushed him away. "Don't bother," she cried.

He shrugged. "She is not bright. Beauty without brains is hardly attractive. And she simpers, by God." He shook his head.

For one more moment, Annabel stared, almost ready to believe him. And then she recalled how he had been fawning over her all night long. "Uh-huh." She knew she was being coarse, but could not help herself. She continued down the path.

He strode alongside her.

And then it struck her, hard, so hard that she halted in mid-stride, facing him in amazement. "If you are not interested in her as a paramour, you must be interested in her as a thief!"

He did not blink. "You always were astute."

He was not even denying it! And all Annabel could think of was that he would get caught, this time, in the act of burglary. "Are you mad? Why do you do it? Surely by now you have stolen enough to live like a king for the rest of your life."

He smiled slowly. "I have."

She stared, shaking her head in disbelief. "Then why, Braxton, why put yourself in danger, again and again?"

"You know why." He was smiling, his gaze direct. "And my name," he said softly, "is St. Clare."

And her heart turned over, but hardly with revulsion. "The thrill. It is the danger which motivates you, thrills you."

"Yes," he said, "it is because of the thrill."

For one more moment Annabel held his gaze, and then she looked away, remembering how exciting that day had been when they had eluded the police after he had robbed her father's safe. Her pulse raced. He would never quit his habit, he was addicted, no less so than some poor wretch addicted to opium. But she understood.

"It's not safe for you here," she finally said. "Someone is bound to recognize you, especially if you rob the countess. Perhaps even someone from my family."

"Perhaps I will be long gone by the time that happens," he said smugly.

She looked at him. He returned her regard. "I think you care, more than you will ever admit," he said after a long pause. "You are afraid for my safety."

"No. No." Annabel shook her head adamantly, knowing he was right, but refusing to accept it. "I don't think we should be meeting like this," she said.

He chuckled. "Why not?" And he caught her hand. "Why not, Annabel?" His smile was gone.

His touch undid her. Desire she had no wish to ever entertain consumed her, but because Lizzie had been right, because she loved this man, she pulled her hand away. If she succumbed to his charm, he would love her and leave her again. He had killed her once. She could not survive a second time. "I am going swimming. Go back to the countess and plan your next escapade."

"Perhaps I will swim, too. With you."

Annabel stared, horrified. And then she enunciated every word as clearly as she could. "Go away," she said.

"I cannot seem to resist you," he said without hesitation. "I could not resist you then, and I cannot seem to resist you now." He was grim. "For better," he said, "or for worse."

Annabel stared. It had become crystal clear to her where this chance encounter was leading. She lifted her skirts and ran.

Chapter Eight

"Adam, Annabel is not in her room."

Adam laid a reassuring hand on his wife's small shoulder. "Why don't I take Evan for a walk and we will see if we can find her? I thought I saw her leaving the hotel earlier, although I am not sure."

Lizzie stood with her husband and her son just outside of the dining room, which was mostly empty at this time of the day, for the hotel guests preferred taking toast and coffee or cocoa in their rooms. "It would be just like Annabel to go walking at such an early hour!" Lizzie cried. She wrung her hands. "I am worried about her. Something is going on. I know her. She is hiding something from me," Lizzie said, frowning.

"Darling, I do not want you to worry about anything other than having an enjoyable vacation and taking plenty of rest." Adam kissed her mouth lightly and hoisted his son up onto his shoulders. "Remember, you are bearing our second son."

Lizzie smiled. "I am with our first daughter, dear."

He grinned. "We shall see." He left his wife after he had seated her in the dining room, Evan on his shoulders. "If you see Annabel, Evan, let me know."

"Anbel, Papa," Evan replied happily, clutching his father's head.

But Adam was no longer smiling. He was positive that he had glimpsed Annabel hurrying across the back lawns half an hour ago, when he had casually glanced out of the window of his dressing room. He believed his wife to be correct. Annabel was hiding something, and because he had grown very fond of her in the past five years, he was as concerned as his wife.

He strode across the back lawns, which were damp from yesterday's rain and the morning dew, with Evan in his arms. Ahead, emerging from the brush, he espied a tall gentleman, coming in his direction.

Adam did not slow his pace. The gentleman, clad casually in tan slacks and a tweed hacking coat, was close enough for Adam to recognize him as the fellow who had so enamored the Countess Rossini last night. They nodded to one another as they came abreast. Last night they had not been introduced.

"Good morning," Adam said, carefully extending one hand, the other firmly upon his son's ankle. "Adam Tarrington."

"Wainscot," the gentleman replied, his blue eyes unwavering.

"Have you by chance seen an attractive blond lady strolling these grounds?"

"No, I have not. Sorry I cannot help you." Wainscot smiled at Adam and his son and continued on.

But Adam did not move. He turned to stare after him, consumed with an odd feeling. Last night he had also felt perplexed. He knew this man, he was almost certain of it. Yet he could not place him, and did not recall his name as one he had already known.

"Papa? Anbel, Anbel!" Evan shouted with glee.

Adam shoved his thoughts aside just in time to see Annabel trudging up the same sandy path, barefoot, her skirts wet. Her shoes and stockings were dangling from one hand. Had she been swimming? He smiled reluctantly, shaking his head. Annabel would never change.

No, I have not. Sorry I cannot help you.

Adam froze, his smile gone. The stranger's words echoed in his mind. How could he have not seen her? Adam had taken this path several times; it led to the inlet, and that section of beach was small. It was impossible that they had not seen one another.

Suddenly he was angry, imagining the stranger spying upon Annabel while she swam. He hurried forward. "Annabel! We have been wondering where you were."

She faltered, seeming paler than usual. "I . . . I . . . decided to walk on the beach."

She was lying. He had not a doubt. And suddenly another scenario occurred to him. He stiffened. Had she just had a rendezvous with the gentleman he had so recently spoken to?

She was a grown woman. In all likelihood, she would never settle down and wed. It was not his place to judge, much less interfere. "Are you all right?" he asked carefully.

"I am fine," she said, far too brightly.

He studied her, but saw no sign of tears. He became certain that she had been involved in a tryst. "Will you join us for breakfast?" he asked. But now he was more perplexed than before. He could not shake the stranger's gray-haired image from his mind. He was more convinced than ever that he knew him, but from where? And why was it so damn important—and so damn disturbing?

"I would love to," Annabel said with obvious relief.

Lizzie was right. She was hiding something. An affair with the stranger?

"You are staring at me," Annabel said, fidgeting.

And then it struck him. He felt his eyes widen as he froze in shock.

He had changed his appearance. But the stranger was Pierce Braxton, the man who had abducted Annabel on her wedding day.

*   *   *

"I think you should sit down," Adam told Lizzie after they had finished breakfast and were alone in their rooms.

"You are scaring me! You behaved so oddly all through the meal. What is wrong?" Lizzie cried, gripping his arms.

Adam led her to an overstuffed chintz chair and pushed her gently down. "Darling, prepare yourself. I have recalled how I know that gentleman who joined the Rossini party last evening."

Lizzie blinked. "What? Oh, you mean Mr. Wainscot? Adam, that is hardly of importance—"

"I last saw him at Annabel's wedding, Lizzie," Adam said softly. "He has changed his hair, done something to his nose. But it is Braxton."

Lizzie turned starkly white. "You mean—"

"Yes. It is that damn thief himself."

He was walking through the lobby when Annabel saw him. Although he was clad as a respectable valet, Annabel would have known him anywhere. Her eyes widened and she froze, then she ran after him, grabbing his elbow from behind. "Louie!"

He whirled. And glanced all around them before holding her gaze with his own. "The guvnor told me you had met 'im, Miz Boothe, but by Gawd, we can't be seen together." His silver front tooth flashed.

Annabel's heart continued to pound. "I want to talk with you. I have to talk with you." She could hear how low and strained her voice sounded. But she was tense. How could she not be? She was caught in a terrible dilemma, harboring affection for a man whom she should hate and even wreck vengeance upon. Instead, she was obsessed with him once again, or perhaps she had never stopped being obsessed by him, not in two achingly long years. Perhaps she had only deluded herself into thinking she was over him after he had abandoned her and she had returned home.

In the interim since her aborted wedding, she had buried herself in one pursuit or another, keeping herself so occupied that she could not dwell on the past, feel the pain of the present, or think of the future. So she could not think. But his appearance had changed all of that.

There was no denying it, and no way to convince herself to feel differently about him: she was drawn to him against all common sense, against her very will; somehow, in some way, her heart was irrevocably attached to him. And now Braxton was here, and he was in danger and she was terrified for his safety. "Louie, come with me," she said firmly. She felt as if she were on a path of self-destruction, but she could no more stop herself than she could halt a locomotive flying down the Union tracks.

He shook his head, but she took his arm and began propelling him through the lobby and out the front door. When they were outside, and standing some distance from the two stone urns guarding the hotel entrance, Louie shook her off. "Are you still a madwoman?" he cried.

Annabel folded her arms and stared. How fortunate that Louie was once again aiding Braxton. "When is the robbery to take place? And how is he going to pull it off?"

Louie gaped at her. When he had recovered his surprise, he said, low, with a frantic glance around to see if anyone was watching them, "I don't know wot yer talkin' about!"

"Ha! Of course you do! Pierce already admitted his plans to me. He will get caught, Louie, this time he will be caught. I have such a bad feeling about this!" And it was true. Ever since that morning she had been sick at heart, thinking of the robbery that would soon occur. This time, she had a horrid feeling that he would not get safely away. She could even envision him being led away by the local sheriff in leg irons and handcuffs.

"We must stop him, Louie, from doing this." Annabel heard her own voice crack.

Louie stared. "You thinkin' of tellin' gents 'ere who 'e is?"

She flushed. "I can't do that, even though I should. Louie, talk him out of this. Either that, or let me help." The moment she had spoken, she was stunned by her own words.

"No one can change 'is mind when it's made up," Louie said matter-of-factly. "An' 'e would never let you 'elp us, by Gawd."

Annabel stared. She had no doubt that Braxton intended to rob the countess, and that Louie was right, his mind could not be changed. What if she could help, somehow, to insure that he did get safely away?

Annabel bit her lip. Something *was* wrong with her. She was now planning to help the very man who had betrayed her and broken her heart!

"Guess you still care about 'im, now don't you?" Louie was saying slyly.

Annabel stiffened. "He does not deserve to rot in jail for the rest of his life. And he certainly helped me avoid marriage to that mealy-mouthed Harold Talbot."

"That 'e did," Louie said with a grin and a wink.

"I want to help," Annabel said, suddenly meaning it. And her blood raced. Her skin tingled. Her mouth became absolutely dry. She was breathless, recalling their getaway on the day of her wedding. Perhaps she was too much like Braxton, and that was the source of her fatal attraction.

"Never," Louie said firmly.

"Annabel!"

It was Lizzie, and Annabel turned, to see her sister waving at her from the hotel's wide front steps. She faced Louie again. "Go! Quickly! And do not say a word to Braxton about this or I'll wring your neck!"

Louie hurried off. Annabel inhaled deeply, composing herself before facing her sister as she crossed the shell-covered drive. Annabel managed a bright smile. "I thought you were going to take a nap."

Lizzie looked gravely from Annabel to Louie's departing form. Her brow was creased with worry. "Who is that?" she asked, her tone unusually sharp.

Annabel stiffened. "A servant. I was asking directions—to town."

"Were you planning on walking the five miles from here to there, Annabel?" Lizzie asked, her tone high with uncharacteristic sarcasm.

Annabel stared. Lizzie was not given to mockery, and not only was she wounded, she was alarmed.

"Don't lie to me!" Lizzie cried angrily. "And you have been lying to me, haven't you?" Suddenly tears were spilling down her cheeks.

"Don't cry," Annabel said, aghast.

Lizzie sobbed into a linen handkerchief. Annabel watched, feeling horrible, and filled with an equally dark inkling about what this was about.

Lizzie stopped, and sniffing, she looked up. "Braxton is here, and you met him at the beach this morning."

Annabel's heart dropped like a boulder to her feet. For one moment, she could not breathe or speak. Then, through stiff lips, she managed, "That is absurd."

"Don't lie to me!" Lizzie shouted. "Adam recognized him."

Annabel began breathing harshly. She felt dizzy, faint. "I was as surprised as you. Please, Lizzie, don't say anything, please!" And Annabel gripped her hands.

"You are in love with him! I can see it in your eyes! Oh, God!" And tears fell from Lizzie's eyes again.

"I am not," Annabel tried, aware of how pathetic her lie was. "Lizzie, he does not deserve to spend the rest of his life behind bars. Surely you can agree with that."

Lizzie wiped her eyes. "He is a thief! He stole Mama's necklace. And he ruined you. He is guilty of at least two crimes. He should be incarcerated and you know it, Annabel. How can you say otherwise? How?"

Annabel was shaking. "Lizzie, he is a thief, but he is not a bad person. He never hurt me. Actually, he is a gentleman."

"A gentleman! How can you defend him after all that he has done?"

Annabel wet her lips, her pulse pounding. She was desperate. For the hour of Braxton's doom seemed to be at hand. "I have never really told you, or anyone, the truth. But listen to me now. He did not want to abduct me. He tried to leave me in some barn on the West Side of Manhattan, but I refused. Lizzie, *I refused*. And he would not have touched me, except that . . ." She faltered, afraid to continue.

Lizzie's gaze was glued to her face. "Except that what?" she whispered, her eyes wide and mirroring something close to horror.

Annabel wet her lips. "I seduced him."

"You what?"

"I seduced Braxton, Lizzie, it was not the other way around. Because I wanted to be ruined, so I would not have to marry Harold Talbot or some other idiot like him." Annabel stared. She could not quite believe that she had told her sister the truth, no matter how much she loved her and how close they were.

Lizzie gaped at her.

Annabel shrugged, tears filling her own eyes. "Something is wrong with me, isn't it? As Missy keeps saying? Reckless, that's what they say. Reckless, impulsive, headstrong."

Lizzie was crying again, but quietly. She hugged Annabel hard. And when she pulled away, she said, "You are different, there is no question of that, but there is nothing wrong with you." Her gaze was searching. "I hope you are telling the truth. But I cannot think of why you would lie about something like that in order to protect him. Oh, Annabel!"

"I am telling the truth. He is not a cad." Annabel smiled and sighed. "I wish he were, for then this would be so very easy." For then she would not be in love with him.

"But he is here," Lizzie said after a pause. "Braxton is here, and you were with him at the beach. Annabel, what are you doing? Please, just this once, stop and think! You must stay away from him."

"I have been thinking. The truth is, all I have done since he arrived yesterday was to think. Will you keep my secret?" Annabel asked. "Will you keep our secret? Please?"

Lizzie did not speak at first. "I could never betray you, you know that."

Annabel hugged her in relief. And when she opened her eyes, she saw Melissa standing behind them, staring at them with wide eyes.

Chapter Nine

Annabel stared at her sister. Melissa smiled and came forward. "I was about to take a walk and I saw the two of you standing here," she said. "Are you about to stroll? May I join you?"

Her relief knew no bounds. It did not seem as if Melissa had overheard their conversation. Unfortunately, though, Annabel did not completely trust her sister—she had eavesdropped far too many times. She regarded her closely. "Actually, Lizzie merely wanted to speak with me—about my walk earlier this morning on the beach."

If Melissa knew that the subject of their conversation was Braxton, or that Annabel had met him on the beach, she gave no sign. "Oh. Well, I do not want to walk alone. Lizzie, will you join me?"

Lizzie shook her head. "Actually, I have a horrid headache and I must lie down." Not looking at Annabel, she lifted her skirts and hurried toward the hotel entrance. Both sisters watched her go.

"What is wrong with her?" Melissa turned wide eyes upon Annabel. "She is so upset. What have you said, or, what have you done now?"

Annabel smiled and said calmly, "We had a very private conversation, and I think I shall go to my rooms now, too."

Melissa did not reply, but this time, from the look in her eyes, Annabel had the awful feeling that she knew everything.

From across the dining room, Braxton smiled at her.

Annabel's nerves had been on edge ever since she had come down to supper, both wishing that he would be there, and wishing that he would not be so foolish. Now her heart went wild. She looked away, feeling her cheeks burning. Then, from the corner of her eye, she saw that Lizzie had noticed the entire intimate exchange.

Annabel quickly looked at Melissa. But if she had noticed, she gave no sign. She was enjoying her prime rib.

Annabel swallowed, the hair on her arms still raised, and cautiously looked his way. He dined with the countess, what nerve! Did he intend to rob her this evening?

And would he make love to her in order to do so?

Annabel thought about their conversation on the beach that morning. It was unforgettable, like the man himself. But she would be an idiot to believe anything that he had said about his feelings for her.

"You have no appetite, Annabel. In fact, you seem upset," Melissa remarked, laying down her knife and fork, having finished most of her course.

Annabel's food was untouched. "I'm afraid I spoiled my appetite this afternoon with a box of chocolates," Annabel lied, her gaze straying of its own volition toward Braxton again.

The countess leaned against him, regaling him with some tale or another. Her blond escort, Sir Linville, was openly annoyed. Braxton appeared completely at ease— and seemed to be thoroughly enjoying himself.

Melissa turned and stared at the Rossini party. "How fascinated you are by the countess," she said. "Or is it that handsome Englishman she seems so enamored of?"

Annabel could hardly breathe. "A rich Italian widow hardly fascinates me." She forced herself to eat.

"I am fascinated by the countess," Lizzie interjected a bit too quickly. "Imagine being that beautiful, and having so many men falling all over themselves for your attention!" She shot Annabel a warning look. Her cheeks were highly flushed.

"You are that beautiful, and you hardly need more than one man falling all over himself for your attention," Adam said. "And that man is myself."

Lizzie smiled at her husband. He smiled back at her. Annabel watched them, wondering what it would be like to be so cherished by a wonderful man—and to cherish him in return. She did not dare look at Braxton again. But she had to face her innermost feelings. She wanted Braxton to be that enamored of her, the way Adam was of Lizzie, so much so that he would hardly glance at another woman.

She reminded herself that he was going to burglarize the countess, and then he would be on his way. If he was not caught, that is.

And if he did escape, then she would never see him again.

And suddenly Annabel felt as if she were on the vast precipice of life. The future loomed before her, a huge and dark void. Alone, she thought. She would forever be alone.

Unless she took her destiny into her own hands.

She lurked in the shadows at the end of the hall. It was close to two in the morning, and the last of the hotel's festive-minded guests had gone to bed—except for the countess and Braxton.

Annabel had been hiding on the hotel's top floor for over two hours, waiting for them to retire. She heard the elevator whirring and stiffened, crouching down low. She was rewarded when the elevator's brass door opened and Braxton escorted the countess out. She was exquisite in a red lace evening gown, but she was also tipsy, and clinging firmly to his arm.

Annabel bit her lip hard, tears stinging her eyes, thinking how easy it would be for him to seduce her now, let her fall asleep, and make off with her jewels. Her heart hurt.

The countess was laughing huskily at something he had said. She could not seem to find her keys in her beaded purse, and she swayed a bit on her black satin high-heeled shoes.

"Allow me," he said with a smile. In a moment he had found her keys and opened the door to her suite.

She smiled at him, poised to enter her apartments.

"Good night, Guilia," he said.

Annabel's eyes widened in shock.

"Pierce? Surely you wish to come in?" The countess was as surprised as Annabel.

He smiled again and tilted up her chin. "My darling lady, I have no wish to be dangled upon your strings like the other men you collect."

Her eyes widened, and then she smiled, rubbing his chest beneath his black dinner jacket. "Do I dangle men?" she purred.

"You do."

"Perhaps it would be so very enjoyable for both of us," she whispered, staring up at him.

"I imagine so, but in truth, Linville is smitten with you, Guilia, and you would be foolish to throw such a gentleman away. His intentions, I believe, are honorable. Unlike mine," he added wryly.

She stared. "You amaze me."

He laughed, kissed her lips lightly. "Good night."

"Good night, Pierce," she said.

Annabel continued to watch them, no longer shocked but elated. The countess disappeared behind her closed door. Pierce turned and sauntered down the hall, back toward the elevator. He seemed to be in exceedingly good spirits.

As was Annabel. She grinned to herself, and a chuckle escaped her.

Pierce froze in mid-stride.

Annabel shrank back against the wall.

He turned. And he saw her immediately.

His expression was comical. His eyes went wide.

There was no point in hiding anymore, so Annabel straightened, her heart pounding like a damnable drum. Her color, she knew, was high. He strode forward. "Well, well," he said, his gaze taking in her appearance. "So you have gained employment in the hotel as a housemaid?"

Annabel thought she blushed again. She was wearing a black dress with a white apron, borrowed from the laundry room. "This is a disguise."

He folded his arms and chuckled.

"How are you going to rob her if you do not sleep with her?" Annabel asked very directly.

His smile vanished. "That idea is highly repugnant. How little you think of me."

"But you have to get inside her apartments, and she has locked the door."

He smiled at her.

"Oh." Annabel smiled back, suddenly feeling quite happy. "A locked door hardly interferes, I do see."

"Perhaps what I want is not in her suite," Pierce said softly. He stared directly at her, his smile gone.

Annabel understood. She did not move.

Pierce suddenly shook his head, as if catching himself in an unplanned act. "Go back to your rooms, Annabel. And back to bed. I have work to do."

Now she started. "So it is tonight." Which explained his good mood, she thought.

"Yes." He stared.

"Let me help."

"That is out of the question."

"Why?"

"You will cause me to bungle the job."

"That is not fair," Annabel said angrily.

"But it is true. You would only distract me. And I have a partner."

Annabel did not know what to say. So she spoke the truth. "I will never see you again after tonight."

He hesitated. "It would be unlikely."

She crossed her arms, hugging herself.

For a long moment, he did not speak. "You are wearing your heart upon your sleeve—for me to see."

It was hard to speak. "I don't care," she said hoarsely.

"Annabel, this is insane." His gaze was glued to hers. His facial muscles were set and tensed.

She swallowed with difficulty. "What is insane?"

"This." And he swept her into his arms.

Annabel could hardly believe he was kissing her, that finally, after two horribly long, endless and lonely years, she was in his embrace. His mouth claimed and held hers. She gripped his shoulders, his back, her mouth tearing at his. How unbearable, how good, this was.

And then his lips were on the soft underside of her throat. Annabel's hands were in his hair. Her back was against the wall. His palms slid over her breasts. His mouth, kissing and nibbling on her throat, finally found a tiny area of exposed flesh on her collarbone. It was sheer and wonderful torture.

He pulled her hard against him, burying his face in her hair, groaning.

"Don't stop. Please, Pierce, I will never see you again!" Annabel cried.

He pulled away from her, only to clasp her face with his strong hands. Their gazes locked. "I want you," he said.

*   *   *

There was a soft rapping on the door.

Annabel lay naked in Pierce's arms in his bed. She was panting, her heart just beginning to slow from their frenzied and rushed lovemaking. He had not even moved off her, and like herself, was breathing quickly and harshly. The knocking came again. It was soft and low, but insistent.

For one instant, his arms tightened around her. Then he slid off her and sat up.

Annabel became lucid. She could guess who was knocking on his door at perhaps two-thirty or three o'clock in the morning, and she sat up, clutching the covers to her chest. Pierce stood, reaching for his drawers, which he stepped into. He strode to the door and opened it.

"Guv, wot yar doing? Did you forgit we 'ave a job to do this night?" Louie asked in a low tone of voice.

"I do believe I briefly lost my head," Pierce said wryly. "With good cause." And he looked over his shoulder and smiled at Annabel.

Annabel could not smile back. This was happening too swiftly. She did not move.

That was when Louie saw her and his mouth dropped open. "Guvnor, it's late. We got to get going. Forget 'er."

Pierce stepped aside so Louie could enter the room, and he quickly dressed. His expression had changed, hardening. Watching him, Annabel felt the glow of their glorious lovemaking vanish, replaced by dismay, dread, and fear. "I want to help. At least let me keep watch."

"No." Pierce buttoned his white shirt deftly, slipping on his jacket.

Annabel stared, and then she flung aside the covers and stepped from the bed. Louie cried out. Pierce whirled.

Annabel leapt into her drawers and chemise. "I am going to help!" she cried.

And for one instant, as Pierce stared, she thought his gaze was admiring, and knew it had nothing to do with her body. Then he stepped to her and gripped her shoulders. "No. I know you are headstrong and brave, but not this time, Annabel."

"What if she wakes up and catches you while you are robbing her?"

He flung on his jacket, and as he did so, Annabel saw it was the one with the specially sewn interior pockets. Then he bent over the trunk and produced a small black satchel from it. Annabel realized he was about to leave, without answering her, and frantically she shimmied into her black dress. Would he abandon her once again without even a good-bye?

But if he did, it would be her own fault, for allowing this to happen—and for not seizing her own fate.

She was so upset, she could not do up more than a single button. "Goddamn it!" she cried.

He paused at the door, and when he finally turned, his face was grim. Annabel had not taken her eyes off him, even as she tried to struggle with the damned buttons on the back of her dress. Their gazes clashed and locked.

Pierce dropped the satchel. He strode to her, grabbed her and kissed her hard. "Good-bye," he said, his gaze intense.

"No!" Annabel said.

He retrieved the satchel and, without a backward glance, moved to the door. Annabel knew he was about to exit not just the room, but her life, and that this time it would be forever. She knew she must act.

Her gaze swung around the room wildly and settled upon a blue and white vase filled with flowers. She grabbed it, running after the two men. And as she hefted it, Pierce turned. His eyes widened with surprise and comprehension. "No!"

But it was too late. Annabel crashed it down upon the unsuspecting Louie's head.

Chapter Ten

They both watched Louie sink to the floor, his eyes rolling back in his head.

Annabel grimaced, hoping she had not hurt him, and when she looked up, she saw Pierce staring at her. "I want to help," she said.

"Good God," he returned. Then, ruefully, he half smiled. "Very well. But only this once."

Annabel could not believe her ears. She felt herself smiling.

And for one moment he stared at her. Then, "Turn around." His tone was brisk. "It is late and we are behind schedule."

Annabel turned. He quickly buttoned up her dress and she stepped into her shoes. Then they slipped soundlessly from the room. Annabel had a hundred questions to ask, especially once she realized they were going downstairs and not up to the floor where the countess's suite was, but she did not dare. She knew Pierce would strangle her if she made a sound. She was determined to be an extraordinary accomplice.

A few small lights flickered in the lobby as they hurriedly approached. Annabel's heart lurched when she realized a clerk remained behind the front desk, and even though he was sleeping, his head upon his folded arms, she gripped Pierce's arm from behind with alarm. Pierce looked at her, one finger to his mouth, having lost none of his composure. Annabel nodded, aware of perspiring. Perhaps, she thought, the clerk would be the one to discover them in the midst of this criminal act. Her pulse was racing with both fear and excitement.

They left the stairs and started through the lobby. It had never seemed larger to Annabel and traversing it seemed to take an eternity. They were halfway across the room when the clerk suddenly stirred, making a sound.

Annabel froze. The clerk mumbled to himself. Pierce grabbed her and they ran the rest of the way, when Annabel would have turned and fled back to the stairs. She flung a glance over her shoulder. The clerk, Annabel saw, continued to doze.

They paused just around the corner, outside the manager's office. Annabel trembled, her fear warring with relief. She could hardly believe they had not been caught, could hardly believe Pierce was so bold. Then she saw Pierce extracting a bit and brace from the satchel. He did not look at her, but Annabel was in shock. They were breaking into the manager's office, just steps away from the front desk and the sleeping clerk? Was he mad?

Very quickly, Pierce drilled the bit into the wood around the lock. Annabel's heart continued to thunder and her mouth was painfully dry. He finally looked at her with a smile, standing and jimmying the doorknob off the door. He pressed it open and bowed as if they were at a ball. Annabel shook her head—now was not the time to clown—and together they went inside. Pierce closed the door carefully behind them.

"Yale locks," he whispered. "Impossible to pick." He winked.

Annabel was sweating; he was enjoying himself. And she felt like breaking into hysterical laughter. Instead, she pointed at the door and at herself.

"Good girl," he mouthed, patting her back. He handed her the knob and walked behind the desk. Annabel realized his goal was the huge cast-iron safe set in the wall. She watched him extract some kind of small brass horn from the satchel. As he placed it against the safe, the other end to his ear, he began to twirl the large black dial.

Annabel realized she was so fascinated with what he was doing that she was not keeping guard as she was supposed to do. She turned and cracked the door slightly and peered out of it. The lobby was empty.

Her pulse continued to race. She heard a click from behind. It seemed ominously loud in the silence of the night. Pierce had opened the safe. The horn had disappeared back into the satchel. He was groping through the vault's dark interior.

Annabel heard a footstep. She whirled, but saw no one, and only silence greeted her now. And then there was a tap on her shoulder from behind.

Annabel almost jumped out of her skin, but she faced only Pierce. He was smiling at her, holding out the largest ruby she had ever seen. It dangled from a strand of glistening, perfect pearls.

"Oh, my God," she heard herself whisper. And then she heard the footfalls outside in the lobby again.

Pierce heard them, too, because the necklace disappeared. A small pistol had appeared in his hand in its stead. He shoved Annabel behind him.

The door began to open.

Annabel was so tense she thought her body would snap. Sweat poured down her face and limbs in streams.

A slender man stepped into the room.

As he did so, Pierce grabbed him, clapping a hand over his mouth and pressing the muzzle of the gun to his head. "Louie." He released him.

Louie glared at Pierce, and then at Annabel. If looks could kill, Annabel would be dead.

Annabel wanted to tell him how sorry she was, but on the other hand, she wanted to throttle him for scaring her to death. But she could do neither. Pierce was signaling to them and his meaning was clear—it was time to go. He shoved first Louie and then Annabel from the room. They melted against the wall, waiting to hear any sounds from the front desk. The clerk was now snoring.

Annabel could not believe that their good fortune continued unabated. Her eyes met Pierce's.

He smiled at her and waved them forward. And as one, the trio raced across the lobby and upstairs to the safety of his room.

The clock in Pierce's room read three fifty-five. Pierce was grinning and holding up a bottle of champagne. As he popped the cork, he said, "I seem to recall that you are fond of champagne, Annabel."

They had done it. They had burglarized the countess, and escaped without mishap. She laughed in delight. "I am."

He handed her the bottle, sliding his arm around her. His tone low, he said, still smiling, "Even if it is warm?"

"Even if it is warm," she said, her smile fading.

His also dimmed. Annabel forgot to think. He bent and kissed her, long and slow, tongue to tongue.

"Now hold on," Louie cried, arms folded across his chest. "She's got some explaining to do."

Pierce released her. Annabel felt drugged from the kiss and what they had just done. It was hard to think, for all she wanted to do was to jump back into bed with Pierce and touch him everywhere, allowing him the very same liberties.

"Here," he said softly. "Ladies first."

Annabel accepted the bottle and took a long swig of champagne. How delicious it was, even at room temperature. And then she thought again of what they had done, and her part in it, and she grinned. Living dangerously was definitely in her nature.

"You seem very pleased, Annabel," Pierce said softly.

She met his blue gaze. "I am."

His gaze was probing.

"An' I got a headache you couldn't believe." Louie scowled at Annabel.

"Louie, I do believe the lady meant no harm," Pierce said, handing him the bottle.

"I'm sorry," Annabel said, meaning it. "But I was so afraid for the two of you and I wanted to help." Suddenly her elation died. They had done it, pulling off the burglary with ease and even aplomb, but what would happen now? Her heart lurched with sickening intensity. She turned to Pierce, only to find him watching her extremely closely, and he was no longer smiling, either— as if he could read her thoughts.

"Now what?" she asked with real trepidation.

"In a day or so we will check out," Pierce said easily. "After the ruby is discovered missing, after the police come, question everyone, and fail to find either the thief or the jewel."

"You will stay here?" Annabel was aghast.

"Yes. If I leave now, in the thick of the night, I will be the obvious culprit. You are the only one who knows who I am, Annabel." He was smiling.

Annabel was ill. So much so that for a moment, all words failed her. She sat down hard on his bed. Where, so recently, they had been passionately entwined. She looked at the mussed covers, recalling the intimacy they had shared.

"What is it?" His tone was sharp.

"Oh, God. I should have told you this before." She looked up. "Adam and Lizzie know who you are, Pierce. Adam recognized you and told my sister."

Pierce stared.

Annabel rubbed her temple. "She agreed not to say

anything, but I do not think she can keep her silence once this theft is discovered. And Adam, why, I am certain he will come forward."

Pierce cursed.

Annabel had never heard him use an epithet before, and oddly, it seemed incredibly out of character. "We are blown," he said grimly to Louie. "And we must leave right now."

Annabel started.

"An' how are we going to do that?" Louie said. "The staff'll be up in another two hours, we won't even be out of town by then."

Pierce was grim. His gaze found Annabel.

And ridiculously, she felt as if this were her own fault. "You knew the risks," she said defensively.

"I knew the risks," he agreed.

"There wasn't time to tell you sooner," she said. Thinking about why there hadn't been time—because they had been in bed together.

"They're going to catch us," Louie said, pacing. "Even if we make the next train out, when they finger us, they'll be stoppin' the train to arrest us."

"Actually, I am in agreement with you, Louie."

The situation was horrid, and getting worse with every moment. "I will beg them not to say a word," Annabel cried.

"Adam Tarrington has too much integrity. He will point his finger at me the moment Guilia cries theft."

Annabel was of the exact same opinion. "So what will you do?"

"I will run. And with a little luck, Louie and I shall escape."

She was frozen. His words echoed. Unable to restrain herself, filled with dread, she asked, "And what about me?"

He hesitated. "History seems to be repeating itself, does it not?"

She told herself she would not allow even a single tear to fall. "I am an accomplice."

Pierce gave her an odd look and Louie snorted in disbelief.

He wasn't even going to suggest that she run away with him. Annabel could not move. She loved him, dear God, she did, but he did not return her feelings, or not to the same degree. So, once again, he would abandon her, and in doing so, kill her heart another time.

"Annabel."

She looked up.

"It would never work."

She inhaled. "Why not?"

His jaw flexed. "The risk of being caught is high now. I cannot let you take that risk, Annabel."

"You are taking that risk," she said, her tone oddly fragile.

"I am. But I am different from you. You belong here, with these people, with your family, your own kind."

And tears filled her eyes. Her own kind. The kind who preferred the drudgery and predictability of marriage and society fêtes, the kind who loved nothing more than to point and whisper, judge and condemn. Poor, poor Annabel Boothe. Why couldn't he see that he was her kind? Not those other, horrid, gossiping folk?

They were one of a kind! How blind could he be?

"Annabel. One day you will fall in love with some proper but brilliant fellow, and you will marry. I am certain of it." He knelt before her. "I know you do not understand. But you are young, and one day you will thank me for what I have done."

Annabel laughed, without mirth, through her tears. I am in love, she thought miserably, but did not verbalize her thoughts.

"Let's go, me lord," Louie cried. "Afore we got no chance at all."

Pierce took her hands in his. "I will never forget you."

Annabel could not speak.

He stood. Their gazes held. Then he walked out of the room with Louie, betraying her almost exactly as he had done two years ago. But this time, Annabel knew she would never forgive him, and that she would never see him again.

Chapter Eleven

The banging on her door was terrific. Annabel had cried herself to sleep. Now she opened one eye and saw the sunlight streaming into her room. It was mid-morning.

"Annabel! Open this door immediately!" Lizzie cried, pounding on her door again.

Lizzie was the last person Annabel wished to see. She sat up slowly, and was overwhelmed with grief again. The tears fell and she could not stop them. She flopped back on the bed, this time rolling onto her stomach and sobbing into her pillow.

"Annabel! Annabel! Are you in there?" The knob rattled wildly.

Suddenly angry, Annabel threw her pillow aside and stood, striding to the door. She swung it open. "I am sleeping," she cried. "Go away!"

Lizzie gasped. "You are crying? Oh—what has he done now?"

And at her sister's open display of genuine sympathy, Annabel collapsed into her arms, sobbing uncontrollably.

Lizzie held her. Eventually, Annabel pulled away and walked back to the bed, sinking down tiredly upon it. Lizzie closed the door, locking it, and came to sit down beside her. "The countess was robbed. An extraordinarily valuable ruby, worth a king's ransom, they say, was taken from the safe in the manager's office last night."

Annabel looked at her. Recalling the theft caused the tears to fall again. She had never cried so much in her life—not even the last time. She had never felt so heavy, so lifeless, so exhausted.

"It was Braxton, wasn't it? Has he run away already?" Lizzie asked.

Annabel wiped her running eyes with the back of her hand. "Yes, it was Braxton, and he is gone. And actually, the burglary took place at three-thirty this morning, not last night."

Lizzie blinked. "How would you know that?" But now she was staring at Annabel's black dress. "And why are you wearing a housemaid's uniform?"

"Do you really want to know?"

Lizzie stood, her color shocking in its pallor. "Oh, dear Lord. Oh, please, please, tell me you did not get so involved with him that . . . I cannot even think it."

Annabel did not bother to reply. She was too despondent. She choked on another sob.

"Oh, Annabel, he is such a horrid man, do not cry this way over him." Lizzie hugged her hard.

Annabel did not reply. A part of her was still ready to defend him, but she refused to do so, by damn. She would never defend him again. But she heard herself ask, "Adam? Is he going to the authorities?"

"How can he? We have discussed it at length. He and I should have come forward with the truth about Braxton immediately, but we did not, and he is a wanted felon, Annabel. And where would such a confession leave you? Why, it would make you seem to be his accomplice!"

Annabel could not laugh, not even mirthlessly. "I am his accomplice," she muttered.

Lizzie moaned. "Do not say another word! Do not tell me another thing! Please, do not!"

Annabel looked at her sister, who was extremely distraught, and fell back onto the bed, reaching for the pillow, which she placed over her head.

She could not even hate Braxton. All she could do was grieve. She had loved him and lost him a second time.

"Annabel." Lizzie's tone was firm. "Adam has already wired Papa. I imagine that he will arrive tomorrow."

Annabel sat up, eyes wide. "You're going to tell him, aren't you? You're going to tell him everything."

"Yes," Lizzie said. "For your own sake."

Her father arrived late the following day. Annabel had not stepped out of her room since Braxton had left. But she had learned from the housemaid assigned to her floor that the local police were sweeping the area for him, suspecting him of the theft because of his abrupt departure in the middle of the night. As yet, no one seemed to have connected Wainscot with Braxton. In spite of herself, Annabel was relieved.

Her father had only just checked in, but Annabel was already summoned to his suite by a porter. She took one glance at herself in the mirror over her bureau and winced—she was a terrible sight, her eyes and nose swollen and red, her face pallid and white. Summoning up her courage, she left her room and went to his suite on the fifth floor. Anxiety filled her. She could not imagine what he was going to do to her now. He would probably disinherit her and throw her out of the house. That did not scare her as much as facing his wrath did. Finally, fearfully, she knocked.

"Enter," he barked.

She winced. His tone of voice told her that he had no patience left for anyone, and that her situation—her future—was dire indeed. She walked into the wood-paneled sitting room of his apartment.

He turned. "What do you have to say for yourself?" he demanded in another bark.

He looked extremely tired—and extremely angry. "How are you, Papa?" she ventured.

"Do not inquire after my welfare or my journey, by damn! He was here, and you are here, and I am in a state of disbelief!" George Boothe roared. "Were the two of you carrying on?"

Annabel cringed, tears filling her eyes. But they had nothing to do with his anger—and everything to do with her loss, her love, and her grief. "Yes," she whispered. "He was here. We were carrying on."

He stared, wide-eyed, as if he had expected her to deny it. For a long moment he could not speak. "How could you? He abducted you, Annabel, and you just forgave him?" He was incredulous. "You are an intelligent and strong woman. You allowed him to seduce you?"

"Yes," she whispered brokenly.

He stared again, as if doubting his own ears. "I will kill him when he is caught!"

"I love him!" she cried back.

"Oh, God!" he cried.

Annabel collapsed onto an ottoman, weeping against her own volition.

George turned back to her, towering over her. "Annabel, you cannot possibly love such a man. Not only is he a complete stranger, he is a thief. He breaks the law, by God. Did I not raise you to know the difference between right and wrong? How is it possible that you just stood by and allowed him to rob the countess?" He was grim. "How could you not have turned him in?"

"Even now, as hurt as I am, I pray he eludes the police," she whispered, not daring to look up. Had Lizzie told him everything? Did he know that she had participated in the theft? It did not seem so, thank God.

"If you were a child, I would turn you over my knee and give you a serious spanking, Annabel. Perhaps this is all my fault." He threw his hands up into the air. "By allowing you your wild ways as a child, by never striking you, not even once!"

"It's not your fault," she managed hoarsely. "It is my fault. Something is wrong with me, Papa. Pierce and I, we are alike."

"You are alike?" he shouted. "You are not alike, Annabel. He is a thief. You, by God, are a Boothe."

Annabel hugged herself. "I am sorry, Papa, for failing you and for protecting him, but where he is concerned, I cannot help myself. Do you know that he is the only person I have ever met who admires me for my outspokenness, for my determination, for my courage?" She covered her face with her hands. "I cannot seem to stop crying," she moaned. "If only I could stop crying!"

Silence filled the room. Boothe went to her, lifting her to her feet and taking her into his arms. "Oh, Annabel. I will kill him for breaking your heart, that I promise you."

She managed to look up at her father. "No. You see, he never made me any promises, Papa. I wanted to go with him. But he refused. He would not let me go with him. He did not want me to suffer the risk of being captured and incarcerated, and he even told me he expected me to find love with another man one day. Yes, he has broken my heart—yet again. But you should thank him for refusing to take me with him, instead of vowing to kill him."

"You are defending him." Boothe stared, and finally he sat down hard on the sofa. "You love him still. Oh, Annabel. What am I going to do with you?"

"It doesn't matter," she said. "My life is over. Pierce is wrong. My future doesn't exist."

"No." Boothe stood. "You have committed a grave error of judgment, but affairs of the heart are rarely wise. Your future begins today. I have never dictated to you before, and as much as I comprehend your grief

now, I will do what is right for you—as I should have
done two years ago."

Annabel was alarmed. "What do you intend?"

"You will marry, my dear, like every other proper
woman, and one day you will thank me for it."

Two days later, Annabel stood at the altar in the reception hall of the hotel, which had been festively decorated
with flowers and candles for her wedding to Thomas
Frank. Her entire family was present, as was the countess and her entourage and most of the hotel's guests.
Annabel was numb.

She would do as her father asked, because she did not
care about her life anymore and she did not have the
strength or the inclination to fight with him. Lizzie had
pointed out that Thomas Frank was besotted with her,
and she would probably be able to do as she liked once
married—that this was, for Annabel, a very good match.
Annabel had looked at her, wondering if she were out
of her mind. Lizzie had married for love after a brief but
stormy courtship. She and Adam remained in love four
and a half years later. Who was Lizzie fooling?

Melissa had been more rational. "Papa is right. The
time has come for you to settle down and grow up, Annabel. You could have found someone to your liking if
you had tried, but you never tried, so now you have no
choice."

Annabel did not dare look at the groom now, but she
glanced at Missy, who seemed pleased by the turn of
events. It struck her then, for the first time in her life,
that her sister did not wish her well, but she could not
fathom why.

Suddenly Annabel realized that the minister had
paused and was staring at her. She began to flush. She
had been so immersed in her thoughts—and her misery—that she had not been paying attention to a word
he said. Thomas nudged her.

"I do," he whispered.

Oh, God. Annabel froze, unable to speak. She realized now what stage they had reached in the ceremony—just as she realized she could not go through with this.

"She does." Her father stepped forward from where he stood just behind Thomas with her mother and her sisters and brothers-in-law. "Annabel?" He stared commandingly at her.

Annabel opened her mouth. No words came out.

The white-haired minister looked at her, his eyes kind. "My dear, do you, Annabel Boothe, take this man to be your husband? In sickness and in health, in good times and in bad, for better or for worse?"

Annabel wet her lips. A huge silence filled the reception hall.

And a cramp seized her. She gasped.

The minister smiled, apparently misinterpreting the sound for an affirmation, and he turned to Thomas quickly. As quickly, Thomas reached for and took her hand, clearly saying, "I do."

Annabel closed her eyes in disbelief. In another moment they would be man and wife.

"If there be any man present who objects to this union, set forth your objections now, or forever hold your peace," the minister intoned.

The hall was silent.

I object, Annabel thought wildly. I object!

The minister smiled and opened his mouth to pronounce them man and wife.

"I object," Pierce cried, striding down the aisle.

Annabel cried out and turned as the crowd gasped. Her eyes widened and her knees buckled. She could not believe her eyes—she had never wanted to behold anyone more.

He had come—he had come to rescue her.

"I beg your pardon?" the minister asked, bewildered.

Pierce paused beside Annabel. "I object," he said, his

rich voice carrying. "Annabel Boothe cannot marry this man."

George came to life. "Arrest him. It's the thief who stole the Rossini ruby!"

And several members of the hotel staff came rushing forward from the very back of the hall, including the manager. The five men grabbed Pierce and immobilized him. But he did not struggle. Finally, his gaze met Annabel's.

She was crying. How she loved him. She had never loved anyone more.

"Get the sheriff," the manager was ordering one of his bellmen. The young bellhop ran off.

"Wait!" Annabel cried.

The bellhop actually faltered and stopped halfway down the aisle, for her tone had been so sharp.

Annabel looked at Pierce. He smiled at her, calm, composed, filled with assurance. She tried to smile back, but her rioting emotions—and her fear for him—made it impossible. She faced her father and their guests. "Mr. Wainscot did not steal the countess's ruby," she said firmly.

"Annabel," George began warningly.

"No." Annabel shook her head. She did not hesitate. He had come to rescue her—and she would rescue him. "He could not have stolen the ruby that night. It was a physical impossibility." She looked at Pierce again.

He was staring, his smile gone, as if he knew exactly what she would say.

Her pulse was deafening her. Annabel wet her lips. Raising her voice, she said, "He was with me the entire night, until well after sunrise. With me—in my bed."

George turned white. Lizzie cried out. Missy gasped. Lucinda slowly crumpled to the floor. John and Adam, apparently paralyzed by Annabel's declaration, failed to catch her. And the crowd began talking wildly.

"It's the truth," Annabel said, aware of her burning cheeks. But she held her head high.

"Annabel," George said harshly, "do you realize what you are saying?"

She looked at her father, wishing desperately he would come to her aid, would understand—would bless them. "Papa, I have spoken the truth. Pierce was with me, he could not have stolen the ruby."

The crowd continued to whisper among themselves. Annabel and her father stared at one another until Annabel turned to Pierce. She finally smiled at him.

He did not smile back. But the look in his eyes was so powerful that she felt her knees buckling all over again.

Suddenly the countess was pressing through the crowd and coming up the aisle. "Pierce Wainscot is my friend," she declared. "He would never steal from *me*." And she smiled at Annabel.

Annabel stared. And slowly, she smiled back.

The countess turned to George and the manager of the Acadia. "As far as I am concerned, the ruby is a thing of the past," she began.

"Contessa, Contessa!"

Annabel blinked. One of Guilia's companions was running up the aisle, holding something in her hand. Annabel saw the pearl necklace with the Rossini ruby and whirled to face Pierce. He grinned.

"I found this in your chamber when I was preparing your evening clothes for supper tonight," the woman cried.

For one moment, Guilia stared, and then she took the necklace and beamed. "I think there has not been any robbery, after all." And she shrugged, in a very European, elaborate manner.

George said slowly, looking now from Annabel to Pierce and back again, "Apparently not."

"Well." Pierce now spoke up. "If you good men would release me so I might continue?"

He was released. And he now had the attention of everyone: the minister, Thomas, George, the countess, the Boothe family, the entire crowd. "I love this woman," he said. "And I believe that she loves me. Which is why she cannot marry Thomas. I wish to marry her myself." He faced George. "But perhaps I should introduce myself first. My full name is Pierce Wainscot Braxton St. Clare. The Viscount of Kildare." And he bowed.

Annabel was stunned. "You are titled?"

He smiled at her. "Unfortunately, yes. You see, a year ago my older and only brother was killed in a hunting accident."

He was titled. He was aristocracy. In fact, Kildare was in Ireland—he wasn't English at all. Annabel's gaze swung to her father. How could he refuse Pierce now? And suddenly there was joy and elation.

"Wait one moment," George was saying. "Are you by any chance related to the Marquis of Connaught?"

"Julian is my cousin," Pierce replied quite smugly. "My first cousin. I take it you are acquainted with the family of his wife, the Ralstons?"

Even Annabel blinked. "Lisa is a friend of mine," she whispered.

Pierce's smile seemed to widen. "It is such a wee world," he said, lapsing into a hint of Irish brogue.

"I would like a private word with you, sir," George said stiffly.

"Actually, it is 'my lord,' " Pierce said. The two men stepped aside. Annabel had no intention of being left out, and she hurried around the side of the altar where they were speaking in whispers. As she did so, she glimpsed poor Thomas Frank, bewildered and morose, and she felt sorry for him. But he would not have been happy with her as a wife. Within weeks he would have realized that she was far too high-spirited for him.

"Why the hell are you a thief?" George demanded keeping his voice low.

"I suppose there are two explanations," Pierce said calmly. "I have a faulty character—and it has to do with my family."

"Do you care to explain yourself, sir?"

"My father was quite accomplished, actually," Pierce said with an apologetic shrug. "But in reality, I steal for more 'respectable' reasons. I've been retained by the British Museum for the past five years in order to restore the collection of jewels that once belonged to Catherine the Great's nephew. It was stolen twenty-five years ago and the museum wants it back, piece by piece, if necessary. It's been quite an exciting vocation."

Annabel felt herself begin to giggle. But only Pierce heard her, and this time, the look he gave her made her melt inside.

"My dear man," Pierce said. "I have finally met my match in life—your daughter. I love her and I wish to marry her. If you will allow me the honor, I will give up my career," he said flatly, "and live a more conventional life."

Annabel moved to his side and they clasped hands. She could not believe her ears—or what he was prepared to do in order to spend the rest of his life with her.

She looked at her father. "Papa, please."

George hesitated, and nodded gruffly. "Given today's turn of events, I do not think I have a choice in the matter."

Annabel clapped her hands, excitement filling her.

"I would like to do the deed now," Pierce said. He turned. "Mr. Frank, I am so sorry for the inconvenience, but would you mind stepping aside?"

Frank looked from Pierce to Annabel. "I knew it was too good to be true. Good luck, sir. Annabel—I wish you so much happiness."

"Thank you," Pierce said.

Impulsively, Annabel went to Thomas to hug him. Then she returned to Pierce's side as her father took his place with her family. Her mother was being revived by Missy.

"You, Reverend, may marry us now," Pierce instructed.

The minister stared, wide-eyed and flushed.

"Go ahead," George said, nodding.

Annabel and Pierce, hand in hand, faced the minister, who was recovering his composure. "This holiest state of matrimony," he began.

Annabel hardly heard. Pierce was gazing tenderly at her, and she could not look away.

"No one," he whispered low, as the minister continued to speak, "has ever made me contemplate changing my entire life, other than you."

Annabel gripped his hands. "I love you, too. But Pierce, I do not want you to change your ways," she whispered.

"What?" He was both perplexed and amused.

"I should be unhappy if you changed your ways," Annabel said, smiling but deadly earnest.

And he understood. He tipped back his head and laughed.

The minister coughed.

Annabel started. "I do," she said, firmly and loudly.

"Do you, Pierce Wainscot Braxton St. Clare, take this woman," he began.

"I do," Pierce said, cutting him off. "I take her for now and forever to be my wife and my partner in all deeds, good and"—he grinned—"bad." And he pulled her forward while she stood on tiptoe and they kissed, for a very long time.

"Excuse me, my lord, we are not done," the minister cried.

But neither the bride nor the groom heard him. The

kiss went on and on. And slowly, the audience began to clap, until applause filled the reception hall.

Lucinda and Lizzie were crying. Adam and John were as obviously moved. Tears even appeared in George's eyes. And Melissa was smiling, albeit reluctantly.

"I now pronounce you man and wife," the minister said, somewhat glumly.

Annabel pulled away from her husband. "So when," she whispered, still on tiptoe, "is the next caper?"

And he laughed and kissed her again.

THE LOVE MATCH

Rexanne Becnel

For the new girls,
Dominique, Savannah, and Simone

Chapter One

Jinx Benchley spoke before her housekeeper could. "Whoever it is, say that I am indisposed."

"But Miss Jinx, he said—"

"I don't care what he said. I cannot possibly see him, or anyone else, this morning."

Although Jinx's voice was firm, her hand shook—as did the single sheet of parchment she grasped. She didn't look at Mrs. Honeywell when she spoke to her, a behavior considered perfectly acceptable among the gentry when dealing with the help. But Jinx had always considered it inexcusably rude to treat anyone so carelessly, be they royalty or humble farmer. Today, however, she could hardly think straight, let alone behave as normal. Disaster had struck, and she did not know how to undo it.

She stared at the letter her younger brother had left on her desk. What had he been thinking?

She pushed away from her desk and the myriad papers so haphazardly stacked upon it, and stared up at the portrait of her parents. How would they handle this situation, if they were still living? It was clear she must do something, but what? Perhaps she should send for the solicitor in Fiddle Crossing. "Send one of the stable lads to me," she told Mrs. Honeywell. "I need someone to deliver a message right away."

"Yes, miss. But about the gentleman in the parlor. I don't think you can ignore him, you see—"

"A gentleman should know better than to call this early in the morning."

"But we've always been early risers here—"

"He can leave his card. Just . . . just tell him whatever you must!" she exclaimed with an agitated wave of her hand.

"Is everything all right, Miss Jinx?" the housekeeper asked, a frown increasing the lines on her brow. "You're not acting at all yourself."

Jinx heaved a great sigh, then slowly turned to face Mrs. Honeywell. The stout little housekeeper had been with the Benchleys for over twenty years. She'd proven her loyalty through the fat years and lean, through good times and bad. In truth, there was no reason not to tell her what Colin had done. Perhaps she might have some idea where to begin.

Jinx held the crumpled letter out to her. "Colin has done something so stupid, so outrageous, that it defies the extremes of every Benchley eccentricity to date. And as you well know, that's saying quite a lot."

Mrs. Honeywell took the letter and, squinting to see, pored over the words. "He's in love. What's so terrible about that for a lad of three and twenty? Oh." She grimaced. "He's run off to Gretna Green. Still and all, though you mayn't have wanted that for him, Jinx girl, I wouldn't call that the most outrageous thing a Benchley's ever done. Have you forgotten that your grandfather married his second wife on board a ship bound for India? And your father—"

"No, I haven't forgotten," Jinx interrupted. "But finish the letter. Finish it. See whom he's run off with? This

Lady Alice. Oh!" She grasped her head with both hands. "How could he?"

Mrs. Honeywell frowned. "I don't believe I know a Lady Alice."

Jinx began to pace. "Of course you don't know her. I don't know her either and it's because her family is not the sort to stoop so low as to hobnob with families such as ours."

"The Benchleys are a fine family, gentlemen and ladies all, and as good as anybody," the housekeeper stated. "Besides, your uncle's a viscount and your father was a great scholar."

"Thank you, Mrs. Honeywell. Your loyalty is commendable. Unfortunately, Lady Alice's brother is not likely to be impressed with any young gentleman whose uncle is a mere viscount. He'll never countenance an untitled and penniless gentleman farmer for a brother-in-law. Here. Look." She rustled around on her desk, toppling a stack of articles about water rights in her agitation. When she found the two-month-old edition of the Sunday *Times*, she stabbed a finger at an item on the front page. "She's practically the most eligible young lady who came out last year. Why would she choose to run off with our Colin?"

But Jinx knew the answer to that. So did Mrs. Honeywell. "Because he's the most charming lad in the world," the older woman said, beaming with so much pride you'd think the rapscallion was her own flesh and blood. "Handsome, good-hearted, and with the most winning ways. Any sensible girl would want our Colin for a husband."

Jinx rolled her eyes and threw the outdated paper down. "Well, it won't do her a bit of good to marry him. For when her brother learns of this, he'll kill Colin. Mark my words, he will *kill* him."

"Now, Miss Jinx. Don't carry on so. It'll turn out all right. You know, you might take a lesson from your brother and reconsider that offer Mr. Tonkton made for you—"

"I am not interested in marrying Herbert Tonkton and that is not the point. The situation with Colin and this Lady Alice will not turn out all right. Her brother is not the type to let it turn out all right. You forget, I had two seasons in town, and while I never met him, I saw him several times. He was the one who fought three duels and was banished from court for as many years."

That got the housekeeper's attention. "The one who fought the three duels? Oh, my. I do remember. Oh, my!" she repeated. "*That's* why his name sounded so familiar." She pressed a knotted handkerchief to her lips. "Oh, my. Whatever are we to do, miss?"

Jinx plopped down onto the only clear space on a settee stacked with books opened to various pages. "I don't know. That's why I thought I might consult with our solicitor. He may have some idea of how to proceed."

"Oh, but there isn't time for that!"

"You may be right. Perhaps I should start after Colin right away." She jumped to her feet again. "I could take the curricle. It's old, but it's fast."

"No, no, miss. You don't understand. There's no time for that!"

"Well, what else am I to do?" Jinx exclaimed, exasperated by the fix Colin had put them in. "He's certainly not going to come back on his own."

For some reason, Mrs. Honeywell was pointing at the door, and her eyes were round as saucers. "Your gentleman caller."

"I told you, I don't have time for visitors today. I should think that perfectly obvious by now."

"But it's *him*."

"Him? Him who?" Then a terrible thought occurred to Jinx. A frightening thought, so awful she dared not believe it possible. "Him who?" she asked again, though this time in a whisper.

Mrs. Honeywell thrust a card at her. Jinx took it with trepidation. An exquisite example of the stationer's art. A simple, elegantly printed script. *Harrison Stirling, Marquis of Hartley*.

"Bees knees!" Jinx exclaimed, then sat down hard. Harrison Stirling. The murderous marquis, he was called, and hot-blooded Harry. The man was already searching for his sister—and for Colin.

And he was in *her* front parlor!

Everything she'd ever heard about the man flashed through her head. A terrible temper. A vengeful nature. He had money and power enough to buy his way back into Prinny's favor, it seemed. Six years ago he'd been considered quite the catch, though most of the young ladies had been in awe of him. Still, money and a title were a heady lure. Added to that, he was also devastatingly handsome. He'd never lacked for female companionship. But so far as she knew, he hadn't yet married. If he was that particular for himself, how much more so must he be for his only sister?

Jinx swallowed hard and tried to curb her runaway emotions. She must think! If Colin were to survive this dreadful incident, Lord Hartley must be put off the trail. The fact that he knew enough to come to Benchley House was not a good sign, but Jinx could not let that deter her.

She pushed to her feet and nervously smoothed her old kersey skirt. She must send Lord Hartley off in the wrong direction, then immediately go after Colin herself.

And once she found her charming fool of a brother and had him safe, she would wring his handsome neck—that is, unless Lord Hartley beat her to the task.

Heads would roll, Harrison vowed as he waited impatiently at the parlor window. If his information was right and Colin Benchley had run off with his sister . . . His hands tightened into fists. There would be hell to pay.

By rights he should have been exhausted. He'd spent the entire night grilling anyone who might have some inkling of Alice's whereabouts. Her maid had kept mum, weeping incessantly as he alternately cajoled her, then threatened her. That had been the first clue: Alice had sworn the misguided maid to secrecy. But the girl's father had proven more forthcoming. Three gold sovereigns in the man's hand, and he'd convinced the daughter swiftly enough to talk.

Still, all he'd gotten was a name. Colin Benchley. A few more inquiries at his various clubs, and he'd learned that the cad was one of the Hampshire Benchleys. The eccentric ones, not the titled ones.

He'd have strangled the man, had he been anywhere to be found in town. But Benchley was not in London, and at four in the morning Harrison had set off for Hampshire, his valet in close pursuit. A shepherd boy had directed him to Benchley House; a milkmaid in the courtyard had informed him that Master Colin was not presently in residence, but that Miss Jinx was.

Miss Jinx. What sort of name was that? he fumed. And where in hell was she?

The door creaked and he turned, and for a moment—just one, very brief moment—he forgot what had brought him racing through the night to such an out-of-the-way place. For that one fraction of a second, he just stood there, transfixed by the woman who glided into the room.

She was not what he'd expected.

Not that she didn't live up to her odd name. But he'd expected someone older, someone frivolous and flustered because a marquis had come to call. By contrast, Jinx Benchley was young and slender, and possessed of the most outrageous mane of auburn hair he'd ever laid eyes on. She was dressed all in lavender, with splashes of yellow and green. A gypsyish scarf was draped over her shoulders. A bright ribbon fought to hold back the masses of her long, thick curls.

He caught the fragrance of her perfume, a blend of flowers and exotic spices. And with every step she made, tiny bells tinkled.

Then she spoke, and he blinked and came back to reality.

"I hope you've come to advise me where my brother is," she stated in a calm, well-modulated voice, tinged with irritation.

Harrison frowned at the woman's abrupt remark. No introduction. He gave her a curt bow. "I regret to impose upon you so early in the day, but you plainly know my mission. I am Harrison Stirling, Marquis of Hartley."

"Yes, yes. And I am Jillian Benchley, sister of Colin. Do you bring me word of him?"

"I was advised to speak with a Miss Jinx Benchley."

She waved one hand. The bells trilled again. Where did she wear them? "I am Jinx. 'Tis a pet name given me by my father. But tell me, what word have you of Colin?"

Jinx waited breathlessly for the marquis's response. It had taken but one glance for her to know he deserved every bit of his reputation. Tall, well built, and furious. His eyes were black with suppressed rage. His hands flexed and tightened into fists, as if he imagined them wrapped around Colin's throat.

Poor Colin, she fretted, worrying her lower lip. What had he been thinking to antagonize a man like the Marquis of Hartley? But it was too late to regret Colin's folly. Now she must somehow work to ameliorate it.

She willed herself to be calm. She must do whatever necessary to divert the man, and that meant preventing Lord Hartley from setting off for Gretna Green in pursuit of the wayward couple.

She crossed the room toward him, beating back the

absurd impression that she was entering a lion's den. This was her house, not his. No harm could befall her at Benchley House. "I should like to find them as soon as possible and bury any word of this unfortunate incident before it gets out," she said breezily. "As, I'm certain, do you."

He crossed his arms, presenting a truly threatening image. "I'd like to bury something, all right."

"There's no cause for such talk as that," she snapped at him. "We are dealing with two foolish young people who, no doubt, think they are in love."

"In love with her money," he scoffed.

Jinx smiled, a deliberately smug, superior smile. "You do not know my brother very well. if you think that. Money does not count with him."

"Really? Then he's the only young man in England to feel that way."

She meant to control her temper. Truly she did. But rudeness toward her darling Colin, and in her own home, was too much for anyone to bear. She tilted her chin up. "Pray tell, is that why you remain unwed? You've not yet found a woman rich enough to please you?"

His eyes narrowed and for a moment Jinx thought he might loose his famous temper upon her. But what could he do, she thought, bolstering her courage. Strike her? He would not dare. Threaten to ruin her family? The Benchleys were so far removed from the Hartleys' rank in society that she was surprised he'd managed even to find Benchley House.

That left only insults and verbal sparring, and in that venue Jinx trusted herself to hold her own.

To his credit, he did not resort to any of those. Still, the frost in his voice was enough to chill her to the bone. "It is not my motives which are in question, Miss Benchley, but your brother's. Do you perchance know where he is?"

"No." *Not specifically.*

"But you knew that he was gone and that I had reason to be searching for him. Did he inform you of his plans to run away with my sister?"

With a great show of frustration, Jinx turned and walked to the window. In truth, however, she needed desperately to break the hold of Lord Hartley's intense gaze. She feared he would see through any small fib she made, and even though her motives were pure—to save her brother's foolish skin—she did not want to lie to this man. After all, his motives were also commendable: to save his sister from a marriage few guardians would approve. She could not find fault with him for that.

Perhaps she should take a different tack. She turned to face him again. "I learned of this unfortunate situation just minutes prior to your arrival." She sighed. "My first thought was to go after him and stop him, but then you appeared. Tell me, what do you plan to do when you find them?"

When his jaw began rhythmically to clench and release—clench and release—she went on. "I know your reputation, Lord Hartley. Even here in the hinterlands we've heard tales of the murderous marquis. You will understand, therefore, my extreme interest in your answer. What do you intend to do?"

Their eyes locked. Jinx fancied she saw the workings of his mind. He weighed her value to his search against his need to vow his vengeance. She saw clearly the moment he dismissed her impact on his plans.

"I intend to challenge him to a duel," he stated calmly. Coldly. "I intend to do my level best to rid me and my sister of him forever."

Fury banished every other emotion Jinx felt. She drew herself up, jerking her shawl closer around her shoulders. "I'll thank you to get out of my house. This very minute," she ordered.

"Not until I see the letter he left you. The one you apparently discovered this morning."

"I didn't say he left a letter. For all you know, he told me himself."

In a moment he was across the room, mere inches from her. He was so much taller, so much more threatening up close. She would have stepped back, but he caught her by the shoulders. "Is he here? Is Alice here?"

"How dare you lay hands upon me, sir! Release me at once!"

"The truth, Miss Benchley. Where are they? What do you know about this affair?"

"Enough to know I will not cooperate with the likes of you! Enough to understand why your poor sister would flee your protection for Colin's!"

He let go of her with an oath. "Alice is not fleeing me, though you may console yourself with thinking so. She no doubt fancies herself in love—an honest error for an innocent such as she. But I've learned enough about your brother to know he is not so innocent. You Benchleys have a reputation for being outlandish. Eccentrics. You do not fit in with the rest of proper society."

Jinx rubbed her hands over the places he'd held her. Though he'd not hurt her, the press of his fingers yet left their mark. "If we are eccentric, it is only because the rules of your society are so stifling as to kill any hope of creativity and happiness. Your rules are for small minds, and we Benchleys do not have small minds. Go on," she ordered. "Leave here. Chase after your sister. She has obviously made a love match with my brother and I have no doubt that she and Colin are supremely happy together, else they would not have risked your anger. But what have they to fear?" she added bitingly. " 'Tis clear Alice is possessed of a much broader intelligence than her narrow-minded brother. I should think she and Colin will have no trouble at all outwitting you. Good day, sir. I have nothing further to say to you."

Chapter Two

Jinx watched from the parlor window as Harrison Stirling stalked across the gravel front court, toward the stables. A little shiver snaked through her, and she rubbed her arms distractedly. The Marquis of Hartley would make a dire enemy. Did Colin have any inkling of the danger he'd put himself in?

Bits and pieces of old gossip filtered up from her memory. Lord Hartley had been quite as terrible a rake as society had ever seen. Drinking. Gambling. Whoring. Not to mention the dueling. And he had the gall to think Colin unsuitable! Then again, she'd heard reformed rakes made the strictest fathers—or guardians, in this case.

Except that Harrison Stirling hardly appeared to be reformed. The man was all temper and muscle and ruthless determination. Up close she'd been too involved in their confrontation to notice details of his appearance. But from the safety of her parlor window she could now be more detached.

In truth, Lord Hartley cut a most impressive figure—not unusual for a rake of the sporting set. The long, muscular legs of a horseman. The broad shoulders of a fencer. The powerful arms of a boxing enthusiast.

Colin did those things, too, she reminded herself. But

Harrison Stirling was half a head taller than her brother, and fairly two stone heavier, she'd wager.

If Lord Hartley caught up with him, Colin was a dead duck.

But only if Hartley caught up with him.

Her eyes narrowed, following the arrogant marquis until he disappeared beyond her prized topiary clipped in the shape of dragons. He would assume Colin and Alice had set off for Gretna Green as, according to her brother's letter, they had. But there were two main routes headed north, and any number of lesser routes. Colin would not wish to be caught. So which route would he take?

She bit her lip and fiddled with the lace curtain, still staring at the leafy dragons that formed an arch with their tails. She should have asked Lord Hartley where Lady Alice had disappeared from, London or a country estate. Colin had last been at home on Friday. Then he'd departed for town to meet their cousin Alfred—or so he'd said. He'd known she meant to spend a long weekend in Caulfield with her friend Virginia, who'd recently had her third child. That's why the wretch had left the note on her desk. He'd counted on her not finding it until Tuesday morning. It was pure chance she'd cut her visit a little short. Still, he had three days' head start on her.

"Lizard legs," she swore. She was wasting time. She needed to get under way, but only after Harrison Stirling was well away from Benchley House.

But he didn't leave and didn't leave, and when Jinx could bear to wait no longer, she stormed out to the stables. She found him in the carriage house, with the stable workers lined up, thoroughly cowed by his relentless questioning.

". . . so no carriage is missing?"

The three stablemen nodded their heads in unison. Jinx wanted to scream. She would have asked them the very same thing, had she been provided time enough to think of it. But if Lord Hartley thought he could instigate a private inquisition on her property, he was very much mistaken.

"Darren. Clifton. Rob. You are all dismissed. Go about your work," she ordered in crisp tones. Grateful, they bobbed their heads and practically sprinted from the shaded carriage house. Then she turned on Lord Hartley and his man. She crossed her arms and gave him her severest look. "I believe I asked you to leave."

He raised one dark brow in a maddening display of arrogance. "So you did. And in so doing, you no doubt think to delay my search. But I caution you, Miss Benchley. Do not think a relationship to the Hartley name will benefit either you or your brother."

"Hah! I'm hardly so delusional as to believe that. Though you may find this difficult to comprehend, not everyone finds a connection to the upper nobility an asset. If the truth be told, I cannot imagine a less welcome notion. You as my brother-in-law." She forced a visible shudder.

Unfortunately, the insult she implied just ricocheted off his superior attitude. "So you say. But the two carriages you keep appear older than you." He gestured around them. "There's a hole in the roof, judging by that spot of sunshine next to your foot. And the entire premises, both house and outbuildings, are in need of a fresh coat of paint. You do not keep a butler. 'Tis obvious your finances are not entirely in order. Added to that, the Benchley penchant for investing in ridiculous inventions is well-known." He crossed his arms across his chest, mirroring her pose. "Did I leave anything out?"

Jinx trembled with outrage. How dare he reduce her family to the status of lowly money grubbers! She advanced on him, fists knotted and eyes blazing. "How like an *aristocrat* to focus purely on the physical—and the monetary. You have indeed left something out, something which defines the Benchleys much more clearly than our financial condition. We have a long history of making love matches. We Benchleys always marry for love."

"For love?" he snorted. "Perhaps. But love of what?"

Though it was clear she would have no influence on his poor opinion of either her brother or her family, Jinx's dander was up. She could not ignore his sarcasm. "I'll confess, I too find it hard to imagine Colin falling in love with your sister. Given what I know of you and your horrid reputation, I find myself hard-pressed to believe anything good of your sister. Had Colin asked my opinion, I would have advised him to avoid any connection with the Hartley line. But he did not ask my opinion, and so I can only assume that he sees something in her worth loving. Despite all the liabilities attached to her name, she must possess some redeeming grace for them to have made a love match. At least I dearly hope so."

The words had tumbled out in a violent rush, a sarcastic sermon that left her breathless. But as she came up for air, she realized he was staring at her with a strange glitter in his eyes—and that she'd advanced far too near him.

"Were you a man," he said, "I'd call you out for insulting my family in such a manner."

Jinx swallowed hard. "Were I a man, I would already have called you out," she vowed. "If you will recall, *you* insulted my family *first*."

"But you're not a man, are you?" he observed in a voice that no longer sounded angry. It was no longer loud, either. In fact, there was a disturbingly husky quality to it which, when coupled with his intent gaze, seemed more seductive than anything else.

And she could feel herself responding to it.

Oh, help! a little voice cried from somewhere inside

her. While she trusted herself to match wits with the man, she'd not considered that he might try to seduce her. Stupid, stupid girl. He was not considered a rake for nothing!

She took a hasty step backward. "I think you should leave, Lord Hartley. Colin is not here and I cannot help you."

"Cannot? Or will not?" His eyes ran over her in a slow perusal that shot the most inappropriate prickles of awareness through her. He was trying to disarm her with his famous charm. And she'd almost let him.

But not anymore.

She wrapped her arms around her waist and when his eyes locked once more with hers, she deliberately let her eyes go crossed. It was an old childhood ploy, one she'd often used to distract Colin. Now, though, she used it to distract herself. If she could not see Lord Hartley's handsome face and slumberous gaze, they could not affect her.

"What are you doing?"

Jinx started at his sudden question, again stepping backward. But her crossed eyes made her awkward. She lost her balance and might even have fallen had not Lord Hartley caught her. By the time her eyes were straight, he had her laid down on the dusty stable floor.

"Are you all right?" He knelt over her, his face but inches from hers. "Can you hear me?" He patted her cheek rather sharply. "Miss Benchley, can you hear me?"

"I can hear you!" She batted his hand away.

He looked immeasurably relieved. "It appears you may have fainted."

"I did not faint." She struggled up on her elbows. "I never faint. Would you please move?"

"Are you subject to fits, then? Your eyes went crossed."

"I know they did," she fumed, feeling like an idiot.

"I see. Do they do that often?"

She glared at him. "It depends on whether or not I want them to." She crossed her eyes for emphasis, then uncrossed them.

His brow furrowed as he stared at her, and all at once Jinx became acutely conscious of their odd position. She lay on the carriage-house floor with a stranger kneeling over her—a famous town rake, no less. Pray God none of the servants were near enough to see. Of course, it might be better if someone were nearby, for Harrison Stirling was again studying her with that disturbingly intent gaze of his.

Then his eyes crossed and she couldn't help it. She burst out laughing.

He started laughing, too, and for a moment, at least, the two of them were in accord. But when he helped her upright, their humor could not last. The dire circumstances of their meeting precluded it. Slowly their laughter faded, and she took a careful step back from him.

"We are agreed that a marriage between Colin and Alice is unwise," she said, sober now. "Can we not also agree on how to deal with their reckless behavior?"

His jaw became stern. "I cannot allow them to wed, and I will do whatever I can to prevent it."

"And if you are too late to prevent it?"

Their gazes locked, and the most ludicrous thought leapt into Jinx's head: if only they'd met under different circumstances. Then reason prevailed and she buried that insane notion. This was Lord Hartley, notorious rake, deadly duelist. Holding her breath, she repeated her question. "What if you are too late?"

After a long, tense moment he replied. "I won't be."

She heard the threat in his voice and chose to read the worst into his words. What else could she do? "I think it's time you left."

He made no move to comply. "They went to Gretna Green, I take it."

"I imagine so. Good day, Lord Hartley." She turned to depart but he caught her by the arm.

"It would be better if you cooperate with me, Miss Benchley. It would be in everyone's best interest if I found them before he has the chance to completely ruin her."

"By society's standards—your society—she is ruined already."

"I have the wherewithal to remedy that."

"Oh, yes. Your famous riches. All that money that you have and we Benchleys do not." She gave him a tight smile. "I have no information that can help you. He did not take one of our carriages, but that signifies nothing. Perhaps your innocent little sister provided the equipage."

"She did not."

"Then they rented a hack. Or could they have chosen to travel by horseback?" she added, hoping to gain some snippet of information from him.

He frowned and thought for a moment. "I do not think Alice so adept a rider as to attempt such a long journey by horseback."

But *she* was, Jinx thought. On horseback she could make much faster time than could a hired hack. But first she must rid herself of Harrison Stirling.

"However they travel, you but waste your time speaking with me, Lord Hartley."

"Perhaps so. Then again, perhaps not. I caution you, Miss Benchley, not to aid the runaways. You may delude yourself into believing it possible to marry purely for love, but the rest of English society is far more practical."

"Indeed. Since you are so practical, then, you must realize that you do but waste your time lingering here. Get on with you, Lord Hartley. Rescue your sister before a man who loves her can make her his wife. Then hurry back to London before all the wealthy heiresses are stolen out from under your nose. Be practical," she taunted him. "Time is wasting."

Harrison bided his time, but not easily. The quick-tempered Miss Jinx Benchley was right. Time *was* wasting. He needed to be practical, he needed to be on his way. And yet something made him linger.

He'd ridden out of the gravel courtyard fronting the Benchleys' very odd manor home with its myriad turrets and steep roof walk. He made his way furiously beyond reach of the towering yew dragons, past the half-sized Dutch windmill, and the miniaturely proportioned replica of the classic Greek Pantheon. But once beyond the strange house and the collection of outlandish follies that dotted the otherwise serene landscape, he doubled back through the hunting park, his jaw grimly set, his frown securely in place. Now he waited, along with Rogers, his valet, to see what Miss High-and-Mighty Benchley was up to.

Though he did not like to admit it—and would do so only to himself—the feisty Miss Benchley had scored a direct hit with her pronouncements regarding the state of society matrimonies. He doubted her claim that everyone in her family had made love matches. Still, it raised the question of whether it was possible these days for *anyone* to marry for that nebulous reason.

He stared beyond his sheltered bower and across the damp meadows, just rousing to the bright sunlight burning through the morning fog. But he did not see the sheep that dotted the lush green landscape, nor the meandering stone walls that marked fields in use for a thousand years and more. Instead he pictured his sister, Alice, and their last conversation.

She'd been very upset, almost to the point of tears. But she hadn't cried, even when he'd browbeaten her about Arlen Forrester, Lord Meever. That had been eight days ago. He'd gone blithely on to Winchester afterward, sure in his conceit that she would come around to his way of thinking. After all, Lord Meever was not too old—her objection to Lord Barton. He was not a sot—her objection to Lord Tinsdale. Nor was he a womanizer—her objection to Lord Lamkin. Barton, Tinsdale, and Lamkin had each been well connected, with solid family names and deep pockets. But Harrison recognized now that none of them had truly been right for his sweet younger sister.

Arlen Forrester, however, had no such flaws.

Alice had called the man dull as dirt, and perhaps he was. But that was hardly a fatal flaw, and indeed, he might make a better husband for it. He was a conscientious fellow who took his responsibilities seriously.

Yet the thought of marrying Forrester had sent Alice straight into the arms of a penniless opportunist who'd promptly dragged her off to Gretna Green.

No doubt she believed herself in love with the man, and for that Harrison was prepared to forgive her. Benchley, however, would receive no such leniency. For Colin Benchley had taken advantage of a green girl, and Harrison meant to punish him dearly for his audacity.

Unfortunately, Harrison could not escape some portion of the blame himself. He'd left Alice alone too much. Then when he'd decided she was ready for marriage, he'd tried to rush her into it.

He, of all people, should have known that the selection of a mate could not be rushed. It had been three years since he'd decided to select a wife and produce the heir he knew his position demanded. Three years, three seasons, and not one eligible miss he'd go so far as to actually commit a lifetime to. Whether silly or serious, titled or merely wealthy, not one of the many young women he'd danced and flirted with had moved him to propose marriage.

Not that he was waiting for love to strike, as Jinx Benchley obviously was. She was already old enough to be considered on the shelf. Before long she'd be a confirmed spinster. And all in the name of love.

But that was not his problem. He was not waiting for love.

The fact remained, however, that he'd not found the right woman for himself. So why had he presumed he could find the right man for Alice? That didn't mean he could allow Alice to choose her own husband without some guidance from him. This disaster with Benchley was proof that she was not capable of it. Still, Harrison knew he'd been a lackluster guardian to his much younger sister. He'd not sufficiently considered her feelings regarding marriage. He would have to do better in the future.

He waited silently in the woodland bower. Above him a pair of mating squirrels tore around the trunk of a towering oak, chasing one another in a dizzying upward spiral. His sleek mount stamped one foot and nickered softly to Rogers's placid mare. Love was in the air. Then he grimaced at such an idiotic notion. Not love, but lust.

He frowned and shifted uneasily in the saddle. Squirrels. Horses. Young men. Did Alice feel lust for this Benchley? Was that what she found missing in Lord Meever?

Harrison didn't like to think of his sister that way, nor of any innocent young woman of good breeding.

You thought of Miss Jinx Benchley that way, a silent voice accused.

His fist tightened on the reins. The horse tossed its head, restless from the wait. Maybe for a moment or two he'd thought of Miss Benchley that way. But then, why shouldn't he? She was not, after all, your typical gentleman's daughter. Her wild red hair, her eccentric wardrobe. The intriguing fragrance that clung to her.

Those bells that tinkled when she moved.

Any right-thinking man could be forgiven for harboring less-than-wholesome thoughts about such a vibrant creature. Even her temper had sparked his interest, for she was no shy, mumbling child, intimidated by either his anger or his physical presence.

And her voice, confident and yet musical—

"Look, milord," Rogers called, interrupting Harrison's inappropriate musings. "Someone's leaving the manor grounds."

Cursing himself for a fool, Harrison leaned forward, focusing at once on the distant rider. At first he was disappointed. It was a man, for he rode astride. Then his eyes narrowed. The rider's hat nearly fell off and a long knot of hair unfurled down his back. *Her* back, Harrison realized when the sunlight struck sparks off the rich red mass. Jinx Benchley, riding astride in some sort of combination of breeches and skirt. He could hardly believe it! She thundered down the road, trailed by another rider. One of the stable men, he would guess.

So, she was off to find her brother herself—no doubt to warn the wretch that someone was hot on his trail. Harrison had been right to wait, and now he meant to follow her straight to the runaway pair.

But as he turned his horse and picked his way along the edge of the woods, following the direction Miss Jinx Benchley took, he resolved to put aside the baser feelings the woman had roused in him.

Yes, she was attractive, but it was in an exotic sort of way. Yes, she was quick-witted, but she was also a sharp-tongued shrew, far too argumentative for his taste. And though she sat a horse admirably, almost as if she'd been born astride, that was not a talent a proper young lady need possess.

But for all her oddities, she was still a gentlewoman. She was young and well bred, despite her odd manner, outspoken ways, and outrageous behavior. Besides that, she was Colin Benchley's sister, and the last woman he should get involved with. He meant to follow her, that was all, and to use her to find Alice.

He leaned forward, urging his horse forward. The chase was on and, like a hound sharp on the heels of a wily red-haired vixen, he meant to pursue his quarry until he had her trapped—and with her, her brother and his foolish sister.

Chapter Three

Colin Benchley made his way down to the stables, ostensibly to check on the horses. But in truth, he needed time alone to debate his next move.

The first night he and Alice had stayed at an inn outside of Oxford. Alice had slept in the bed; he'd shifted fitfully all night on a chair that had long lost its padding. The second night they'd rested at an out-of-the-way abbey, passing themselves off as brother and sister. If the good brothers had suspected the truth, they'd kept it to themselves. He'd slept but little on the lumpy pallet given him in the men's quarters.

Two miserable nights. Two pitiful accommodations. His exquisite Alice deserved so much better. That's why they'd stopped earlier this evening, at a prosperous-looking coaching inn near Ballycoat. He'd taken a suite of rooms more in keeping with what Alice deserved.

And yet, wasn't he deluding himself? He could never provide for her as she deserved. And though he loved Benchley Manor and it was his home, he knew it did not begin to compare even to the least of Alice's brother's holdings.

He had no right to deprive her of her family wealth. How could he ever have been so selfish as to think he did?

He looked in on his team of weary horses, then gave the stable boy tuppence for extra rations. But instead of returning to Alice, he hesitated in the musty stable.

He wanted her so badly, he ached. But he'd vowed not to dishonor her by taking her innocence outside the bounds of matrimony. She was so beautiful, though. He wasn't sure he could bear another night sharing a room with her and yet not sharing a bed.

God, but he was so confused! He loved her and he wanted to marry her and take care of her and spend all the days of his life with her. But he was going about it all wrong. He could see that now. Despite her objections, he should have gone to her brother. It was the right thing to do, and it was still not too late to do it.

Resolved, he turned and strode back toward the inn. They would start back in the morning. He would have to make her understand that no matter how her brother might react, they must return and ask his approval.

She did not answer when he knocked. He knocked harder; still no reply. Alarmed, Colin turned the latch and peered inside. What he saw set his heart racing and blood rushing to his loins. For Alice stood in the window, backlit by a stupendous sunset which made her lounging gown all but disappear.

He saw a tiny waist and sweetly rounded hips outlined beneath the diaphanous fabric. He saw long, shapely legs. His honorable intentions turned to mush in the face of her innocently silhouetted femininity. The words he meant to say evaporated in the heat of the moment. Then she spoke, an angel who was more tempting than even the devil, and he was finally and irrevocably lost.

"Colin, I cannot wait any longer. I cannot bear to delay until we travel all the way to Scotland, my love. Please, Colin, make me your wife tonight. Now. Please . . ."

*   *   *

Jinx sat at the crossroads, staring first down the road to Logan Fields, then down the one that led to Martinton. Her horse blew and stamped, and she patted its neck. "Not much farther today, Daffodil," she murmured to the tiring mare. "You'll have your dinner and your rub-down soon enough. But where?" she added to herself.

She heard Rob approach on his slower horse. "Miss Jinx, this ain't right, an' well you know it. You can't be ridin' across the countryside this way. Why, if himself was here he'd be—"

"If my father were still alive, he'd be doing exactly as I am," she vowed. She fixed a fierce look upon the aging servant. "I am grateful for your loyalty, Rob, but I will not have you lecturing me all the way to Scotland."

"There you go again with Scotland. We can't go gallivantin' all the way to Scotland. Don't you know them Scots is a bunch of madmen, wearin' skirts, screamin' like banshees?"

"Mama was half Scots," Jinx reminded the squat stable master.

He frowned, for he'd dearly loved Jinx's mother. " 'Tis only the men as is mad," he grumbled.

"Be that as it may, I'm going there. Colin must be prevented from marrying this girl."

"Ah, but miss, what if we get there too late to stop him?"

She stared down the two roads again, one wide and well traveled, the other a rough choice for a carriage. She could not be too late. But if she was . . . "If we're too late to prevent Colin making such an unwise marriage, then we'll probably be just in time to prevent him being murdered by his new wife's brother."

On that grim note she turned onto the wider road. Colin would not want his true love jounced about in the carriage. He would want to provide for the easiest journey possible, wouldn't he?

"Bee's knees," she muttered, then urged Daffodil on.

"We make for Logan Fields," she called back to Rob. "Turn back if you like, or follow along. But do not annoy me with advice I refuse to heed, else you will find yourself picking berries for your supper and bedding down in the fields with the hares and field mice."

Not that she would follow through with her threat; not that Rob believed a word of it. But it was a measure of her determination to save her love-struck brother from a disastrous match—and a fatal confrontation with Lord Hartley—that she would even vow such a thing.

As the sun lowered over the pastoral lands of northern Oxfordshire, Jinx made for Logan Fields with Rob following along behind her. She was hungry and thirsty and her bottom ached from long hours in the saddle. She'd made very good time, but all she wanted now was a hot bath and to never wear these chafing breeches again.

Unfortunately, tomorrow promised only more of the same, and the next day as well. It would take all her energy to reach Gretna Green before Colin did.

She fumed angrily as she rode. The list of grievances against her brother mounted steadily. When she finally found the wretch, he would have much to account for.

She only prayed he lived long enough to do it.

Harrison stood before her door. The hall was dim. The hour was late. Miss Benchley's servant had bedded down in one of the crowded attic rooms. She had taken a moderately priced single room on the third story. As for himself, he'd taken finer accommodations on the second story, but he'd not been able to sleep. A coin here and there, and he'd discovered all he need know: she'd taken supper in her room; she'd paid extra for a bath. She did not know he trailed her and, on the whole, he was satisfied with this day's work. But he was restless. A bottle of red wine had not deadened his mind. Rather than start a second bottle—and pay dearly for it with a headache on the morrow—he'd stalked up the stairs and stood glaring at her door.

He ought to pound the door until it rattled on its hinges. He ought to startle her awake and make her tell him where the runaway pair were, for he was certain she knew more than she'd revealed. The fact that she'd undertaken this insane journey proved that.

He raised his fist to the door, then with a shuddering sigh, spread his fingers and instead pressed his palm flat against the wooden barrier. He was behaving like a madman. Too much wine, too little sleep, and more frustration than he was accustomed to. These Benchleys were even more outrageous than the gossips made them out to be. Brother and sister alike, they were impulsive, shortsighted, and selfish.

He slid his hand back and forth, the width of the wood panel, and his thoughts grew even more churlish. It was his damnably poor luck that Jinx was so unexpectedly attractive. Not that she was the sort that usually drew him. He preferred cool, elegant blondes, with an occasional vibrant brunette thrown in for variation. Redheads, particularly eccentric ones, had never been to his taste.

Unfortunately, he found this particular redhead precisely to his taste. She was smart and loyal and not easily intimidated, a combination not often found in a woman, especially in a young, beautiful one. Added to that, she triggered the most primitive reaction in him. He'd had the entire day to ponder that fact, and now just the thought of her made him hot. Standing outside her room, knowing she lay unclothed in her bed, sent a river of fire coursing to his loins.

"Bloody hell!" he muttered, yanking his hand back from the door. He was behaving like a fool, and all on account of her. If her brother possessed even half the allure of his sister, it was no wonder innocent Alice had run off with the man.

But his goal was to follow Jinx Benchley, not seduce her—or be seduced by her.

Knotting his hands, he thrust his fists into his pockets and turned away. He needed more wine, and damn the consequences!

The morning was dreadful. Jinx got an early start. She'd not slept well. Though she had never displayed the same predisposition for visions or predictions that her mother had, all night she'd been bothered by a series of confusing dreams. Colin and a faceless bride. A baby in her own arms. Lord Hartley laughing in a joyful manner. He'd looked so much younger laughing. But what had he been laughing about? And whose baby had she held, Colin and Alice's, or her own?

So she'd risen gladly from her restless bed and before the sun had appeared above the Chiltern Hills she'd been on her way, with Rob trailing unhappily behind her. There had been one bit of good news, however. The stableman on duty remembered Colin and Alice. A tall auburn-haired young gentleman and a china-doll beautiful young lady.

She'd picked the right road. That was something, at least.

But then the rains had come, turning the road to slop, and it had become hard to remain optimistic. She was wet and hungry when they made Bicester, but she did not linger any longer than necessary to eat, and to refresh the horses. Just beyond the village the drizzle eased. But within an hour another mishap: Rob's mare came up lame.

"The ostler said Banbury was a four-hour ride in good conditions. It makes more sense for you to return to Bicester," Jinx told Rob.

"And what of you, miss? Surely you cannot plan to go on with this chuckle-headed scheme. Not alone."

"I most certainly can. Here." She dug into her hastily

packed portmanteau, tied behind her saddle. "Here's coin enough to take care of both you and Dolly. If you just follow the same path south, you should find your way home once her leg is better."

" 'Tis not meself I'm worried about!" the man cried. "You cannot mean to ride on alone, and all the way to the Scots land."

The truth was, Jinx did not want to go on alone. The farther north they rode, the less sure of herself she became. But she refused to reveal as much to Rob. The fact was, she had no choice. If she could not prevent Colin from acting on his foolish scheme, at least she could stand beside him when he faced the dangerous Harrison Stirling.

She peeled a still-damp lock of hair from her neck and thrust it behind her shoulder. "It's pointless to argue with me, Rob, for you know I will do precisely as I please. Soon enough I will find Colin, and then I will be perfectly safe."

Harrison watched the tableau being played out in the curve of the road below him, and though he could not hear them, he could imagine full well the drift of the conversation. The stableman's horse was limping, and the poor fellow thought a practical argument would sway his mistress into turning back. Hah! After only two conversations with the woman, Harrison knew better. Miss Benchley meant to press on alone, leaving the worried servant to tend the lame horse. Foolish girl! Had she any idea the myriad disasters that might befall a woman traveling alone?

Except that she would not be alone, for he was right behind her. He grinned and glanced over at his unhappy valet. "Take heart, Rogers. From this point on I'll not require your company. Provide Miss Benchley's servant with whatever assistance he requires. Meanwhile, I will go on alone and tend to Miss Benchley's needs myself."

*   *   *

It was nowhere near sunset. Jinx tilted her head up, gauging the bruised-looking sky. It was only the low-hanging clouds that gave the impression of impending night. They were heavy with rain, threatening at any moment to douse her once more.

How much farther to Banbury?

This part of Oxfordshire was not nearly so well populated as the southern portion. She'd passed near a tiny village some miles past, and had spied a pleasant farmhouse down one hill. If worse came to worst, she could seek shelter in some respectable-looking rural household.

Then again, what respectable household would welcome a woman traveling alone?

For the hundredth time she regretted her hasty decision to send Rob back to Bicester. If the weather would only cooperate, her journey would not be so difficult. But the rain had made the roads treacherous as well as dampened her enthusiasm for her task.

She tugged her scarf over her head. At least she was not totally soaked. Yet.

The road turned and she urged Daffodil up the incline. The game little mare was as tired as she, but she responded with renewed effort. They had nearly surmounted the hill when the animal lost its footing in a patch of slick gravel. Daffodil nearly went down, and if she had, it might have been disastrous. But the horse managed to stay upright. It was Jinx who could not keep her balance.

She grabbed wildly for the saddle horn, but it was useless. With a shriek of frustration and a whoosh of skirts, she landed hard in the middle of the sodden road. Added to that ignominy, the clouds chose at that very moment to spill their unhappy bounty.

It was as if the storm mocked her, she fumed, lying flat on her back, trying to catch her breath. First the clouds tittered, then they chuckled. Finally they guf-

fawed, buckets and buckets of drowning laughter rain-
ing down upon her.

Jinx turned her face aside and covered her eyes with
one drenched arm. Nothing was broken. She'd scraped
one palm and her bottom would surely be bruised. But
other than that she was unharmed. Yet she continued to
lie there, pelted by the storm, wallowing in a trough of
self-pity. How had she come to such a pathetic pass as
this?

A streak of brilliant light and a violent crack of thunder startled her out of her misery. Daffodil snorted and
shied, and before Jinx could grab for the reins, the mare
was off, tail raised like a flag as she skittered over the
crest of the hill and vanished from sight.

"No. No!" Jinx scrambled for footing, trying to give
chase. But her soaked skirts were too heavy, even without petticoats. She slipped and stumbled again, cursing
the horse, the weather, and most of all, her idiotic, love-
struck brother.

She didn't hear the rider until he was almost upon her,
and when she whirled about, she lost her footing again.
Down she went, this time in a thicket of heath. At least
it cushioned her fall, but her most comfortable riding
suit would never be the same. "Bee's knees," she swore,
wiping rain from her brow. Then sheltering her eyes
from the driving rain, she looked up from her humiliating position—and nearly swooned!

Harrison Stirling! What was he doing here? And why
must he come along now, when she looked like a fool,
a pathetic, bedraggled fool? She let out an audible groan.

He dismounted, then bent over her. "Are you all
right?"

Though his face showed the appropriate amount of
concern, Jinx was not impressed. He wore a wide-
brimmed hat and an oil-cloth cape, and though he was
somewhat damp, he was not drenched, nor humiliated,
as was she.

He crouched beside her and touched her shoulder. "Are you hurt? Can you stand? Here, let me help you."

Gritting her teeth, she brushed his hand aside. "If you will fetch my horse, I can manage the rest on my own."

By the time he returned with Daffodil, Jinx was upright once more. But barely. The rain had ceased its initial rush and had found a pace more to its liking. Had she been at home, she would have stood in a window enjoying the pleasant drumming against the glass. She would have listened for the gurgle of roof water angled with gutters and fanciful spouts into a veritable fountain, a project of her grandfather Benchley.

But here, on this sodden hill, in who-knew-where Oxfordshire, she took no pleasure at all from the rain. She was cold and drenched to the bone. She could hardly move, her clothes weighed her down so. Added to that, she was exhausted and mortified—and the day was not yet done!

If he laughed at her, or tried to browbeat her, or so much as raised one of his arrogant brows askance . . .

To his credit, he did none of those. "Are you able to ride?" he asked.

"Yes." But she could not quite haul her sodden self up into the saddle. "I can manage," she insisted, when he dismounted to help her. A second try and a third, however, yielded no different results. But still, she refused to beg his assistance.

Then she heard a muffled oath. Something about women and insanity, and she whirled to take umbrage with him. Unfortunately he was already upon her, reaching for her waist to hoist her into the saddle, she presumed. But once he clasped his hands on her waist, he didn't lift her at all. Instead, for an endless, breathless moment, they stood stock-still, facing one another much too close. *Much* too close.

The rain pelted them, cold and chuckling once more. His hands were warm on her waist. Warmer than made

any sense. She felt the distinct outline of his wide palm
and strong fingers. He stared down at her and she up at
him, and suddenly everything changed. It was no longer
about Colin and Alice. It was about him and her. He
was impossibly handsome. Ridiculously tall. A man, not
a boy. And he was going to kiss her.

Had she been logical she would have turned away,
even though she was a Benchley and Benchleys were not
above kissing in the rain. She believed in love among the
unlikeliest of people. Her scholarly father had loved a
butcher's widow. Her grandfather had wed a Gypsy.

But a marquis?

No Benchley of her lineage had ever been so unwise
as to fall for a man that far above her in station.

But she *was* falling, like one of Newton's apples, hard
and fast and unable to stop. He was arrogant and determined, but he could also be gentle and considerate.
He was vengeful, but that was merely an extension of
his loyalty to his family, wasn't it? She gazed up at him,
blinking against the rain, mesmerized by the look in his
dark eyes. Then he bent nearer her. Their lips almost
touched—

And rain from the brim of his hat dumped into her
face, very nearly drowning her!

"Oh!" she sputtered, coughing and wiping her face.
She heard him curse—an exceedingly foul string of
words he should not say in front of a lady—and she felt
like echoing him. Then his grasp tightened and in a tri-
fling she found herself mounted on Daffodil and staring
down into his grim features.

"We'll find shelter somewhere ahead. Then you and I
will have a heart-to-heart talk, Miss Benchley."

"About why you are following me?" she snapped
back, determined that he never have the last word in an
argument with her.

"About why you lied to me," he growled.

He mounted his horse and started forward, still head-

ing north, she noticed. Well, that was something. But if
he thought she would help him find Colin so that he
could challenge him to a duel, he was more than wrong.
He was completely mad.

"I didn't lie to you!" she shouted, urging Daffodil forward. Benchleys did not lie. They were too honorable to
do that. "I never lie!" she vowed.

But commit murder? She glared at his unyielding
back, so straight and arrogant—and dry beneath his
cape. At least one Benchley she knew was tempted to
commit murder. Sorely tempted.

Chapter Four

They sought shelter at a farmhouse, a substantial, though somewhat shabby, establishment. Jinx waited alongside the pigsty while Harrison approached the main house.

She didn't want to stay anywhere with him, yet the long hour's ride she'd just endured had taken its toll. Pride was all very good, but practicality sometimes took precedence. Like now. She wanted a bath, a meal, and a bed, in that order. Her only satisfaction was in knowing that Lord Hartley was not happy to be taking such mean lodgings for the night.

But the farmer's wife was certainly happy, Jinx surmised when the woman began to bow and curtsy, attempting both actions at the same time.

"We're to have the best rooms in the house," Harrison said when he returned.

"How much did you pay her for the privilege of putting her out of her own home?" Jinx asked, annoyed with him despite her eagerness to gain access to those very rooms.

"A sovereign, and I rather doubt she considers it a hardship," he retorted.

"Of course she doesn't. The sovereign you so care-

lessly toss about is worth a month's labor to folk such
as she."

"I'm well aware of that, Miss Benchley. I'm also cognizant of the fact that she would have been grateful to
receive one shilling."

Jinx glared at him. She wanted to stay angry with him
but it was hard, for to be honest, a sovereign was a very
generous sum, and she well knew it. Still, she was not
about to heap praise on him for it. "If you'll excuse
me?" She urged Daffodil past him, toward the open stable.

But he caught the mare's bridle. "Not so fast, Miss
Benchley. Her son will take the horses. You and I are
overdue for a chat." Then without so much as a by-
your-leave, he hauled her down from the saddle.

"I'll thank you to keep your hands off my person!"
She jerked back from him, tilting her chin up to a fighting angle.

A boy edged up, curious but cautious. "Rub them
down well and give them each an extra portion of bran,"
Harrison told the lad. "And bring the bags up to our
rooms."

"I'm quite capable of carrying my own bag now."
Jinx unfastened the portmanteau and started for the
farmhouse. "If you wish to speak with me," she called
over her shoulder to Harrison, "it will simply have to
wait until I get out of these wet clothes."

"Gladly," Harrison murmured, watching her march
like a bedraggled queen across the sloppy yard. Her
skirts dragged, a pitiful muddy blue train. Her wet hair
clung like a bronze curtain to her slender back. She was
stubborn and haughty—and he'd give far more than
merely a sovereign to see her out of her wet clothes.

The very thought of the creamy skin that lay beneath
her muddy blue riding suit heated him like roofing pitch
brought to a boil. She disappeared into the farmhouse,

with their hostess fluttering about her as if she were visiting royalty.

What was it about Jinx Benchley that drew people as disparate as a farmer's wife and a marquis? He could not deny that the troublesome redhead had confounded him from the first moment he'd laid eyes on her. She had an air of self-possession that befitted a well-heeled matron, though she was neither well-heeled, nor a matron. She could not be above five-and-twenty, and he knew the Benchleys had limited funds and only a mediocre estate. Neither was her confidence dependent upon her appearance—which was a far cry from the accepted norms of beauty—nor on her position in society—which was negligible.

That was not to say that she wasn't a proper lady, for she was a gentleman's daughter. But she was an odd bird, and from an odd family. He frowned in frustration and concentrated on the facts. And the fact was, aside from her unwarranted ego, Miss Benchley possessed no particular presence, save that attributable to any attractive female. Redheads were said to have volatile tempers—and volatile passions. He knew she possessed the former. But did she possess the latter?

"Bloody hell," he muttered as desire struck him with embarrassing results. Angry at his reaction to the troublesome wench, he grabbed his leather valise and strode purposefully across the drenched yard to the house. Chickens scattered out of his path.

Jinx Benchley's sexual appeal was not the point, he told himself. The woman obviously thought she could protect her brother from the consequences of his actions. Otherwise she would not be galloping north to find him. While he admired her loyalty and found her adventurous nature intriguing, that changed nothing. She knew where her brother was. He was sure of it. He had only to be patient, to beat her at her own game.

How difficult could that be?

*   *   *

Removing her ruined traveling suit was a lesson in frustration. The wet wool clung to the soaked linen beneath it, which clung to her shivering skin below that. She removed her grandmother's anklet with its tiny Gypsy bells. Her stockings peeled reluctantly from her legs, like a second layer of ice-cold skin, leaving her flesh prickling from the chill. Jinx wrapped up in a blanket as she awaited hot water and a tub, and only then did she examine her surroundings. The room she'd been given was spacious, albeit with a low, sloping ceiling. The rain leaked in over the window; a pot caught the drips with wet, rhythmic plunks.

This was not the owner's bedchamber, she decided. No doubt the high-and-mighty Lord Hartley claimed that. Holding the blanket secure with one hand, she pushed her clothes into one sodden heap. She needed a bucket for them, otherwise they would leave water marks on the old wooden floor.

The housewife came and, aided by a dairymaid, dragged in a huge tub. At the sight of it Jinx finally found something to smile about. It was almost as large as the porcelain tub her mother had installed in a special upstairs bathing chamber at home.

"Water's heating, miss," the woman said. "I'll have it up directly," she added, bobbing and bowing. It took six hot buckets and six cold to fill the tub. The woman even had a block of hard soap, and once Jinx slid into the steaming stew, she let out a groan of utter contentment. If only she could sleep here, immersed in warmth, cocooned from the cold and bitter realities of the world outside this tub. No Harrison Stirling hounding her. No runaway brother foolishly enamored of a woman he should not want.

She closed her eyes and began to lather her hair. When this was over and she returned home, she wanted to investigate the possibility of an upstairs stove with a large

water tank that could empty directly into the bathing
tub. The water could be supplied to the heating tank
from the roof gutters, she speculated. And perhaps she
should consider a special drain to carry the used bath-
water directly outdoors. That way Mrs. Honeywell
would be saved the task of heating and fetching and
carrying away. And that way Jinx could bathe as often
as she liked—daily would be absolutely wonderful—and
feel no guilt for the burdens it placed on their limited
household staff.

She'd sunk down to her chin, and only her knees
showed, pink and warm, above the faintly soapy surface.
Her mind filled with details of plumbing and a system
for hoisting firewood up to the second floor, when a firm
knock disrupted her reverie. She sat up with a correspondent slosh of water. "Who is it?"

"Harrison. May I come in?"

"No!" She sank down again, down until her chin and
ears were halfway beneath the water. "No," she
squeaked. "I'm almost finished here and I'll be downstairs directly—"

The door opened, she shrieked, and then it closed
with an ominous thud. For a moment, all was absolutely
silent. But though Jinx's back was to the door, she
knew he was inside the room. He was inside the room,
and she was naked, and she had no idea what to do
about it.

She did know, however, that to react passively would
only encourage him to bully her further. Though it took
more courage than she thought she possessed, she forced
herself to sit up, just enough so that her head was completely out of the water. Then she shifted to one side,
fixed him with her most lethal glare, and said with a
completely false calm, "Get out of this room. Now."

"Not until you and I have had a little talk."

"If you wish to speak to me, you will gain no satisfaction by behaving like a ruffian. I refuse to speak to you under such unseemly circumstances."

The unconscionable wretch only deflected her glare with a smug grin and advanced farther into the room. He dragged a straight-backed chair into the middle of the floor, then, straddling it backward, faced her across a mere three feet of distance.

It was such an arrogant male gesture, she wanted to throw the soap at him. And yet that same arrogance, the very maleness of his behavior, sent a shiver of both fear and awareness through her. She sank deeper into the water, crossing her arms over her chest and cursing herself for a full-fledged fool. Toad eggs! What was she to do now?

"I do not negotiate with ruffians," she muttered, averting her gaze.

"You have no choice but to negotiate with me, Jinx."

"From one presumption to the next you leap! I am Miss Benchley to you."

He chuckled. "I have difficulty with such formalities when I'm in a lady's bedchamber, especially when she's—"

"No woman who welcomes the likes of you into her bedchamber could possibly be termed a lady."

"Some are. Some aren't." He grinned. "Which are you?"

The water had begun to cool. Now, however, it felt warm again. Hot. Positively steaming. He was enjoying himself entirely too much!

Jinx weighed her options. She could hold this conversation with him while sitting in the bathtub. She could refuse to speak to him at all, so long as she was sitting in the bathtub.

Or . . . She could get out of the bathtub.

He expected her to refuse to speak with him, and then eventually, to give in, and it galled her to let him best her that way.

So she considered the alternative. Did she dare exit the tub, allowing him to see her naked, even if only for a moment or two? She was not an excessively modest person, and yet . . .

Ego won out over modesty. She sank completely under the water, rinsing the last of the soap from her hair—and gathering her courage. Then, not giving herself time to reconsider, she surged to her feet, stepped out of the tub, and snatched up the towel lying across the bed. She was covered in a moment, at least her torso was. Her arms and legs remained bare, but she could deal with that, she told herself. Finally, she steeled herself and turned to face him.

"Now, what was it you wished so urgently to discuss?"

Harrison closed his gaping mouth with a snap. Had she just done what he thought she'd done? Jinx Benchley sat on the bed. She was wrapped in a generous length of toweling, and as he watched, she reached up and began to apply another towel to her dripping mane of copper-colored hair.

She was the picture of composure, a lady at her bath. But the image of her smooth pink skin, a narrow waist, and dimpled derriere, were burned into his brain.

He'd bullied her, but she'd turned the tables and bullied him right back. Quite a feat. But he was not calm enough yet to fully admire her ability to outbluff him. He was too overwhelmed by the desire to unwrap the towels that hid her luscious body. He wanted to see the rest of her, the breasts he'd not really glimpsed, the softly rounded belly. The feminine vee between her legs.

"Lord Hartley?"

Harrison blinked, only belatedly coming back to awareness. As he watched, she stood and, still wrapped in the towels, slipped her arms into her wrapper. Then turning her back to him, she did a little jiggle, and from beneath her wrapper, the towel fell to her feet. She tied the wrapper in place, then finally turned back to face him, completely covered, neck to wrist to toes. But she was still naked beneath that one layer of cloth.

She planted her fists on her hips. "Now what was it that was so important I must waste a perfectly good tub of water?"

Indeed, what had been so important? He couldn't remember.

Maybe he'd only hoped to catch her at her bath and see some portion of her unclothed. But never in the wildest of his fantasies had he expected her to be so bold as to rise gloriously naked from her bath, like some Venus on her shell of a bathtub.

Perhaps she was not the innocent maiden he'd assumed her to be.

His eyes narrowed. "I confess, you have taken me quite by surprise, Miss Benchley. Unfortunately, I was so stunned I did not entirely appreciate your little display. Would you consider repeating it?"

A faint blush rose in her cheeks. So, she was not so blasé in her behavior as she pretended. He found an immense satisfaction in that knowledge. He went on. "You see, Miss Benchley, all I truly wanted was to discuss the matter of our wayward siblings. But if you have another sort of . . . *discussion* in mind, I'd be more than happy to join you on the bed."

She popped up from that bed like a fox who'd just stumbled into the hound. For all her bravado, Harrison was reassured that she was still an innocent. She had a boldness to her, and courage of a sort seldom seen in a woman. But that smooth pale skin had not yet known the touch of a man. He would swear on it.

"I do not wish to talk to you at all," she vowed. " 'Tis you who have forced your unwelcome presence on me. Your implication is exceedingly coarse and completely unappreciated. Pray, sir, say your piece, then leave."

Harrison thought of himself as a practical man. Despite his reputation to the contrary, he took matters of family and money deadly serious. That's why he needed a wife. That's why he wanted Alice to wed a well-connected man.

But the three duels he'd fought—and won—had stained his reputation forever, even though they'd all been unavoidable. The men had challenged him. Each one of the fools had been jilted by spiteful women who'd then goaded their former lovers to fight their current lover: himself. The women had done it for the pride of knowing men had shed blood for them. The men had done it because male pride would not allow them to back down. Foolish men fighting to regain frivolous women. And he'd been the most foolish of all.

Still, he'd never ruined an innocent woman. He'd never even contemplated doing so—at least not since he'd reached his majority. But this woman—this beautiful, headstrong redheaded woman whom he'd known but two days—she was driving him to distraction!

He wanted her. It was that simple and that complicated. And now he was afraid to stand up, for the proof of his desire would be painfully apparent. He'd often had this problem when he was twenty. But he was thirty now, a jaded thirty, at that. No untried virgin should affect him so.

But this one did. Perhaps it *would* be best if he just said his piece and left.

He cleared his throat. " 'Tis apparent from your curious behavior that you seek to alert your brother to my pursuit. But it will do you no good, Miss Benchley. He cannot evade me forever."

"I'm certain he does not expect to."

"Then what do you hope to achieve with this mad dash you've made to find him before I can?"

"To save his hide from the murderous marquis!" she exclaimed. Her eyes flashed with anger, a clear aqua-green anger. Her breasts heaved with emotion beneath the flimsy linen wrapper. She was magnificent, he thought. She'd been magnificent in every incarnation: her early-morning attire; her bedraggled riding outfit; and now, wet and unadorned, fresh from her bath. How would she look draped in teal silk or cloth of gold, with diamonds sparkling in her hair or a web of gold and pearls draped around her throat? How he would like to find out.

"Well?" she demanded. "Have you no reply to that? Do you admit you mean to murder my brother, simply because he is so unwise as to love your sister?"

Harrison was not a man particularly given to impulsive behavior, no matter what other people thought. But when Jinx stared at him so belligerently, making accusations uncomfortably close to the truth, he reacted impulsively. The chair crashed down when he rose to his feet. Before she could do more than gasp with alarm, he pulled her into his arms.

"What—What are you doing?"

"You're a smart woman, Miss Benchley. Jinx. Figure it out." Then he silenced the protests rising from those pouty lips, from that petulant mouth. He kissed her and realized only then how much he'd wanted to do just that. From his first sight of her, all during the hard riding of the past two days, and culminating in her daring removal from the tub, he'd wanted to kiss her. He wanted to do even more, but kissing was a good start.

So he kissed her as if he and he alone had the right to do so. His lips captured hers in a carnal quest, and after a moment she began to kiss him back. As if he'd thrown down a gauntlet, she rose to the challenge he set.

She was not sure of herself, but she learned very quickly. Her protests died unsaid and softened into little sighs of acquiescence. She was damp and lithe, a soft, strong armful, and when he pressed her fully to him, she arched nearer, intensifying their embrace. Her arms circled his neck, her lips parted to grant him entrance, and he feared he would embarrass himself then and there.

His hands roamed freely down her back, circling her waist, learning the curve of her derriere. She gasped against his mouth, and he groaned. "Feels good, doesn't it?"

"Yes," she breathed. "Better than ever I would have guessed."

Harrison deepened the kiss, for he was heady with desire, and drunk with the passion her honest words roused in him. He devoured her mouth, sliding his tongue in and out, trying to rouse her as she roused him. He knew he was going too fast, and he didn't want to frighten her off. But he couldn't stop. His hands explored her sweet body while his mouth demanded she submit.

When she mimicked his caresses with caresses of her own, he nearly came undone. She was sweet and honest, and long overdue for her first sexual encounter—

Her *first* sexual encounter.

Was he insane?

With a groan he broke their kiss. With a curse he broke their embrace and thrust her away from him. But he did not let her go. He just stood there, holding her shoulders in a stiff-armed stance, his breathing harsh and ragged.

"What are you trying to do?" He glared at her, appalled at what had just occurred between them. What had *almost* occurred between them. "What in bloody hell are you trying to do?"

For a second she looked stunned. Her mouth gaped open. Her lips—her sweet, rosy, kissable lips—actually trembled. Then the moment passed, her jaw snapped shut, and the passionate sheen in her eyes turned to venom.

"What am *I* trying to do? *Me?*" She jerked free of his hold and backed as far away from him as she could.

"The better question is what are *you* trying to do? First you intrude on my privacy. You interrupt my bath. Then you proceed to kiss me—" She broke off. But though her face colored in a heated blush, her fury did not abate. "You do all that, then you have the gall to accuse *me* of trying to do something to *you*!"

She was right on every count. She knew it and so did Harrison. And yet he could not explain the idiocy of his behavior with any amount of logic. So he chose to blame her.

"If you think to lure me into some sort of compromising position and thereby gain a better bargaining position for yourself, it will not work."

"Are you accusing me of trying to gain a husband by such nefarious means? Is that what you are trying to imply?"

"No. That's not what I meant!" Harrison thrust his hands angrily through his hair. It was either that or grab her and silence her in the one way he now knew worked. Except that kissing her again would not be a good idea. "I didn't mean that you wanted to put me in a compromising position then force me into marriage. Not exactly," he added less forcefully.

"Then what exactly did you mean?" she demanded, glaring at him, her fists once more knotted on her hips.

Damn, but he was handling this badly! He didn't want to make it worse now by insulting her, or hurting her any more than he already had. But he didn't trust himself to keep his hands off her, no matter how stupid an idea it was.

Then again, if he angered her sufficiently, she would be the one to avoid him.

He didn't like the idea, yet given the messy circumstances of their acquaintance, it seemed to be the best option open to him.

So he answered her question though he no longer believed his own words. "When it comes to protecting your idiot brother, you have already shown yourself to be bolder and more daring than any woman I've ever met. It can be no wonder, then, that I assume you would be willing to buy your brother's safety with the use of your body."

She slapped him.

He deserved it. But though he wanted to apologize to her, he did not. This attraction between them must be killed. It had begun too abruptly. It would have to end in the same manner. So he stepped back from her and gave an abbreviated bow. "I'll leave you now."

When he reached the door, however, she called out. "I'm not turning back, Lord Hartley. You can't scare me off so easily as all that."

He did not think he had. But Harrison kept his own counsel. He did not look back at her or respond in any way. He left and sought his own room where he and a bottle of whisky proceeded to spend a long, restless night together.

How was he to get rid of the difficult Jinx Benchley? He'd kissed her, a stupid move, given who she was and the circumstances of their relationship. He'd seen her naked and run his hands over her delectable body, compounding his stupidity tenfold. Still, he'd not totally compromised her. Somehow he'd managed not to do anything he could not undo.

He stared up at the ceiling, disgusted with himself. He wanted her even though he knew she was not the sort of woman a man could seduce with impunity. But logic fell short when it came to his reaction to Jinx. Though he should put her out of his mind, he could not. He wanted her still.

He heaved a great sigh and lifted the whisky glass once more to his lips. The only solution was to get rid of the difficult and delicious Miss Benchley before he gave in and did something that he could not undo.

Chapter Five

She should have slept the sleep of the dead; she'd been that exhausted. But Jinx was too upset to sleep. Too agitated and bewildered and furious.

By midnight she was seething. How dare he burst into her private chamber?

By two A.M. she was ready to commit murder. How dare he kiss her, then turn around and accuse *her* of trying to distract *him*!

By four o'clock, she was sick with shame. How could she have risen, wet and naked from the tub, with him right there? How could she have kissed him so passionately? And why should he not question the purposes of any woman who behaved so?

When the downstairs clock chimed half past four, she decided she must do something, else she would tear her hair out in utter frustration. So she dressed in her wrinkled, barely dried riding costume, pulled on dry hose and wet boots, then wound her hair into a serviceable knot and tied on her hat. She would not subject herself to Harrison Stirling's distracting presence one moment longer. Nor him to hers. She would go on alone. According to their hostess, Scotland was another two-day ride—assuming the weather cooperated. With the slower carriage, Colin could not be too much ahead of her.

Perhaps she might even catch up with him today.

She paused at the door. Lord Hartley would be furious and he would be after her with the same vengeance he felt for Colin. He was not a man accustomed to being thwarted. But that only intensified her resolve. He deserved to be thwarted. He deserved to have his sister wed someone he refused to approve.

Jinx's brow creased in a frown. In a way it was ironic, for in theory, her goals and Lord Hartley's were the same: prevent the union in marriage of their respective siblings. But her primary reason for wanting to prevent it was to avoid Lord Hartley's revenge upon Colin. If his nature were not so vengeful, she would not be so opposed to Colin marrying his sister.

But why should she help the arrogant Lord Hartley achieve his aim? Why should she seek to prevent Colin and Alice marrying? They were adult enough to make their own decisions, and if they were in love, who was she to gainsay them? Rather than join with Lord Hartley in thwarting them, it behooved her to rush to their aid— and thereby thwart Lord Hartley.

Her hand tightened on the ceramic doorknob. She would find the wayward pair before he could, she vowed. And if necessary, she would hire Bow Street runners to protect them. And she would laugh in Harrison Stirling's face and bring his sister home to Benchley Manor and all its charming follies.

Feeling much better than she had in hours, Jinx shoved the door open—and promptly sent a tower of pots clattering onto the floor.

"Lizard legs!" she swore as one of the metal vessels careened down the hall. So much for making a silent getaway.

When the last lid stilled its wobbling spin, she heard the creak of a door and the thud of footfalls on the bare wood floor. But Jinx did not want to hear the triumph in Lord Hartley's voice, or see the gloating look in his eyes. She slammed her door, then leaned back against it, breathing hard. Blast the man for foiling her escape. And blast him for being the most difficult, frustrating, stubborn oaf she'd ever had the misfortune to meet!

"Good try." His voice came through the door, and she jumped like a startled cat. "Good try, but you can't escape me that easily," he continued.

If it weren't that his voice was so unnervingly husky, Jinx would have snapped some sharp retort at him. She would! The trouble was, his voice *was* unnervingly husky. It was dark and warm and as luscious as velvet pouring over her naked skin.

"Bee's knees," she breathed, afraid for her own sanity. She lurched away from the door, one hand at her throat, the other holding on to her valise with a death grip. This was insane. Insane! She could not be having such an improbable reaction to this man. Such a primitive and visceral reaction.

But she was. There was no denying it. And that, more than anything else, kept her somber and silent in her room the long remainder of the night.

The farmer's wife came at dawn with a tray. Jinx ate because she knew she must. The stable lad brought the horses around to the front door, but still she sat in the room. Only when Lord Hartley knocked at her door did she rouse. "Go along without me. I'm not accompanying you any further."

He came straightaway into the room, as she should have known he would. "Are you ill?" he demanded to know.

"Yes. Ill," she responded, refusing to look at him. She was afraid to.

At once he pressed his hand to her brow. Jinx leapt back, a difficult feat, considering she was sitting on the bed. She glared at him. "Who taught you manners? This is not your room, nor am I your concern. Go." She waved her hand. "Go on about your fool's errand. As for me, I am returning home."

"To Hampshire? To Benchley Manor?" he asked, fixing her with a suspicious gaze.

She nodded. Now that she was looking at him, it seemed she could not look away. He was so tall, and so beautiful, she conceded, in a harsh, masculine sort of way. Why must he be the one man to move her?

By rights he should be the very last man to attract her. Other than his manly appearance, he had nothing to commend him. He was too arrogant, too high-handed, and too rich, and she had no inkling whether he possessed either intellect or common sense, both of which she admired in a person.

But he is a loyal brother, the small voice of reason reminded her. Rightly or wrongly, he took his sister's welfare most seriously.

Too seriously, she decided when he crossed his arms and stared down at her. "I am not fool enough to leave you here alone, Jinx, neither for my sake nor your own."

"Don't call me that. And I hardly believe you have any concern for my welfare."

"I am not leaving you here and that is final. For one thing, you cannot travel all the way back to Hampshire unescorted. Not that I trust you to go home. By the same token, I cannot let you travel on to Gretna Green alone, either."

"I told you. I've changed my mind. I'm not going on to Gretna Green."

"Yes you are." So saying, he caught her wrist in one hand and pulled her to her feet.

"Stop that! Who do you think you are?" she sputtered. "No—"

But Lord Hartley was stronger than she and bent on ignoring her. He snatched up her portmanteau and, deaf to her complaints, hauled her out of the room, down the narrow stairs, and out to the waiting horses. He rudely put her on Daffodil and then mounted his own steed. The farm wife thrust a bundle of bread and cheese into her hands, then they were off, with the farmer, his wife, and their three workers waving them down the road.

Jinx plotted revenge the whole day long. Over every hill, through every valley. Beneath clouds and sun and the occasional drizzle, she plotted revenge against the despotic Lord Hartley. They rode swiftly, he goading her horse before him when she did not ride fast enough. But to his every remark, she turned a cold shoulder.

"How did you get the name Jinx?" he'd asked at one point.

When she did not reply he answered for her. "Oh, I was a troublesome child, almost as troublesome as I am now."

She stared straight ahead, vowing to remain angry with him. Unfortunately, the ridiculous falsetto voice he'd adopted made it hard.

"You, troublesome?" he said in his own voice. "Oh, yes," he replied, mimicking her once more. "Women who are hardheaded and unreasonable generally behaved the same way during their childhood—"

"I am not unreasonable," Jinx stated in a haughty tone.

"So you admit that you're hardheaded."

"You are hardheaded. I am merely determined."

He had dropped back so that they now rode side by side. "Most people would agree that a young woman sallying forth alone to find her brother is more than merely determined."

She shot him a glare, her anger restored by his patronizing tone. "I was not brought up to be a slave to what 'most people' think. I do what I believe is right."

"As do I."

Frustrated, she urged Daffodil on. She would not ride beside him, conversing as if they were on an afternoon's pleasure ride. She would not exchange banter, nor even insults with him, for it did no good.

But it did not sit well for her to be silent in the face of frustration. She was more wont to lash out with her quick tongue than suffer in silence. Unfortunately, her reactions to Harrison Stirling were simply too irrational. She tried to stay angry, but he charmed her. She tried to shock him and he kissed her. She still had not recovered from that!

Oh, but he was the most arrogant, high-handed, egotistical . . . She couldn't find words remotely adequate to express her fury. He was the most egotistical man she'd ever had the misfortune to know. So she rode and she fumed and she bided her time. She would have her revenge, one way or another, she vowed. One way or another.

Late afternoon the rain resumed. They were well into the north country now, a pretty land of mountains and lakes, but few villages. They'd made good time, for the road was well maintained. But as they descended into a shallow valley, her captor, as she'd begun to think of him, turned off the road into a private park. Jinx had been riding rather dispiritedly just a little behind him. Now she straightened and peered out from beneath the drooping brim of her bedraggled bonnet.

"Where are you taking me now? Not calling on some friend or another, I hope." The last thing she wanted was for anyone to hear of this incident. Bad enough that everyone thought the Benchleys odd. If it got out she'd spent all this time alone with Lord Hartley, her reputation would be in a complete shambles.

Though her friend Virginia and the housekeeper, Mrs. Honeywell, feared Jinx meant never to marry, that was not so. It was only that it was difficult to find the right man. But ruining her reputation with Lord Hartley would make it utterly impossible to find a husband.

That thought caused her to straighten even further.

Harrison Stirling was obsessed with his sister's reputation yet he did not mind playing fast and easy with hers. Perhaps it was time that *she* present a threat to *his* reputation.

"Where are we going?" she repeated. "This is not the way to Gretna Green. Why have we turned off the main road?"

He shot her a damp, disgruntled look. "So you're speaking to me again."

She tilted her chin to a lofty angle. "I have my reputation to protect. The last thing I want is to be caught in a compromising position with you. I should think you would feel the same."

A muscle began to twitch in his jaw. "The last thing, you say? It didn't feel like the last thing on your mind yesterday."

She fought the rise of color in her cheeks. "If you were a true gentleman, you would not bring that up!"

"If you were a lady, you would not be traipsing across the countryside alone!"

"But I'm not alone, am I? I'm stuck with a vengeful brute who's bent on murdering my brother—my *only* brother—and bent on ruining me as well!" She wheeled Daffodil around so abruptly the little mare nearly sat down on her haunches. Then she was off, flying down the gravel drive, back toward the main road.

He caught her, of course. His steed was bigger and faster—and probably would not dare to disappoint his demanding rider. He caught her and hauled her right out of the saddle as if she were a sack of some useful victual or another—potatoes or radishes or leeks. Her struggles ceased at once, for she did not want to fall beneath his mount's heavy hooves. But though she clung to the arm wrapped so unrelentingly around her, her verbal protests did not abate.

"You wretched, wretched man!" she shrieked. "What do you think you're doing? Stop this very minute, you barbarian. You brute! Let me down." She batted futilely at him. "Stop and let me down!"

"Not until we reach the house," he muttered. He shifted her higher, so that she now sat across his lap.

"I'll not go riding up there carried in your arms like this for the entire world to see," she swore. "I won't. Do you *want* to start talk about us? Is that your aim?"

"This is *my* house. No one will talk."

His house? That put a rather different slant on things. Still, Jinx felt a jolt of alarm. Why was he bringing her to his house?

"To obtain a chaperone," he answered when she questioned him. "For both you and my sister."

"Oh." Though she hated to give him credit for anything, the idea of a chaperone was a very good one. So Jinx sat in silence, with no further struggles as they made their way up the drive. Lord Hartley's horse nickered and Daffodil responded, then turned and ambled along behind them. The park was pretty, with ancient hornbeam and mature oaks and an allée of lime trees. Then they made a turn past a small lake and she saw the house, a handsome three-story country house with chimneys and eyebrow windows aplenty, but no turrets or fanciful downspouts. Still, it was a singularly lovely place and beautifully sited.

They were met in the forecourt by two grooms, while a third ran to alert the housekeeper.

"Miss Benchley is hurt," Harrison blithely fibbed when the two men stared in astonishment at Jinx riding before him. He slid off his horse, still holding her as if she were an invalid. "A twisted ankle from a fall," he said, embellishing his tale. "Ask Mrs. Downy to prepare the room off the terrace for her. And you," he muttered in Jinx's ear. "You'd best be still if you value your reputation so highly as you profess."

What a fuss! Unfortunately, he made a good point. So Jinx ordered herself to relax in his arms. It was all for the best, and he *was* trying to protect her reputation. Besides, their delay here would afford Colin and Alice more time to achieve their aim.

But it was exceedingly difficult to relax when Harrison Stirling had one muscular arm cradling her back and the other one curved under her knees.

He carried her up the stairs and down a hall, not waiting for the housekeeper to appear. It was a goodly distance, and Jinx was by no means petite. Yet he seemed unfazed by her weight. She, however, was hardly unfazed. She should not have been. After all, his ability— or inability—to lift her weight was hardly pertinent to the situation. Yet the fact remained: she could feel the muscles in his arms bunch and shift; she could feel the heavy thud of his heart. And with her every breath she caught his scent, a confusion of horses and sweat, and soap and rain. It made her slightly dizzy.

He made her dizzy.

By the time he kicked open a door and deposited her on a settee draped in furniture cloths, her anger at him had turned into aggravation at herself. When had she become so muddleheaded?

She looked up at him as he pulled away from her. He was in the act of straightening up, but when their gazes met, he froze. He cleared his throat. "Just pretend your ankle is injured, Jinx."

She nodded.

"It's only to protect the reputation you value so."

Again she nodded. Lizard legs, but his eyes were beautiful. Dark as night, yet with a sparkling depth to them.

"Don't look at me like that," he muttered, his voice lower. Huskier.

But she couldn't *not* look at him like that. He infuriated her and yet he also managed to rouse emotions in her that no other man had ever touched upon. For whatever reason, he fanned to roaring life some small, primitive flame that until now had lain happily dormant.

It was dormant no more.

Their eyes held and he groaned, and she knew he meant to kiss her. Then a knock sounded, he jerked away, and the housekeeper scurried into the room.

" 'Tis sorry I am, sir, to keep you waiting." She curtsied while her curious gaze flitted back and forth between her master and his guest.

Jinx didn't know whether to laugh or cry, the situation was that ludicrous. If only the woman had not come in at just that moment. Jinx needed to find out what was happening between Harrison and her. At the same time, though, she wanted nothing more than to flee and never be tempted by him again. It seemed ridiculously ironic that she could do neither.

So she sat there as he introduced Mrs. Downy. Then he backed away while the housekeeper bustled about, directing two maids to pull back the drapes, open the windows, and remove the furniture cloths.

"I have not been to Grassymere in a while." Harrison spoke into the awkward silence.

When had she begun to think of him as Harrison? "It must be pleasant to have so many estates," she murmured.

He frowned, then signaled to the housekeeper. "You may go. We shall want supper in the dining room. Something simple will suffice." When the woman and her maids left, he faced Jinx from his place across the room from her. "Having so many estates is more duty than pleasure," he said in a tone that sounded awfully defensive.

"I wasn't being critical. I was just . . . just trying to make polite conversation. You shouldn't be in here alone with me," she added.

He stood stiffly with his hands clasped behind his back, ignoring her last comment. "You weren't implying that my sister need not marry for wealth?"

She stood up, suddenly weary of this debate they

waged. "My brother has an estate of his own, as you
well know. And while it may not be so grand as this—
or as any of your other estates—it is comfortable enough
for our needs, despite its peeling paint and ancient carriages. It provides an adequate enough living for a man
to bring a wife home," she added, crossing her arms,
daring him to disparage Benchley House.

His gaze narrowed. "Two days ago you seemed as
determined as I to prevent a marriage between my sister
and your brother. Yet now I detect another mood. First
you want to abandon the chase. Now you tout your
brother's ability to provide for Alice. You aren't recon-
sidering your position regarding a union between them,
are you? Are you?" he repeated.

When she did not respond, but only pursed her lips
and looked away, he groaned. "If nothing else, consider
this, Jinx. Their union would make us in-laws. Is that
what you want?"

"No." She looked back at him. "No." She did not
want to be related to him in that way. But the thought
occurred to her that unless the marriage went through,
she was very likely never to see Harrison again. The
shocking truth was, she didn't want that, either.

So what did she want?

He must have sensed her confusion, for he crossed the
room until they were less than an arm's length apart.
She should have stepped back, but she could not. Then
he breached the failing space between them and grasped
her by the arms.

"What do you want, Jinx?"

She stared up at him and tried to be honest. "I want
none of this ever to have happened."

He grinned, a half-smile that was, temporarily at least,
free of all the strain between them. "Do you really?"

"Don't you?"

Slowly he shook his head, and just as slowly, his grin
faded. "No, I don't think I do."

Chapter Six

He should know better. He *did* know better. But that did not alter Harrison's behavior one whit.

As he pulled Jinx nearer, he consoled himself with the knowledge that he would stop if she protested. But she didn't protest, as he'd known she would not. If she were waiting for him to stop this mad, spiraling desire between them, her trust was sorely misplaced.

So he pulled her nearer, until their breath mingled. Until her thighs brushed his, and the press of her breasts burned his chest. Her eyes, so vividly blue, remained locked with his, as innocent and sultry as a schoolgirl courtesan's. Worldly he might be, but he flung himself headlong into the dangerously deep emotional waters of those eyes. He lowered his head and captured her mouth, and vowed then and there not to give her time to change her mind.

She tasted like no other woman, he dimly realized as he pressed her boldly to him. Nor did she respond like other women, for there was no coyness in her, not an iota. She was who she was, sweet and feisty, strong and innocent. He kissed her, devouring her mouth, invading her with his tongue, and drawing her tongue into his mouth for the heated dance of lovemaking. He would have this woman now.

But what of later?

He hesitated and raised his head. She began to kiss his chin, his neck, and his Adam's apple, however, and the last shreds of logic fled his brain. With one swift motion he lifted her into his arms, while she held his face with her hands and kissed him without ceasing. He lowered her to the bed and lowered himself over her, and still the kiss went on and on. Down the hall a clock began to chime. Up close he was enveloped in the unique scent that perfumed her. Sweet, earthy. Fresh as rain, wild as the forest.

"I will not let you go," he growled.

"You need not."

"You drive me mad with wanting you."

" 'Tis I who must be mad," she murmured, nibbling the words against his mouth, then nipping his lower lip for emphasis.

He covered her breast with one hand and swallowed her little gasp with a hungry kiss. After that there was little room for speech. His clothing and hers were stripped away, sometimes a frantic struggle, other times a torturous peeling away. He found the mysterious bells around her ankle and, in the process, kissed every bit of skin she revealed, every sweet, supple inch of her, from her pink toes, to her luscious mouth, from the anklet of bells that made her every movement musical, to the masses of fiery hair that drew him like a beacon.

Her little cries and artless moans urged him on. Creamy thighs, sweet belly. He traced a circle around her navel with his tongue, then slid farther up her lithe torso, anointing each rib. He lay between her legs, braced on his elbows. Before him her breasts were exposed to his gaze, lovely pale flesh crested with taut, rosy buds that attested to her arousal. Her breaths came short and shallow. Her eyes were glazed with passion.

She was his now. His.

His own breathing was ragged. "Unloose your hair,"

he said. "It's so beautiful. Unloose it for me, Jinx."

One of her hands cupped his face; the other rested on his bare shoulder. He saw her uncertainty, so he dipped his head and circled one nipple with his tongue. Then he kissed it, tugging it up into his mouth. She arched up with a cry of acquiescence.

When he raised his head again she began shakily to release her hair from its twists and coils. With her arms extended above her head that way, she looked like a wanton creature, a pagan offering to the gods of earthly delights. He actually hurt with his need to possess her. He captured her raised wrists with one hand, and with the other drew her flame-colored tresses down across her shoulders and chest and breasts. The ends curled near her waist, showing only tantalizing glimpses of her delicious skin between the tendrils.

If his violent desire frightened her, her fear was overcome with passion, for she groaned when once more he teased her nipples with his tongue and lips and teeth.

"Harrison." She breathed his name, and he nearly embarrassed himself, so profoundly did that single sound affect him.

"I cannot go slow," he muttered, half in warning, half in apology.

"Then don't."

It was the last straw. He slid up her, letting her feel the strength he meant to release upon her, giving her one last chance to stop this insanity they'd plunged into. But she only gazed up at him, wide-eyed and accepting. Eager. So he drew her legs up and then, capturing her mouth with his, he pressed into her.

Her welcome was sweet and oh, so hot. He slid inside her and she began to writhe. He grew bolder, met with resistance, then thrust past it. She shuddered. He felt it in their kiss. But he worked to rouse her further, sliding his tongue in and out until she melted once more. Then he began the same rhythm with his hips.

Such a fire. Such a raging inferno. His passion was a mad beast, possessing him. Possessing her. But as he plunged, deeper and deeper, faster and faster, she met his passion with an equal passion of her own. Her legs wrapped round his hips. Her hands slipped over the damp skin of his back and arms and shoulders. She roused him as he roused her. But still he struggled to restrain himself.

Then he felt it, in every part of his being: she was near. He could bring her there, this innocent wanton he'd discovered in the unlikeliest of circumstances.

Her cries became more helpless. Her body tensed. Then she arched in that exquisite culmination, and he could hold back no longer. He plunged even deeper than before and exploded into her with as much pride as desire, and with as much satisfaction for her as for himself.

Afterward he held her as she eased down from the euphoria she'd found—that they'd found together. He wrapped his arms around her and held her against him, reveling in the warmth of her damp flesh against his, breathing deeply of the fragrance of man and woman joined at last. He would have to make this right, he told himself as she fitted herself more comfortably in his embrace.

Her breathing slowed; she'd fallen asleep. Harrison pressed a kiss into the heavy tangle of her glorious hair. He would have to make this right. It was one thing to carry on with your mistress, or a widow, or even someone else's wife. But to ruin an innocent young woman? No, a gentleman could not do that. He must make it right.

Yet instead of feeling trapped by that knowledge, Harrison felt the oddest sense of relief. Of freedom. He ran his hand down her arm and wove his fingers between hers. How many years had he searched for a woman to wed?

Then he sighed and smiled, and drifted into peaceful slumber.

Jinx awakened to absolute darkness and complete disorientation. Her stomach growled. She was starving. She must have missed supper. Where was she? What room was this? What bed—

What man?

There was only one man it could be, and in a tumble, everything came back to her. She and Harrison had—

"Bee's knees. Toad eggs. Lizard legs! What have I done?" she muttered into the night. She tried to think and to avoid the panic that theatened to overwhelm her. But she couldn't think while lying so intimately in his arms. First she must get out of the bed.

But when she tried to slide away from him, Harrison sighed and shifted with her. She was nestled up to him, her naked backside against his naked front side. For a moment she hesitated. Had it truly been as wonderful as she remembered? A spiral of lingering passion answered yes, it had been that wonderful. That stupendous. That unbelievable.

But that did not mean it had been right.

She groaned and, for one minute only, succumbed to utter despair. What must he think of her now? And what in heaven's name was she to do?

She was saved pondering that ghastly thought by the sound of footfalls in the hall and the worried voice of a woman.

". . . but it might be better if I fetch her, sir."

"Which room?" a man's voice demanded. An angry man's voice. A familiar man's voice.

"Please don't be hasty, dear," another woman pleaded.

"I'll handle this, Alice."

Alice?

Colin?

Jinx leapt upright. Colin was here? Now?

Her heart sank even as her body sprang to life. She must stop him! She must avert this disaster.

"Not so fast," Harrison mumbled, catching her around the waist and pulling her down on top of him. He was warm and strong and her body reacted most perversely to him. "You're not ever to try to escape me again," he murmured, nuzzling her neck.

Then the door burst open, a lantern cast the room in wildly careening light, and Jinx shrieked and dove beneath the covers.

"What in bloody hell!" Harrison roared, bolting upright.

"I'll see you in hell this very night!" Colin roared back. "Get away from him, Jinx, so that I can kill him!"

"She stays right here," Harrison vowed. "Who in the hell are you?" Then he spied his sister. "Alice?" Then in the next breath, "Benchley? You bastard!" he yelled, leaping from the bed with only a pillow to cover his naked state. "I'll have your head on a pike!"

"And I'll skewer you for ruining my sister!"

Jinx peered out at the scene from beneath the rumpled bed linens. Beside the bed, tousled from sleep and from their lovemaking, Harrison, naked as the day he was born, stood tensed as if for battle. Across the room, just inside the doorway, stood Colin, livid with anger. A petite blonde clung with all her might to his arm, managing but barely to stop him from attacking Harrison.

So this was Alice. No wonder Colin had fallen in love with her. If she was even half so good-hearted as she was lovely, he'd done very well, indeed. Still, Alice was not her immediate concern.

Though it was the most humiliating moment in her life, Jinx squared her shoulders, drew the sheet up to her chin, and rose awkwardly to her knees on the mattress. "That will be quite enough from you two."

Colin transferred his furious gaze from Harrison to her. "Jinx—"

"Not one word from you," she snapped. "Not one word. How could you do it, running away like that?"

"Because we love one another," he snapped right back. "And she feared her brother would not approve of me. What are you doing here anyway?"

"Searching for you!"

"In his bed?" Colin spat. He surged forward again with knotted fists, but Alice planted herself firmly in front of him. She was tiny, but she was determined.

"I will not have my husband and my brother fighting," she swore. "I will not allow it."

"Your husband?" Harrison shouted.

"You're married?" Jinx cried.

"This morning. We're just back from Gretna Green," Alice replied. "So you see, Harrison, it is too late for you to interfere."

"Not if you haven't—" Harrison broke off and his voice dropped. "You haven't, have you?"

Alice gave him a smug smile. "We have," she replied. Colin wrapped an arm about her and looked down at his pretty new bride with such pride and love shining in his eyes that Jinx wanted to cry with happiness. Colin was such a dear. A hardheaded, opinionated dear, but a dear just the same. He deserved every happiness and she had the warm feeling he would find it with Alice.

But then Colin glowered at Harrison, and Jinx knew this mess was far from resolved.

"We are wed," Colin said. "But I doubt you two can claim that. Not yet, anyway."

Harrison had wound a section of sheeting around his hips. Unfortunately it was the end of the same sheet that shielded Jinx from view. She tugged and he tugged back, and they had no choice but to both edge nearer one another.

"This is not what it seems," Jinx began.

"Yes it is," Harrison said.

She glared at him. Whose side was he on? "This is all Colin's fault. It would never have happened if he hadn't run off with Alice."

Colin's eyes bulged with outrage. "He did this to you for revenge? You out-and-out bounder—"

"I didn't say it was revenge. And I won't have such language!" Jinx shouted.

"Nor will I!" Alice concurred.

"I did not do . . . did not take . . . did not—Bloody hell," Harrison swore. He glowered at Colin. "I fully intend to marry your sister."

"I should hope so," Colin muttered, but his tension did seem to abate somewhat.

Jinx's, however, did not. Marry her? Harrison would do that? She felt a surge of emotions: relief, joy. Then, swiftly, gloom. She did not want him to marry her out of a sense of duty.

"I believe it takes two to marry," she said. "And I'm not likely to agree to such a union between us."

"You agreed the moment you accepted him into your bed," Colin stated, stalking right up to the footboard. "It's too late for you to say no now."

"I will not allow you to arrange my life for me, Colin. Not you, nor anyone else."

He threw his hands up in the air. "You must marry him, Jinx, or else you will be ruined. Can't you see that?"

"I must do no such thing!" she retorted.

Then a hand caught her by the arm and her argument was no longer with her brother. Harrison stared down at her, his face serious. "Why won't you marry me?"

"Because . . . Because . . ." She swallowed hard, searching for words. "For one thing, you haven't asked me. You just announced that you would marry me, without ever consulting me about it. You're far too high-handed to make a good husband—"

"Will you marry me?"

That shut up her nervous babbling.

"I . . ." She shook her head and frowned. "I don't think that would be at all wise. We don't get along very well. You know that's so. We disagree about everything."

"The only thing we have disagreed on was whether your brother and my sister should wed. And that has just become a moot point."

"We hardly know one another," she said.

Colin let out a snort, while Harrison grinned at her. "We know each other well enough."

Her cheeks grew hotter still. He had her there. "But . . . but I'm not rich enough for you," she said, beginning to run out of excuses and afraid to point out the only real reason she had to object: that he didn't love her.

Then again, did *she* love *him*?

As Jinx stared at him, at his bare chest and broad shoulders and casually tousled hair, the oddest feeling settled over her. He was smart and loyal, and honorable. He was a generous lover and had a wry sense of humor, and he had the knack of surprising her. Plus, he set her heart to racing and her stomach to churning in ways she couldn't begin to understand.

Did she love him already?

She knew at once she did.

But instead of allowing her gracefully to accede to his request, the fact that she loved him only strengthened her resolve not to let him marry her out of a sense of duty. She shook her head once more and fought back the sting of unexpected tears.

"I don't need a rich wife," he said, scowling now.

"You don't need a wife at all," she whispered.

"Perhaps we should leave," Alice suggested.

"Are you mad?" Colin exclaimed. "Look at them. They're naked."

"Yes. They are," she agreed, taking hold of his arm and steering him toward the door.

"Wait a minute, Alice—"

"No, Colin. Trust me in this. They must settle this between themselves, just as we made our decision absent of the interference of others."

A nervous shiver snaked up Jinx's spine. "I don't think you should go," she said.

But it was too late. Something had passed between Alice and Colin, some shared look that lightened his mood considerably. "Perhaps you're right after all, my dear." He glanced over at Harrison and actually smiled. "I hope you can convince her to marry you, Hartley, else I'll be forced to issue you a challenge, come the dawn."

It was all too ludicrous, Jinx thought as the couple departed, closing the door with a decisive click. All along she had feared Harrison challenging Colin, but instead, her brother had issued Harrison a challenge—albeit a friendly, grinning one.

Oh, but men were a perverse lot.

Still, this madness was not yet done, for she must deal with Harrison and his dutiful, and therefore unacceptable, proposal. She cleared her throat. "You needn't offer for me simply because of what has happened here between us."

"That's not why I offered for you."

He dropped the end of the sheet and sat down beside her. She scooted to the opposite side of the bed, still hiding her nakedness.

"While it's very nice of you to say that, and I appreciate the gesture, we both know the truth."

"No, I don't believe we both do."

She chanced a sidelong glance at him. "What does that mean?"

"It means that you could not possibly know why I

want to marry you. I'm only just figuring it out for myself."

Jinx clutched the sheet tighter around her and tried
not to notice how magnificent he looked in the altogether. "If you mean sex, well, yes, it was very nice. Very
nice," she repeated. "But there should be more to marriage than merely procreation."

At that he started to laugh. "What we did in this bed
was not 'merely procreation.' That was making love,
Jinx. Love."

Love? She couldn't help it. She stared at him wide-
eyed, knowing her emotions were bare to his examina-
tion, knowing that with one glance he would be able to
guess all her secrets.

"Yes, love," he said, answering her silent question. "I
know all about duty, Jinx. I know I must wed and create
an heir for the Hartley line, and I've searched diligently
for a woman to fill the role of my wife. But I was always
looking for her with my head, not with my heart. Only
now do I see that."

He sat there staring at her so earnestly, so sincerely,
that Jinx was overcome. She was not a weeper; she never
had been. Yet tears welled in her eyes, then one by one
spilled over.

He reached out and with his thumb gently smoothed
them away. "I love you, Jinx. I love you wet and bedraggled. And angry and obstinate. And even cross-eyed.
Your every incarnation managed to trap me more and
more securely in your web until now . . ." He lifted his
arms and let them fall in a gesture of helplessness. "I
love you. I only hope you can learn to love me, too."

"I do. I do love you," she blurted out. Then not allowing herself time to think, she launched herself into
his arms. In a moment they were locked in an embrace,
legs, arms, and sheets, all tangled together.

"I love you, Harrison," she murmured between sweet

kisses and hot kisses and seething, writhing kisses. "I love you."

"And you'll marry me?"

She drew her face back from his. She lay on top of him yet she knew she was as trapped by him as if he held her down by force. Love had caught her in its snare. How lovely a thought that was.

"I'll marry you, but on one condition."

He did not look in the least surprised. "And what is the condition?"

"You'll approve of Colin and Alice's marriage."

He laughed. "Oh, that. I conceded that battle to you yesterday."

"You did?"

"When I decided I could not let you go, I knew I would have to accept the rest of your family as well."

"You decided that yesterday?" When Harrison grinned and nodded, Jinx smiled at him, certain she'd never at any moment of her entire life been happier than she was now. Without planning to do so, she'd somehow fallen in love. And so had her soon-to-be husband.

A love match. Fancy that.

Epilogue

THE SUNDAY *TIMES*
LONDON, MAY 30, 1824

These are shocking times, dear readers. Shocking times, indeed.

On Wednesday past, Hartley Hall, that grand manse on Grosvenor Square, was the scene of unanticipated excitement. The Hartley mansion is renowned for its collection of classical bronzes and early weaponry, and also, in years past, for the exquisite balls and receptions hosted by the late Marquis and Marchioness of Hartley. The ceremony on the evening in question, however, was of another sort entirely: the newest Marchioness of Hartley made her unannounced entrance.

Yes, dear readers, your eyes do not deceive you. Harrison Stirling, Marquis of Hartley, is wed, a fact many will find even harder to credit, once advised of the scandalous circumstances of his marriage. But be in no doubt. It is a *fait accompli*. The eligible Lord Hartley is eligible no longer.

Your faithful correspondent has learned that the new marchioness is the former Miss Jillian Benchley, eldest daughter of the late Honourable Stanley Benchley and his late wife, the former Violetta Greenleigh. While I will allow that the bride is rather striking, tall with a graceful carriage and a crown of blazing tresses, she also has an odd air, rather exotic and foreign. One would swear bells tinkle in her wake. If nothing else, she will be a most entertaining addition to town society. No doubt invitations to Hartley House will be greatly in demand for the remainder of this season.

One wonders, of course, about such an unseemly haste to wed. Responding to inquiries about why no announcements were made prior to their union, Lord Hartley remarked only that his marriage is his private concern—his and his wife's.

It is speculated that Lord Hartley purchased a special license to wed in Derby, where he has a fine estate. But others whisper that the wedding took place in Gretna Green. Shocking, if such is true.

Compounding the scandal further, Lady Alice, Lord Hartley's only sister, wed the new marchioness's brother, Mister Colin Benchley. Rumors associated with the second couple had abounded in recent weeks, but as in the case of Lord Hartley, no announcement was made prior to the wedding.

This writer went so far in the search for the truth as to question Clarence Benchley, Viscount Geffen, regarding the sudden marriages of both his niece and nephew into the exalted Hartley line. There was no mistaking Lord Geffen's shock to hear of it, nor his extreme pleasure at the advantageous matches the younger Benchleys had made.

Advantageous, indeed! The Benchley siblings come from a long line of eccentrics who seek out mates in unlikely quarters. However, the current generation seems to have come to its senses. (Though whispers of *arriviste* are bound to be heard.)

As for the Hartley siblings, one must ponder the reasons that led them to the altar. In Lord Hartley's case, he has exercised the right of any well-fixed young lord to marry beneath him if he so desires, assuming the lady is presentable in society. For that same lord to allow his sister to make such a match, however, is far less comprehensible.

However, your faithful correspondent has discovered the true reason for the hasty weddings. The handsome Benchley siblings have apparently captured the hearts of Lord Hartley and his sister. Lord Hartley did not respond directly to my queries, but as he escorted his bride up the steps of her new home, he paused, and in plain view of neighbors, journalists, and servants alike, kissed her.

A love match? Draw your own conclusions, dear readers. But remember always that you have read it first in the Sunday *Times*. Harrison Stirling, Marquis of Hartley, former rake and man-about-town, has been landed by an eccentric country miss, with love as her only bait. A curious situation, indeed. A veritable scandal.

It remains now to be seen whether this year's crop of eligible misses will take a page from Lady Hartley's book. While the mamas angle for titles and the papas root out deep pockets, will the daughters chase after love? This writer certainly hopes so. For the fact remains that this season has, until now, been frightfully dull. *Ah, la barbe!* A trifle more love in the London air might liven matters up considerably.

· · ·

A WEDDIN' OR
A HANGIN'

Jill Jones

For my sister, Janet,
Of th' ancient clan of Frazer.

Chapter One

"A weddin' or a hangin'. What'll it be?"

The clan members gathered closer to the fire, laughing and speculating as they waited for the verdict, although Meredith guessed they knew what was coming. She could scarcely conceal a grin. These people must have heard this folk tale a thousand times, but still, the old storyteller held them rapt.

She was held rapt as well, by his story, by the night, by the enchantment of at last arriving on Scottish soil. It was a long way from where she lived in the mountains of North Carolina, but it felt like home, for since her childhood her grandfather had regaled her with stories such as these about Scotland and their kinsmen, the Clan Macrae. Meredith Macrae Wentworth, the American cousin, now sat with those kinsmen around a bonfire in an open field near the village of Corridan on the northern coast of Scotland. In front of her lay the North Sea, behind her rose the Highlands. Above, the aurora borealis shimmered, punctuated frequently by shooting stars.

She had arrived, she decided, in heaven.

That heaven consisted of more than beautiful scenery,

however. Today, she'd cheered these Macraes through the local Highland games and forged the beginnings of a heartfelt bond with her clan. She gazed into the fire-warmed faces of the people with whom she shared an ancient and honored bloodline. Ruddy cheeks and sun-bleached hair bespoke their rugged outdoor lives. Broad smiles and genuine affection for each other said even more about these gentle giants who had treated her like a true daughter of Scotland. They embodied a noble character, were dignified in their own rustic way.

Until they hit the playing field.

In spite of her enthusiasm for her clan, Meredith was troubled by what she'd witnessed earlier in the day. Unlike the games she helped organize in the States, which were played in a spirit of sportsmanship and camaraderie, the competition today between the Macraes and their rival clan, the Sinclairs, had been fierce and uncompromising, bordering on violence, with insults flying between the players.

Her gaze wandered into the darkness beyond the fire circle where across the field another bonfire lit up the night. Gathered around it were the Sinclairs. The Macraes had filled her ears with tales of an ancient feud between the two clans and made it clear that although the bloodshed had ceased, the enmity had not.

She'd seen the leader of the Sinclairs today, a tall, robust, darkly handsome man who defeated every opponent he faced. Although her clansmen had denounced him, he didn't appear to have horns and a tail as they would have had her believe. He was, in fact, one of the few who had displayed gentlemanly behavior. She'd also found him downright sexy in his traditional Scottish attire. She thought about crossing over to his bonfire to congratulate him on his victories but decided she didn't need to complicate her life by indulging her passing attraction to the Sinclair chieftain. For as much as she would like to remain in this quaint seacoast village, soon she would have to return to North Carolina.

Meredith returned her attention to the storyteller as he completed his yarn. It was a humorous tale, and also sadly poignant, about a young outlaw who was caught stealing cattle from a wealthy laird and who was thrown into the castle dungeon to await hanging. The laird's wife, however, offered to save his life if he would marry their oldest, and very ugly, daughter. The girl was so hard to look at that the thief at first chose hanging, but after several days' consideration in the dark dungeon, he decided instead to let the earl tie the other kind of knot to seal his fate.

Meredith joined in the laughter at the story's end and watched in merriment from the edge of the circle as a bottle of whisky was passed around. She needed no whisky to warm her, for although she was weary, she was suffused with a glow as radiant as the flickering fire. This was all she'd dreamed of and more. At last she was truly a part of the Clan Macrae. And unbelievably, at last she owned a piece of her beloved Scotland. For last night, in a formal ceremony performed entirely in Gaelic, she had inherited the property once belonging to the former clan chieftain, her great-uncle Archibald Macrae.

Uncle Archie, as she'd known him, was her grandfather's brother. He'd kept up with the American side of his family and knew of Meredith's passion for Scotland. She was deeply touched that he would bequeath his belongings to her. She was also pleased that she had managed to follow the Gaelic ceremony. As a hobby she had learned to read and write the ancient language of her forebears, but until now she'd had little opportunity to experience it as a living language.

Along with a small parcel of land and the cottage in which her great-uncle once lived, she had inherited a number of historical artifacts that had been handed down through generations of Macraes. Although honored to be the recipient of these treasures, Meredith wondered if anyone resented them going to an American. That did not appear to be the case, however, for after the ceremony, she had been given a shawl woven in the plaid of the Macrae tartan and wished well by everyone in the community. That's when she'd learned that the village of Corridan was populated mainly by her kinsmen. She smiled to herself and drew the shawl over her shoulders, turning to go. She'd longed for clan kinship; now she belonged to an entire town of Macraes!

Ian Sinclair wished he could share in the enthusiasm of his fellow clansmen as they celebrated their many victories in today's games with drams from his personal stash of fine Duneagen single-malt whisky. He wished, in fact, that he relished the competition as much as they did. As head of the Clan Sinclair, he felt obliged to participate, but a part of him resented the waste of a day. He had so many other, far more pressing problems on his mind than defeating the Macraes on the field of play. He found it depressing, too, that his fellow Sinclairs persisted in perpetuating that age-old feud. At least, he thought, casting a dubious eye on the men who were growing increasingly drunk, in recent years the feud had been confined to this arena. Better that than the sniping and harassment that had gone on before.

Ian turned away from the fire and walked down the lane toward his car, feeling the effort of the day in every muscle. It was nearly midnight, and the sun had at last descended, leaving a twilight sky illuminated with a brilliant show of the mystical northern lights. He was forever awestruck by the aurora borealis and overwhelmed by the majesty of the Highlands of his birth.

He loved this land, fiercely, protectively, although lately he'd begun to wonder why he gave a damn at all. It wasn't a happy land, but rather one that seemed to breed strife. Since he'd become the Sinclair clan chieftain, he had been constantly embroiled in land disputes between his own clansmen. Senseless squabbles, since the land itself had little other than scenic value. Still, Scotsmen would be Scotsmen, he thought morosely. They simply loved to fight.

Then there was the castle. Duneagen, the crumbling ancestral fortress, loomed above him, high on a craggy cliff overlooking the serene bay of Corridan like a dark stain on the night. He had inherited the gloomy pile of stone upon his father's death, and being young and eager, he'd vowed to restore it to its former glory. He hadn't known that like a rapacious monster, it would swallow his already diminished family fortune and wash it down with the profits from the Duneagen Distillery.

Now at age thirty-two, he regretted making that commitment, but he couldn't quit feeding the beast. Ian had dumped so much money into the place in the past seven years, he couldn't afford to stop now and let it fall into ruin after all. He maintained quarters in the one habitable wing of the hulking old palace but most of the time stayed in his small apartment on the estate where he operated the distillery. That way he didn't have to go to bed with his folly every night.

Caught up in his thoughts, Ian didn't see the woman until he collided with her in the darkness, almost knocking her down. Instinctively, he took her elbow. "So sorry. How clumsy of me. I wasn't watching where I was going."

When she turned her face to him, he recognized her instantly—the tall, extraordinarily good-looking redhead he had fancied had been watching him all day. This close to her, even in the dim light, he could see that she wasn't just good-looking; she was beautiful. The fine features of her face were accented with high cheekbones and flawlessly arched brows. Her nose, turned up ever so slightly, appeared dusted with faint freckles, her cheeks burnished by a day in the sun. Although he couldn't discern their color, her wide eyes seemed to reflect the luminescence of the aurora, and her hair spilled in sunset disarray from where she had it fastened on the crown of her head. She had an essence of freshness about her, like the wild wind in the heather, a radiance that seemed to shimmer directly into the darkest corners of his heart. He swallowed hard, confused at the inexplicable emotions she evoked. "Sorry," he managed again.

She offered a tentative smile from the fullness of her lips, but her eyes reflected alarm. "No problem," she replied, drawing her elbow away. "I should have been paying more attention, too."

The woman's lilting accent captivated him further. "You're a stranger in these parts," he said, awkwardly stating the obvious. "An American?"

Cocking her head to one side, she replied curiously, "American in residence, but Scottish at heart." She gave no further explanation, nor did she offer her name. She merely gazed steadily into his eyes for a long moment with a look that turned Ian's insides to molten ore. She blinked at last and smiled a little uncertainly. "I have to go."

Ian didn't want her to go. Women like her were few and far between in northern Scotland, nonexistent in his life. "May I escort you to your car?"

"Don't have one," she answered, turning again to the path. "I'm staying in the village. It's just a short walk." Her tone was dismissive, and Ian got the message. *Thanks but no thanks.*

Discouraged, he watched her go. Only then did it register that she wore the Macrae tartan draped over her slender frame, and he recalled that she'd been with the Macraes all day. So that was it. She knew he was a Sinclair, and she didn't want to be seen with him.

Ian shook his head in disgust and took a shortcut across the field to where his Land Rover was parked. This was the twentieth century, for God's sake. Almost the twenty-first. When were these people going to grow up?

Chapter Two

Meredith was breathing hard by the time she reached the cottage. She closed the door behind her and leaned against it, her heart pounding heavily, not only from the brisk walk in the thin Highland air, but also from her reaction to the tall, solidly built Scotsman with the deep, resonant voice and rich Scots accent. That accent still echoed in her mind, confounding her that she found it so appealing.

She'd known him immediately. Ian Sinclair. The man she'd watched intently all day. He had been handsome seen from afar. He was drop-dead gorgeous close at hand, with dark, piercing eyes and thick black hair tossed across his forehead by the wind. For the slender space of time that he'd held her by the elbow, she had taken in the breadth and squareness of his shoulders, the well-proportioned height of his body, and had been rendered nearly senseless by the raw power of his masculinity. It had taken several long moments and a lot of willpower to gather her wits and move on down the road. She would have liked to have lingered with him there in the darkness, but he was a Sinclair, and she hadn't wanted any of her clansmen to come upon them together. Being literally the new kid on the block, she didn't want to do anything that might jeopardize her new relations with her blood kin.

Removing the shawl and hanging it on a peg by the door, she admitted that she would love to learn more about Ian Sinclair. Maybe she could ask around about him, quietly, discreetly. For something in his touch and in his eyes had reached into the depths of her being, shaking her, awakening her, seeming to call her to yet another aspect of her Scottish destiny. She knew that was nothing more than a fanciful notion, but she was unable to shake it.

The hour was late and she was tired, but Meredith was too keyed up to sleep. She decided instead to examine the treasures she had inherited. Going to the small wooden chest that sat on a stool in one corner, she raised the lid. At a glance, the Macrae treasures didn't look like much. A battered pewter quaich, the traditional Scots drinking vessel. A dirk with a handle made of a stag horn. A scarred old belt buckle. A rag of a scarf in the colors of the ancient Macrae tartan.

At the bottom, carefully folded in tissue paper, was a tablecloth woven of rough wool reputed to be over two hundred years old. Meredith stroked it with the back of her fingers but did not remove it. She'd wait until bright daylight to take it out. An article of that antiquity was surely fragile, and she didn't want to damage it by over-handling. She gazed at the other items, sending a silent thank-you to her departed great-uncle, for he'd given her far more than these material things, more even than the walls that surrounded her. He'd given her a sense of belonging to the clan.

Looking around the small dwelling, Meredith felt more at home than in any other place she could remember. She'd been in Corridan less than three days, and already her Scottish roots were tickling the bottoms of her feet. She knew she must return to North Carolina, but she wished suddenly that she could just stay here.

It wouldn't be that hard, she mused as she heated water for tea. Other than the tiny Scottish specialty shop she owned in her small mountain town, there was nothing for her in the States. Her parents had both died, her best friend had married and moved away. Although she had many acquaintances, primarily through her work organizing the Highland Games each year, she was close to no one. She'd had one love affair during college, but after graduation, he'd wanted the city life, and she couldn't bear to leave her beloved mountains. Since college, there had been no "significant other."

It wouldn't be that hard to just stay here, she thought, where the mountains were even more magnificent, her family ties stronger even though her kin were still unfamiliar. She was getting to know them better each day. Meredith poured hot water over a tea bag, her mind traveling eagerly down the path she'd cleared for it.

It would be easy, actually, she told herself. She could sell the business. She already knew someone who wanted it. The house where she lived was a rental, whereas she owned this cottage. She added rich local cream to the cup, along with a pinch of sugar. Sinking into the pillows of the worn sofa opposite the fire, she sipped her tea, thinking of possibilities. Unbidden, the image of Ian Sinclair popped into her mind. Meredith sat up with a start. He was *not* a possibility.

And yet . . .

She allowed her mind to wander in his direction. What if she hadn't taken off so quickly back there in the parking lot? She closed her eyes, feeling his closeness, remembering the intensity of his eyes gazing into hers. What if . . . Ian Sinclair had kissed her? An involuntary shiver of delight ran through her, and Meredith opened her eyes again with a sigh. Her thoughts of moving to Corridan had made her delusional. He was a Sinclair. She was a Macrae. Their families had fought each other for over two centuries. What made her think that things

could be different between them? The feud was so in-
grained in the minds and hearts of both the Sinclairs and
the Macraes it might even be in their genes by now.
Forget it, sweetheart, she scolded herself, and for God's
sake, get those thoughts of Ian Sinclair out of your mind.

She finished her tea, turned out the lights, undressed
and slipped between the cool sheets. But as she drifted
off to sleep, those thoughts of Ian Sinclair crept back
again and made themselves at home in her dreams.

After a restless night pervaded by dreams of a chance
encounter with a gorgeous American woman, Ian awoke
with the strangest sensation that his left big toe was leaking. He edged himself up on his elbows and looked with
bleary eyes to where his feet had kicked away the covers
sometime in the night, and he saw that indeed his toe
was wet. He flinched as another drop splashed against
it. He looked up. It wasn't the toe that was leaking. It
was the ceiling.

"Damnation!" He leapt out of bed and hastened into
the clothes he'd dropped on a nearby chair the night
before. They smelled of yesterday's games, but he didn't
care. He had to find the source of the leak and stop it
before it sent the ceiling onto his bed in a soggy plaster
rain. He'd just had the roof repaired, and it wasn't rain-
ing outside. That left only one possibility as the source
of the leak. One of the upstairs bathrooms.

Cursing under his breath, he raced up the stairs, feeling the stone floor cold and hard beneath his bare feet.
As he'd feared, water was trickling from one of the five
guest suites his grandparents had created on the second
floor of the old castle and pooling in the central hall.
The prewar plumbing was just one of the many headaches he faced in this renovation project from hell.

Ignoring the frigid water, Ian splashed through the
puddle and went into the adjoining bathroom to find
water spewing enthusiastically from a rusted split in a

pipe. With a jerk and a curse, he closed the cutoff valve, then stood back to survey the damage and decide what to do about it.

The closest plumber was in Corridan, but he disliked calling on the villagers for help. They would come, but in their own sweet time, for they were Macraes, always on the lookout for an opportunity to annoy the Sinclairs. His own neighboring clansmen were spread out over many miles, and he didn't recall there being a decent plumber among them. He decided at last to send one of his engineers from the distillery over to patch things up. That was the trouble with the whole damnable place, he thought, throwing towels on the floor to soak up the water. It was one big patch after another. He didn't have the funds to replace everything that needed it. There was just too much. Roof. Windows. Plumbing. Electric wiring. Stone work. Not to mention furniture and fixtures.

He returned to his quarters below and chanced a quick, hot shower, praying the antiquated pipes would stand the strain. He dressed for work and half an hour later slammed out the door of the only relatively modernized wing of Duneagen Castle. Behind him the once-proud fortress was now a sad mass of weathering stone walls, a legacy he both loved and hated.

Ian considered stopping at the pub in Corridan for a cup of hot coffee to sustain him on the forty-minute drive to Duneagen Distilleries, but as it was already late in the morning, he decided he'd better hurry along to dispatch help for the ailing plumbing in the castle.

The road from the castle wound down from the high promontory and through the village, passing by the cottage once owned by Archibald Macrae. Ian glanced at it as he drove by, wondering if what he'd heard was true, that the old clan chieftain had left it to a distant relative. He gave a silent, sardonic laugh, doubting that a newcomer would be much welcomed in this tightly knit community.

The thought of a stranger in town reminded him of the American woman who had lingered at the fringe of his consciousness all through his morning's difficulties. Who was she? She'd told him she was Scottish at heart, and with her looks, he thought it likely there was Scottish DNA in her genes. From her scarf and her association with his rival clan at the games, Ian guessed she was a Macrae and wondered again if she had dismissed him so abruptly last night because he was a Sinclair. Had this newcomer already let tales of the feud set her against him? If so, she was a fool. A beautiful fool, but someone just as well avoided.

Rounding a corner, he caught his breath, for there, striding into the village on long legs, was the woman in question. She wore close-fitting jeans and a white turtleneck sweater topped with the shawl she had worn last night. Her hair was piled casually onto her head, adding to her height and accentuating the length of her graceful neck. His reservations of only moments before fled, replaced by rekindled curiosity about her.

As there was but a single road through Corridan, he had no choice but to pass by her, and as he did he slowed and glanced through the car window into her face. She looked toward him and their gazes met, only for an instant, but long enough for him to know that if he weren't careful, he could drown in the sea-green depths of her eyes.

He pressed the accelerator and passed her but caught sight of her again in the rearview mirror. He thought she was watching him, as well. A strange sensation stirred within him, as if he had just seen into his future, and he sensed that somehow his fate was entwined with that of the American stranger. Ian looked away, telling himself that was a ridiculous notion. When he looked back again, she was lost from view.

Chapter Three

Angus Stewart pulled his mid-sized Nissan off the main roadway onto a narrow overlook above the village of Corridan. He killed the engine and got out of the car, stretching his arms and legs. It had been a long drive from Aberdeen. The day was fair and breezy, and he took off his hat and turned his face to the warmth of the late morning sun.

Below him, the unspoiled village looked picture-postcard perfect. Like a movie set. The pristine waters of Corridan Bay sparkled and glinted in the bright summer day, and the beach arched in a shimmering crescent between the protective arms of two promontories that rose steeply from the edge of the sea on either side. Perched on the far cliff, hulking over the harbor like a bird of prey, was an ancient weather-beaten castle.

Angus lit a cigarette and surveyed the area appreciatively. New Horizons Cruise Lines had chosen well. Corridan was an excellent site for their project. The deepwater harbor was both scenic and protected, not large but sufficient to accommodate two of the behemoth liners at a time. The village could be renovated just enough to retain the authentic feel of the past and yet provide the amenities wealthy cruise customers would expect. And the castle. It looked like something out of a storybook. Or would, he decided, after extensive refurbishing. It would cost a bundle, but the investors who had hired him seemed not to care.

"We want to create a fantasy port of call that will give our cruising clientele a taste of 'auld Scotland,' " they'd told him. They planned to bring thousands of international tourists each year to what they envisioned to be a first-rate resort that exuded Highland charm and offered a taste of the past. There was to be a world-class golf course, five-star dining, offshore fishing. The castle was to be the playground of patrons who wanted to experience the life of a Scottish laird or lady, at least for a night or two. Angus smirked. The cruise line specialized in making such fantasies come true. All it took was money.

The cynical solicitor had no reservations about what he'd been hired to do, telling himself the resort was a much more profitable use of the land than it had known in the past. The old crofters who lived here were an anachronism, and the land was nearly barren except for the few scraggly livestock they owned. Far better to turn it over to tourism.

Angus finished his cigarette with one long last drag, then flicked it over the railing where it rolled down the steep hillside. He didn't really give a damn what his clients did with the land. All he wanted was to successfully complete his assignment and collect his pay. He'd been hired to purchase the land for the American-owned company, and he was determined to do it quickly and economically, for his fee was based on a sliding scale. The better the price he negotiated for the houses and farms and businesses of Corridan, as well as the castle and its environs, the more money he would make on the deal.

It would be tricky, he knew, for it was an all-or-nothing proposition. He had to convince every single villager to sell out and move away. The same with the chieftain of the Clan Sinclair. Unless he could secure the entire area, the owners of the cruise line could not implement their plans.

Angus Stewart smiled to himself, returned to his vehicle and headed down the hill into the village. He would succeed, for he had worked out an ingenious plan of his own. He was nothing if not one of Aberdeen's most creative solicitors.

Not knowing how long she might stay in Corridan, Meredith had not yet bought groceries for the cottage. With only a cup of hot tea for breakfast, by eleven o'clock she was ravenous. Donning her new shawl, she'd set out on the short walk into the village, wondering what time the little pub served lunch.

About halfway to town, she'd heard a car approaching from behind her, too fast, it seemed, for the narrow road. She turned and watched as a dark green Land Rover careened around a turn in the road. It slowed as it came nearer, and her heart lurched as she recognized the driver.

Ian Sinclair.

He made no attempt to stop and greet her, but she was not surprised after the way she'd hurried away from him the night before. He did, however, cast a glance her way, and his face seemed set in a scowl. A most handsome scowl, but unfriendly nonetheless. She jumped as he suddenly accelerated and wondered if the getaway gesture was in reply to her own abrupt dismissal of him the night before.

Perturbed more by her undeniable attraction to the man than his abrupt exit, Meredith continued on, reaching the old whitewashed pub only moments later. She immediately noticed a bright red Nissan sedan in the adjacent car park. It stood out from the rest of the vehicles not only in color, but also in size and youth. Curious, she wondered if a tourist had wandered off the beaten path or gotten lost. Corridan was remote, and the roads leading here were rough.

She pushed open the door and walked in on a heated exchange between three local men and a stranger who sat at a table in the corner. He was a small fellow, with thinning brown hair combed back from his forehead to hide his encroaching baldness. His beaked nose, slanting forehead, and weak chin gave him the look of a rodent, she decided. Meredith ordered a ploughboy sandwich from the bartender, a man she knew only as "Mac." He nodded, but she could tell he was distracted and had one ear tuned to the men in the corner. She turned her attention to them as well.

"I'm telling you, you have no legal claim to this land," the stranger said emphatically. "I've searched the historical records of ownership of this entire area, and you Macraes were all run out, quite legally, by the Earl of Sinclair in 1815. Back then, it was called a 'clearing,' and the earl cleared the lands around Duneagen Castle as far as the eye could see to run sheep. Any of your families who came back on the land since then did so illegally. You have no valid title of ownership." That said, he sat back with a defiant glare, daring them to challenge him.

The locals rose to the bait. "You're a liar," Sandy Macrae growled, his already ruddy face turning an even deeper shade of red. "Who are ye, and what'd ye come here for? Why are ye sayin' these things?"

Meredith's pulse quickened. Who indeed was this odious little man, and what did he hope to gain by stirring up trouble with such preposterous claims?

He reached into his jacket pocket and took out some business cards and spread them on the table. "The name's Stewart. Angus Stewart. I'm a solicitor, but I'm not your enemy. I came here because I've learned that history may be about to repeat itself, and I want to help you."

"What in th' name of Saint Brigid are ye talkin' about?" Fergus Macrae demanded, standing with legs apart and arms folded, blocking the rear exit with his bulk.

"The Sinclair may be going to do it again. A clearing, I mean. Not for sheep this time, but for tourists."

Meredith's eyes widened even as her heart plummeted to the pit of her stomach. Surely she wasn't hearing correctly.

"Go on with ye," Mac yelled from behind the bar. "There's no such thing in these times."

Angus Stewart gave him a knowing look. "I wouldn't be so sure, if I were you."

The front door opened and several more men from the village hurried in, along with a boy who had been sent to fetch them. "What's up? Why'd y' send for us, Mac?"

"This here bloke's tryin' t' convince us th' Sinclair's about t' do a clearin' round here," Mac filled them in. "Says we don't have legal claim t' our land and that we're about t' be run off it."

Meredith couldn't believe her ears. Surely everyone had some kind of legal title to their property. These families had been here for eons. But then she thought back to the ceremony of two nights ago, when her great-uncle's property was transferred to her. There had been no transfer of a deed. Simply a reading of the will and the consensus of the clan.

Where was the paperwork?

As if reading her thoughts, Angus Stewart asked the villagers, "Where is the proof that you own your land? The papers that verify it was purchased legally? I have searched every kind of record I can think of in towns from here to Aberdeen," he said, then added with a hopeless shrug, "I've not found one shred of evidence that any of this land was ever purchased from the Earl of Sinclair."

The room grew quiet. Meredith saw the men exchange troubled glances, and a terrible fear began to gnaw at her. Could this man's claims possibly be true? Was there a threat of the villagers being evicted? If so, what would he gain from coming to warn them?

Years of fending for herself in the world gave her the courage to confront the man. She edged off the stool at the bar and moved to the front of the crowd. "Who sent you here?"

The man jumped to his feet, obviously surprised at being challenged by a young woman. "The name's Stewart, ma'am. Angus Stewart. I represent a landowner in Aberdeen who, hearing of the plight of the people here in Corridan, has generously offered to relocate all of you at a most reasonable cost."

Meredith heard the rumble of disbelief from the men assembled around her. She herself found it difficult to believe the man's scam was so transparent. "So you're here to sell land?"

She saw the blood rise to redden his face. "I'm here because I'm a decent chap," he replied defensively. "I've gone to a lot of trouble to check out the rumor that there are plans to develop this land into a tourist resort. It's not just a rumor, ma'am. It's a project that's already in the planning stages. And if, as I believe to be the case, the Sinclair does indeed hold legal title to this land, there is nothing to prevent him from evicting all of you to make way for the resort." He turned sympathetic eyes to the villagers.

"For my whole career, I've made my living representing the common man," he told them, "and I'm a Scotsman born and bred. I don't want to see my country invaded by hordes of foreigners in a commercial venture such as this that will mean nothing short of the rape of this glorious land. I undertook my research thinking I could prevent it by disproving the Sinclair's claim of ownership. Then, when I discovered that his claim might stand up in court, I searched for ways to lessen the blow to my countrymen—you, the common people, who will suffer, just as your forefathers did two centuries ago at the hands of the Sinclair."

Meredith looked around and saw that Stewart was punching the right buttons to stir the Macrae hatred of the Sinclairs. But his words rang false to her. She listened carefully as he continued.

"That's when I approached my client to see if he could help. This good man has created a pleasant subdivision on the outskirts of Aberdeen and has not only offered to sell you a plot of land with a new cottage on it at a very reasonable price, he's willing to give each and every person in this village who is being so brutally uprooted a moving allowance."

Angus Stewart dropped his head and studied his hands. Then he returned his gaze to the crowd who stood before him stunned and speechless. "It's not much," he said in a voice just above a whisper, as if emotion were caught in his throat. "But it's something at least to make up for the land you'll be losing. Please, I beg you, consider my offer. Let me help you."

Chapter Four

All hell broke loose in the pub after Angus Stewart left the premises. Mac had sent the boy to the fishermen at the seashore and the farmers in the fields, to alert those who hadn't been in the impromptu meeting that something bad was afoot. In a few minutes, the tiny public house was bulging with men and women wanting to know what was going on.

Robert Macrae, the clan chieftain, moved to the far side of the room and, placing a finger at each side of his mouth, emitted an earsplitting whistle that immediately commanded everyone's attention. When the room was quiet, he briefly repeated Stewart's story.

"Could it be true?" asked one woman, and Meredith heard the edge of hysteria in her voice.

"Of course it's not true. Th' man's off his head," said another, although not sounding convinced.

"It's th' curse . . ." came from a woman standing nearby, an utterance that renewed the general commotion.

The Macrae gave another whistle. "Quiet, all of you. There's no need for panic," he told them. "We own this land. We've lived on it for generations and there's never been a question about it. This is likely some scheme made up by that weaselly solicitor to make a fast quid at our expense."

"Maybe," said Mac, his voice heavy with suspicion, "but then again, maybe he's tellin' th' truth. Maybe th' Sinclair is plottin' t' take over our land."

"If he wants mine," vowed Sandy Macrae, "he'll have t' kill me for it."

"I'll kill him first," shouted another, and the rest echoed the sentiment.

Meredith felt sick to her stomach. This wasn't the Scotland of her dreams. This was more like a nightmare. These people . . . her people . . . had suddenly been transformed from respectable, hardworking Highlanders into a murderous mob by the words of a solicitor. An outsider. Why were they listening to him? Did they think for one minute that they did not legally own their land? Did they believe Ian Sinclair and his clan might actually try to take it from them? Or were they just reacting from the inbred hatred in their hearts for the Clan Sinclair?

She pushed through the crowd and out the door. Leaning against the cool stone wall of the building, she inhaled deeply of the rarefied Highland air, trying to settle her nerves and sort things out. A thousand questions assailed her. *Did* she, or any of them, have legal deeds as proof they owned their property? Were the clans about to go to war? And what on earth did that woman mean by "It's th' curse"?

The biggest question in her mind was, who had hired Angus Stewart? Did he represent some altruistic land developer in Aberdeen? Meredith doubted it. It made more sense that Stewart was in the employ of the man who stood to benefit from taking their land virtually for free. Ian Sinclair. He owned the castle. Now he wanted the village. She'd heard the upkeep of the castle kept him nearly broke, and it made sense that he might try to develop a resort to fund the preservation of his fortress high on the hill. Squinting into the hazy sunlight, she could see it from where she stood and could tell even from a distance it was in sore need of major restoration.

Why didn't he just offer to buy the property from the villagers? But she knew the answer almost as soon as the thought occurred to her—the Macraes would never sell an inch of their soil to a Sinclair.

No, he would logically have had to resort to some more devious plan. Meredith suspected that Ian Sinclair had negotiated with the developer of the Aberdeen subdivision to subsidize the cost of that property, hoping the Macraes, in fear that their land was not their own, would take up the sweet deal and relocate with little resistance. Stewart was just the go-between.

But why, she wondered again, would the Macraes fear for ownership of their land? Unless . . .

Her earlier question reared its head again. Where was the paperwork?

Ian Sinclair looked at the business card his secretary handed him. Why in God's name was a solicitor from Aberdeen calling on him? He had little patience with solicitors even on the best of days, and today wasn't one of them. His engineer had called from Duneagen with an exorbitant estimate of the cost of repairing the plumbing, and a large pallet of his finest Duneagen single-malt had fallen from a forklift while being loaded into a shipping container and crashed onto the dock. Insurance would cover the financial loss, but the thought of the exquisite eighteen-year-old Scotch dripping away between the boards of the creosote-covered wharf was almost enough to make him cry.

"Show him in, but ring me in ten minutes," he instructed his secretary, who gave him a knowing smile.

Angus Stewart cut neither an impressive nor threatening figure. He was short, unhandsome, and seemed somehow . . . oily. "What can I do for you, Mr. Stewart?" Ian asked politely, indicating for the man to take a seat.

The solicitor sat down, placed his briefcase on the floor at his side, and then turned a warm smile on Ian. "The question is, Mr. Sinclair, what can I do for you?"

"I beg your pardon?"

"I know you are a busy man, so I'll get right to the point. In addition to being a solicitor, I am also an ardent fan of Scottish history. I am particularly interested in the preservation of the ancient architectural treasures of our nation, such as Duneagen Castle. I have learned, sir, that you have expended commendable effort, not to mention substantial private funds, to restore Duneagen."

In spite of the man's ingratiating words, Ian was irked that the solicitor had been poking around in his affairs. "And how, may I ask, did you come to know this?"

Stewart's eyes pierced him with a calculating gaze. "As you will discover, sir, research is my forte. It's my job to learn many things on behalf of my clients. I apologize if I have intruded unwittingly into forbidden territory, but please hear me out. I'm here, sir, as the representative of a group of investors who are interested in purchasing Duneagen Castle with the intent of completely restoring it to its former glory."

Ian thought his ears deceived him. "You want to buy Duneagen Castle?"

"My clients do, yes. Might you possibly entertain an offer?"

After the morning's frustration with the plumbing and the prospect of yet another major expenditure on the castle, Ian was almost ready to give the bloody thing away. But his suspicions were aroused. "Perhaps," he replied, "but as you undoubtedly learned in the course of your . . . ah . . . research, it will take a veritable fortune to achieve those ends. What do your clients plan to do with the castle once it is restored?"

Stewart rubbed the palms of his hands together and

gave him another solicitous smile. "Ah, I detect a kindred spirit, a loyal Scot, someone who cares what happens to our historical treasures," he said. "Although it is not of high priority to them, once the structure is sound and the decor authentic to the date of its construction, I believe they will open it to the public, much like Stirling or Holyrood."

The thought took Ian by surprise. He'd never considered anyone would pay to look at Duneagen, it was so remote and inaccessible. Yet, so was Dunnottar, on the eastern coast, and it had become a tourist attraction even in its state of ruin. "They'd have to charge a lot of money to make it pay for the renovations," he remarked.

"Yes," Stewart agreed, "they would."

Ian leaned back in his chair and furrowed his fingers through his hair. "I don't know, Mr. Stewart. That castle is part of the Sinclair heritage. Technically, I am the Earl of Sinclair, although I don't go in for titles. Still, I'm not inclined to sell my clan's crumbling legacy at any price."

He heard Angus Stewart exhale a deep breath. "That is unfortunate, Mr. Sinclair. For if we could work out an arrangement, it wouldn't be necessary to bring to light the rest of what I've discovered in my research."

Ian's head snapped up at the threat inherent in his words. "And what would that be?"

"In delving through the archives of the past two hundred years," Stewart said slowly, "I found something very interesting that took place around the turn of the eighteenth century." He paused, as if for effect. "In 1811, to be exact. Before that date, Duneagen Castle and all the lands surrounding it belonged to . . . the Clan Macrae."

Ian leaned forward, incredulous. "What? What are you talking about?"

"Your forefathers stole it." Stewart smiled pleasantly.

"It never belonged to the Sinclairs, and it doesn't to this day. Duneagen Castle is rightfully owned by the Macraes. Now, that being the case, I could, and should, I suppose, make my offer to the Macrae chieftain down in Corridan. But it's easier sometimes just to go with the status quo. Some things are best left alone, don't you agree, Mr. Sinclair?"

"You're insane."

"I thought you might have a little trouble believing my research, so I took the liberty of bringing along photocopies of the papers I found to prove my point." He snapped open his briefcase and took out a thin sheaf of paper attached with a metal clip. He threw it on Ian's desk.

"When you've had time to study this, I will contact you again," he said, rising. "My clients are prepared to make you a reasonable offer, Mr. Sinclair, but they hope to buy it for a reasonable price. They will, after all, be investing a great deal more than the initial purchase price to bring the castle back to life." He went to the door, then looked back over his shoulder. "Look at it this way, Mr. Sinclair. Something is better than nothing."

Chapter Five

It had been nearly a week since the solicitor named Angus Stewart had dropped his little bomb on the villagers, but nothing had been resolved, and rumors flew thick and fast. Meredith had tried to gain information from Robert Macrae, but he'd explained little, making her feel like an outsider again. Discouraged, Meredith wondered what, if anything, she could do to protect the interests of her clansmen. She wasn't a solicitor, just a twenty-nine-year-old woman with a lot of common sense and a good head for business. She was unsure what good that would do her, a foreigner not only to this country but also to its culture, but she was determined to try to get to the bottom of this. She hoped a walk on the beach might clear her mind and give her some inspiration.

The sun was high in the sky, golden against brilliant blue. To one side, blackened granite cliffs rose in a sheer vertical wall. To the other, the ocean lapped placidly at the coarse sand and splashed over mossy shards of rock that had long ago tumbled from the cliff. Seagulls chattered noisily as they plunged into the frigid waters in search of dinner. But her mind was not on the dramatic natural beauty that surrounded her.

She was worried sick about the solicitor's threat. Her newfound relations were in a turmoil, as not a single one could produce a deed to their property. Although Robert Macrae had assured them that their ownership could be proved by the long history of their possession, Meredith thought he was being naïve.

These people lived a simple, remote life. She doubted that there was even a computer in the village. There were only two telephones, one in the pub, the other in a traditional red phone booth at the center of town. The people of Corridan were provincial and vulnerable, ripe pickings for an unscrupulous solicitor like Stewart and his client, Ian Sinclair.

She was also deeply disturbed by what she'd learned about Ian Sinclair from Robert Macrae. He had told her of the man's almost obsessive determination to renovate the castle and of his cutthroat business practices. She was convinced the Sinclair chieftain would stop at nothing to achieve his goals and believed he might be capable of evicting the villagers to create an income-producing resort property.

She heard barking and looked down the beach, where she saw a black-and-white dog racing back and forth, playing in the shallow waves. Meredith smiled for the first time that day. She recognized it as a border collie, one of those highly intelligent animals used by the Highlanders to tend their sheep. So taken was she with the antics of the dog that she failed to realize that it was followed by a man walking toward her on the beach.

A tall man, with dark hair and broad shoulders. Her heart skipped a beat. Ian Sinclair.

Her first instinct was to run, but suddenly she decided to hold her ground. Maybe this was providential. She wanted answers. Here was the man to give them to her. That was one thing she could do with her common sense. Ask questions. She leaned back against a large boulder, one leg bent and propped on the rock, arms folded, and waited.

If Ian Sinclair saw her, he didn't show it. He walked

slowly but steadily, his hands in his pockets, head down, as if deep in thought. He wore a dark fisherman's sweater and jeans. He didn't look like a villain. He looked, in fact, like a man with troubles as worrisome as her own. For an instant, she considered that maybe he wasn't at the root of this business with Stewart after all.

Surprised by the momentary flash of sympathy she felt for him, Meredith frowned and reined in her feelings. Of course he was behind Stewart. Who else could it possibly be? Her momentary lapse in reason was caused by nothing more than her physical attraction to him. *That,* she told herself sternly, was something she would just have to get over.

The dog spotted Meredith long before its master did and came bounding toward her. She reached down with one hand and petted its head. "Hey, boy. Or are you a girl?" she said, scratching the animal behind the ears. She heard a sharp whistle and the dog took off, racing back to the man who had come to a standstill about twenty yards away.

"I'm sorry if he was bothering you," he said.

"He wasn't. I love dogs. What's his name?"

"Domino. He's not a pet."

Meredith felt as if she'd been scolded for being friendly to the animal. "Then I won't pet him," she returned, annoyed, but she held his gaze defiantly. Silence stretched awkwardly between them, and she became aware that her heart was thundering in her chest, not from fear or intimidation, but from an altogether different emotion. A physical reaction to his presence surged from somewhere deep inside, a totally inappropriate emotional response considering the circumstances. A response called desire.

"What are you doing here?" he asked brusquely. Desire beat a hasty retreat.

"Why?" she replied sharply, recovering quickly. "Is this your private beach?"

He stepped closer, his dark eyes riveting hers until she thought she might squirm. "In Corridan, I mean. What are you doing in the village?"

Meredith was confused by his question and the challenging attitude behind it, but she refused to be bullied. She lifted her chin. "I'm visiting my relatives."

His frown deepened and he gave her a look that said he clearly disbelieved her. "Visiting? Are you sure you're not here on some other . . . business?"

Running into the American woman on the beach was just the perfect capper for the Week from Hell. Ian had nearly exploded in anger after Angus Stewart left, but the questions the solicitor had planted in his mind had disturbed him all week, making it difficult to concentrate on work, which irritated the hell out of him. He'd come to the castle for the weekend to rest and think, and this morning he'd set out early to walk the moors above Duneagen where he usually found solace and peace of mind. He had hiked vigorously for hours, up over the crest and down the far side, his mind so intent on discrediting Angus Stewart's claim that he was unaware that his cousin's dog had joined him.

Unfortunately, instead of finding some reason to believe Stewart was mistaken, Ian had only managed to conclude that the solicitor's claim could be true. His ancestors *could* have stolen the property from the Macraes, although in the ways of the clans of old, possession equaled ownership, and winning a battle was an accepted means of transferring property. After two hundred years of claimed ownership, however, Ian believed the land would be considered Sinclair property, regardless of any lack of official documentation. Still, he'd set his family's barrister onto it just to make sure.

The question remained, who was behind Angus Stew-

art? Who were these investors, and were they as be-
nignly benevolent as he'd maintained? Ian's gut told him
that wasn't the case.

A bothersome thought had occurred to him somewhere along the way. Odd, that two strangers would
suddenly appear in the vicinity within a day or so of one
another. Angus Stewart and the American woman
whose name he still did not know. Was she somehow
involved in this? If she was like so many Americans of
Scottish descent, she was probably a passionate student
of Scottish history. She might have poked into the troubled history of her clan, found one of those instances of
"change of ownership" on the battlefield, and come up
with the charge that the Sinclairs had stolen Duneagen
Castle from her ancestors. Was she rich, though? Did
she have the money to pull off the extensive restoration?
Or was it just a scam to get him to part with his family's
ancestral castle for pennies on the pound?

The irony was that at this point Ian Sinclair would
have welcomed help in restoring the old castle. But he'd
be damned if he'd be bulldozed by anyone, solicitor or
lady, into selling Duneagen Castle.

And now, here he was, face-to-face with that lady,
challenging her with all the raw anger he had built up
over the afternoon. "Are you sure you're not here on
some other . . . business?" He'd blurted the question
that had been on his mind more bluntly than he'd meant
to, and he saw defiance ignite in her deep green eyes.

"What other *business* would that be, Mr. Sinclair, and
why is it any *business* of yours?"

He regretted his brusqueness. He suspected her, but
she hadn't been proven guilty. Hell, he knew nothing
about her. The wind stole a wisp of her russet hair from
its nest and teased it against her fair face, and suddenly,
irrationally, Ian wanted to reach out and touch it. "I'm
sorry," he said, easing out of his frown. "I was out of
line." He attempted a smile. "Ye have the advantage of

knowing my name." His eyes fastened on the flutter of the coppery strand of hair. "May I know yours?"

She tucked the hair behind her ear. "I'm Meredith Wentworth. Meredith *Macrae* Wentworth." She pushed away from the rock and walked toward the shore. "My great-uncle was Archibald Macrae, chieftain of the Clan Macrae until his recent death."

So she was the distant relative . . . "I knew the Macrae," Ian said, watching as she slipped her hands into the hip pockets of her jeans. "He was a reasonable and respected man. My condolences."

She turned to him with a look of surprise. "I didn't know the Macraes and the Sinclairs were on speaking terms."

"Your uncle helped me forge what precarious peace we have between the clans," he told her. "He was a good man. Did ye know him?"

She gave him a dubious glance. "Unfortunately, I never met him. We talked on the phone from time to time, when my grandfather, his brother, was still alive."

" 'Tis too bad ye couldn't come to Scotland before he died."

She dropped her gaze, and he saw a shadow of sadness on her face. "Yes. I regret that I never took the time, and now he's gone." She looked up at him, her expression bleak. "He left me a legacy," she said at last in explanation of her belated visit. "His land and cottage and a few other items of Macrae memorabilia. He knew how much I loved my Scottish heritage."

Enough to have come up with the claim being made by Angus Stewart? Ian wondered. His earlier suspicions came charging back. She might have come to Corridan to claim her inheritance, but he wasn't convinced that was the only reason for her visit. If he could keep her talking, perhaps he'd learn the rest.

"Would ye care to walk down the beach with me?" She shrugged. "Sure. Why not?"

"I take it from your comment about the Macraes and the Sinclairs that ye've been told about our feud. Maybe ye wouldn't want to be seen with me?"

"Clan feuds are, or should be, passé," she told him as they hit a stride along the sand. "I mean, this is 1998."

"Tell that to our kinsmen," Ian laughed, liking her good sense, wishing both their clans shared it. Wishing, too, that he could take her hand as they walked. In spite of his doubts about her, she was the most engaging woman he'd met in years. Maybe ever. It wasn't just her looks, although he was completely taken with her sexy, fresh-faced appeal. She was also bright, sharp-witted. He suspected she could hold her own in any conflict or debate.

Too bad that despite her appeal, despite her talk about feuds being outmoded, she might be behind an action that would undoubtedly ignite a new conflict between the Sinclairs and the Macraes. She would need all those sharp wits and more if she dared pursue the backhanded affair presented to him by her agent, for he would fight her with every ounce of Sinclair blood in his veins. Keeping pace alongside her, enjoying her company, he hoped it wouldn't come to that.

Chapter Six

Later that night Meredith soaked in the old claw-footed tub, wishing she had some of her favorite bath salts to ease the stiffness in her muscles. She was unused to such strenuous exercise. So engrossed were they in conversation, she and Ian Sinclair had walked miles before she realized it.

Meredith ran some cool water and splashed it in her face, thinking about Ian Sinclair. She didn't know what to make of the man. She wanted to distrust him. Did distrust him, actually. Yet, his entire manner was that of a man who cared as deeply as she did about Scotland and his own heritage. Although she'd been unsuccessful in ferreting any suspect plans out of him, he'd told her some remarkable stories about recent flare-ups between their clans, before the two chieftains had worked together to arrive at an agreement that all future conflict would be confined to the playing field. He'd said that like her, he deplored the futile family feud and told her he hoped that the new Macrae would continue to enforce that policy.

He hadn't for a minute sounded like a man about to evict the people of Corridan.

Yet she knew it could only be a bluff, an outward show of goodwill to cover his real intent. She just wished she knew what that intent was. It would help her decide her own intentions toward Ian Sinclair.

Giving up the bath at last, she shivered into a towel and then into a long wool skirt and sweater. The purple and blue Pride of Scotland, a new tartan, had become a favorite, and she loved the way the long full skirt felt almost like a cozy blanket around her legs.

Her stomach growled, and she realized how hungry she was. She took the small leg of lamb she'd purchased earlier at the village store from the tiny fridge and seasoned it with garlic and rosemary. It was too much for one person, but she could make sandwiches from the leftovers. Placing the roast in the oven, she poured herself a glass of wine.

Only then did she allow thoughts of Ian Sinclair to wander through her mind again. How could she learn the truth about the man? Not from her kinsmen, she was certain. They were so prejudiced against the Sinclairs that no one, not even Robert Macrae, seemed to be able to think objectively about them.

She'd learned a little about him on their hike. He was thirty-two, had never been married, and appeared to be a classic type-A workaholic. In addition to Duneagen Castle, he had inherited his family's distillery business, and if what he said was true, he'd managed to turn it from a small "boutique" operation into a firm that exported quality aged single-malt Scotch to countries around the world. Apparently in the process, he had undercut some smaller distilleries, which would have gone out of business if he hadn't bought them out instead. Cutthroat business practices?

In the conversation about his business he'd given her the only hint that he might be inclined to be involved in the plan that Angus Stewart had said he threatened. He'd remarked that the castle renovations drained the profits from the distillery and said that he had to find another way to fund the restoration. By turning Corridan into a tourist trap?

He'd acted strangely about the castle, too, probing her with questions about its history, as if she should know all about it. She'd been annoyed at first, wondering why he was bent on testing her knowledge of the area, but he'd backed off when she'd admitted how ignorant she really was about the history of Corridan. "I didn't even know there was a feud before I came here," she'd pointed out.

He'd grown quiet after that. Introspective almost. He was an interesting man, she decided. And very sexy. Her heart did a little flip-flop at the thought of his dark blue eyes and truant black hair that insisted on falling in disarray across his wide forehead. His ancestry was obviously the dark Celtic Scots, while hers was the fair-haired Vikings. Was the conflict between their families that ancient?

The aroma of garlic and rosemary began to permeate the small cottage, and Meredith started toward the kitchen nook to peel some small potatoes when she heard a knock at the door. Maybe it was Robert Macrae, checking on her. He and his wife, Anne, had been so kind. Not only had they driven all the way to Aberdeen to pick her up from the airport, but they had treated her as if she were close kin. She had grown fond of them in the short time she'd known them. When she opened the door, however, it was not Robert Macrae who greeted her.

"I hope I'm not intruding. I would have called, but there is a definite lack of telephones in the village." Ian Sinclair handed her a large bundle of wild heather, rich and purple in full bloom. "I gathered it from behind the castle. There's also a lack of florists around here."

The earlier flip-flop of her heart turned into manic palpitations. The man at her door was a blend of Prince Charming and the boy next door. He wore a white shirt and tie with a tweed jacket, but instead of slacks, he had on a tartan kilt and knee socks that outlined the muscles of his calves. His hair blew in the light evening breeze, and his eyes twinkled.

"I was hoping ye might go to dinner with me over in Craigmont," he said.

"Please, come in." Meredith found her breath at last and struggled to regain her senses. "I . . . I've already put on a leg of lamb. But there is plenty. Won't you join me here instead?" *Oh, my God, what am I doing?*

He stepped through the small door, filling the cottage with his size and presence. "Are ye sure? It smells wonderful, and I rarely have the pleasure of a home-cooked meal. We can go to Craigmont another time."

"I would enjoy the company," she replied weakly, her defenses destroyed by his good looks and the charm of his decidedly Scots accent. She took the heather and deposited it into the only thing she could find large enough to hold it, a pewter pitcher that stood on the mantel. Then she turned and asked, only half teasing, "You don't think I'd poison a Sinclair?"

He just grinned in reply. "What can I do to help?"

You can leave and let me come back to earth, she thought, but aloud she said, "I'm not used to these chilly summer evenings yet. Would you see to the fire?"

Meredith Wentworth was more beautiful than ever, Ian thought, questioning again the wisdom of his call at her cottage. But it seemed as if he couldn't help himself. His body appeared to be functioning independently of his brain and had brought him here even against his better judgment. Seeing her before him now, a vision in a heather-purple tartan skirt and angora sweater, he wasn't sorry.

After they had parted on the beach, he had returned to the castle intent on doing some book work he'd been unable to finish during the week. Instead, he'd showered and shaved, his mind filled with images of a tall, lithe redhead striding alongside him on the beach, thoughts that tantalized him in a most sensual manner. From there, he'd gone to gather heather, as if it were the most natural activity in the world. He'd never taken heather to a woman in his life.

She might be his enemy, but while they were together, she had given him no indication that she knew enough to be behind the plot to obtain Duneagen Castle. If she knew anything at all about the old fortress, she'd hidden it well behind a screen of feigned ignorance. He hadn't invited her to dinner to continue to probe her for guilt in the matter, however. He found he simply wanted to be with her again. All the same, he planned to keep his ears open.

Ian stoked the fire, then turned to face her. "It's a nice place. What do ye plan to do with it when ye return to the States?"

He saw her hands pause in the stirring of the potatoes she was sautéing on the kitchen stove. "I . . . I don't know."

"I suppose ye could rent it out."

She turned and gave him a slight smile. "Or, I could just stay here. Actually, I've been thinking about that."

Ian was surprised but at the same time strangely pleased at the prospect. The woman looked as if she belonged here, in these mountains, among the wind and heather and wild open spaces. "But what would ye do?" *Restore an old castle?*

"I haven't gotten that far," she laughed as she finished cooking. "It's probably all just a pipe dream anyway." She brought the platter of lamb and potatoes to the table. "Come. Dinner's ready." She indicated a chair. "Will you pour the wine?"

"It was good of ye to have me on such short notice," Ian said, refilling her glass and pouring the stout red liquid into another that was set at his place.

Their eyes met, and he saw a lovely blush color her cheeks. "It was good of you to invite me out," she said at last and raised her glass to his. "I'll take a rain check."

Warring emotions stirred within him as Ian took a seat at her table and tasted the succulent meal she was sharing with him. Even though he suspected she had hired Angus Stewart and had designs on his family legacy, he was at the same time drawn to her so strongly it almost hurt. She was the woman he'd dreamed of someday having in his life, and yet if she were deceiving him with her innocence and charm, that could never be. He had to know the truth.

"Delicious," he complimented her.

"Thanks. Lamb is one of my favorite dishes, but it's hard to find in my small town in North Carolina."

"What's it like there?"

"I live in the Blue Ridge Mountains. They're very much like these mountains, only not as grand. I run a little shop in a small town near several ski resorts, specializing in Scottish gifts and apparel."

Ian nearly dropped his fork. This woman was a shopkeeper? She looked more like a princess. This bit of information, however, gladdened him, for a shopkeeper would surely not have the money to undertake the restoration of a crumbling castle.

"I was wondering where ye got such a bonny tartan skirt," he said. "A person doesn't find that kind of weave in these parts."

Again the rosy blush. My God, but she was beautiful.

"It's not a clan tartan," she said. "It's a new design—"

She was interrupted by a sharp rap at the door, and Ian saw the color drain instantly from her face. "Oh, dear," she said. "That must be Robert and Anne."

Ian understood her distress. Likely she didn't want her clansmen to know she was entertaining a Sinclair. It could be awkward for her in spite of her egalitarian attitude toward the feud. But another thought suddenly occurred to him. What if it wasn't her clansmen who had come knocking? He stood, half expecting to see Angus Stewart at the door.

"Robert!" Meredith greeted her caller over-enthusiastically. "Come in. Have you had supper? I've a leg of lamb on the table. There's plenty."

Robert Macrae removed the flat cap from his head and came into the single living area of the cottage. "Thanks, but Anne's just fed me fine. I just stopped in to see if ye needed—" He broke off in mid-sentence when he saw Ian. The two clan chieftains stared at each other mutely for a long moment, then Robert turned to Meredith, and Ian saw the man's face grow fiery red.

"Sorry. I dinna know ye had company."

Chapter Seven

She had nothing to feel guilty for. Nothing! And yet Meredith could have died when she saw the look on Robert Macrae's face when he'd realized who was dining with her in the cottage. The Macrae had departed immediately without saying another word, leaving Meredith with the distinct impression she had in some way betrayed her clan. It infuriated her.

She turned to Ian and raised her chin just a little. "Shall we finish supper?" she asked, angry at her kinsman, not her guest. If her clansmen would spend more time talking with the Sinclairs and less time fighting, maybe the rivals could at last resolve their differences.

"I'll leave if it would help," Ian offered.

Meredith glanced at the door. "No, damn them. I'm a Macrae, but I refuse to get involved in this ridiculous clan war."

She saw a glint of humor in his eyes. "If ye're a Macrae in these parts, ye'll have little choice."

"Then maybe I'd better just go home." She took her seat and reached for her wine glass, but his hand covered hers and enveloped it in its warmth and strength.

"Or stay and try to put an end to it."

Meredith looked up at him in surprise, wondering if

he could feel her pulse racing. "What on earth are you talking about?"

Ian did not reply immediately, but his fingers caressed her hand, and his eyes probed hers. "I'm talking about giving up certain . . . plans . . . and picking up where your uncle left off in the peacemaking process."

What plans was he talking about? Her plans to return home? Her heart skipped a beat at the thought that he wanted her to stay. "Do you think anyone would listen to an outsider?" she asked, finding the idea of being a peacemaker between the clans appealing. And finding her suspicions of Ian Sinclair melting away. He couldn't be the beast her kinsmen believed him to be. His expression was sincere, his eyes guileless.

"I think you could be very convincing. But it wouldn't be easy. Your kinsmen are a stubborn lot."

"And yours aren't?" Meredith grinned and withdrew her hand at last, not because she took offense at his comment about her relatives but rather because holding hands with him made her feel a little too vulnerable.

They returned to the interrupted meal that was now nearly cold and ate without talking for a few minutes. Then Ian asked, "What is it about Corridan that makes you think you want to stay here? It's a rough place, almost uncivilized in some respects."

"That's its appeal." Meredith busied herself removing their empty plates. "I love the very wildness of the place. I like this rustic cabin. I like the simple ways of the people." She seized the opportunity and added pointedly, "I like the fact that it's not spoiled by tourists and commercialism."

She saw a frown cross his brow, but it vanished as swiftly as it appeared. "I thought Americans worshiped tourism," he said, and she heard an unpleasant sharpness in his voice. Had he thought she might condone such a plan as he had in mind for promoting tourism in Corridan?

"Some do, I suppose. But I don't. I can't bear to visit some of the tourist towns near where I live. They've turned into nothing but streets lined with souvenir shops selling rubber tomahawks and moccasins made in China."

Ian stood and went to stir the fire. "I'd hate to think what tourism would do to Corridan. Those kinds of shops would be selling little plastic replicas of Duneagen Castle. Or fake brass letter openers with the castle on top."

Meredith heard the bitterness in his tone and couldn't believe he was pretending. If this man planned to clear the village to make way for tourism, he was certainly putting on a convincing act to cover his scheme. Perhaps he was not Angus Stewart's employer after all. But if not, who was?

She joined him in front of the fire. "Tourism would ruin this place, Ian. Don't . . . don't ever let that happen."

He moved closer and touched her cheek, sending a delicious shiver down her spine. How she hoped he wasn't working with Stewart.

"It'll not happen as long as I have a say in what goes on around here. But there may be others with different ideas." He looked deeply into her eyes, his expression troubled. What was he implying?

She didn't have time to ask, for slowly, resolutely, he lowered his head until his lips met hers, and when they touched in the most tender of kisses, she forgot all about tourism and clan feuds. His arms enfolded her and drew her against him, and she leaned into the breadth of his chest, closing her eyes to all but the moment. The warmth and strength of his embrace filled some deep emptiness within her, a loneliness she had successfully ignored until now, and she opened her lips to him. His kiss deepened, replacing tenderness with a heightened passion that only whetted her appetite for more.

Then as suddenly as it began, it was over. Ian released her and stood back, holding her away from him. "Why did you let me do that?" he whispered hoarsely.

She couldn't reply, as raw emotion seized her breath and tightened her throat. She hadn't *let* him do anything. Had she? He had simply taken what he wanted. She found her voice at last. "I think you had better leave now."

The chimes of the clock in the hall rang Westminster style, keeping Ian fully aware in fifteen-minute increments of the night that was escaping him. He tossed on the bed, hammered his fist into the pillow, and cursed himself for ever having called on Meredith Wentworth. Because now there was no escaping her. She was under his skin like a thistle, and try as he might, he didn't seem to be able to go back to the time before the kiss. Or to return to objectivity about her. She was everywhere. In his mind, in his senses, in his very soul, it would seem.

And yet, he mustn't be naïve. She had talked a good line about not wanting tourism to spoil the area, but it could have been just that—a line.

Sometime past two A.M., sleep finally claimed him, but it was a sleep filled with unfriendly dreams about a beautiful but deceitful woman who made love to him while behind his back arranging for his demise. He awoke exhausted and filled with renewed determination to discover who was behind the threats brought by Angus Stewart.

"Has Britton called yet?" It was only eight o'clock on Monday morning, but Ian could wait no longer and telephoned his office.

"It's early," his secretary reminded him.

Ian didn't give a damn how early it was. He realized he'd only given his barrister a few days to investigate Angus Stewart's claims, but he wanted answers. If Meredith Wentworth was in any way connected to the scheme proposed by Stewart, he must know it immediately. Before he let any more of his heart slip away.

"I'm going to Aberdeen," he said, making an impulsive decision. "Would you please place a call to Britton's office and see if he can have lunch with me? I should be there by noon. One o'clock at the latest."

It was half past twelve when he pulled into the parking lot of the law firm. George Britton was waiting for him, but from the look on his face, Ian surmised he did not have good news.

"Let's discuss this whole thing over a pint," Britton suggested gently.

They walked the short distance to a nearby pub and ordered lunch, then the elderly barrister held up his pint of dark Scottish stout. "Here's luck to you, Ian. And it looks as though you're going to need it. I've done the checking you asked of me, and what Angus Stewart claims appears to be true. Your ancestors stole Duneagen Castle from the Macraes." Ian stopped drinking the bitter ale in mid-sip and stared at his longtime legal representative.

"You're joking."

Britton set his pint down again and waved a hand in the air. "Now, don't get all upset. That's not to say you don't have legal ownership of it. Lots of land and properties changed hands that way back then. It could, however, mean a court battle to prove your right to the title and castle, and that takes time and money, not to mention the headache."

Ian groaned. "Who's behind it? Who hired Stewart?"

"Stewart's a lowlife. No self-respecting Scotsman would employ him. He works primarily for foreign interests. Does lots of work for American oil companies."

"So who hired him?" Ian asked again.

"I can't prove it, but word is around that a consortium of American investors who own a large cruise-line company has eyes on Duneagen Castle and the town of

Corridan. They want to turn it into some sort of resort, a fantasy port of call that will give their rich customers a trip back in time, so to speak, so they can play at being in olden-day Scotland. It sounds like the kind of thing Stewart would get involved in. What's he offered you?"

Cold disappointment knifed through Ian. An *American* cruise-line company? Did Meredith work for them? She claimed to be the heir of Archibald Macrae, but the arrival of an American in Corridan at this time seemed just too coincidental. His suspicions that she was somehow involved in this development scheme were too strong for even the memory of her kiss to overcome.

Ian answered Britton's question, and the barrister winced. "Sounds like it's time for pre-emptive action."

Ian listened distractedly as George Britton rambled on, assuring him that the court would uphold Sinclair ownership of Duneagen Castle, but his mind was on Meredith Wentworth. *Please don't let her be involved in this,* his heart pleaded. *Don't be a fool,* his mind warned.

At last he could stand it no longer. He laid a twenty pound note on the table and stood to go. "Sorry, old chap. I can't wait for lunch. By all means get the ownership thing sorted out with the courts as quickly as possible. And keep an eye on Stewart, won't you? He seems a devious little devil. Call me if you learn anything more about these Americans, too."

Before George Britton could overcome his surprise at his client's sudden departure, Ian was out the door, car keys in hand. Nothing, not even ownership of the castle, was more important to him at the moment than to hear from Meredith's lips that she was not involved in any of this. He only hoped he could tell if she were lying.

Chapter Eight

The grocer was polite but not friendly. The people she passed on the street either barely nodded, stared at her openly, or looked the other way. No one greeted her warmly as they had done previously. Meredith knew she was being shunned. It didn't take long in a little town for word to spread that she'd been seen with the enemy.

She'd thought Robert Macrae was her friend, but she'd quickly learned that even within a clan there were limits. And she'd gone over that limit last night in inviting Ian Sinclair to dinner.

After her brief and somewhat unpleasant visit to the village to pick up a few supplies, she returned to the cottage and donned her hiking boots, then set out with a sandwich and a bottle of water to climb into the high moors. Maybe up there at the top of the world, the brisk wind would clear her mind, and she could put things into perspective again.

Her mind wouldn't let her wait until she had reached the heights, however. It kept going over and over her dilemma with each step she took: she was a Macrae wanting to be friends with a Sinclair. The clan's treatment of her angered her, for although Ian's visit hadn't been planned, she'd had every intention of using it to find out what he was up to, which would have helped them all. They had been discussing tourism, edging around the subject, when, well . . . the kiss had gotten in the way. Meredith blushed at the memory but didn't try to chase it away. At the moment, she felt far friendlier toward Ian Sinclair than she did toward her own clansmen.

The fact was, however, she'd missed her chance last night. The opportunity had come and gone for her to ask Ian point-blank for a straight answer about his intentions for the village. She wanted to see him again but had no idea if that would happen. And if she did, what made her think he would tell her the truth if she asked? Her feelings for Ian Sinclair were dangerous, for she was strongly attracted to him, and she was liable to believe him no matter what he told her. It horrified her to think she might truly be consorting with the enemy.

By the time she reached the crest of the moor high above Duneagen Castle, she was miserable and conflicted. She sat on a rock and bit into the sandwich but found it hard to swallow. She considered just packing up and leaving Corridan. Maybe she didn't belong here after all.

She didn't want to go, though, until she knew the fate of her own property, if nothing else. There was little she could do to defend it from the other side of the ocean if Ian tried to remove the villagers. She had to find out what was going on. But how? She had no car. She couldn't just pop over to Aberdeen and check out Angus Stewart. Nor did she have any idea how one went about going through property records in Scotland. Even before last night, Robert Macrae had not wanted her involved, and she was certain he would not welcome her intrusion into village affairs now. It seemed there was only one option. Ian. She must find him again and demand the truth. And be strong enough to handle it if he told her he *was* behind the plan to evict the villagers. She just couldn't believe it of him, but then, she didn't know him very well.

A drop of rain splashed against her face, then another and another. Meredith looked up. The sky was boiling with dark clouds. A storm had brewed over the mountain without her even being aware of it. She swore under her breath and started back down the slope along a path. The rain fell in large, cold drops, pelting her and soaking her light cotton sweater and jeans. She quickened her step, hurrying as fast as she dared, and slipped on the slick mud and fell. This time she swore out loud. She was unhurt, except for a scrape on her right palm where she'd tried to catch herself, but her jeans were slimed with mud.

With greater caution, Meredith descended the moor, keeping to the path, although it was not the way she had come. She rounded a large boulder and to her surprise found herself squarely in front of Duneagen Castle. Without thinking, she dashed for cover beneath an eave. Maybe she could wait out the storm here instead of squishing her way home in the rain.

Meredith shivered in her wet clothes and wondered if Ian might be at the castle. His Land Rover was nowhere in sight, but there might be a garage somewhere. She felt her hair and knew it was disheveled. Her hands were dirty from her fall and wiping them on her grimy jeans didn't help. She decided not to knock on the door after all. If he were home, she didn't want him to see her in such a mess.

After fifteen minutes, the rain showed no sign of letting up. Uncomfortably cold and damp, Meredith decided she had little to lose by going on to her cottage. At least there she could take a hot bath and have some tea. Clenching her jaw, she stepped out into the downpour and walked as fast as she could down the road that led to the village. She'd gone less than half a mile when she saw the headlights of a vehicle coming toward her, and she moved to the side of the road. The driver slowed as he approached her, and she saw with dismay that it was a dark green Land Rover. The laird had returned to his castle.

He opened the passenger door. "Get in."

Numb with cold and weary to the bone, she didn't argue. He turned up the heater and continued on up the hill.

Meredith had thought he would take her home. "Where are we going?"

"To the castle. We have some talking to do."

She looked like a drenched urchin as she shivered in the seat next to him, and Ian wished that he could comfort her rather than accuse her. He longed to hold her and kiss her as he had last night, but before that could happen again—ever—he had to know who she really was and why she was really here.

He parked as close to the front entrance of the residential wing as he could and helped her inside the castle. "Here," he said, covering her shoulders with a throw that was slung over the back of a sofa. He led her to a chair by the fireplace. "I'll start a fire. It'll help dry ye out." He saw her trembling uncontrollably and knew a fire wouldn't do it. She needed dry clothing. Now.

"I have another idea, if you're comfortable with it."

She turned her enormous green eyes on him, and he felt his heart go into meltdown. "What's that?" she asked.

"Ye, uh, ye need to get out of your wet things. Obviously, I don't have anything your size, but I do have a large robe ye could wear until your clothes dry out."

"Do you have a hot shower to go along with?" She gave him a shy grin. "I'm freezing."

Ian thought about the plumbing and prayed that it would hold together for her. "Aye, sure. Come along. I'll build that fire while ye bathe." He led her up the stairs to one of the guest rooms, his mind overheated with thoughts of Meredith Wentworth naked in the shower. "There's soap and shampoo and the like in the bathroom. Please make yourself at home. I'll bring the robe and hang it in the bedroom."

He left her and went down to his room where he found a heavy woolen robe in his closet. It was over-sized, a dark brown plaid, not at all feminine. So much the better, he thought, returning upstairs with it and hanging it on a valet stand. As sexy as she was even in dirty jeans, he would need all the defenses he could muster to stay objective. They would be together only for a short time, but there was little chance of being inter-rupted. He must use this opportunity to learn whether or not Meredith Wentworth had come to Corridan in the employ of the cruise-line company.

When she returned to the large main hall, Ian had a fire blazing in the huge stone hearth. He looked up and knew his first line of defense had failed. Fresh from the shower, she was more beautiful than ever, despite the drab brown robe. Her damp hair fell in golden-red waves past her shoulders and played seductively around the open neckline of the robe. Beyond that neckline, he caught a hint of the delectable curves that he knew lay hidden beneath the woolen fabric. She gave him a smile that finished his destruction.

"Got socks?" she asked, curling one bare foot across the other.

He went to her and picked her up, carrying her easily to the overstuffed chair closest to the fire. He took the bundle of wet clothes from her and set it on the hearth. "Your feet must be like ice. Wait here a minute." He dashed back into his bedroom and found some heavy, ugly brown boot socks that would complete her ensem-ble perfectly, he thought wryly. It didn't matter. The woman was stunning in anything she wore.

And in nothing at all, he imagined. Damn. He

shouldn't be thinking things like that. Stay in control, he warned himself as he returned with the socks. But he felt the hard evidence that his body wasn't listening to him.

He watched as she put on the socks and longed to run his hands over the smooth skin of her exposed calves. He fought to stay composed, but it was a losing battle.

"I'd offer ye tea, but I don't think I have any in the place. I don't stay here often."

Meredith stood up and adjusted the tie belt, the only thing that held the robe closed. "I don't need tea, thanks. The bath took away the chill. But I need to get these things dry. May I hang them by the fire? I can't very well go home in your bathrobe," she added with an uncertain, almost embarrassed little laugh that he found endearing.

Ian didn't want her to go home. At all. Ever. Odd, he thought, how she seemed to light up this gloomy old place. He rigged a line of twine between a table and the back of a chair, and it sufficed to support her jeans, sweater, and delicate lingerie. He turned his eyes away from the latter. It made his already urgent problem even worse.

"No tea, but how about some whisky? I have a store of Duneagen's finest." He needed a drink whether she did or not.

"Okay, but just a tot."

He filled two small dram glasses with the finest single-malt Scotch available anywhere and was suddenly proud that he could offer it to her. He'd screwed up a lot of things, but his management of the distillery had led it to a worldwide reputation for excellence. He handed her one of the glasses, then raised his to her.

"Here's te us, fas like us, damn fa, and they's all deed."

She laughed out loud. "What's that?"

"Why, an 'auld Scottish toast.' I'm surprised ye

haven't heard it." He savored her childlike delight.

"I'm sure there's lots I haven't heard," she murmured, taking a sip. "But I'm willing to learn."

Her eyes held his, and the room grew so quiet all that could be heard was the sound of their breathing. "I'd willingly be your teacher," he whispered. He knew better than to step closer, but he did anyway, and suddenly she was in his arms. He tasted the drink on her lips and it was sweeter than anything he could imagine. "Ah, Meredith Macrae," he breathed. "What is it you're doin' in my arms?" He ran one hand through her silken hair, and she tilted her head back and looked up at him with eyes that reflected a passion as hungry as his own.

"Weren't you going to teach me something?"

Chapter Nine

Meredith seemed consumed by heat, from the bath, the fire, the whisky, and the desire that raged through her body. She hadn't meant for anything like this to happen, but now that she was in Ian's arms, she never wanted to leave. She let him take the dram glass from her, then lift her gently and carry her into an adjoining room where he laid her on an enormous bed.

"Meredith?"

She heard her name spoken from somewhere that seemed far away, but when she opened her eyes, Ian's face was intimately close to hers, his eyes seeking permission.

"Yes, Ian." She splayed her hands over the strong features of his face and drew it to hers. "Yes, please." As she kissed him, she heard a small groan escape his throat. She felt his fingers loosen the tie belt, then draw the robe away, exposing one side of her body. While his lips explored her mouth, his hand explored that side, slowly, tantalizingly, moving with exquisite deliberation down the length of her neckline, across her breast, past the curve of her waist, over her hip, and back around, coming to rest on the soft mound of her pubic curls. With a sharp intake of breath as he began to intimately explore her, she arched against him, something deep within craving the fulfillment promised by his touch.

Moments later, she felt him shift his weight across her body. He removed the other half of the robe and performed his magic on that bare skin. Meredith thought she might die from the need he was building within her. Never had she been loved like this. It was as if he were worshiping her with each caress, and with each caress, her desire flamed, obliterating her reason, destroying all caution.

Just when she thought she could take no more, he stopped and drew away from her. "I want to see ye," he said, kneeling beside her, removing her arms from the huge sleeves of the robe. His voice was thick with his own desire as his eyes wandered from the top of her head to the tip of her toes. She lay naked and unashamed before him and let him devour her with his gaze.

"I want to see you, too," she murmured at last and watched in pleasure and anticipation as he removed his shirt, then stood and took off his pants and shorts.

His body was as magnificent as the Highland mountains themselves. Broad shoulders settled across a muscular chest before his torso tapered toward his hips. His legs were long and well formed, his arms brawny. She saw the strength of his desire and held out her arms to him, for it was her desire as well.

He knelt across her and entwined her fingers in his, his eyes never leaving hers. He entered her gently, easing into her with the same slow deliberation, driving her passion out of control. Again she arched into him, and she felt the first flicker of that sweet satiation her body demanded. She wanted more, but he moved away, only to return with a deeper thrust, and she rose to meet his lover's assault. He smiled down at her, and she felt their bodies begin to move in a rhythm that carried her higher and higher with each stroke. She tried to keep her eyes open, locked on his, but the sensation was too exquisite, and she closed them as she cried out when he brought her to a crescendo of delight. He crested the wave with her, and she felt the delicious pulse of his body within her, filling her, making her whole.

He lay down lightly upon her, wrapped one leg around her, then turned to one side, holding her against him in their intimate embrace. "Oh, my God, Meredith," he whispered, "what a woman ye are."

She was unable to speak or move or think or scarcely even breathe. He was everywhere she wanted him to be. Around her, within her, in her mind and heart, body and soul. She may have made a terrible mistake in this, but this was an experience she would cherish for the rest of her life, no matter what the consequences.

"I . . . don't generally fall into bed with virtual strangers," she said, finding her voice at last, teasing the hair on his chest with one finger.

"Nor I." He drew her even closer with his leg. "You've made me lose my mind, lass."

She looked into his eyes. "Lass. I've never been called a lass before. It's so . . . Scottish."

"Do ye like it?"

"I do."

"Hmmm. Did ye hear what ye just said? Ye said, 'I do.' I like the sound of that."

Meredith blinked. He couldn't mean . . . "What are you talking about?"

He kissed her forehead. "Do ye suppose a Sinclair could marry a Macrae without everyone in the territory taking up arms?"

Meredith held very still. Marry? Was he serious? "Is that a proposal?"

"Aye, 'tis."

"But . . . but we barely know one another."

"I thought 'twas rather well-acquainted we just became."

Meredith's heart began to race all over again. This couldn't be happening. She'd known this man less than a week and, although she was overwhelmingly attracted to him, there were still many things about him she distrusted. Falling into bed with him might be bad judgment, but marrying him so hastily could be disaster. She placed her hand on his chest and drew away slightly.

"When you picked me up on the road, you said we needed to talk about something. Is this what you meant?"

Ian shifted and they separated. Meredith felt the loss and shivered. He threw the bedspread over them and drew her back into his arms. "No, actually, it wasn't what I had in mind."

No one was more surprised than Ian Sinclair when the proposal of marriage came out of his mouth. Marriage was something he'd thought he might consider one day, but not for years yet. He'd been married to his work and to the ongoing project with the castle. There simply hadn't been time to think about it, or a woman worth thinking about.

Then along came Meredith Wentworth, Meredith *Macrae* Wentworth, and suddenly marriage seemed the most logical step in the world. If, that is, they could settle the rather major issue that still loomed between them. He held her close and jumped into it with both feet.

"Ever heard of a company called New Horizons Cruise Lines?"

"I've seen their ads on television. Why?"

"They want to buy this castle."

Meredith turned wide eyes on him. "What on earth for?"

"The same reason they're after the land in the village. They want to run us all off and create a vacation resort here as one of their fantasy ports of call."

He jumped when she bolted out of his arms and sat up, clutching the bedspread to her. "Why, that little weasel. He's playing both ends against the middle."

"It wouldn't be Angus Stewart of which ye speak?"

She jerked her head toward him, and he saw the fire in her eyes. "What did he offer you? Or should I say threaten you with?"

Ian knew in that instant that Meredith had nothing to do with Stewart's deceit, and joy surged in his heart. He told her the details and watched as her eyes widened in astonishment and then narrowed again in disgust.

"Why, he's the sleaziest, slimiest bastard I've ever run across."

"And I thought ye were a lady," Ian teased, but agreed wholeheartedly with her opinion. He was curious, though, as to how she knew about Stewart. She must have heard something in the village. "Your turn. What do ye know about him?"

"He came to the village and informed my kin that they don't own their land, and that you, the mighty Earl of Sinclair, were about to enforce another clearing. He said you were going to turn the village into a tourist attraction. He failed to mention New Horizons Cruise Lines."

It was Ian's turn to explode. "I would never dream of such a thing . . . even if I owned the land! Which as far as I know, I don't."

Meredith snuggled down next to him in the bed. She was quiet for long moment, then whispered, "I owe you an apology, Ian. Like the rest of the Macraes, I've doubted you. I didn't know if Stewart's claim was true or not. That's what I was trying to find out last night when I started talking about tourism."

Ian drew her closer. "I owe ye an apology of my own," he said softly, kissing her hair. "Stewart showed up in my office just a day or two after ye arrived in Corridan. When he made his threat, I concluded that it was just too coincidental that ye both came to this remote little village at the same time. I thought ye must somehow be involved with him, maybe had even hired him."

"What! You couldn't—"

"Wait a minute. It gets worse," he added unhappily. "Last night, ye convinced me that ye couldn't possibly be involved in a scheme to promote tourism. By the way," he added with a small laugh, "ye also stole my heart." He felt her move closer, but it didn't make his confession any easier. "Today, when I found out that the cruise-line company was American, I was suspicious all over again. It was one thing to think ye, a stranger, might be about to betray me, but after last night, ye weren't just a stranger anymore. Ye see, I'd fallen in love with ye, and I couldn't bear it if ye were really only just a beautiful enemy." He paused, then added, "That's what I wanted to talk about."

She looked up at him with a bemused smile. "So what am I? Friend or foe?"

"Would I propose to a foe?"

"I'm a Macrae," she reminded him, "and you didn't know the truth about Angus Stewart's scheme when you proposed."

"I knew ye, and that's all I needed to know."

Chapter Ten

The rain relinquished its stranglehold on the mountains, and Meredith let go of her last doubts about Ian as the two of them lay on the bed, intermingling discussion of the solicitor's scheme to take Corridan and the castle with lovemaking and talk of what-ifs that only the day before would have seemed impossible. With some effort, she managed to convince him that they should postpone any talk of marriage until the issue of land ownership was clarified and any misunderstandings sorted out between the Macraes and the Sinclairs. "It would just give the clans something else to squabble over," she pointed out. "Neither clan is going to like the idea."

She didn't tell him that her real reason for deferring his proposal was that everything had moved too quickly where her heart was concerned. She knew she'd fallen in love with Ian, but marriage, so hastily . . . that was something else.

She watched him now as he drove away and missed him immediately. *Is that what it feels like to be married?* Closing the door to the cottage behind her, she looked around the cozy dwelling. Only days before she had considered how easy it would be to remain here. Now she was trying to talk herself out of it. Why? The answer, she knew, was fear. She thought of Ian's proposal, delivered in a moment of profound intimacy. Had he really meant it? They scarcely knew one another.

Yet, she could not dismiss his proposal out of hand, for Ian Sinclair was unlike any man she had ever met. There was something, some invisible tie, some bond, that had stretched between them the moment they'd met. Had he felt it, too?

Rattled, Meredith changed clothes and made tea, marveling at how her priorities could shift in so short a time. Her gaze came to rest on the chest in the corner containing her Macrae treasures. *Could* a Sinclair marry a Macrae without creating trouble? She recalled the dark look on Robert Macrae's face and the way she'd been shunned by the villagers simply for having dinner with a Sinclair. What on earth could have caused such a lasting feud in the first place? With a rueful shake of her head, she lifted the chest and brought it to the table. She opened the box and removed the items one by one. She was proud of her heritage but not proud of the continuing involvement of her clan in a feud. Because of it, the treasures in this chest seemed somehow tarnished.

At the bottom of the chest nestled the ancient woolen tablecloth. She eased it out and carried it carefully to the couch where she unfolded it to its full size and draped it gingerly over the sofa. Although it had yellowed with age, after two centuries it was still a piece of great beauty, handwoven and decorated with a wide band of embroidery around the hem.

Meredith held it up to examine the fine stitching but could find no familiar pattern to the work. Extending her arms, she studied the overall effect and suddenly realized that the border wasn't sewn with any ordinary embroidery stitch. The design was created from ancient Gaelic symbols strung together into words, words that were in turn stitched into sentences. Her breath caught in her throat.

Locating the beginning of the embroidery, she slowly

began to read the words aloud. The style was foreign to her ears, the words difficult to translate, but as she worked her way around the cloth, she was astounded that she was reading the story of the young cattle thief who avoided hanging by marrying the laird's ugly daughter!

At first she thought the tale must be a well-known folk story that someone had whimsically turned into an embroidery pattern, until she came upon the name of the laird—Duncan Macrae. And that of the thief—Peter Sinclair.

She murmured a quiet expletive and read on. The embroiderer apparently was none other than the ugly bride herself, and she stitched a far less humorous tale into the following lines. According to her account, her father and mother both died shortly after her marriage to the thief. Her new husband then murdered her brother, the legitimate heir, and claimed the land and the castle for his own.

Duneagen Castle.

Meredith's hands began to tremble. Peter Sinclair soon after cleared his newly acquired land that was occupied mainly by Macraes. The towns were sacked and burned and were replaced with huge flocks of sheep.

Dropping the edge of the cloth, she gazed unseeing into the room. So Angus Stewart wasn't lying! If this were the truth, a Sinclair *had* stolen the castle and land from the Macraes. Maybe Ian did not own the castle after all.

But if Peter Sinclair's clearing had been somehow sanctioned by the government, as many were in those days, then the villagers might have no claim to their land if they couldn't prove it had been purchased from the Sinclair.

Meredith was dumbfounded. No wonder the Macraes hated the Sinclairs. Even she felt indignant. But these events had happened some two hundred years ago, she reminded herself. It was time for both clans to get past them.

Meredith bent her head to translate the remaining short lines. That Peter Sinclair's wife had hated him was evident from what she read next:

> May the dark of the night curse the name of
>   Sinclair,
> May strife on the land be his penance,
> 'Til the day comes to pass that a true-blooded
>   heir
> Of Macrae returns to the palace.

Strife on the land. The feud. Until recently, continuing bloodshed on both sides. *Was* the land cursed? Meredith tried to dismiss the thought, but couldn't. What was a curse except something that when believed often came true, like a self-fulfilling prophecy? She recalled the woman at the pub saying it was "th' curse" that had brought Angus Stewart and his threat to their doorsteps. If these people had believed in such a curse for all this time, it would take nothing less than changing the complete mind-set of two clans of very stubborn-headed Scots to make peace between them. It seemed impossible. Her eyes fell on the final two words of the embroidery, the signature of the writer: Megan Macrae. The ugly bride. Meredith could almost feel her pain.

The thought of Megan Macrae, however, also gave her an idea. A Macrae had cast the curse. Could another Macrae dispel it?

Ian left Corridan both encouraged and anxious. It had been three days since he had asked Meredith to marry him and though she had not turned him down, still she had not agreed. He knew she was wary of such a hasty wedding, but he had no doubts in his heart whatsoever that she was the woman destined to be his life's mate.

In addition to her concern about their brief courtship, Meredith had also remained adamant that the feud be resolved before they wed. "How can we expect to live happily ever after if neither of us can be part of our clans?" she asked, and he knew it was a valid concern. At first, uniting the Sinclairs and the Macraes had seemed an impossibility. Then she'd shared with him the archive she'd discovered embroidered into the hem of the tablecloth and with her innate good sense had suggested a plan that might resolve both his and the village's problems with Angus Stewart. It was not a solution to the two-hundred-year-old feud, but it had led to surprising cooperation between the clans.

He accelerated and climbed the steep grade that led out of the village. He had just enough time to drive to Craigmont, pick up his special guest, one that no one, especially Meredith, expected, and return for the meeting that had been called at the church.

An hour and a half later, he pulled into the car park beside the small white chapel, and his heart gave a little lurch. Would it work? Not just Meredith's plan, but his own as well? He turned to the man who sat next to him. "Wish me luck, Reverend."

Inside, Robert Macrae stood at the front of the church. His clansmen had claimed the pews on the right-hand side. On the left, a surprising number of Sinclairs had gathered. Neither group was cordial to the other, and the Macrae wore a skeptical frown. Ian took a deep breath and strode to the front to greet the rival chieftain. Where was Meredith?

Moments later, the door opened again, and Ian looked up to see a familiar, beloved figure enter the church. Meredith was more beautiful than he'd ever seen her, with her hair falling in coppery waves over the purple angora sweater and the tartan skirt flowing to her ankles. She looked at him with unmistakable love in her eyes, and he took heart.

Behind her followed a not-so-beloved figure. Angus Stewart. Ian enjoyed watching the confident smirk on his face shift to shock and concern at seeing the clan chieftains together. Robert Macrae had invited the solicitor to the meeting at the church, telling him that the villagers had come to an agreement. Ian had then called him and asked for a meeting just two hours later. Obviously, Stewart had come to Corridan believing he had two deals in hand, one to complete at the church, the other just afterward. Ian laughed. His deals would be completed, all right.

"Now see here, Sinclair," Angus Stewart called out, pushing past Meredith and hurrying down the aisle. "Just what do you think you are doing here?"

Ian let him get almost to the front, then replied coldly, "Lower your voice, Mr. Stewart. Ye are in the house of God. Please take a seat."

Stewart stopped in mid-stride, glaring at Ian. "What the hell do you think—"

Ian, a full head taller than Stewart, glared down at him. "Shut your mouth, Mr. Stewart. You've had your turn at talking. Now it's time to listen." Ian took Stewart by the arm and forced him to take a seat in the front pew. Then he looked up and nodded to Meredith to join him. When she reached his side, he took her hand, and he heard a communal murmur from both sides of the church.

Ian gave her hand a reassuring squeeze, although his own pulse was beating rapidly. He turned to the congregation. "I thank ye all for coming," he began. He looked from one side to the other. " 'Tis been a long time since the Macraes and the Sinclairs shared a house of worship." He heard a rustle of disconcerted laughter before he went on. "It's been too long. And for too long our clans have fought one another. 'Tis time to put an end to these useless hostilities. The Macrae and I, and this lovely lass, are here today to ask ye to bring this feud to a close."

Meredith was deeply touched by the sincerity in Ian's plea but even more by the effort he had made to honor her wishes. She knew it had taken a lot of both courage and patience to work with Robert Macrae over the past few days to bring this meeting about. None of them had any idea whether their plan would be successful, but they had all three agreed that the time had come to bring everything into the light of day and try to get their fellow clansmen to see the futility of their ongoing quarrel. They had chosen the church for the meeting place, doubting that anyone would resort to violence within a house of worship.

In the silence that followed Ian's startling request, Meredith saw people lean forward, astonishment written on their faces but curiosity precluding them from interrupting Ian. Pride swelled in her heart to see that he had the power to influence both clans and the integrity to use that power for peace. He was a man she would be proud to marry. One day. She listened as he continued.

"For two centuries, this feud has cost both our clans the blood of our brothers. More recently, it might have cost us all everything we own." He nodded at Stewart. "This . . . ah . . . gentleman"—he emphasized the last word cynically—"almost managed to use our animosity toward one another to steal away your village," he said to the Macraes, "and your clan's castle," he added, addressing the Sinclairs.

Angus Stewart burst to his feet with indignation, but Ian pressed him back into the bench with firm hands on both shoulders. " 'Tis your turn to listen, remember?" At the clear threat in his voice, the man retreated, and Ian continued.

"On Monday last I was visited by Mr. Stewart, who informed me that he represented a group of investors who wished to buy Duneagen Castle and restore it, purely from their loyalty to Scottish heritage. But he also threatened that if I didn't sell it, and at a 'right' price, he would reveal that his research shows that the Sinclairs don't own the castle at all."

The silence was shattered with a buzz of amazed speculation, but Ian held up his hands and continued. "Mr. Macrae, would ye be so kind as to tell my kinsmen exactly what Mr. Stewart offered your people?"

Ian's rival turned to the Sinclairs and repeated the solicitor's claim that the Macraes did not own their land and that the Sinclair was preparing to execute a clearing to make way for a tourist resort. He concluded by outlining the offer of their relocation. "I doubt if it would bring tears t' any of yeer eyes to see us go," he added with a sardonic laugh, "but I can clearly see Mr. Stewart's scheme, and I for one would like t' see th' lout at th' end of a rope for tryin' t' stir up trouble between us again."

A rumble of agreement issued from both sides, and from the corner of her eye, Meredith caught the distress on Stewart's face. *Let him squirm,* she thought. *Let the little worm squirm.*

Ian took the floor again. "The only thing that needs clearing here is the air. As long as we're at it, I'd like to ask, does anyone know what caused the feud in the first place? What have we been fighting about all this time?"

The members of both clans stared at him blankly. Then one young man from Sinclair country stood. "I heerd it was because a Macrae killed a Sinclair."

"Well, ye heerd wrong," challenged a strapping jumbo-sized Macrae. "It's ye Sinclairs that murdered our brethren." Meredith cringed, half expecting a brawl to break out in the church after all.

"Quiet!" Ian's voice boomed above the din of the commotion. The crowd calmed and turned toward him again. "If we're ever to get this settled, we must know the history. This woman," he said, turning to Meredith, "holds the truth in her hands. Mr. Macrae, she is of your clan. I ask permission that she be allowed to reveal what she has discovered."

"Ye have it."

"I also must seek your agreement that whatever is revealed will be considered strictly as the history of the matter, not an incitement to new hostilities." Ian extended his hand to Robert Macrae, who accepted it.

"Agreed," said the Macrae, and the two men shook hands.

Emotion tightened Meredith's throat, but she cleared it and explained briefly about the message she had discovered embroidered into the hem of the tablecloth. Then she began to read the story of the beginnings of the feud. At first she heard a titter of laughter when the listeners recognized the familiar story of the ugly bride and the doomed bridegroom. But as she continued, the room grew deathly quiet as the folk tale turned from mere legend to harsh history. She was nearly finished when a ruckus broke out again, the Sinclairs claiming it to be a lie, the Macraes indignant at the wrong perpetrated by Peter Sinclair. With difficulty, Ian managed to quiet them.

"Finish," he told her, and Meredith read aloud the curse of Megan Macrae:

> *May the dark of the night curse the name of*
> *Sinclair,*
> *May strife on the land be his penance,*
> *'Til the day comes to pass that a true-blooded*
> *heir*
> *Of Macrae returns to the palace.*

She looked up, wondering what would happen next. Ian cleared his throat. "Whether a true curse was cast against my kinsmen, or whether 'tis the curse of hatred

that has blighted both our clans, there's been enough
strife on this land. Our stubborn resentment against one
another almost allowed this outsider to steal away our
lands and our heritage."

Robert Macrae stepped forward. "Aye. What th' Sinclair says is true. And if it hadn't been for another outsider, this lass who had the courage to challenge
tradition," he said, placing his hand on Meredith's
shoulder, "we might have succumbed to this man's plot.
'Tis time t' vow an oath t' end th' feud, now and forever.
Do I have your pledge?" he demanded of his clansmen
in a voice strong and resolute. After a moment's hesitation, each person rose and nodded, murmuring a com-
mingled "Aye." ·

Ian charged his own clan with the same oath, and they
in turn stood and agreed. Tears filled Meredith's eyes.
Could this be happening? Could they be making peace
at last? She had every reason to believe so, for Ian had
told her if they could get the clansmen to commit in
public, their honor would hold them to their vows. She
felt Ian's hand slip into hers.

"Very well, then. The feud is ended, by our word of
honor." He turned to her, and in front of the entire congregation said, "Will ye marry me now, lass?"

Meredith's cheeks burned, and she heard the murmur
of amazement rustle through the crowd, an astonishment that matched her own, but she looked into his eyes
and saw the love of her life who had just moved heaven
and earth for her. "Yes. I will marry you."

Ian turned to those gathered in the little church. "If
there ever was a curse, it will be broken now forever,
for tonight a true-blooded heir of Macrae will be returned to the palace."

Meredith jerked her head. "Tonight?"

He grinned at her. "Ye said ye would marry me.
Now." He turned and motioned toward the side door.
"I've brought Reverend Fraser from Craigmont to join

us in holy matrimony. 'Tis living proof the Macraes and the Sinclairs can dwell together in peace. Will ye?"

Meredith's heart pounded, but her fear dissolved. Only she and Ian, and perhaps Robert Macrae, knew that ending the feud was not her reason for marrying him, but she didn't care what the rest thought. Feud or no feud, the love that had sprung so suddenly between them could not be denied. It was a love that she felt deep in her heart, a love that transcended time and place, that demanded fulfillment in their marriage. "Yes," she whispered.

"This is an outrage!" Angus Stewart jumped to his feet. "I object. This is not a sacred marriage. It's a farce and a blasphemy, a last-ditch effort by the Sinclair to manipulate the Macraes." He turned to that faction. "Don't you see he's just marrying her to gain your sympathy? She's not even one of you."

Robert Macrae charged at Stewart and grabbed him by the lapels on his jacket. " 'Tis too late, Stewart," he snarled. "Your little scheme didn't work. Meredith Macrae *is* one of us, and this wedding will bring us together once and for all. You're the outsider here, and you're not wanted."

"Hang him!"

Stunned, Meredith looked toward the man who'd called out. It was the old storyteller from whom she'd first heard the tale of the cattle thief and the ugly bride. He pushed through the crowd until he reached Robert Macrae, who relinquished his hold on Stewart and stepped aside.

"We still hang thieves in these parts," the storyteller hissed into Stewart's alarmed face. "And ye're nothin' but a thief, tryin' t' pit us against one another again so ye can steal our land. Give up your objection, Mr. Stewart, and let this weddin' commence."

Meredith's pulse thrummed in her ears, and the rest of the church stared at the two men in uneasy anticipation. Angus Stewart, wide-eyed and pale, was too tongue-tied to answer. The old man moved his face even closer.

"A weddin' or a hangin', Mr. Stewart, what'll it be?"

Angus Stewart's beady eyes darted from one face to another, and Meredith saw a sheen of sweat on his forehead. He picked up his hat, and, with an anxious glance over his shoulder, hurried down the aisle and out the door of the church.

She turned to Ian and saw amusement rather than triumph in his eyes, and her heart swelled once again. Even though he had defeated the solicitor, Ian Sinclair showed no sign of malice toward his enemy. He was the kind of man who would always play fair with his opponents, and she knew without a doubt she could trust him with her heart. Taking a deep breath, Meredith let go of her earlier apprehensions about marrying so hastily. She didn't know if the wedding Ian had arranged on the spot would even be legal—didn't they have to have a license or something?—but it didn't matter. A true-blooded heir of Macrae would indeed return to the palace tonight. They could take care of the details later. She smiled up into the handsome face of her very own Scotsman, and in the strongest imitation of his accent she could muster, she said, "I think 'tis th' weddin' he's chosen."

BEAUTY AND
THE BRUTE

Barbara Dawson Smith

Chapter One

The third disaster of the day occurred when Lady Helen Jeffries found herself stranded in an unseasonal blizzard.

Shivering outside the broken coach, she clutched the ermine-trimmed hood tighter around her blond hair. The wind plucked at her crimson cloak. Specks of ice peppered her cheeks. Heedless of her own discomfort, Helen waved a cheerful farewell to her footman as he rode off into the blinding snow.

For a moment she stood there, gripped by cold and fright. It was mid-afternoon already. Even if Cox reached the village before dark, would there be time for a rescue party to set out?

Possibly not. She and Miss Gilbert and the injured coachman might be forced to spend the night here with no fire to warm them. The spare horse, tethered in the shelter of the rocks, could not carry all of them to safety.

And this predicament was her fault.

Heartsick, she climbed into the coach, which lay tilted in the ditch. At least the plush blue interior felt marginally warmer than outside. M'lord yapped excitedly. Helen scooped up the little brown-and-white dog and took comfort from his warm body.

Miss Gilbert had tucked a spare blanket around the coachman's hurt leg. With her arms fluttering beneath her cape, she looked like a plump brown wren. "Oh, my lady," the old governess chirped, "whatever are we to do? Poor Cox will freeze to death. And so shall we!"

"It's not as bad as all that," Helen said reassuringly. "He'll ride to that hamlet we passed a mile back, and then we'll be rescued in a trice. Mr. Abbott, are you in pain?"

"I'm well enough," the coachman said, though his grizzled face showed tension around his mouth. " 'Tis sorry I am for running us off the road."

"It was an accident," Helen soothed. "Certainly we've survived worse. Remember that sandstorm in North Africa? And the earthquake in Turkey?"

"Lord Hathaway saved us from those catastrophes," Miss Gilbert said worriedly. "He led us to safety. How can we manage without him?"

Helen wondered, too.

Her father, the Marquess of Hathaway, often accompanied Helen on the journeys she had taken over the past five years. After the disastrous end to her betrothal, she had left England, restless to seek a new life. She had traveled the world, and as time passed, she had come to relish her freedom.

Lord Hathaway had intended to join her on this tour of the Highlands. But as they had been about to depart at dawn, a messenger had arrived from the docks. A fire had broken out on a ship belonging to his lordship, and he needed to assess the damages. Helen wanted to delay the trip, but her father insisted he could catch up to the party later.

That had been the first disaster of the day.

The second had occurred after luncheon, when a few pale flakes had drifted from the leaden sky. As it was too early in the season for a storm, Helen had insisted upon pressing onward. She was enthralled by the rugged scenery, so ancient and natural, the trees displaying their autumn brilliance. Except for the occasional croft with smoke drifting from a stone chimney, the Highlands were a rough masterpiece untouched by man. Great crags of rock towered over heather-carpeted moors. Once she glimpsed a herd of red deer grazing deep in the shadows of a pine forest. Another time, a waterfall shimmered against the mossy rock of a hill.

As the coach climbed higher into the mountains, the powdered-sugar dusting of snow had thickened into a dense white blanket. The wind whipped the flurries into a frenzied dance, but even then Helen had been enchanted by the savage splendor of it all . . .

"M'lady," said Abbott, hanging his head, "I humbly beg your pardon for leadin' you into such trouble. When his lordship hears what I done—"

"You shan't lose your post," Helen said, anxious that he would fear so. "It's *my* fault. We ought to have turned back when you first suggested it."

"Oh, we shall all perish." Miss Gilbert dabbed at her red nose with a handkerchief. "They will find our poor frozen forms with the spring thaw."

"Please," Helen said in exasperation, "there's no need to be theatrical."

"But listen to that wind. I do believe the storm has grown worse." Quivering, the governess peered out the window. "One might think an evil sorcerer has cast a spell over this uncivilized land."

A flurry of goose bumps crept across Helen's skin. "That is nonsense," she said crisply. "We are safe here with enough food in the hamper to tide us over. Now sit back and relax. I shall read to all of us."

The crazy angle of the coach made it impossible for more than one person to comfortably occupy each blue-cushioned seat. Cradling M'lord in her lap, Helen sat down on the floor, reached into her valise for *Rob Roy* by Sir Walter Scott, and read the book aloud. The well-worn pages provided a distraction from the howling of the blizzard. After a time, a light snoring emanated from Abbott, and his chin slumped onto his broad chest. Even Miss Gilbert huddled in the corner with her eyes closed.

The scant daylight had begun to wane. Soon it would grow dark. To allay her fears, Helen stroked the dog. Her fingers and toes felt numb from the cold. Had Cox reached the village yet?

She prayed so. The thought of spending many more frigid hours here daunted her. What if the snow continued throughout the night? What if rescue did indeed come too late?

Immediately she scolded herself. Who was she to complain when Abbott lay senseless with pain?

Helen leaned her head back and stared out the window, where snowflakes cavorted in a highland jig. The branches of a bush scraped somewhere outside. The wind lamented like a lost soul.

A sense of utter aloneness crept over her. She had the uncanny impression it had nothing to do with being stranded on this remote road, that the emptiness had been there for a long time, buried deep inside herself. She felt lacking somehow, unsatisfied with . . . what? The direction of her life?

Surely not. She liked being free to go her own way, to discover new places. And yet . . . she thought of her visit a few weeks ago to her half sister. Isabel and Justin lived on an estate in Derbyshire with their three young children. Their happiness had lingered like a rich essence in the air, and Helen recalled the time when she had come upon husband and wife kissing in the garden. The tender passion of their embrace made her heart ache.

How would it feel to be held by a man, to let him caress the secret places of her body, to join with him in the mysterious act of mating? She had traveled the world, seen more exotic sights in the past five years than other ladies did in a lifetime, but she did not know the touch of a man.

At one time she'd had that chance, but she hadn't been ready for it. Now she feared she might never again have the opportunity. She had no wish to marry a dull English lord, and her father would be terribly disappointed if she wed beneath her station. Besides, having a husband would put an end to her independence, and that thought was sufficient to douse any romantic yearnings. She wanted to live life to its fullest. Never again would she be the naïve girl whose sole relief from boredom was to visit London for the Season.

Of course, there were drawbacks to adventure. Her quest for new experiences had left her stranded in a raging snowstorm.

The reminder of her predicament sobered Helen. Because of her selfish folly, she had endangered her loyal servants. Yet she felt almost fated to fall in love with the wild grandeur of the Highlands. If she still believed in fairy tales, she might have fancied these mountains enchanted . . .

M'lord lifted his silken head and growled at the door.

An instant later, a dark shape appeared outside the window. And Helen found herself staring at the hulking form of a monster.

Chapter Two

The door handle rattled.

A scream strangling her throat, Helen jolted upright. Her half-frozen fingers gripped the leather-bound book, and she wished it were a pistol. It was up to her to defend Gillie and Abbott.

In a blast of icy air, the door flew back. The dog barked. Miss Gilbert came awake and squealed in surprise. A loud snort emanated from Abbott.

The beast thrust its head and shoulders inside, blocking the meager daylight. His shaggy black hair was mantled by snow, and a length of plaid cloth draped his brawny chest. Dark eyes glowed in a face of uncompromising masculinity.

A *man*, Helen thought in relief. The beast was merely a Highlander.

"Hello," she said, extending her gloved hand to him. "I am Lady Helen Jeffries. And you are . . . ?"

Muttering under his breath, he glowered as if she were his worst enemy.

The coachman rubbed his eyes. "Here now. What's this?"

"We've been found, thank heavens," Helen said briskly. She braced her hand on the velvet-covered wall and struggled to stand in the tilted vehicle, her half-numb legs tangling in her heavy skirts. "Have you come from the village, sir?"

The Highlander grunted what sounded like an assent. In one giant step, he entered the coach, and it rocked beneath his weight.

Helen's heart beat faster as she backed up to afford him space. He dwarfed the interior, and she was pressed against Miss Gilbert's plump form. "You must have seen Cox, my footman," Helen said. "Is he all right?" When the stranger didn't reply, she went on, speaking slowly for his benefit. "Surely he must have given you directions, told you where to find us."

Another grunt. Was the man a simpleton?

He turned his broad back to her and examined the coachman's leg. Abbott winced at his touch. Then the Highlander retreated outside and returned with a short, straight branch. Taking a long strip of cloth from the pouch hanging at his waist, he secured the branch to the coachman's lower leg.

" 'Tis broken, your ankle," he said, rolling the words in a gravelly Scottish burr. "You shouldna ha' been moved without a splint."

At least the man could speak. "Are you certain it isn't just a bad sprain?" Helen asked in concern.

The stranger cast an accusing glance at her, as if he knew the accident was her fault. "Aye. The temporary splint will protect the leg for now."

She stifled her guilt. "Thank you. We should be on our way if we want to reach the village before dark. I can't imagine we have more than an hour of daylight left. If you'll be so kind as to help Mr. Abbott climb out."

Sheltering M'lord within her cloak, she clambered past the Highlander to open the door of the coach. Snow needled her face and the wind snatched at her cloak, but she gritted her teeth and stepped outside. The gale blew worse than before, the snowflakes falling thick and icy.

Slipping and sliding, Helen hurried to the horse tethered in the lee of the rock cliff. The gelding nuzzled her cloak, clearly looking for his dinner.

"Sorry, darling," she murmured. "You've a bit of a load to carry first." Even as her numb fingers fumbled to untie the leather lead, she felt herself brushed aside. She looked up into the harsh face of the Highlander. His features were as rough as these wild hills, with a stark, compelling beauty.

"The injured man rides," he stated. "Not you." Before she could react, he led the mount away.

He thought *she* meant to claim the horse?

His rude assumption startled Helen, but she was too cold to stand there framing belated retorts. Returning to the coach, she helped Miss Gilbert disembark as the Highlander hoisted the burly coachman onto the horse. Then he poked around the luggage that was lashed to the back of the vehicle. Suspicious, Helen went to him. "May I help you find something?"

"Food. You canna be daft enough to set out with no provisions."

His criticism made her bristle. "There's a hamper inside the coach, secured beneath the seat. If you need anything else, you have only to ask—"

He didn't stay to listen. Striding to the door, he went inside and emerged a moment later with the large basket. He thrust the hamper at Helen. "Here, make yourself useful," he growled. "I'll lead the horse."

With a jerk of his head, the stranger motioned for the women to follow. Then he guided the horse and coachman toward a cleft in the rock.

Helen blinked the icy flakes from her eyelashes. Holding the dog in one arm and the basket in the other, she hastened to follow. "The village is back that way," she called, pointing down the road in case he was slow-witted.

"Too far," he snapped. " 'Tis almost dark."

He started to turn, but she caught his sleeve. His muscles felt hard beneath her fingertips. "Wait. What is your name?"

He muttered an answer, but she couldn't have heard him right. "The *brute*?" she repeated.

"MacBrut"—he cast her a brooding look—"without an *e*."

He could spell, too. She wanted to proclaim it the perfect name for an unfriendly lout. But whatever his faults, Mr. MacBrut had come to their rescue. "How did you find us?" she asked.

"Your footman."

Exasperated, she said, "Then why didn't you say so in the first place?"

"I dinna have time for chatter."

He directed the horse up a steep track into the hills. Miss Gilbert fell into step behind him. Lugging the heavy hamper in one hand and the dog in the other, Helen hastened to catch up to the small party, already barely visible through the falling snow. She slogged through drifts higher than her ankle boots and felt icy trickles down her silk stockings. Within a short time, her hem was sodden and the freezing dampness dragged at her skirts. Miss Gilbert was struggling to keep up, so Helen lent her aid, though it was awkward while holding the dog in the crook of her arm.

"Bless you, my lady," the governess panted. "And bless our rescuer. Aren't we lucky he happened along?"

"Lucky, indeed." Helen didn't want to alarm the older woman. But something about MacBrut made her uneasy. How did they know they could trust this stranger? He might be a bandit, leading them to his lair . . .

Quickly she banished the morbid thought. She was no longer a silly girl who spun fancies. Better she should praise him for being a good Samaritan.

MacBrut. That must be his clan. What was his first name?

She watched his wide back as he led them steadily higher into the mountains. A thick wool plaid wrapped his massive torso. Now and then, she caught a flash of strong, bare legs beneath his knee-length kilt. The sight caused a peculiar tension in the pit of her stomach. If he had any sense, he'd wear trews in such weather. Though perhaps the storm had caught him by surprise, too.

Where *was* he taking them?

She had her answer a few minutes later when she spied a castle through the snow. The dark monolith reared against the sheer rock face of a cliff. There was no drawbridge or moat, only an arched gate with a raised portcullis. Through the dimness of dusk, Helen glimpsed twin towers guarding either end of the walled yard.

Picking a path through the scattered rubble, MacBrut guided the horse toward a tall stone keep. Helen could barely feel her feet as she trudged across the bleak courtyard. The basket of food dragged on her arm, but she spared only a fleeting thought for her own discomfort. From the way Miss Gilbert clung, her round body quivering, Helen knew the cold upland trek had been hard on the aging woman.

The keep was chilly and dark inside, but at least the walls provided protection from the wind and snow. Helen gratefully set down the hamper and tilted her head back, turning around for a dizzying view of a cavernous room. The faintest light seeped through the high window slits.

She looked at MacBrut. "What is this place?"

"My castle."

"*Your* castle?"

"Aye."

"Do you live here alone?"

"Do you see anyone else?" he snarled back.

He probably couldn't get a dog to stay with him, Helen decided. He had brought the coachman in, horse and all, and now he lifted Abbott down, setting him on the stone floor so that he could sit propped against the wall.

Worried, Helen crouched beside him. "Poor Abbott. How do you fare?"

"Fine, m'lady," he said, though pain roughened his voice.

She looked up, seeking their host. "He needs warmth. Can we—"

Before she could suggest a fire, MacBrut strode into the murky shadows of the hall. His heavy footsteps echoed through the gloom. What a rude, exasperating man! Then came a rustling noise and the hollow thump of wood being tossed onto a grate. Within moments a cheery blaze sent light and warmth radiating into the hall.

No, he was a *wonderful* man.

She helped Miss Gilbert to the massive stone hearth and seated her on a three-legged stool. Smiling, the governess stretched out her mittened hands to the fire. "Oh, this is lovely," she said, looking as pleased as a pudgy mole invited to the drawing room of a duke.

Helen set down M'lord, who scooted close to the fire. She turned her back to the blaze, soaking in the blessed heat, but only for a moment. Seeing MacBrut half carrying the coachman, she removed her fur-trimmed cloak and made a pallet close to the hearth. "Have you any blankets?" she asked him.

"The trunk upstairs. In the first chamber." With a tilt of his head, he indicated the darkness. Gruffly, he added, "Take a candle."

She found a stub of wax in a basket beside the hearth, and touched the wick to the fire. It was torture to leave the blazing warmth for the icy bowels of the keep. Shivering, she clenched her teeth to keep them from chattering.

The meager circle of illumination wavered over the stone floor, without penetrating the dense gloom elsewhere in the vast chamber. She could see only a short distance in front of her. The place smelled musty and ancient. She lifted the candle and searched for the stairs. Rusted armor hung on the walls alongside huge faded tapestries. A dull layer of grime coated the few chairs. If this was MacBrut's home, he sorely needed a housekeeper.

Better yet, a wife to sweeten his sour disposition. Unless he already had one—imprisoned in the dungeon.

Just as she started toward the arched opening of a stairwell, a peculiar sight distracted her. On a dais half-hidden in the shadows, a long trestle table was draped in yellowed linen and set for a dinner party. Dust shrouded the fine porcelain plates. Cobwebs stretched from the filthy crystal glassware to the tarnished silver candlesticks. Dark lumps sat upon serving dishes, and only when Helen walked closer did she realize it was petrified food.

She stood riveted, her skin prickling from more than the frigid air. The ghostly dinner waited as if the residents of the castle had been called away in mid-meal. What could have happened? A clan war perhaps? It must have been a tragedy if even the servants had not come back to clear the table.

"The stairs are that way."

The harsh echo of MacBrut's voice startled her. She spun around, the candle flame guttering. He stood pointing, a mythical beast outlined against the fire. His body cast a colossal shadow across the floor.

Still shaken by the strangeness of the abandoned meal, she mounted the winding stone staircase, half expecting to meet the specters of those long-forgotten diners. The upper corridor loomed dark and eerie, but she prodded herself along with the reminder of Abbott's injury.

Venturing through the first doorway, she found herself in a spacious bedchamber outfitted as finely as any London house with silk hangings and exquisite wood furniture, sadly begrimed now. At the foot of a massive four-poster bed stood a trunk of carved mahogany. She leaned down and blew a cloud of dust off the top. The leather hinges creaked when she opened the lid, and the musty odor of wool long shut away drifted to her, tinged by a certain subtle sweetness. Helen inhaled deeply, but couldn't quite identify the pleasant scent. Having no desire to linger in the lonely dark room, she grabbed an armload of blankets and hastened back downstairs.

Amazingly, the sound of laughter came from the group around the fire. A smile wreathed Abbott's broad face, and even MacBrut relaxed his unsociable scowl as he encouraged Miss Gilbert to accept a silver flask. She stared askance at the vessel before taking a dainty swallow. She coughed delicately, then drank again, more deeply.

Helen reached the welcome warmth of the fire and set down the blankets. "What is that you're drinking?"

Miss Gilbert dabbed her lips with a handkerchief. "A medicinal tonic. Mr. MacBrut recommended it to ward off a chill."

Helen sniffed the flask and almost reeled from the strong aroma. "Why, it's spirits."

"The finest Scots whisky," MacBrut said. "I'd offer you a nip, m'lady, but others need it more." He rudely plucked the flask from her and handed it to Abbott. "Drink this down, man. 'Twill dull the pain."

Like Miss Gilbert, the coachman obeyed MacBrut without question.

Of course, Helen reflected, perhaps they didn't catch the hostility burning in his eyes whenever he glanced at her. And they must not have noticed the hint of contempt in his voice. But she had noticed—especially the mocking way *m'lady* rolled off his tongue. He resented her presence in his ruined castle. Why?

The question piqued her curiosity. If they had intruded upon his solitude, she could understand his displeasure. But why single her out as the recipient of his ill humor?

Kneeling beside Abbott, the Highlander removed the makeshift splint. "I'll ha' to cut awa' your boot," he said, drawing a dirk from the sheath at his waist.

Abbott nodded, and took a long pull from the flask. "Do as you must."

MacBrut wielded the knife with an expert hand. Steel flashed as he sliced into the leather and neatly removed the boot. He sheathed the dirk, but not before Helen saw the gleam of a large cabochon sapphire decorating the scrolled hilt. Why would this rough Highlander have a weapon fit for a prince?

"It's a fine dirk," she said. "Where did you get it?"

His gaze met hers. In the light of the fire, his eyes were not black, but a deep midnight-blue that quite took her breath away. "I didna steal it."

"I never said you did." But she had felt a fleeting suspicion, and his frank scrutiny made her blush and turn away.

She busied herself folding one of the blankets into a compact square, then knelt down opposite MacBrut. "Here, we can prop his leg on this."

MacBrut frowned, but made no comment as he helped her position the support. Then he examined the coachman's ankle, probing so carefully that the coachman scarcely winced.

His deft movements fascinated Helen. She found herself studying his large hands, the long fingers and clean, trimmed nails, the broad, strong backs. They were not the soft hands of an aristocrat, but showed the talent and dexterity of a man accustomed to physical labor. She had the sudden, inexplicable image of him using those hands to pleasure a woman, his fingers dark against the fairness of her bosom, his touch tender and loving . . .

Loving? Surely not this curmudgeon.

"The cold has kept the swelling down, at least," MacBrut pronounced. " 'Tis something to be thankful for."

As he spoke, he took the stick and wrapped a piece of yellowed linen around it to make a padded splint, which he placed against the injured limb. Abbott sucked in a sharp breath, his weathered cheeks gray with pain.

"Oh, dear," Miss Gilbert said, averting her face and covering her eyes.

"Now, dinna trouble yourself, ma'am," MacBrut said with surprising kindness. "You might fetch the food from the basket. Once we're done here, Mr. Abbott will need some nourishment."

The older woman hopped off the stool. "I should be happy to do so." She trotted away.

MacBrut's gaze took on a distinct hostility as he looked at Helen. "Go on and help her," he said. "This is no place for an English *lady*."

Helen refused to let him scare her off when she might be a comfort to Abbott. "I'm staying here."

"Suit yourself. But if you swoon, I'll leave you lying where you fall."

"I never swoon."

Abbott attempted a jovial laugh. "Rest assured, sir, her ladyship is not one for hysterics. She never quailed the time we faced brigands in the Alps. She jabbed one in the belly with her umbrella, and the others ran away." The coachman fell silent, the corners of his mouth pinched with pain.

"Swallow that whisky," MacBrut said. "Every wee drop of it."

While the coachman was occupied with drinking, MacBrut turned his penetrating gaze on Helen. "Scared off the brigands, did you?" He looked her up and down, and lowered his voice to an undertone. "And here I thought Sassenach women had but one use."

His gaze ogled her bosom, leaving no doubt as to his

meaning. Helen told herself to feel outraged, but a tingling warmth filled her instead. The sensation had little to do with thawing skin, and everything to do with a shocking awareness of him as a man. A big, bold rogue of a man.

MacBrut focused on the task of splinting the injured limb. " 'Tis a clean break, I trow. At least you willna be getting the fever."

Helen felt as if she were the one with the fever. The firelight caressed his clean-shaven cheeks and strong jaw. Melted snow glittered on the night-black hair that brushed his shoulders. For so large a man, he had a remarkably gentle touch. What a curious mix of barbarian and healer he was.

"Where did you learn to set a broken bone?" she asked.

"Here and there." His blue stare bored into her. "So far from the city, we canna send down the street for a doctor."

"I don't suppose you can." And that made him all the more fascinating. He had skills unknown to the civilized gentlemen of London. His rough-edged manner only made her wonder what other unique abilities he possessed. An insistent curiosity settled low in her belly. In truth, he was unlike any other man she had met in her travels.

She helped to lift Abbott's leg so that MacBrut could pass the strip of linen bandage around the splinted ankle. As they worked together, she grew more intensely aware of him. Aware of the quirk of his hard mouth. Aware of the lock of black hair that had tumbled onto his brow. Aware of the clever movements of his hands, and how perfectly her breasts would fit his palms—

"That's quite enough," MacBrut said.

Flustered, Helen moistened her dry lips with the tip of her tongue. "I beg your pardon?"

His gaze narrowed on her mouth, and his scowl deepened. "I'm finished. You can lower his leg, careful now."

"Oh." Helen saw that the bandage had been tied
neatly. She eased Abbott's leg back onto the blanket.
"How are you doing?"

The coachman sighed as if glad the ordeal was over.
"Ready for that bite to eat, m'lady."

With the timing of a stage actress, Miss Gilbert trotted
back with the provisions, and Helen helped her set up a
picnic by the fire. She found herself seated beside
MacBrut. A strange aching tension distracted her from
any interest in food. While everyone dined on cold ham,
bread, and cheese, she merely nibbled at her meal, feeding small bites to M'lord. She stole sideways glances at
MacBrut, at the muscled bare legs beneath the kilt and
the way his rough linen shirt and black and red plaid
clung to his chest. He was so different from the elegant
noblemen that Papa too often steered into her path. Was
MacBrut thinking of her, too?

No. He had made it clear he despised her.

When she reached for the wine flask, their hands
bumped and the contact prickled up her arm and into
her bosom. His gaze jerked to hers, and for an un-
guarded moment she glimpsed a burning intensity in
him, something vastly different from hatred, something
deep and rich and mysterious. Elation swept like wildfire
through Helen. She'd been around enough men to recognize the truth.

MacBrut desired her.

Though he turned abruptly away, she reveled in the
feminine thrill of conquest. MacBrut wanted her. He
wanted to take her to his bed. He wanted to do wicked
things with her.

Things she wanted desperately to experience.

The heat within her flared into a pulsebeat. She had
the spark of an idea so outrageous she doused it at once.

But the thought took hold like tinder, burning brighter until she could deny it no longer.

MacBrut was the perfect man to show her the secrets of physical love.

Chapter Three

The deep hush of night shrouded the castle.

As Helen slipped out of bed in the small upstairs chamber, she could hear only the whine of the wind down the chimney and the soft snoring of Miss Gilbert, who lay burrowed beneath the pile of blankets. Nestled at the foot, M'lord lifted his head and wagged his tail, but Helen whispered, "Stay," and he obeyed, his liquid brown eyes watching as she crept toward the door.

The fire had burned down to smoldering embers during the hour she had waited to make certain her companion was soundly slumbering. Helen had spent the time in dreamy romantic fantasy until her every nerve hummed and she could bear the suspense no longer.

It was now. Or never.

The icy floor caused her toes to curl inside her thin silk stockings. She'd left off her shoes, which were still damp from the snow. Luckily, she had retrieved her cloak when Abbott had been moved to a bedchamber, for the air held a frosty nip that penetrated her thin shift and petticoats.

When Gillie had innocently suggested she remove her gown and corset before retiring, Helen had complied. She had also unbound her hair and let it tumble to her waist. Now she felt deliciously daring as she opened the door and stole out into the gloomy corridor.

Where did the master of the castle sleep?

MacBrut would have chosen the best room for his own—the laird's chamber. This was his castle, after all. Questions clamored in her. Where were his servants? Did he have another home elsewhere? Who *was* he, really? Helen sensed there was more to him than he let the world see. Much more.

With one hand on the cold stone wall, she slowly felt her way through the darkness. A frisson of excitement scurried over her skin. She could scarcely believe she was on her way to meet a man in his bedchamber. Such scandalous behavior could ruin an unmarried lady.

And if all went as planned, who would ever find out? Certainly no one from her social circle. This was her one night of adventure, her one chance to learn the truth behind the mystery of the sexes.

After tomorrow, she would never see MacBrut again.

She stumbled into a chair, and the legs scraped the floor with a loud screech. Helen froze, her heartbeat surging. The passage was pitch-black; belatedly she realized she should have brought a candle. She had the eerie sense of being watched by a ghostly presence, and the image of that dusty abandoned table in the great hall flitted to her. But she deliberately put it out of her mind. She would let no morbid thoughts intrude upon her quest.

Carefully she moved on until she reached the bedchamber. The door stood halfway open. Feeling giddy, she tiptoed closer. From within came the glow of a fire and the faint crackling of logs. Helen pictured MacBrut lying sprawled in the four-poster bed. His eyes would widen with surprised appreciation when she walked into his room. He would be stunned by her offer; then he would sweep her into his arms and kiss her and do the wicked deed and at last she would *know* . . .

It would be as simple as that. Or would it?

She paused, her palm frozen against the studded oak door. All she had to do was to push it open and walk inside. But her hand disobeyed the edict of her brain. Her legs had all the strength of frostbitten flower stalks. What if MacBrut scorned her overture? What if he gave her that stony look of his? What would she say to persuade him?

Hello, I wondered if you would mind taking my virginity. Too blatant.

I thought you might be feeling as lonely as I am. Too dreary.

It's frightfully cold. May I join you in bed? Too childish.

A draft of chilly air eddied down the corridor and slapped her cheeks. Helen shivered, hugging the ermine-trimmed cloak in an effort to contain the heat of her fantasies. Now that the moment was nigh, however, cold common sense asserted itself. What madness had brought her here?

She was no seductress. She couldn't offer herself to a stranger. Especially not a Highlander who hated her. What if MacBrut treated her ill?

Perhaps she had only deluded herself into believing he had a kind nature beneath his gruff exterior. Caring for an injured servant didn't necessarily make MacBrut a hero.

Perhaps she should find another man to be her teacher. A civilized gentleman whom she could trust.

She turned to go. And ran smack into the solid bulwark of a man.

He crowded her against the wall, and her mind registered danger in the fingers gripping her upper arms. In the musk of his male scent. In the massiveness of his muscled chest pressing into her soft bosom.

Tilting her head back, she could discern only his large black outline against the gloom. But she didn't need to see his face to identify him.

MacBrut.

A secret thrill pulsed deep in her belly. It was part fright and part fascination. Like a wolf, he'd crept up and caught her. "What are you doing out here?" she asked in a breathy voice.

"Better I should ask that of you."

His deep, rolling brogue stirred her senses. The heat of his large body sparked a blaze of carnal curiosity, the feeling so powerful she forgot her change of heart. In a rush she blurted out, "I came to see you. To be with you."

Would he understand her meaning? Would he accept her bold offer? She waited in agonizing hope.

Silence throbbed around them. The tensing of his fingers betrayed a response in him, though whether it was disgust or desire, she could not tell. In contrast to the furnacelike warmth of him, the frigid stone wall pressed into her spine. From a distance came the scolding of the wind like the voice of her conscience. *Turn back, make an excuse, flee while there's still time . . .*

He parted her cloak and cupped her breasts. A shocking fervor melted the remnants of her resistance. His touch felt so right, so perfect, and she leaned into him, wanting more.

Abruptly he ground his hips against hers. "Out whoring, m'lady? I shouldna be surprised."

"Don't speak to me like that." She drew an indignant breath at his crude remark. "I'm not what you think."

" 'Tis pretty words you ladies want. And fancy trappings for your lust. But underneath you're all the same."

His hands descended, following the curve of waist and hips, moving downward over the layers of petticoats until he captured the prize between her legs. Gasping, she instinctively clamped her thighs together, but succeeded only in trapping his hand in place.

She shoved at his arm, a futile effort against iron muscles. *"Don't."*

"Don't? You came here wanting this." He rubbed slowly, provocatively. "But perhaps my manner is no' so genteel as your other lovers'."

This was how a man touched a woman? With harsh insistence? And to her utter shame, why did she like it? "I have no lovers. And I won't tolerate you acting like a brute." She gave him another, harder push. "That's brute *with* an *e*."

He jumped back half a step, removing his hand but remaining so close she could feel his body heat. His grimace flashed through the darkness. "You've a husband, then, I trow. Well, it doesna matter to me how many men you've had in the past."

"I have no husband, either," she retorted. "I've never done this before."

"You've never sought out a man in his chamber?" He fingered a silky strand of her hair. "No doubt the rutting curs grovel at your doorstep."

"Blast you." Helen slapped at his hand. "The truth is, I was curious. I'm twenty-four years old, and I've never been with a man. Not *ever*."

He stood unmoving. "You. A virgin."

She hated the skepticism that roughened his voice. She hated *him* for ruining her golden dream of discovery. "Step aside. I was mad to come here. If you must know, I was returning to my room when you appeared and started pawing me."

He didn't budge. Rather, he placed his hands on the stone wall to form a prison around her. "Were you now?"

"Yes, this was all a mistake. A momentary loss of reason." She ducked under his arm, but he moved with the swiftness of a predator, catching her against his hard form, his grip deceptively loose.

"Coward," he said softly.

Was he laughing at her? Certainly not MacBrut; he didn't possess a smidgen of humor in his muscle-bound body. She tugged at his arm to no avail. "Let me go."

"Not so quickly, lass. 'Twould seem I must voice an apology."

"So say it and be done."

"I shouldna ha' spoken so ill to you just now. If you are truly untouched—"

"There's no *if* about it."

"Then you canna be used to a man's ways. I shouldna ha' fondled you so." He was fondling her now, his fingers sliding beneath her cloak to trace her waist and spine with masterful delicacy. In contrast to his earlier scorn, his voice was pure honey, sweet and thick and addictive. "But you canna blame a man for going a bit daft over you. You're soft and curvy and warm the way a woman should be."

Her legs felt weak again, but she clung to her displeasure. "Release me. I wish to return to my room."

"First, here's something to take back to your lonely bed."

His dark head swooped down and the heated pressure of his mouth met hers, his tongue nudging apart her lips. The surprise of it held her motionless; her mind resisted his appeal. But her body thought otherwise. Her arms slipped around his neck and she gave herself up into the deep pleasure of his kiss. He tasted of the wine they'd drunk at dinner, and she could feel herself growing warm and giddy. All the while he caressed her in loving strokes that caused her skin to tingle and her blood to surge. She touched him tentatively at first, then with bolder forays over his chest and shoulders. His strength awed her, the muscle and sinew beneath the roughness of male skin. She loved the differences between them, the way they complemented each other, man and woman. This was what she had dreamed of, being kissed with passion and tenderness, held as if he could not bear to let her go.

He slid his mouth to her ear. His hand kneaded her

breast and stroked the aching tip. "Tell me to stop, lass. Tell me lest I do more."

A small shuddering sigh eased from Helen. She arched up on tiptoe and nuzzled his throat. "Do more, please. Do whatever you like."

His breath hissed out through his teeth. His arm tightened in a fierce grip. For a moment he didn't speak; then he muttered, "As m'lady wishes."

Taking her by the waist, he drew her into his chamber and kicked the door shut. A fire burned low on the stone hearth, casting a glow over the stately four-poster with its tall canopy and tattered silk hangings. Rather than lead her to the bed, he brought her to a pallet of blankets he'd laid out before the fire. He released her, went to the woodpile, and tossed several logs onto the hearth. The flames leapt, biting and hissing in a shower of sparks.

Despite the radiant heat and her enveloping cloak, Helen trembled. She felt awkward and uncertain without the reassurance of his arms. It was not that she regretted her decision. It was that she did not know what to *do*. Should she undress? Should she lie down?

MacBrut unwound his plaid and cast it onto the blankets. His coarse linen shirt outlined the solidity of his shoulders and chest. As he kicked off his boots, her gaze was riveted to the long, bare legs leading up to his kilt and she wondered what—if anything—he wore beneath.

"Having second thoughts, m'lady?"

That mocking note was back in his voice. She lifted her chin and decided to be honest. "No. I . . . just don't know how to seduce a man."

His lips quirked to the verge of a smile—but not quite. Yet it was enough to soften the fierce angles of his face. "Aye, lass, that you do."

Striding to her, he undid the fastening of her cloak and let the garment fall to the floor. His hand lingered a moment on the curve of her neck, beneath the curtain of her hair. Then his moody blue gaze moved lower, and she felt the brush of his fingertips as he let down the sleeves of her shift. The loose fabric clung protectively until he peeled it to her waist and bared her breasts.

Flushed with embarrassment and desire, she lifted her hand to her bosom, but he caught her arm before she could cover herself. His thumb caressed the tender inner skin of her wrist while he gazed at her. How strange to let a man look at her so. It made her feel wicked and wonderful. The frank admiration on his face was gratifying, especially when he slid an arm around her waist and pulled her close against him, using his other hand to stroke her.

Sighing, she leaned her head onto his wide shoulder and closed her eyes. Her self-consciousness faded as she focused on the tactile sensations aroused by his callused fingertips. Then something wet and warm closed over her nipple. *His mouth.*

"*Oh . . . I never dreamed . . .*"

" 'Tis no dream. Remember that." And he blew on her dampened flesh.

While she whimpered from the rush of delight, he untied the tapes of her petticoats, pushed his hands inside, and found the curve of her bottom. He squeezed gently, setting off a reactionary tightening deep within her, and he caught her up in another long, openmouthed kiss.

Sweet heaven, she had been right. So right about him. Despite all his gruffness, MacBrut could be tender and loving and oh so exciting.

Somehow her undergarments fell away and she stood naked and unashamed in his arms. The world tilted as he pressed her down onto the pallet, and she felt the softness of his plaid beneath and the roughness of his clothes against her front. His kilt had ridden up, and a rodlike shape pressed into her thigh. Helen felt breathless and wanton just thinking about it, wondering why she ached to touch it, wondering what exactly he would do next. Then she could think no more when he brought his hand to her leg, smoothing up and up until his palm rested lightly at the top of her thighs, where he had handled her so crudely out in the corridor.

She stiffened, but he showed no anger now, only finesse. The tip of one finger moved . . . and touched a place so private and sensitive that she cried out, clutching at his arm.

"Sshh, lass. Let me stroke you. Let me prepare you."

"Prepare me?" she asked, mystified.

"Aye . . . I'll show you now."

He caressed her again, and the tension inside her dissolved, generating a moist heat coaxed forth by his skilled hand. She meant to lie quietly on the blankets, but her hips moved in rhythm to the rising beat of pleasure, and MacBrut crooned encouragement, his breath hot against her ear. Never had she imagined allowing a man such intimacy . . . or enjoying it so greatly. She shuddered with pleasure when he settled himself between her legs, his body comfortably heavy. Something hot and hard probed her tenderness, and before she could wonder at his intention, he entered her.

It hurt. Especially when he plunged deeper, driving himself to the hilt. He lay still then, his arms braced on either side of her. His chest heaved, the muscles in his neck straining as if he fought for control. In the firelight, strands of black hair gleamed around the harsh beauty of his face and the midnight eyes that gazed intently at her. Helen only realized she was biting down on her lip when he leaned down and brushed his mouth over hers in a soothing gesture.

"Steady, lass. Give yourself a moment, and you'll like it more."

She did already. His size stretched her to a pleasant fullness, and a sense of awe enveloped her. So this was how it was done, this mysterious act of mating. Never had she dreamed of such an intimate joining, or the warm, insistent yearning that made her reach out and draw him down onto her.

"I do like it," she whispered. "Very much."

He nestled his face in her hair, his voice husky in her ear. "And now I'll make you love it."

He moved slowly. In and out, commencing a rhythm that called to a primal craving buried within her. She lifted her hips to take him in deeper, but it wasn't enough. She wanted . . . something more. Something beyond her reach . . . something that wrested small moans of frustration from her as she surged with him, clinging to his shoulders, feeling the urgency build and build in her. She closed her eyes, focusing on the place where they were linked, the place that clenched to a tightness beyond belief.

"Let go," he said, panting. "Fall into it, lass."

"Into . . . what?"

Even as she asked, she knew. Rapture flooded her body, and she cried out with the swift plunge into paradise. She lost herself in the pulsations of pure white light, barely conscious of his final drive, his savage shout.

Limp and replete, she drifted by degrees back to herself. The fire crackled into the silence, enhancing the sense of cozy well-being. She knew a contentment deeper and richer than anything she had experienced in her life. And it was all due to the massive man who lay sprawled atop her, his body still joined to hers in that wondrous way.

MacBrut. Who would have thought she could find such incredible joy with a man she'd met only hours earlier? A man who hid his true sensitivity behind the bristly skin of a beast.

A great tenderness washed through her, a feeling of closeness to this man who had initiated her into the secret society of womanhood. Snuggling against him, she

breathed in his scent along with that ineffable sweetness . . .

"Roses," she murmured in surprise. "These blankets
smell of roses."

He said nothing, his face turned from her, his cheek
resting on her hair.

Helen glanced past him, at the chamber with its fine
mahogany furniture in contrast to the rough stone walls.
"These blankets must have belonged to the lady of the
castle. What happened to her?"

The muscles of his back tensed beneath her hand. Still,
he did not raise his head, though he grunted his displeasure.

His refusal to speak only endeared him to her. He was
a pussycat beneath that lion's growl. Then a horrid
thought struck her: what if this room had once belonged
to his wife? What if he had suffered the terrible loss of
her?

Sympathy brought tears to Helen's eyes. If he didn't
wish to be questioned on the matter, then she owed him
the courtesy of turning her curiosity elsewhere. And she
did have so many questions. She ached to learn everything about him.

She stroked the rough silk of his hair. Softly, she said,
"I don't even know your first name."

He mumbled something indistinct.

"I beg your pardon?"

He lifted his head slightly and shot her a wary glance.
"Alexander."

"Alexander." She smiled, studying his fierce features
and deciding the name fit, for it reflected the blend of
civilized man and wild beast. "Alexander MacBrut."

"Nay. Alexander, *the* MacBrut. 'Tis the way the laird
of the clan is known."

Startled, she blinked. Of course. He was no ordinary
Highlander.

And that explained why he lived in this castle. Why

he carried himself with an aura of command. "If you're the laird, then where are your people?"

"They live in the village."

"But they must have lived here once. That pitiful dining table—"

"Enough of your bletherin'." His expression hardening, he levered himself to his feet. "Women like to natter on about matters that dinna concern them. 'Twould seem you're the worst of the lot."

In half-naked magnificence he towered over her, and Helen could scarcely think. "I merely wondered—"

"Then take your wondering back to your own bed." He snatched up her shift and tossed it at her. "*Now.*"

As she sat up, the chill of the air seeped into her, chasing away the warmth and lassitude of their lovemaking. "How can you speak so harshly after what we just shared?"

"I had my pleasure, and you had yours. But 'tis over, and I've no stomach for useless chatter." Pivoting away, he turned his attention to adjusting the folds of his kilt.

Despite her determination to see the good in him, his rejection hurt. How could she explain her longing for romance, for soft words and parting kisses? She hadn't anticipated this brutal ending to her night of discovery. It left her feeling vaguely used and unclean.

With trembling fingers she donned her clothing, covering herself with the cloak. She paused a moment, looking at Alexander the MacBrut, who had shown her such ecstasy.

He stood gazing into the fire, one of his hands braced on the stone chimneypiece. She had a hundred questions she'd like to ask him, to enable her to understand him better. But he acted as if he'd already forgotten her presence and the deeply personal experience that had seared her soul.

After tomorrow, she would never see him again.

The knot in her throat prevented her from saying

good-bye. She left quietly, slipping out into the cold, dark corridor and feeling her way back to her bed, where Miss Gilbert still snored in blessed oblivion. M'lord awakened and wagged his tail, and Helen hugged him briefly before crawling beneath the covers. She closed her eyes, remembering the joy and beauty the MacBrut had shown her. No, not the MacBrut.

Alexander.

Alexander had made love to her. With his tender touch, he had transported her to paradise. Belatedly she realized the folly of believing she would be content after learning the mystery of it. Once was not enough. Already she missed the warmth of his arms and the excitement of his kisses. Already the place between her legs ached to be filled by him. Only him.

Alexander.

She turned restlessly, hugging her pillow. It was foolish to desire the unattainable. She would leave here on the morrow and never return. She'd had her adventure and now it was over.

Yet as she fell asleep, Helen wished with all her heart for the chance to charm him into doing it again.

Chapter Four

He wanted to do it again.

That was Alex's first thought the next morning on seeing her emerge from the stone keep, the little spotted lapdog trotting at her side. Alex was returning from the stables where he'd tended to the horse, using physical activity to block out all memory of his mistake the previous night. Now that mistake was walking straight toward him.

Lady Helen Jeffries.

He stopped dead in the middle of the snowy courtyard. Half of him wanted to turn and run, but not his lower half. The sight of her transfixed him: the sunshine gilding her fine blond hair, the jaunty spring to her steps, the crimson cloak skimming a figure that had haunted his dreams.

He should never have touched her. He should have listened to logic instead of thinking with his cock. The last complication he needed in his life was a freshly deflowered female—especially when she was a fashionable English lady.

He should stride away in the opposite direction. Better he should follow her lapdog that bounded away to examine the perimeter of the yard. But Lady Helen waved a gloved hand at Alex, and the smile brightening her face caught him with the force of a steel trap.

"Good morning," she called gaily as she picked a path through the drifts. Her boots crunched on the snow, and a band of white bordered the hem of her cloak. Without warning, she skidded on an icy patch.

Alex sprang to save her from a nasty tumble. His arms shot around her, and he found himself holding her close to his swiftly beating heart. Despite his resolve, he was seduced instantly by her slim, curvy form and womanly scent, her rosy face and dancing eyes.

"Goodness," she said, laughing. "I didn't know the ground was so slippery."

He grunted, hoping she would take the hint that he didn't want her company. But even as he stepped back, she chattered on.

"What a fine day it is." Opening her arms wide and tilting her head back, she turned to survey the blue sky. "There isn't a cloud to be seen, and the wind has died down. Have you checked the road yet?"

He gave a curt nod.

"And? Is it covered in snow?"

"Aye," he admitted grudgingly.

"Oh, do let's have a look."

She took hold of his elbow, and he had no choice but to walk her to the arched gate. He felt the softness of her breasts as she leaned into him for support. He glanced at her suspiciously, wondering if she were playing the seductress again. But she was gazing ahead, making sprightly comments on the weather and the scenery.

He had ruined her. With no more than a twinge of conscience, he had plucked England's fairest flower. Lust and a twisted need for revenge had overridden his scruples, and he had seized the chance to claim a prize from the country that had stolen so much from him. If anyone in London society were to find out, she would be shunned, ostracized.

Never would he forget his shock on finding her standing outside his bedchamber. Or his swift, searing response to hearing her hesitant explanation: *I came to see you. To be with you.*

There was no need to feel at fault. She had, after all, sought him out.

Yet guilt sank its teeth into him. She didn't deserve to be punished. She'd had nothing to do with the pain in his past.

"Oh, dear," she said. "You're right."

Alex blinked, realizing they stood at the verge of the steep, downward slope. Snow sparkled on the forested mountains as far as the eye could see. "Right?" he said cautiously.

"The road looks quite impassable. We are snowed in." She sounded cheerful, like a child freed from performing her daily chores. "We daren't transport Mr. Abbott down this slippery hill. That means we shall have to remain here for at least another day. Don't you agree?"

Being stranded here in the company of Lady Helen Jeffries only made Alex more testy. Rather than admit she'd surmised correctly, he said, "The snow willna last. 'Tis beginning to melt already."

He could hear the drip-drip of icicles from the castle walls and the surrounding trees. Gold and red leaves peeked from beneath the blanket of white. It was far too early in the season for the freezing temperatures to continue. By tomorrow, the road would be clear.

In the meanwhile, he had no intention of enduring the company of an Englishwoman. Especially not one who posed a damnable temptation to him. He had been too long without a woman, that was all.

"I've work to do," he muttered, and stalked away.

"Wait," she called from behind. "Don't go yet. I wanted to tell you something. It's about last evening."

He froze. "There's naught to tell."

"Please, Alexander. This is important."

The husky way she said his name made him turn uneasily to see her standing in the opening of the gate. The high stone arch and iron portcullis made her appear more dainty than ever.

She clasped her gloved hands in front of her. The chilly breeze tugged at the tendrils of her hair. A rosy hue tinted her cheeks, and she shyly dipped her chin. "I wanted to explain why I came to you last night."

Hell. What was it about women that made them want to analyze an act as natural as breathing or eating? "You were curious," he said bluntly. " 'Tis best forgotten."

Helen nodded. "I *was* curious. I wanted to know what went on between a man and a woman. Because, you see, I shall never marry."

She paused, gazing at him so earnestly he felt the tightening of interest in his chest. But he said nothing. If he didn't encourage her, maybe she would spare him her unwanted confidences.

"Five years ago," she went on, "I was betrothed to the heir to a dukedom. We'd grown up together, and Justin was like a brother to me." She lowered her gaze to her clasped hands. "But only weeks before our wedding, I found out he'd . . . seduced another woman. My half sister."

"The devil!" In spite of his resolve to remain indifferent, Alex had to clench his teeth to keep from denouncing the aristocracy.

"It's for the best, though it took time for me to realize that. Now Isabel and I are the best of friends. *She* belongs with Justin, not me. I was only in love with the idea of being a bride—with planning a big wedding and buying a trousseau." Helen ruefully shook her head. "How silly I was. Now, I *like* my freedom. Instead of being saddled with a husband and a family, I've traveled all over Europe and Africa and Asia. I'm only telling you this because . . ."

She remained silent so long he prompted, "Because."

"Because I wanted you to know how grateful I am to you for making love to me."

He felt as if he'd been punched in the gut. "Grateful?"

"Why, yes." Her voice lowered to a throaty murmur. "You made my first experience so very beautiful. And I wanted to thank you for that."

He had the violent urge to push her up against the wall and show her another beautiful experience, to hell with the cold and the wrongness of it and whoever might be watching. She stood looking at him, admiration and longing in her clear blue eyes. He could feel himself sweating despite the cold. He did not want her to gaze at him like that, as if he were some sort of hero. Didn't she know a heartless rogue when she saw one?

He deserved to be kicked in the balls, not thanked.

"Fine," he muttered. "Now stay away from me."

Pivoting on his heel, he stalked off and left her standing in the gateway. He had no time to coddle ladies who romanticized the act of copulation. Especially not an English lady who was accustomed to being pampered. The sooner she realized sex was not all sweetness and roses, the sooner she would flee back to England and he'd be rid of her—

Something cold and wet slammed into his head. He clapped his hand to the back of his hair and found melting, icy particles that dripped down inside his collar.

The chit had hurled a snowball at him.

He wheeled around. Another cold missile smacked him in the face. He blinked, shaking his head. Sputtering, he wiped the snow from his eyelashes and saw her hastening toward him.

"I'm so sorry," she said, spoiling the apology with a giggle. "I really don't know what came over me . . . Alex, are you hurt?"

A mad impulse made him fake a groan and keep his hands over his eyes as if he were in pain. He waited until she ventured within arm's reach. And then he lunged.

Uttering a cry, she danced backward to elude him, then spun around and ran. She was surprisingly quick on her feet. He didn't stop to wonder what foolishness came over him. He gave chase through the courtyard, pausing only to scoop up a handful of snow which he lobbed at her.

She squealed when the snow rained over her neck and shoulders. The direct hit slowed her as she swiped at the worst of it. She bent down to snatch up more ammunition, but he caught her before she could throw it, tumbling her down into a snowdrift.

She squirmed and fought for freedom, laughing all the while. And to his astonishment, he chuckled along with her. They rolled in the snow like children until he caught her flailing arms and their mock battle altered to carnal awareness.

He looked at her.

She looked at him.

Her bosom heaved from the exertion of their play. Their breaths mingled like fog in the frosty air. Her cloak was twisted around them, lashing him to the softness of legs and hips and breasts. He lay nestled in the cradle of her thighs.

She had ceased laughing. A womanly warmth curved her lips, and her gaze dipped to his mouth. She desired him, he knew it with fierce exultation. A small adjustment of their clothing and he could be inside her . . .

He could let himself be ensorcelled by an Englishwoman.

The thought chilled his hot blood, and he threw himself off her. He abhorred her brand of femininity. It was an invitation to trouble.

She sat up, too, brushing the snow from her cloak. "Alexander?" she said hesitantly. "Why do you dislike me so?"

"I dinna dislike you." His answer came swiftly, automatically.

"You *do*. You're kind to Gillie and Abbott, but you would as soon have left me stranded in the coach. Whenever I come near you, you draw away."

"We fornicated last night. I dinna recall *drawing away*."

She flinched at his crudeness, but kept her eyes on him. "I'm not speaking of physical closeness, but the closeness of friends. I wondered . . . do you fear being hurt again?"

Her words riveted him. "Again?"

"Your bedchamber with all the pretty furnishings . . . and then that abandoned dining table"—she bit her lip— "well, if you lost your wife, it's understandable that you'd feel reluctant to be close to another woman."

Her wrongful assumption hit him like a blow. He shot to his feet. "I've never been wed. So you can keep your foolish sympathy."

He marched away, but her footsteps pattered behind him. "Was it a clan war, then?" she asked. "If your people were called to battle in the midst of a meal—"

"There was no war," he snapped over his shoulder.

"Then what?" she persisted. "Please, I don't mean to pry—"

"Then dinna ask prying questions."

"But we have only this one day together. I want to know how to reach you. I want to understand why you despise me."

In the shadow of the tower, Alex wheeled around to face her. Lady Helen stopped, too, still in the sunshine, snow clinging to her crimson cloak from their mock tussle and bits of ice sparkling in her sunlit hair. Even now, he felt a dangerous softening inside him. Damn her, he had to make her *see*. He had to show her once and for all that he had no use for a female of her ilk.

"I despise you because you're an Englishwoman. Because this is all a game to ladies like you. You want to play with your Scotsman before you go running back to the comforts of the city, just as my mother did."

"Your mother was *English*?"

"Aye." The admission tasted sour in his mouth. He did not wish to probe the chilling emptiness in his chest. But this pesky female provoked him beyond endurance. "She came here, all agog at the romantic notion of marrying the laird of the MacBruts. But one hard winter in the Highlands was enough for her. On the evening of their first wedding anniversary, my father planned a big celebration here at the castle. When he went to fetch her for the party, he found the note saying she'd gone, that she couldna bear the hardships any longer. So she'd fled like a coward back to London."

Lady Helen pressed a gloved hand to her cheek. "You must have been just a baby."

"A bairn only a few months old."

"Did she never come back to see you?"

A hurting, black well opened in him. "Aye, once when I was a lad of eight. She brought me presents, trying to buy my affections, then left again after a week, never to return." Despising the old ache of pain, he slammed a lid over the memory. " 'Tis a blessing the bitch died a few years later, though my father never stopped bemoaning her loss. 'Twas he who ordered the castle left forever as it was when she lived here."

"Did she never write to you?"

"Nary a once. And my poor besotted father kept hoping till the day he died. He couldna believe his pretty wife liked the frivolous amusements of the city better than her own husband and son."

"I'm so sorry," Helen said, her gaze steady on him. "But you're wrong to assume that all Englishwomen are like your mother."

He scorned the false compassion softening her face. She did not understand. She was blind to her own shortcomings, starry-eyed and wrapped in fantasy. "The English try to steal all things Scottish. You wear our plaids and visit our mountains and pretend they're yours. You play here a while, then you scuttle on back to your own civilized world."

Helen shook her head. "I'm not averse to hardship. In my travels, I've encountered far more inhospitable circumstances than a broken coach and a ruined castle." She looked him up and down. "Not to mention a Scotsman with a beastly disposition."

Her flippant rationalizations incensed Alex. He didn't care if she was weak or strong, cowardly or brave. He only wanted her out of his life.

But that might already be impossible.

Taking a step toward her, he voiced his darkest fear. "There's one thing you didna consider when you came to me last night. I could have planted a bairn in you."

For a moment, the only sound was the drip-drip of melting snow. Then she inhaled softly. "A baby? I didn't think . . ."

He couldn't tell by her breathy tone if she feared the notion. But *he* feared it. He stepped forward and impatiently gripped her arms. "When did you last bleed?"

She ducked her head and spoke to his chest. "I hardly think that concerns you—"

"Dinna play the blushing maiden. A woman is fertile midway between her bleeding times." He didn't tell her how he knew that. The less she learned about him, the better.

"My . . . time ended three days ago."

Relief poured through him. He let go of her and stepped back. "Praise God for that."

She stood with her arms crossed over her middle in an oddly protective gesture. "I feel foolish for not considering the possibility."

"Then dinna make the same mistake when next you seek out a lover."

Before Helen could speak, he strode away, a tall angry

man who despised her. Without a backward glance, he disappeared inside the gray stone tower.

He did not want her sympathy; he'd made that abundantly clear. Yet her heart ached for the lonely, hurt boy hidden inside the scornful man. How she yearned to take him into her arms and comfort him, to show him that not all women were so callous as to abandon their husbands and children.

M'lord danced in front of her. She picked him up, brushing off his snow-covered paws and hugging him, her cheek to his velvety ears. The possibility of being pregnant, however remote, frightened and amazed her all at once. She imagined cuddling a baby, feeding him at her breast, and a strange softness came over her, an emotion she denied. Certainly she did not wish to bear a bastard. She would never want to see her son or daughter suffer the censure of society. How lucky that the timing was wrong.

How very, very lucky.

Lost in thought, Helen walked slowly back to the keep. There was a sense of freedom in knowing their lovemaking would not bear fruit. She would stay out of Alex's path for the remainder of the day. She would give him time to get over his anger. And tonight?

A shiver of longing rippled through her. What would happen tonight?

Chapter Five

With a sense of relief, Alex shut the door to the bed-chamber. He had passed the day in a frenzy of chores around the castle, carting piles of rubbish from the towers and sorting through the rusted weaponry in the armory. He had avoided the keep, preferring the frigid outbuildings to facing Helen.

Lady Helen, he contemptuously thought. A pampered aristocrat accustomed to being waited on hand and foot. *He* would not act like her adoring lapdog.

By evening, however, hunger proved a stronger foe than one small female. He stalked into the great hall, led by an enticing aroma. In an iron pot bubbled an appetizing stew made with the last of the ham, and though Helen took credit for it, he doubted her ability to cook. Dinner must have been Miss Gilbert's doing.

Helen appeared to have cheerfully accepted the end to their relationship. She did not flirt with him, though every now and then he intercepted a thoughtful glance from her. To his chagrin, even her coolness aroused him. It made her intriguing, untouchable, mysterious.

During dinner, she had shown far more regard for Abbott and Miss Gilbert, drawing out stories from their childhoods, listening as if they were treasured companions rather than hired help. Only once did she address

Alex, turning her big blue eyes on him. "Will the roads be clear by tomorrow?"

"Aye," he'd replied gruffly. "We'll depart come morning."

For several heartbeats, her gaze had held his, and he'd felt the wild urge to seize her in his arms and carry her upstairs, to push up her skirts and find heaven again. Then Abbott had engaged him in a discussion of the vagaries of Scottish weather, and the moment of madness passed.

Now, alone in the bedchamber, he paced the stone floor. With a cold eye, he studied the room that had belonged to his mother. The tarnished silver brushes on the dressing table. The age-spotted mirror where no doubt she had spent hours admiring her beauty. The window seat where he'd once found his father weeping, a strong man brought to ruin by a woman. An English-woman.

How daft to worship a lady's pale breasts and come-hither smiles. He himself had always practiced more control—until last night.

Alex stopped by the crumpled pallet. In the center, a rusty spot darkened the lighter brown wool. Virgin's blood.

He could have impregnated Helen. The risk of it horrified him. He of all men should know better than to doom a child to be raised without a mother. He should not have given in to his lust. He should not imagine Helen undressing in a chamber close to this one. He should not fancy her coming here again, offering herself to him one last time . . .

Hell. He kicked the blankets, hiding the evidence of his blunder. His mind rebelled at the notion of spending another night on the pallet where he had succumbed to the wiles of a Sassenach lady.

Striding to the big bed, Alex stripped off the dusty counterpane and the yellowed linen sheets that smelled faintly of roses. He snatched up a pile of spare blankets, yanked off his clothing, and flung himself onto the icy bed. The feather ticking sank beneath his weight. The bare mattress had the neutral, vaguely pleasant scent of age.

He sprawled on his back and closed his eyes. With stern willpower, he kept his thoughts clean. He would not dwell upon the illusory paradise he had found with Helen. Rather, he would focus his mind on acquiring a proper Scots wife.

Aye, last night had proven it was long past time for him to wed. He needed the pleasure of a woman more often. There were several suitable prospects in the area, worthy Highland women who had made their interest in him known, and he considered them, one by one . . .

After a time, he must have dozed, for he dreamed of soft arms embracing him, feminine hands roving his chest and waist and legs. *His wife.* She teased him with coy strokes, skirting but never touching the place where he burned. And he could not seem to grasp her wrist and guide her fingers as he wished. He was at her mercy, frustrated beyond belief . . .

With great effort, he swam to the surface of awareness. Groggy, he opened his eyes to the shadowy room. She lay draped over his side, and this time, he could touch her. He groped for her dainty hand and brought it downward, wrapping her fingers around him. The pleasure of it seared him.

Her soft breathy gasp brushed his ear. *Not his wife.* She was an erotic dream come true. "Helen," he muttered.

"Mmmm." She slid against him, her lips nuzzling his throat, her fingers exploring him.

She was naked. So was he.

His loins ached to the verge of pain. His sleep-drugged brain struggled to function, to fight the onslaught of sensual stimulation. Lust won the battle, and he lowered his head to her satiny breasts. "You shouldna be here," he said roughly into the fragrant valley.

"I know," she whispered. "But I couldn't stay away."

The wistfulness in her voice burrowed to a place deep inside him. She was his. His for the taking. He smoothed his hands down her womanly shape, finding lush hills and hidden vales. He could no longer remember all the reasons she was wrong for him. He could think only that he wanted her with a fierceness that defied understanding. "Bide with me then, lass."

"Yes," she said on a sigh.

Their mouths met in silken darkness. He pressed her against the feather mattress for a deep, drowning kiss. Her hand continued to stroke him, driving him mad. *Ah, heaven.* He was surely dreaming now, for nothing had ever felt so good. She made light forays up and down, circling the sensitive tip, teasing him to the verge of climax. He meant to curl her fingers around him, to show her how hard he liked it, but a primal urge beat inside him, and without further play he positioned himself between her opened legs.

Hot. She was hot and tight and wet. A perfect fit. So perfect that when he moved even slightly, he nearly went over the edge. He gritted his teeth and strained for control, reaching between them to caress her, taking fierce satisfaction from her unbridled enjoyment, her unladylike cries of passion. At last she arched against him, shuddering, sobbing out his name in the throes of release. Only then did he give himself into her power and allow the long, long fall into ecstasy.

Night enveloped them. Her soft body cradled him. Against his shoulder, she sighed in sleepy contentment. His insides clenched with something queerly akin to tenderness.

Helen. He had made love to Lady Helen again.

He reached for resentment, but like a stone it skipped away and sank into the endless sea of darkness. Waves of weariness lapped at him, pulling him deeper and deeper until he knew no more.

A loud crash awakened Helen.

She blinked into the brightness of daylight, and for a moment could not place where she was, which foreign country, what rural inn. Her senses absorbed her surroundings. Tattered rose-pink bedhangings. A bare mattress. A chill against her back, while the front of her was toasty warm, snuggled to a hard male body, a soft woolen blanket covering the two of them.

Alex.

Memory returned in a fervid rush. Before she could assimilate the cozy pleasure of waking up in his arms, his grip tightened on her. She glanced up at his face, and his unshaven cheeks gave him a disreputable and dangerous aspect. But he was not looking at her; he stared across the room.

"What the devil?" he growled. "Get out."

Pushing up on one elbow, she followed his gaze. And gasped at the man standing in the doorway. This was a nightmare. She would awaken in a moment . . . Her lips moved, but no sound issued forth.

Papa.

Though small in stature, the Marquess of Hathaway commanded attention like a king. He stood staring at them, his face pale and grim. Dear God. He must have left Edinburgh and followed her. Cox would have told him about the accident, that she'd been stranded here . . .

She saw the moment when his shock turned to rage. His bushy white eyebrows clashed in a thunderous scowl. Redness spread over his grizzled cheeks. From his wind-rumpled graying hair to his snow-caked boots, he radiated an explosive fury.

Alex sat up, naked to the waist, the blanket falling to

his hips. He half shielded her with his big body. "I said, *get out.*"

Lord Hathaway stormed to the side of the bed. His stark gaze flicked beyond Alex to Helen, and she drew the blanket to her chin to hide her nudity. Chills convulsed her body. She wanted to cry out that it wasn't what he thought . . . but it was. She had given herself to a man who was not her husband. A man she barely knew.

Lord Hathaway's expression turned murderous as he focused on Alex. Through gritted teeth, he said, "What have you done to her?"

"I dinna know who the devil you are, but you canna barge in here—"

"You've seduced her. You bloody lecher!"

In a blur of black cape, Lord Hathaway sprang across the bed. His fist connected with Alex's jaw, and Alex went reeling back against the headboard. The bed shook, a fine dust filtering down from the ancient canopy. Alex clapped his hand to his face. For an instant he sat stunned. Then a savage light entered his eyes, and Helen knew she had to act fast.

She launched herself between the two angry men. "Stop!" she cried. "That's enough."

Alex tried to thrust her aside. "I willna have a woman fighting my battles."

She pushed him back. "And I won't have you striking my father."

"Your *father*?" Alex jerked his head toward the visitor.

Lord Hathaway stood by the bed, breathing hard, his fists clenched. "I should kill you. Forcing my daughter into your bed—"

"He didn't force me," Helen blurted out. Regretting the need to cause him pain, she kept the blanket clasped to her taut throat. "I—I'm sorry, Papa. But you mustn't blame Alex. It was I who sought him out."

Hathaway's face went rigid. "I don't believe you."

She couldn't meet his eyes. "It started out as curiosity. I—I wanted to know what love was like—"

"It doesna matter what she did," Alex broke in. "Naught would have happened had I no' permitted it."

"You're damned right about that," Lord Hathaway snapped. "By God, you'll pay the price for ruining my daughter."

Alex said nothing. The two men shared a hard, angry, assessing look.

Confused, Helen glanced from one to the other. "But it's *my* fault," she insisted. "Papa, I won't have you blaming Alex. He didn't compromise me—he had my consent."

"I don't care if he had the blessing of King George the Fourth."

Her father stomped around to her side of the bed, and for one horrible moment she feared he would strike *her*. He had never ill-treated her in all her life, yet never before had she infuriated him so mightily. She would not flinch. Though trembling within, she kept her gaze steady on him, bracing herself for another outburst of wrath.

But he merely tugged the blanket more securely around her, then snatched up the pile of her clothing from a nearby chair. Taking her by the arm, he pulled her from the bed, leaving Alex without covering. "We shall settle this matter immediately," Hathaway told him.

Alex nodded coolly. Helen permitted herself only a furtive glance at him. He looked magnificent in his nakedness, as dignified as any man can be when caught in the act by an irate father.

Heaven help them. If only she had returned to her bed last night . . .

Outside in the passageway, the marquess handed Helen her garments. His skin appeared gray in the dim light. "Dress yourself," he said in a heavy voice. "Then return here in half an hour." He pivoted from her and started back into the bedroom.

Stung by fear, she cried out, "Papa! Promise me you'll not duel with Alex."

Hathaway grimaced. "Murdering the lecher might prove satisfying. But it would never bring back what you've lost."

"You don't understand. If you'll let me explain—"

"No." Cutting her off with a slash of his hand, he gave her a look of contempt and disappointment. "I traveled half the night to reach here, to assure myself of your safety. Instead I find that you have tricked Miss Gilbert. You have ignored your moral upbringing. And you have betrayed my trust. Do not insult me now by making excuses for your misdeed." His boot heels ringing, he stalked into the bedroom and shut the door.

His harsh words hung like a miasma in the chilly air. Helen wanted to run after him, to beg forgiveness for causing him pain, but she knew he would scorn her apologies. Tears blurred her vision. Since her mother's death when Helen was just a girl, she and her father had had only each other to rely upon. Now she had hurt the one man who mattered to her.

She felt mortified and shaken, though oddly unrepentant. The secret truth was, she did not regret making love with Alex. Both times, it had been a beautiful experience, a celebration of human closeness.

But in the doing, she had destroyed her father's faith in her. Somehow she had to show him that she was still his loving daughter. She breathed that fervent vow as she hastened down the corridor to dress.

Whatever punishment he intended to administer, even if he forbade her to travel anymore, she swore she would accept it.

*   *   *

"You and the MacBrut shall marry."

Her father's edict echoed in the laird's bedroom some thirty minutes later. Dumbfounded, Helen glanced at Alex, who stood fully dressed in kilt and plaid and boots, his hands clasped behind his back and his features stony. Forgetting her vow, she sputtered, "That's impossible."

"When we reach the village," Lord Hathaway said, "you and he will be wed. There is no posting of banns here in Scotland, and no cause to delay."

"But . . . I'm not marrying him." Horror rising in her throat, she spun toward Alex. Her fingers clenched the silk of her skirt. "Surely *you* cannot have agreed to this."

"I proposed a handfast." He grimaced, his blue eyes dark with loathing. "But his lordship insists on settling matters the *English* way."

"Handfast is a barbaric custom," her father said with a derisive snort. "Joined for a year and a day without benefit of clergy. And if there is no child, then you go your separate ways—with the woman's reputation in ruins." He shook his head sternly. "No. You took my daughter's virtue. Now you will do right by her."

To Helen's dismay, Alex didn't argue. But she did.

She ran to her father and grasped his hands. He still wore his greatcoat and gloves since it was icy cold in the room. "Papa, you're acting rashly. We can cover this up. No one need ever find out. Miss Gilbert and Abbott are loyal to me. And the village men who guided you here are hardly likely to inform London society."

Her father's face looked haggard. "Helen, I spent most of my adult life hiding a secret and dreading discovery. Five years ago, I swore I would never, ever do so again. It is better face up to the consequences of one's actions than to practice deceit."

Her heart lurched. He referred to the time when the truth had come out about his bastard daughter by a courtesan. It had been both shocking and thrilling for

Helen to discover that she had a half sister, Isabel. Helen knew her father regretted keeping the secret for so long. But she had not realized how deeply it had compromised his sense of honor.

"Besides," he added gravely, "you may be with child."

"No! I can't be. Alex said so."

"I said 'tis no' *likely*," Alex corrected. He stepped away from the hearth, where he'd been contemplating the cold ashes in the grate. "But the risk is there, and I knew it when I bedded you."

She felt crowded into a corner, without ally or weapon. Her father wished her to wed a man who despised her. To live in this drafty castle. To sacrifice her independence. Panic clutched at her throat. Was this, then, the price of winning back his love?

"Papa, I beg you, please think about this for a few more days—"

"Waiting will not change matters." His hands clasped behind his back, Hathaway regarded her with a level, disappointed stare that brought tears to her eyes. "I remember what it was like to be young, hot-blooded. But I also know there are consequences to be faced. And face them you shall."

Alex stood with his bride in the tiny kirk.

It was the same ancient house of worship where he had been baptized, the same stone altar where his parents had been wed, the same place where his father had been buried with the rest of the MacBruts. Alex seldom attended services anymore. As a boy he had lost faith when it had become too painful to watch his father praying, always praying for his wife's return.

Now Alex was taking an English wife.

Despite the chill in the air, his back prickled with sweat. He wanted to turn and run. To flee before the chains of matrimony bound him to a woman he loathed.

Helen wanted this marriage no more than he did. He would be doing them both a favor.

It is better face up to the consequences of one's actions than to practice deceit.

In his wildest imaginings, he'd never thought to find himself agreeing with an English nobleman. Yet Hathaway had challenged his honor. Now, his throat dry, Alex heard himself parroting his vows. And then Helen speaking hers in a subdued voice.

The deed was done.

She turned to him, her face uptilted for his kiss. Wariness clouded her blue eyes, and her fine pale features wore no smile. His wife. Lady Helen Jeffries was his wife now. She looked coldly beautiful with her blond hair swept up and secured with an ivory comb, her curves hidden by an ice-blue gown with a high neckline. But he knew every inch of her shapely body.

Even here, in the sanctuary of the kirk, he felt a dark, damning lust.

Deliberately he did not kiss her. He merely offered his arm as they walked back down the narrow aisle, past Helen's grim-faced father and a weeping Miss Gilbert, and the hastily assembled congregation of his people. They were avidly curious, he knew. Never in his twenty-eight years had he shown any inclination toward marriage.

The bell in the tower pealed joyously. In the chilly sunshine of the kirk yard, Alex had a moment alone with his bride before the guests trooped out. He bent close to her ear, and she smelled faintly of roses. "My people expect a wee celebration. You will behave as if you are enjoying yourself."

She lifted her chin. "And you will do the same."

Her challenge rankled him. Then it was too late for further remonstrations as the congregation filed out the doorway. Lord Hathaway kissed Helen's cheek and shook Alex's hand. "Treat her well," he said gruffly.

Alex comprehended the warning. He couldn't fault the marquess for wanting to protect his daughter. He would do the same for his own child.

If there was a child. Pray God there was not.

The villagers thronged around Helen. At first they were cautious in their greetings, but they warmed up as Helen played the gracious lady, smiling and accepting the good wishes of everyone, from auld Tam the cobbler who pecked her cheek to wee Jessie, thumb in mouth as she stared up in awe at the bride.

Alex and Helen led the winding procession through the village, past the smithy and the bakeshop and the scattering of homes. The setting sun cast a golden light over the verdant valley with mountains rising all around and cattle grazing near a loch that glistened a deep blue in the distance. Melting snow had muddied the path, and he waited for Helen to complain. But she lifted her hem above the muck and showed a bright-eyed interest in the whitewashed stone crofts with smoke drifting lazily from chimneys. The scent of smoldering peat perfumed the brisk air.

"Are we all going back up to the castle?" she asked.

"Nay." He relished her puzzlement and wished he could prolong it. She surely must be wondering which of these humble dwellings could hold so many wedding guests. He wanted to punish her by letting her think the worst—yet he had a perverse need to prove his worth to her as well.

At the other end of the village, they rounded a bend in the path and came upon a stone fence surrounding a rambling estate. Oaks in autumn glory shaded the overgrown garden. Shooing her through the opened gate, Alex watched in cynical expectation as she spied the grand stone mansion that perched atop a low hill. It might have been an English country house, complete with mullioned windows across the front and a score of chimneys rising from the slate roof.

She looked at him quizzically as he escorted her up the wide front steps. He fought the maddening urge to haul her inside to a private corner and consummate their ill-favored union. "Come awa' in," he said. "You'll want to assess the silver and see if 'tis fancy enough to suit you."

"To suit me?"

"Aye." He pulled open the heavy oak door. "Make yourself to home."

Her steps faltered on the threshold. Her chin shot up and she regarded him in accusing surprise. "You live *here*. Not in that tumbledown castle."

"My father built this pile to please my lady mother. But she couldna even wait for it to be finished." Conscious of the parade coming up the walk, Alex spoke for her ears alone. "How long will *you* last, I wonder?"

Chapter Six

Helen resolved to have a good time at her wedding celebration, if for no other reason than because Alex expected her to be miserable.

The villagers had done a fine job on short notice. In the dining parlor, the women laid out baked goods and meat dishes diverted from their own supper tables. In the drawing room, the men moved back the few pieces of furniture to make room for dancing. A trio of musicians played tunes in a curiously pleasing blend of flute, fiddle, and bagpipe.

She recognized only a few of the guests. Abbott sat comfortably on a chaise, his injured ankle propped on a pillow. Cox chatted with a blushing lass. Miss Gilbert poured punch for the throng of merrymakers, while Lord Hathaway engaged several of the men in a discussion of local commerce.

Helen wandered from group to group, determined to remember names and faces. These were her people now, too. She felt awash in a sense of unreality, a strange though not unpleasant feeling of homecoming.

She smiled and chatted, all the while keenly aware of Alex at the far end of the room, filling a glass of whisky, then sitting beside a pretty, black-haired woman who bent her head close to him, engaging his full attention.

A disagreeable jolt struck Helen. Beyond their two nights together, she knew little about his romantic life. Yet certainly he'd had practice in the art of lovemaking. And the pair of them appeared suspiciously cozy.

"Och, dinna look so fierce," said a tall, gaunt woman who introduced herself as Flora, his housekeeper. "Meg is complainin', and the laird is polite enough to listen. But he willna take up wi' the likes o' her now that he has a bonny bride. That auld nag has sent two husbands to the grave already."

Helen could not be so certain of his loyalty. The *auld nag* was flaunting her lush bosom in his face. Gritting her teeth, Helen deliberately turned her back. "How long have you worked here, Flora?"

"Long enough to have changed the laird's nappies when he was a puir, motherless bairn."

Helen's attention perked. "Did you know Alex's mother, then?"

"Aye, she was a frail lady, looked as if a gust o' wind would blow her awa'. And too proud for her own good." The housekeeper stuck her nose in the air and sniffed. "Truth be told, I wasna sorry to see her go."

"I'm English," Helen said. "Wouldn't you want me to leave, too?"

Smiling, Flora wagged a gnarled finger. "I can take a person's measure well enough. Ye're strong like the laird. An' 'tis pleased I am to see him wed at last. He needs a family to brighten up this lonesome place."

"He needs the braw task o' gettin' himself some bairns," said the little man who joined them, his brown eyes twinkling beneath a cap of tight red curls. "Though 'twould seem the MacBrut wasted no time wi' the beddin'."

Helen blushed. Everyone knew she and Alex had met only two days ago. They surely guessed what had happened during that unseasonal blizzard.

Flora chided, "Go awa' wi' ye, Jamie. The lady's too fine for yer stableyard jests."

"An' here I polished up me best manners." Jamie cocked a kilted leg and bowed. "Might I have the pleasure of this dance, m'lady?"

Helen smiled as she dipped into a curtsy. "Why, certainly, sir."

She accepted his arm and went out into the thick of the dancers. It was a lively jig, which Jamie performed with enthusiasm, his bandy legs a blur of motion. Catching a glimpse of Alex still engaged in conversation with the widow Meg, Helen concentrated on the dance steps, moving cautiously at first, then with growing confidence. When Jamie whirled her around, she found herself laughing from the dizzy sensation.

"Ye're a bonny dancer," he said at the end of the set. "Just what the laird needs, I trow."

"He needs a dancer?" she asked in mock innocence.

Jamie flashed his teeth in a grin. "Someone to gi' him a merry chase, that's what. Crivvens! No man ought to glower so on his weddin' day."

She glanced across the long room at Alex. When their gazes met, he scowled. With a pang, she recalled that moment in church when she'd lifted her face for his kiss and he had turned from her. No doubt his male pride was stung by the forced nuptials. Well, she too had never intended to wed, yet *she* saw no reason to sulk. Her life had changed more drastically than his, with her traveling ended for good. But *she* would make the best of their marriage.

Despite her indignation, Helen felt a flare of possessiveness. He was her husband now. Only she had the right to claim his attention, to go with him upstairs. A delicious shiver warmed her inner depths. Tonight they would make love as man and wife . . .

Another man claimed her for a dance, and she tucked away her private fantasies. The party was hardly the lav-

ish festivity she had once envisioned as a starry-eyed girl
of eighteen, in love with the pageantry of being a bride.
Nor was it an elegant affair attended by the cream of
the ton. Yet as the clansmen came one by one to partner
her, she was touched by their efforts to welcome the
laird's lady. Their kindness helped to ease the abrupt
change from independent woman to unwanted wife.

An hour later, as she danced a reel with a gangly
farmer, she noticed that Alex had vanished. So had the
dark-haired Meg.

Suspicion pricked Helen. How long had they been
gone?

At the end of the dance, she murmured her excuses,
then searched the downstairs rooms, peeking into a quiet
library, an empty morning room, a vacant butler's pan-
try. Alex's house—*her* house—was sparsely furnished.
Many of the rooms lacked wallpaper and draperies, yet
she could see possibilities in the airy ceilings, the tall
windows, the finely detailed woodwork. Drat Alex for
letting her believe he lived in that old, drafty castle with
its eerie, cobwebbed table. And now the rascal had gone
off with another woman on his wedding day.

It was time he showed his wife respect.

Her displeasure multiplied when she couldn't find the
missing couple. Nearing the end of the gloomy passage,
she spied one last door at the back of the house. She
was marching toward it when the white-painted panel
swung open, and her husband stepped out, a candlestick
in his hand.

Behind him sauntered Meg. She was looking down
while adjusting her dark green bodice.

A chill crawled over Helen, followed by a flash of
rage. It was one thing to suspect them of a liaison; quite
another to catch them after the act.

Alex halted, the candle flame casting shadows over his
craggy features. He shut the door behind them. His dark
eyebrows were lowered, giving him the aspect of a wary

wolf. "What are you doing awa' from the dancing?"

"I should ask you that question." She glanced pointedly at Meg, who wore a cat-in-the-cream smile. She either used carmine to darken those ruby lips. Or she had just been soundly kissed.

"It isna your place to question me," Alex said ominously.

"Oh? Then I'll issue a few orders instead. Starting with your partner." Helen swung to the widow. "Bother my husband again, and I'll unman him. Now leave this house before I turn my wrath on you, as well."

The smirk vanished. Her brown eyes rounded, Meg scuttled past Helen and vanished down the corridor.

A fierce satisfaction gripped Helen. Before she could revel in her victory, Alex spoke in a low, melodious brogue.

"Unman me, will you?" One eyebrow cocked, he lounged with his shoulder propped against the wall as he looked her up and down. "And just how would a wee lass like you propose to do that?"

His lazy perusal sparked a heat in her that had nothing to do with anger or triumph. He stood so tall and muscled in his linen shirt and fine kilt. How well she remembered the hardness of that masculine body. The memory made her feel weak inside, yearning for his big hands to touch her.

Hands that had just been caressing someone else.

Helen clenched her silk skirt. "Test me and find out," she said with icy bravado. "I will not abide my husband bedding another woman."

He snorted. "I didna bed Meg."

"Then what were you doing with her in there?"

The glower returned, making his cheekbones stark and his expression grim in the meager candlelight. " 'Tis a private matter."

"Obviously. Or you wouldn't have needed to sneak

away." She marched past him. "Perhaps I'll have a look for myself."

He slapped his palm against the door. "Dinna go in there."

"Why not? Have you something to hide? A rumpled bed, perhaps?"

"That room is forbidden to you."

"This is my house now, too. I've a right to go wherever I please."

"The house is *mine*," he corrected. "And you'll keep out where you are no' invited. It shouldna matter when you'll be gone from here soon enough."

"I've no intention of leaving."

"Then think again," he said bluntly. "There's no point to us living together. Tomorrow, you'll go awa' back to London with your father."

Shock reverberated through Helen. She clasped her hands tightly to steady herself. "You can't toss me out. I won't go."

"Suit yourself, then. But you'd best get out before winter makes the roads too treacherous for travel." In the candleglow, his dark blue eyes showed no regret, only an embittered dislike.

Of course. He feared she would behave the same as his mother. The realization eased the sting of his rejection, and without thinking, she reached up and caressed his jaw, sliding her hand to his temple. His skin was taut to her fingertips, his hair like rough silk. Looking up into his stern features, she imagined the lonely little boy he had once been. And it reminded her of why, in the end, she had spoken her vows to him. Because she ached to reach the fiercely guarded softness she had glimpsed inside the virile man.

Her husband.

She pressed herself closer to him, flushed with the desire to bring light and affection into his bleak life. "I don't mind the winter, Alex," she said in a sultry tone.

"I'm sure we can find ways to keep each other warm."

His nostrils flared. His chest expanded against her breasts. His moody eyes glittered down at her, and she knew with reckless delight that he still wanted her. He too wanted to make the best of this marriage . . .

Suddenly he thrust her away. "Nay. I willna risk having a child by you, Lady Helen. So heed me well. I will never, ever touch you again."

Chapter Seven

"Everything will be fine, Papa."

Helen stood with her father on the front porch the next morning. His black traveling coach waited on the drive, beneath the autumn splendor of a huge oak tree. Except for the mountaintops, the snow had melted and the roads were clear. He was taking Abbott back to England so the coachman could recuperate there. Cox and Miss Gilbert would stay on with Helen.

Lord Hathaway gripped her hands. "I mislike leaving you here," he said for the tenth time. "Perhaps I acted too hastily in forcing this marriage."

I will never, ever touch you again.

"Of course you didn't," she said, giving her father a sunny, reassuring smile. "You wanted to protect my honor. And I love you for that."

Worry deepened the lines on his dignified features. "I know the MacBrut can provide for you," Hathaway said, as if trying to convince himself. "I'd stayed the night at this house before setting out for his castle. His people led me to believe he is a fine, worthy man."

He searched her face, and Helen maintained her determined smile. The woeful state of this marriage was her problem, not his. "Yes, Papa, you've told me. And I know Alex is well regarded in the village."

"He's also affluent from lucrative shipping invest-
ments. And you'll have income of your own. The
MacBrut insisted the marriage settlement remain in your
name. That proves he's a generous man."

It proved he wanted nothing to do with English
money. "Then I shan't want for anything." She swallowed hard. "Although I *shall* miss you, Papa."

"And I, you."

He pulled her into a tight hug that Helen wished
would last forever. For as long as she could remember,
Papa had always been there for her. He had been her
companion on journeys to far-flung places. Now she
would be lucky to see him once a year. The magnitude
of that realization threatened to shatter her, but she held
herself together for his sake. He mustn't guess that she
had spent her wedding night alone, that she had lain
awake for hours in the four-poster bed, listening to the
creakings of the strange house and wishing for the warm
comfort of her husband.

When her father drew away, his eyes glistened with
moisture. She fought back her own tears as he gave her
one last gruff kiss. Then he strode down the steps and
entered the coach.

Helen stood waving, smiling bravely as the vehicle
started off into the majestic hills. Only when the coach
vanished around a bend in the road did she let the tears
fall. Warm, wet drops rolled down her cold cheeks. As
if sensing her unhappiness, M'lord bounded up the steps
and whined. She picked up the dog, hugging his small
form as he nudged her with his cold nose.

Leaning against the stone pillar, she blotted her face
with the corner of her apricot cashmere shawl. It was
senseless to weep over matters of her own making. Better
she should carve a place for herself here in Scotland. Of
all the lands she'd visited, she loved these wild, wind-
swept mountains the best.

The door opened behind her. She stiffened, bracing

herself for Alex's ridicule. She hadn't seen him since the
previous night when he had issued his ugly ultimatum.

I will never, ever touch you again.

A hand gently patted her back. But it was only Miss
Gilbert, her plump face soft with concern. "You mustn't
be distraught. His lordship will be back to visit. And
surely you and the laird will go to England sometime."

Alex would sooner journey to the fiery pits of Hades.

And Helen refused to leave the Highlands without
him. To do so would only prove his cynical prediction.
Instead, she would wear him down with her persistence.
Time would show him that she intended to stay.

Holding her beloved dog, Helen took a deep breath
of crisp autumn air. Yes. Time alone might unlock the
bars around her husband's heart.

Helen spent the rest of the day in brisk activity. Guided
by Flora, she toured the house, room by room, assessing
the antique linens in the cabinets and making lists of
items to be purchased in Edinburgh. She would need
drapery patterns and paint samples, furniture catalogs
and upholstery swatches. It wasn't until mid-afternoon,
when the housekeeper went to the kitchen to prepare
dinner, that Helen came upon the closed door.

The one room Alex had forbidden her to enter.

She meant to walk away, to allow him his juvenile
secrets, at least for the moment. But a muffled, whining
voice issued from inside the chamber.

Frowning, she pressed her ear to the door, but could
not make out the words beyond that the speaker was a
man. Every now and then, she heard her husband's deep
voice in reply. His tone had a patient, gentle quality,
almost like a parent soothing a hurt child.

Was this Alex's office? Was he placating a disgruntled
tenant?

Her fingers touched the brass door handle, but she
resisted the impulse to enter. Men didn't care for women

to interfere in matters of business. She intended to win her husband over, not irritate him. There would be time enough later to satisfy her curiosity.

Turning, she started down the passageway. An agonized howl came from the closed room. The sound sent prickles down Helen's spine.

Instinctively she responded to the cry of pain. She raced to the door and wrenched it open, lifting her skirts as she hastened inside.

She found herself in a long, spacious chamber lined by shelves full of apothecary jars and life-sized drawings of skeletons and anatomical forms. The tall windows let in the sunshine. In contrast to the starkness elsewhere in the house, this room contained a comfortable clutter of medicine cabinets, an examining table, and several cots. And Helen could not have been more surprised to discover a sorcerer's cave.

In the center of the room, Alex bent over a man who was stretched out in a leather chair with his white-knuckled hands gripping the arms. A wooden table held a host of metal instruments along with linen bandages and various bottles and jars. Alex straightened, holding a wooden drill-like implement with a wicked-looking hook on the end.

Alarmed, she hurried forward. "Dear God, what is going on?"

Alex pivoted on his heel and glared. "I told you not to come in here."

"I heard a scream." She peered past him and recognized Dougal, the village blacksmith, a sheepish look on his puffy, bristled cheeks. "What are you doing to that poor man?"

"That puir man had two rotten teeth. I removed them." Alex laid the implement on the table and snatched up a wad of cloth. Over his shoulder, he snapped, "Now go awa', you're intruding here."

Helen folded her arms and stayed put. She watched

as Alex finished with the blacksmith, packing the afflicted area with gauze, instructing him to eat only soft foods until the morrow, and admonishing him to use a cleansing powder daily lest he lose more teeth.

After the man departed, she stared at Alex, recalling his skill in caring for Abbott's broken ankle. Abruptly it all made sense. "You're a physician."

He strode to a washstand and soaped his hands. "I trained in Edinburgh. So that my people wouldna suffer from lack of proper care."

"You might have told me." Frustration simmered inside her, but it was overshadowed by sudden comprehension. "You brought Meg in here last night. Did she have a medical complaint?"

"A burn on her abdomen. I thought it wise to have a look."

"In the midst of your wedding celebration?"

A ruddy flush entered his cheeks as he dried his hands on a linen towel. In the late afternoon sunlight, his face had a rough beauty like the craggy mountains beyond the windows. "Our wedding wasna cause for celebration," he said bluntly. "You ken that as well as I."

A tart retort soured her tongue. But she reminded herself that taming him would take patience and persistence. She would not let him draw her into an endless war where they did nothing but fire shots at each other.

"If ever you need an assistant," she said, "I'd be happy to help."

"You'd swoon at the first drop of blood."

She gazed steadily at him. "You're mistaken. After Papa and I survived an earthquake in Turkey last year, I helped care for the wounded."

Alex cocked a skeptical brow. "Did you pat the injured on the hand?"

"Believe what you will. But your clansmen are my people now, too. And they were kind enough to welcome me yesterday—unlike you."

Before he could do more than grimace, a knock sounded.

"Go awa' with you now," Alex snapped to Helen as he crossed the room and opened a door that led directly outside.

In rushed a wild-eyed woman carrying a wailing child. It was Jessie, the little girl who had stared in awe at Helen outside the kirk. Helen's heart lurched. Blood matted the girl's fair hair and trickled down her delicate face.

Alex carried the girl to the examining table. "Here now, lassie. Let me have a look. I willna hurt you."

Using a cloth, he blotted the blood to expose a deep, jagged cut along her hairline. Her mother hovered close, sobbing, "She was playin' in the glen an' slipped on the rocks. Will she die?"

"She'll be fine. But the wound needs stitching." Alex hunkered down to Jessie's level. "You must lie very still, lassie. 'Twill only be a few pricks and we'll be done."

Jessie battered him with her fists. "Go awa'! Dinna hurt me!"

"Jessie!" Her mother helplessly wrung her hands. "Ye must listen to the laird an' do as he says."

Jessie only cried louder and thrashed harder.

Helen took firm hold of the girl's dainty shoulders. "Sshh. Let me tell you a story, Jessie. It's about a beautiful, brave princess who found herself the prisoner of a wicked beast. But you must be quiet now if you wish to hear all the adventures she had."

Jessie took a few hiccuping breaths. Her stiff muscles relaxed slightly under Helen's soothing massage. She gazed up wide-eyed, her face streaked with tears. "W-what was her name?"

"Her name was Helen, just like me. She traveled all over the world with her father, the king, and they visited many strange and wonderful places. Like the ancient pyramids of Egypt and the bazaars of Baghdad. Once, she even fed the monkeys on the Rock of Gibraltar."

"How did the princess get caught by the beast?" Jessie asked. She didn't seem to notice that Alex was carefully cleansing her oozing wound.

"Well, one day while they were visiting the strangest and most wonderful land of all, her father was called back to his kingdom. But Princess Helen was so eager to explore the lovely countryside that she decided to go on without him, though people warned her the mountains were enchanted, and that a fearsome beast lived there. Princesses, you see, are not easily frightened away by fearsome beasts. No matter how loudly they roar."

Helen saw Alex's lips compress, though his attention was focused on the curved needle which he plucked from the tray of implements. Seeing that he was about to suture the wound, she hastily continued. "One sunny morning, Princess Helen set out to explore the mountains. But by the afternoon, when she ventured deep into the forest, an icy wind began to blow and snow fell so thickly she feared she might freeze to death. Just then, she came upon a beautiful castle with lights twinkling in every window. When she knocked, the door opened by magic. She called out, but no one came. So she hastened toward a warm fire crackling on the hearth and a table laden with a fine feast of hot soup and cake and sugar plums.

"After the princess had enjoyed the most delicious meal of her life, a noise came from the shadows. She saw him then—the beast. He was big and fierce-looking, as shaggy as a bear. He said that eating his food had cast an enchantment over her and now she belonged to him forever."

Jessie had her thumb in her mouth, sucking hard while Alex finished the few stitches and knotted the end. From the black look he sent Helen, she knew he understood that the feast was their two idyllic nights together.

"The princess was afraid at first, but though the beast

growled and snarled, he never, ever hurt her. As the days passed she saw kindness in him. And she learned he had once been a handsome prince until an evil witch had hexed him. Only a love pure and true could break the spell." Helen lowered her voice to a husky murmur. "The princess was determined to love the beast. She was the one woman who could heal his heart."

Alex uttered a low, derisive sound. But his hands were gentle as he applied a clean linen bandage with sticking plaster.

Jessie pulled her thumb out of her mouth. "Did the princess ever turn the beast back into a prince?"

Smiling, Helen rubbed the child's small back and ignored a fierce glance from Alex. "Of course, she did, darling. No matter how difficult the task, princesses always accomplish what they set out to do."

Over the next fortnight, his wife was a constant presence and a source of endless irritation. Alex did his best to drive her away, though when it came to bodily tossing her out of his office, he found he couldn't do it. So he raged and snapped, willing her to take the hint and leave him alone.

But nothing he said seemed to discourage her, and after a time, he noticed all the little ways in which she changed his life. She assumed the role of an adept assistant, brisk and cheerful with the natural ability to calm his patients. She rolled bandages, handed him instruments, and gave sympathy to the fearful. On busy days, she brought him a hot lunch on a tray. Somehow she found out all his likes and dislikes—no doubt by gossiping with Flora—and made certain he had bannocks and blackberry jam for his breakfast, cock-a-leekie soup or smoked haddock with his dinner, along with a glass of his favorite ale. On cold, dark days, when the mist came down from the mountains, she brought him piping hot tea with shortbread.

He tried escaping the house, calling on patients. But as often as not, he would encounter his wife in the glen on her rounds to visit the crofters. She delivered broth to the sick and blankets to those in need. Often she simply sat down for a chat, getting to know each and every one of his people.

Her people now, too, she had said.

He seethed with rage at the way she was deceiving them into thinking she truly cared. He wanted to warn them that Lady Helen was only playing at being the laird's wife. When she tired of living her princess-and-the-beast fairy tale, she would go scuttling back to civilized England.

But he gritted his teeth and said nothing. Time would prove him right. He was the MacBrut. He could outwait one paltry female.

If lust didn't kill him first.

She never mentioned their two nights together. Yet with every swish of her silk dress or whiff of her sultry scent, she teased him. With every smile, every casual brush of their hands, she reminded him that she was his for the taking. He could lock the doors and have her right there on the cot in his office. He could go to her chamber at night and lose himself in the sweetest pleasure he had ever known. She was his wife, after all.

But coupling held the risk of pregnancy. He could not condemn another child—*his* child—to a mother's abandonment.

By the time three weeks had passed, he existed in a purgatory of perpetual arousal. Need for her made him irritable and edgy. So did his need to know she had not conceived. By his calculation, she should begin her monthly flow any day now.

One morning, she entered his office looking pale and fragile. It was on the tip of his tongue to inquire about her health when Jamie came knocking on the door. A horse had kicked him. While Alex cleansed the bloody hoof mark on the stableman's shoulder, Helen stood close by to hand him a linen compress, then the basilicum ointment to treat the wound.

He and Jamie exchanged a bit of banter, but she didn't join in as usual. Perhaps she had started her courses. The thought cheered Alex. Women were often peevish around that time, weren't they?

When he held out his hand for the bandage, she didn't give it to him. He shot her a frown, only to see her swaying on her feet. Her face was milk-white, her hand pressed to her mouth.

The signs of illness jolted him. Even as he took a step toward her, she uttered a little sigh and crumpled into his arms.

Chapter Eight

Helen couldn't fathom why she still lay abed when daylight flooded the room. Then Alex's big form moved between her and the window to block the blinding sun. And it all came flashing back to her: seeing Jamie's injury, feeling queasy and light-headed in the moment before all went black.

Alex must have carried her upstairs to her own bed. She blinked at the square canopy with its plain blue curtains. The sheets felt smooth and cool to her perspiring skin.

His face taut, Alex towered over her. "How are you feeling?"

Her head ached. Her palms felt cold and clammy. Worst of all, her stomach churned. Determined not to show weakness, she pushed herself upright. "I feel perfectly fine—" A rush of nausea overwhelmed her.

Luckily, he had the chamber pot ready. Through her misery, she felt the gentle stroke of his hand on her brow. He murmured something soothing, but she felt too wretched to pay attention. When she was done, he handed her a glass of water. "Rinse your mouth," he ordered.

She meekly obeyed. Then she lay back with her eyes closed, mortified that he had seen her at her worst.

Something deliciously cool came down on her forehead. She groped to touch it. A damp cloth.

The mattress dipped as Alex sat down on the edge of the bed. "Now," he said, "how do you really feel?"

"Better."

"And what do you suppose is the source of this illness?"

She had a suspicion she knew. But he looked disgusted, and she didn't feel strong enough to ward off his attack. "There's a family with the croup—"

"You dinna have the croup." He grimaced as if he'd choked on a dose of bitter medicine. "I would guess, Lady Helen, that you're pregnant."

Pregnant.

Rather than face his ill humor, she closed her eyes again. She had wondered about her unsettled stomach. And her monthly time was late by a few days. She had hoped and prayed, and her prayers had been answered with a baby.

Despite her physical discomfort, she felt a great surge of joy. Their lovemaking had started a new life inside her. They would be a family now, and Alex could not send her away. Because in nine months—no, eight—she would give birth to his baby. The sheer wonder of it lent her strength.

"In late June," she said, opening her eyes. Her happiness blossomed into a smile. "So much for your knowledge of fertility."

His mouth twisted scornfully. "Aye, I blame myself for this mistake. I should ha' turned you out when you came crawling into my bed. You're the last woman I'd choose to be the mother of my bairn."

His cruelty withered her smile, and she placed her hands over her womb. "I won't have you calling our baby a mistake. Nor will I let you drive us away with your malice."

"Understand this," he said coldly. "Once the bairn is

born, I dinna care if you go back to England. But you'll leave the child here with me."

"I will never abandon my own baby."

"So you say. But time will tell the truth."

The frigid contempt on his face chilled her soul. *Just love me and I'll stay forever,* she wanted to whisper. She had a dismal flash of their future together, a life without tenderness and joy, without shared happiness in the birth of their baby. Alex was determined to push her out of his world.

And she was just as determined to stay.

From that emotionally charged moment onward, Alex refused to allow Helen in his surgery. Flora would assist him when necessary, he said. Helen should not expose herself to disease and risk harming the baby. She felt too ill to argue. Besides, she had developed an aversion to strong odors. One whiff of the herbs and medicinals on his apothecary shelves would send her running from the room.

So she slept late each morning and took a nap each afternoon. In between, she nibbled on dry toast and sipped weak tea until she could get out of bed. She kept her mind off her queasiness by sewing baby clothes, helping Miss Gilbert with the mending, and planning renovations for the house.

Helen also devoted a few hours each day to writing a journal about her travels, describing the delights of touring a Turkish bazaar, the excitement of mountain climbing in Switzerland, the romance of boating on the canals of Venice. Someday, her child would read these adventures and know there was a vast world beyond these starkly beautiful Highlands.

She wished she could share her experiences with Alex, too. But he wanted nothing to do with her, except at mealtimes when he bullied her into eating a few bites of bland food to keep up her strength.

He spent his waking hours either in the surgery or visiting patients. At times, Helen might have thought she lived alone except for the clothing he left for Flora to launder or the tramp of his footsteps on the stairs at night.

Then, on a cold, crisp evening in late November, he came to her in the drawing room, where she sat reading on the chaise by the fire. Her heart turned over at the sight of his bluntly chiseled features, the muscled body she yearned to be held against.

He announced his intention to leave on the morrow for Edinburgh to attend a series of medical lectures. "The journey is too far for you," he said. "You'll remain here."

The mere thought of riding all day in a jolting carriage was enough to make her stomach rebel. "How long will you be gone?" she asked softly.

"A few weeks. Perhaps longer. And dinna think to run to England. I'll expect a letter from you once a week to prove you're still here."

It was on the tip of her tongue to ask tartly if he would reply to her correspondence, when he turned on his heel and strode out of the room.

Irked, Helen went to bed. After a restless night, she awakened at dawn to the realization that she was playing his game. He *wanted* to make her angry—so he could prove her to be a heartless lady.

Well, she wouldn't let him depart for Edinburgh without a kiss. She would forget her pride and melt this terrible coldness between them. She would show him that despite his ill humor she meant to stay.

But she rose too quickly and suffered a bout of illness. By the time she felt able to run down the icy stairs, hastening out into the blustery morning, her husband was already riding away on his big black horse.

He never even looked back.

*   *   *

Alex delayed his return until well into the new year.

The medical lectures had ended the third week of December. Yet he dallied in the city, tending to business concerns and visiting acquaintances. He hated to admit it, but a part of him ached to spend the holidays with Helen, taking care that she ate during the feasting, making certain she stayed inside during the bitterly cold weather. His concern was only for the bairn, he told himself. Toward his wife he felt nothing but resentment.

And lust.

He lay awake at night in the rooming house and thought about her. He thought about the silkiness of her hair against his skin. The snug velvet glove of her body enclosing him. The soft joyful cry she made when she climaxed. He wanted her with shameful ferocity.

He was a bloody coward, he knew, for lingering in the city. A blasted fool for fearing the effect his wife had on him. Despite all his reasons to despise Helen, he found himself looking forward to her letters. He had expected a few terse lines of complaint, but instead she wrote pages describing the minor illnesses that Flora treated in his absence, recounting amusing incidents in the village, and making light of her own infirmity.

The more Helen breezed over the state of her own health, the more he wondered if her condition had worsened. He imagined her lying in bed, frail and wan. One morning in early February, he read in a medical journal the case history of a pregnant woman who had died from an inability to eat. That very same day he received an unusually brief letter from Helen. If a few sketchy notes was all she could manage, she must be on a decline.

Heedless of the ice and snow, he rode hard for home, arriving late in the afternoon, the winter sun a dying spark beyond the ashen hills. The house shone like a beacon in the gathering dusk. The ground-floor windows glowed bright yellow except for the drawing room, where something covered the glass, a faint luminescence shining from within.

Flora would never light so many candles. Something must be wrong.

In the stable, Jamie didn't come running to take his mount. Cursing in the darkness, Alex led the horse into an empty stall, gave him a quick rubdown and a handful of oats. Then he dashed toward the house.

The kitchen was deserted, too. An enticing aroma eddied from a bubbling pot over the fireplace. A bowl of half-peeled apples sat on the long wooden table, as if Flora had been called away from her baking.

Something must be terribly wrong.

He saw visions of Helen wasting away to nothing. Helen gasping her last breaths. He'd been bloody daft to stay away for so many weeks.

Alex stormed down the corridor toward the front of the house. The chatter of voices pulled him to the drawing room. So did an odd, acrid odor.

He skidded to a halt in the doorway.

The furniture had been pushed into the center of the room and draped in dust covers. Holding a bucket, Cox balanced on a ladder and daubed the wall with a brush. Wielding another brush, Jamie crouched at the baseboard while Flora directed him. Half the walls bore the familiar dull brown; the rest shone a sunny yellow. Nearby, Miss Gilbert and Helen conferred over swatches of fabric, their heads bent together, one gray, the other golden.

The wee mongrel raced toward him, tail wagging, claws clicking on the wood floor. But Alex had eyes only for his wife.

She looked up and saw him. Her lips parted first in surprise and then formed a smile that turned his insides to mush. She bloomed with health, her cheeks glowing pink and her eyes bright. Her sky-blue gown showed the slight mound of her pregnancy.

She dropped the swatches and hastened toward him. "Alex! You should have sent word you were coming home."

A slow burn crept over him. He felt like a daft auld woman for worrying. "You were ill when I left," he ground out. "And you dinna say much in your last letter."

She stopped a few paces away. "I was too busy to write more. But I'm perfectly fine now. In fact, I've been eating rather *too* well." Laughing, she caressed her belly. "Soon you'll be thinking you wed a cow."

Nothing could be further from the truth. She embodied a fantasy with her lush breasts and fertile curves, the delicate beauty of her face framed by spun-gold hair. He wanted to carry her straight up to bed and slake his need. Even worse, he wanted to cuddle with her all the long, cold night.

The others crowded around him. "Is not our lady looking bonny?" Flora said, her hands clasped to her gaunt chest.

Jamie said, "On Hogmanay, I fetched the cream from the well for her."

"She hasn't been ill a moment since," Miss Gilbert added.

Alex knew the old custom. The cream was the first water drawn at midnight on the New Year. Drinking it brought great luck to a person.

"It's amazing," Helen said, beaming at the others, who clearly adored her. "I cannot thank you all enough."

"Dinna be daft," Alex said. "You passed the first three months, that's all. 'Tis nature you should thank, not superstition."

She wrinkled her nose. "Whatever the reason, I feel wonderful after that beastly sickness." She slipped her hand through the crook of his arm. "Come, Alex. I want to hear all that you've been doing."

The last thing he needed was to be alone with his wife. Her radiance drew him like a lodestone. He ached to laugh with her, to share in her natural joy, to let down his defenses. But then she would plunder the most vulnerable part of himself when she left.

She pulled him through another doorway. The morning room too had been renovated. The walls were painted a soft moss green to complement the new striped chairs and rosewood tables. Green and gold draperies framed the tall windows. The cozy aura invited him to sit down and stretch out his cold feet to the crackling fire.

He remained standing. "I dinna give you permission to refurbish my house."

"*Our* house," she said. "And you weren't here to voice an objection." With the loving care of a wife, she removed his wool scarf.

Her floral scent, the brush of her breasts, nearly drove Alex mad. He stomped away from her and jerked open the buttons of his overcoat. Knowing he sounded petulant, he said, "I liked the house the way it was."

"With chipped paint and nary a stick of furniture?" She smiled slyly. "Dinna be daft, Alex."

"Dinna mock me." He threw down his coat. "Once you leave here, I'll be stuck with your changes."

"Then I'll take the new furniture and draperies with me when I depart. Not that I ever intend to—*oh*!" Her hand flew to her abdomen.

Alarm sent him striding to her. "Are you in pain? Lie down and I'll have a look at you."

"I'm fine." A serene softness curved her mouth. She took hold of his hand and spread it over the gentle rise of her belly. "I felt our baby move."

He stood transfixed by her warmth, his hand splayed over her thickened middle. Her closeness bathed him in a sweet rush of wanting, a desire that plumbed deeper than mere lust. He told himself to draw back, to declare she was mistaken.

Then he detected the faintest fluttering against his palm.

The breath snagged in his lungs, and a tremendous awe shook him. In his role of physician, he had often felt the fetus kick inside the mother's womb. But those bairns had not been his own.

Our baby.

Helen's small hand covered his. Their gazes met, and he was aware of a bond between them, a bond more compelling than vows spoken in kirk. The tenderness in her clear blue eyes lured him with rich promise. He wanted to give himself into her warmth, to tumble headlong into the wonder of her love.

Impossible.

Lady Helen didn't love him. She loved playing the laird's lady. The sooner she was gone from his life, the better.

With effort, he restrained his unruly emotions. "The bairn seems healthy," he said.

He started to pull his hand away, but she held on to it, gently massaging his skin. Her fingers looked delicate and pale against his large, chapped hand. "You feel cold from being outside," she said.

" 'Twas a long, wearying ride," he muttered. "I'll go awa' upstairs now."

"I'll go with you." A tender smile bowed her lips. "I missed you, Alex. You should have a proper welcome home."

His body leapt to burning life. Sweat prickled down his back as he fought the urge to pull her close. Then sanity slew his fervor. If he strengthened his attachment to her now, he would damn himself to hell later.

"Nay," he said curtly, pushing her hands from him. "I need nothing from you, Lady Helen. Nothing at all."

*   *   *

As winter slowly passed into spring, Helen remembered her husband's rebuff whenever she felt tempted to seek him out. She should have known better, she chided herself. Why had she pursued a man who already had made clear his scorn for her?

Because she wanted their marriage to be real. She wanted to heal the years-old wound that festered inside him. And she wanted to assuage her longing for the comfort and love of a husband.

It was not that Alex spurned her entirely. He showed a keen interest in the health of their baby, making certain Helen ate properly and got sufficient rest. He answered her questions about the impending birth and counseled her on alleviating the minor discomforts of pregnancy. Yet their relationship was more doctor and patient than husband and wife. His deep-seated distrust loomed like an unbridgeable chasm between them.

With determined cheer, she spent much of her time embroidering tiny garments for the baby and converting a small alcove off her bedchamber into a nursery. Jamie and Cox carried down Alex's old cradle from the attic, and Flora polished the carved oak to a sheen. Miss Gilbert sewed endless sets of bedding and layette items, fussing as if she were the grandmother. They were all her family, Helen thought with pride and appreciation. She would never be alone so long as she had them. Yet wistfully she hoped for more.

Time will tell.

She clung to that thought, stubbornly hugged it to her heart as her body swelled with Alex's child. And sometimes she fancied he was softening toward her. As spring turned to summer, he accompanied her on visits to the crofters. He listened silently while she solicited advice on child-rearing from the mothers in the village. And on the stroll home, he tolerated her delight in picking wildflowers, in walking barefoot through the heather, in stopping for a drink of icy-fresh water from a mountain stream.

Those lazy days encouraged her to hope he might grow to love her. She was content to put off resolving their problems until after the baby was born.

That moment finally came on a sunny day in June.

Chapter Nine

Her laughter drifted through the opened window of his office.

Normally Alex would have ignored his wife. He knew better than to seek out her company lest he be seized by useless longings. But this morning, the infectious sound of her merriment floated from somewhere outdoors, and curiosity proved stronger than his willpower.

Stepping outside, he saw that Flora had set up the round wooden laundry tub alongside the stream that meandered behind the house. Sunlight dappled the two women, both in mobcaps and plain work gowns.

Beautifully pregnant, Helen stood in the tub, her skirts hitched above her knees and her feet plunged into the wash water. The sight of her bare legs caused a shameful response in him. The feeling burned so fiercely he deflected it into anger.

Stones crunching beneath his boots, he strode across the yard. Helen saw him, and her expression lit with pleasure. With her rounded belly and the tendrils of golden hair framing her face, she looked like the goddess of fertility.

"Why the devil are you treading laundry like a peasant?"

The splashing of her feet ceased, though her eyes still

danced. "It's too fine a day to sit sewing. And I was too restless, besides. So here I am."

"You'll fall and harm the bairn."

"Och, dinna be daft, Alex," she teased in a fair imitation of him. "I'm perfectly fine . . ." Her voice trailed off, and she rubbed her tailbone.

Frowning, he slipped an arm around her. "You're having pains."

"Only sometimes in my lower back."

"Since when?"

"Why, yesterday. It's the weight of the baby, Flora says."

"Or the start of your labor," he said grimly. "Step out of there at once, and I'll examine you in my office."

No sooner did he help her over the side of the tub than a gush of liquid ran down her legs and into the grass. "Oh, my," she breathed, her eyes widening in shock.

Willing his hands not to shake, he lifted her into his arms. " 'Tis only your water breaking. The sac around the bairn."

She clung to his neck. "Then the baby will be born . . . today?"

" 'Twould seem so." He didn't mention the fears that leapt out to throttle him. Sometimes labor went on for days. Many women died in childbirth, or from a fever afterward. He had witnessed it himself, those times when even the finest-trained physician could do nothing . . .

Helen sucked in a sharp breath. Her fingernails pressed into his neck, and he felt the sudden tightening of her belly. "Breathe with the pain," he murmured in her ear. " 'Twill pass shortly." Lifting his head, he barked, "Flora, run on and ready the bed."

"Aye, m'laird." The older woman dashed toward the house.

Alex wasted no time in striding after her. Helen sighed

as the cramp eased, and she buried her face in the crook of his neck. His mouth dry, he considered the ordeal ahead of her. She would endure agony in the hours to come. And there was little he could do to help her.

She suffered another pain as he was lowering her to the bed. The swiftness of it alarmed him. While Flora plumped the pillows, he rubbed Helen's lower back. He had seen prospective fathers pacing outside a croft, and he'd felt a mild sympathy. Now already he understood the frustration and powerlessness that a man felt for his laboring wife.

When the pain lessened, he unbuttoned her gown and helped her out of it. Turning to him, she smiled and touched his cheek. "Don't look so fierce, Alex. This is surely a happy occasion, for tonight I'll hold our child."

Her excitement astounded him. She looked determined and unafraid, completely trusting in him. Her tender blue eyes promised fulfillment of the hopes and dreams that had lain dormant within him for too long. He wanted to tumble into her warmth, to believe she would stay with him forever.

Then the pains struck quickly, mercilessly. As morning wore into afternoon, Helen uttered not a word of complaint, begging only a sip of water now and then, or asking him to massage her back. In between, she told him how much she wanted their baby to grow up here in the wild beauty of the Highlands. She talked of seeing him take his first steps and going on picnics. She would start a school so their child could learn in the company of the village children. With incurable longing, Alex wanted to believe her idyllic plans. But a part of him doubted. She could not truly mean to spend her life here.

By sunset, her resilience began to flag, and she closed her eyes between the waves of pain. Her golden lashes enhanced the delicacy of her flushed skin. During each contraction, she clung tightly to his hand, and Alex would have sold his soul to ease her agony. Surely the pains had been too close for too long. Experience told him there were differences in each woman's labor, that one baby came easily while another proved difficult. But the worries crowded in on him. She was so small, so dainty, and he was a big man. What if the infant were too large? What if he lost Helen?

Though the room was warm, a cold sweat caused him to tremble. He mastered himself with effort. It was stunning to realize how empty his life would be without her smiles, her chatter, her endless optimism. Somehow, she had become as vital to him as air.

At that moment, she uttered a fierce cry, her fingers knotting in the bedlinens as she strained to expel the baby. When he sprang to examine her, he saw to his relief the crowning of the head. He encouraged her to focus all of her strength into bringing their child into the world. She did so with great fortitude, and within moments he held a slippery, squalling baby.

" 'Tis a boy," Alex muttered, half dazed with elation.

The next moments passed in a blur. His actions automatic, Alex tied the cord and delivered the afterbirth, then washed up while Flora wrapped the baby in a blanket and brought him to his mother. Helen cuddled the infant in her arms and laughed with joy. "Oh Alex, we've a son. Isn't he beautiful?"

Alex sat down beside her. "Aye," he whispered.

He could trust himself to say no more. Reaching out, he touched the boy's still-damp black hair. He'd always found red-faced, squalling newborns rather ugly. But this one made his eyes burn with fierce, protective ardor.

Helen's radiant smile enveloped him. Seeing her cradling his son, Alex felt giddy, love-daft. Impelled by a powerful impulse, he leaned forward and gently kissed her. For one sweet moment, their lips melded with tenderness and hope.

He knew then that it was too late to fight his feelings for her. He wanted the three of them to be a family. His life—his son's life—would be incomplete without Helen. But he didn't know how to hold her.

Chapter Ten

"I haven't been to Scotland since Justin and I wed at Gretna Green," Isabel said. "Oh, it's such a lovely place."

Sitting on the porch steps, Helen shared a smile with her half sister. The mountainous vista enhanced the delight of enjoying Isabel's company again. With the sun glinting on her loosely upswept copper hair, Isabel looked too young to be the new Duchess of Lynwood. "I'm glad you and Papa came to visit," Helen said fervently. "I've missed you both ever so much."

"And I wouldn't have missed meeting your husband and little Ian for the world," Isabel declared. "I've never seen a man dote so on a baby."

It was true, Helen knew. In the past weeks, Alex had proven himself a fine father, never hesitating to change a nappie or rock Ian to sleep. Now if only he would pay half so much attention to *her*. Deliberately, Helen deflected the conversation away from Alex. "Speaking of doting," she said, "Papa certainly dotes on his grandchildren."

She shaded her eyes to watch Lord Hathaway standing beneath the old oak tree, pushing Isabel's four-year-old daughter in the swing while Isabel's son toddled after the dog. The trill of childish laughter floated across the park. They had been here for a few days, having come six weeks after baby Ian's birth. Justin was due to arrive tomorrow after tending to estate business. And Helen would see Justin and Isabel hug with the tenderness she herself longed for from her own husband.

She felt the soft touch of Isabel's hand on her arm. "Helen? I don't mean to pry, but is everything all right between you and Alex?"

One glance into those sympathetic sherry-brown eyes cracked the dam around Helen's emotions. She spilled out the story of how Alex resented their forced marriage, glossing over the details of who had seduced whom. "We can't truly be a family until he loves me," she concluded with a sigh.

"Oh, but he does! I've seen the way he looks at you. As if he were a starving man and you were a feast."

Helen doubted that. Her throat ached as she remembered their tender kiss after Ian's birth. Other than that brief closeness, Alex had remained aloof. Sometimes he vanished for the entire day, as if he needed time alone.

She turned her gaze to the distant loch, and the deep blue reminded her of his eyes. "You must be mistaken. If he truly loved me, he would want to . . . ." Reluctant to reveal their lack of intimacy, she bit her lip.

"He hasn't shared your bed for a while," Isabel guessed. "Do you know, Justin had a peculiar notion after our first was born. He swore he wouldn't subject me to the rigors of childbirth again. So *I* had to seduce *him*."

She didn't know that Helen had already seduced Alex. Twice. "I wish it were so simple."

"It *is* simple. A man likes to pretend he has a strong will. But he can't resist a determined woman—especially not the woman he loves."

"Och, there ye are, m'lady," said a voice from behind them. Smiling broadly, Flora held out a basket. "Perhaps 'twas forward of me, but I packed a feast of the laird's favorites. I ken ye two need some time alone."

"A picnic!" Isabel exclaimed. Her eyes sparkling, she shooed Helen up from the step. "What a perfect idea. Papa and I shall watch Ian for the afternoon. While *you* take your husband on a picnic."

Half an hour later, Helen stepped into Alex's office. In her damp palm she clutched the basket of food. She didn't quite understand how Flora had come to appear at the right moment, but it all seemed part of the magic of hope. In a flurry, Helen had fed Ian and then put him down for his nap before changing into a rose-pink gown, cut low over her newly maternal bosom. All the while she had trembled to imagine Alex caressing her. Perhaps Isabel was right. If they found pleasure in each other's arms again, perhaps intimacy could mend the terrible rift in their marriage.

He sat writing at his desk, the window open to the balmy August day. As she approached, he looked up sharply and her heart sank. In his rough features she could see no sign of unrequited love. Instead, his dark brows were lowered as if he resented being disturbed.

She would not let him drive her away. Not today. "We're going on a picnic," she said firmly. "Just you and I."

He stared, his eyes enigmatic. She braced herself for a refusal, but he merely said, "On one condition. That *I* choose the place."

"Agreed." *So long as it's secluded,* she added to herself.

He rose from the desk and took the covered basket from her. Without another word, he opened the door and ushered her out into the sunshine.

His easy compliance surprised Helen as he led the way up a gentle slope fragrant with heather. Bees buzzed the pinkish-lavender blooms alongside the dirt path. As the hill grew steeper, Alex dropped back and cupped her elbow, helping her over the rocky, upland trail.

"Where are we going?" she asked.

He shot her a cryptic glance. "You'll see soon."

She took another look, and recognition excited her. The last time she'd been this way, snow had covered the great boulders, and the trees had worn their autumn grandeur. Already, she could see the crumbling gray stones through the trees up ahead.

The castle.

Nestled against a sheer rock cliff, the ancestral home of the MacBruts looked majestic in the sunlight, like an ancient warrior standing straight and tall. The square keep loomed beyond the twin towers. Something sweet and wistful stirred in her breast. Here, Alex had made her a woman. Here, they had conceived their son.

She expected Alex to set down the picnic basket in the meadow outside the stone walls. But he steered her through the open gate and toward the keep with its dismal aura of neglect. Helen slowed her steps. She wanted a new beginning, uncluttered by the past.

"We should have our picnic out on the grass," she protested.

"This willna take long. I've something to show you."

In the sunlight, his features had the rough splendor of an unpolished gemstone. Helen sensed a grim determination in him as they entered the castle. His fingers felt tense and stiff on her arm.

Their footsteps echoed through the vast chamber. Even in the midst of a summer day, the great hall was dim and cool. No cheery fire lit the huge hearth, and she found herself edging closer to Alex's warmth.

To her surprise, he slid his arm around her waist and let his hand rest on her hip. The breath faltered in her throat. She glanced up at him, wondering if his embrace was a thoughtless gesture. But his gaze was focused beyond her.

They stopped before a long table of gleaming oak. The

polished silver candelabra glinted in the sunlight that streamed from the high windows. At one end, two fine china plates with crystal goblets were set as if for an intimate dinner.

Helen blinked at what had once been the cobwebbed banquet table. "Someone's cleaned it," she said in amazement.

Alex set down the picnic basket. " 'Twas me."

"*You?*"

He nodded, his eyes serious. "My father preserved the place because he was brokenhearted. Then I did so too to remind myself of my mother's cruelty. But I didna want Ian to carry on that legacy."

Helen hardly knew what to think. Was it possible Alex had changed? That he would cease to judge her by the mistakes of another woman?

He went on. " 'Twas I who told Flora to pack us a picnic. I wanted to show you what I'd done here." On that astonishing statement, he took Helen's arm and guided her up the winding stone stairs.

In the laird's bedchamber, too, much had been altered. A new mirror replaced the age-spotted one over the dressing table. Lemon-yellow silk draped the four-poster bed with its collection of plump feather pillows. The musty odor of neglect had been replaced by a fresh, flowery fragrance.

"Roses," she murmured. "You've refurbished this room, too. Why?"

"Surely you shouldna have to ask."

He gazed at her as if begging to be spared an explanation. But Helen had suffered too many lonely nights to forgive him so easily. Walking to the bedpost, she leaned against it for support. "I do have to ask. Tell me."

He glanced around as if the walls held the right words. After a long moment, he looked at her, his expression twisted with raw anguish. "I did it for you, Helen. To show you that the past doesna rule me anymore. To convince you to stay with me."

Her heart leapt with hope. Did he truly mean it? She took a shaky breath. "You need a mother for Ian, that's all."

"I canna deny the needs of our son." Alex's voice lowered to a hoarse murmur. "But I also need a wife. *I* need you, Lady Helen."

For once, he spoke her name like a caress instead of a curse. It wasn't a declaration of love, but close enough. She wanted to laugh and weep with joy. Clasping the bedpost to keep from running to him, she teased, "And just how would a big, braw man like you propose to keep his wife happy?"

A gleam entered his eyes. His gaze made a slow sweep of her from head to toe, lingering on places that ached for his touch. Then he strutted toward her. "I've a few notions in mind."

Her pulse beat faster. "Such as?"

He stopped so close she could feel his body heat. With his finger, he traced the edge of her bodice. "We might start by testing the new bed."

Helen drew in a breath. "And then?"

"And then I might spend a long while kissing you . . . touching you . . . pleasing you." He did just that, his mouth moving over the tender skin above her bosom, his hands reaching behind to unbutton her gown.

She tilted back her head, charmed by the magic of his seduction. It was a dream come true after all those lonely months of resolute hope and stubborn prayer. As her gown slithered to the floor, she reveled in the extravagance of sensation, the rare pleasure of his caress.

Her hands rested on his broad shoulders, but not for long. A boundless love overflowed her, spilling through her with the need to gratify him, too. She arched against him and kissed the rough features that had become so dear to her. They undressed each other and tumbled into the feather bed, nestling naked in a pool of sunshine and desire. He sought to go slowly, to prolong her pleasure until Helen writhed in frustration.

"Enough," she whispered, guiding him home. "I want you *now*."

As he joined their bodies, a moan of intense pleasure vibrated from her. He lay still, bracing himself with his hands on either side of her. His eyes were dark with passion—and regret. "I dinna mean to hurt you, lass. To take you so soon after giving birth."

"You'll hurt me only if you dinna *hurry*!"

She moved her hips, wanting all of him, drawing him deeper within herself. He groaned, setting the quickened pace she craved, the glorious friction that took her higher and higher until at last she plunged over the verge into a sea of perfect bliss. She was aware of him falling with her, his harsh cry echoing, his strong body shuddering. The happiness lingered when she came back to herself in the warm shelter of his arms. *Her husband.* She wanted to stay right here in bed with him forever. If only she could.

She stroked his bristled cheek. "We should have our picnic soon."

With a wicked grin, Alex brought her hand to his loins. "Was this not feast enough to satisfy you, wife?"

Helen laughed. "Certainly. I only meant we'll need to return home in a while. Lest our son howl for his next meal."

"Ah, the lucky lad must have his feast, too." Appreciatively, Alex caressed the swell of her breasts. Then he gazed into her eyes. "Helen, you ken we took no risk today. A nursing mother canna get pregnant—"

"Dare I trust your knowledge of fertility?" she teased.

His grin lasted only for a moment. "I dinna like to burden you with another bairn if 'tis not your wish."

"But Ian needs brothers and sisters. And I would like a big family. Wouldn't you?"

"Aye, very much." He cupped her cheek in his big hand, and a look of yearning lit his craggy features. "My dearest lady," he murmured with stirring possessiveness, "I do love you."

Her throat tightened from the fulfillment of her dreams. "You needn't say that to keep me. I love you enough to stay."

"I'm through saying things I dinna mean. And I'm sorry for acting like a daft auld fool." He brushed a kiss across her lips. "I'll keep you happy, I swear it. We'll travel to England if you like, or anywhere in the world if it pleases you."

His willingness to change for her sake touched her heart. "Oh, Alex. I'd sooner stay right here." She moved sinuously against him. "With you, my love, forever."

. . .

Would you like to read the exciting story of Lady Helen's past? Helen was once engaged to wed Justin Culver, heir to the Duke of Lynwood, until a mysterious beauty entered their lives, the half-sister Helen had never known she had.

You can find their fascinating tale of intrigue and love in HER SECRET AFFAIR by Barbara Dawson Smith, published by St. Martin's Paperbacks in May 1998.